GW01454223

The Music
of the Cosmos

Glyn K Green

The Music of the Cosmos

Copyright © Glyn K Green

Published by Showborough Books

www.glynkgreen.com

Showborough Books
Showborough House
Twyning
Gloucestershire
GL20 6DN

"The world is full of magic things
patiently waiting for our senses to grow sharper."
W. B. Yeats

"Yeah, fairies wear boots and you gotta believe me …"
Black Sabbath

Chapter One

Sometimes life drives us down into the basement. Scurrying to avoid the pain, we find a corner, hunker down, lose the will to climb back up the stairs and remain in the half dark like naked mole-rats. Charlie Peterson was in the naked mole-rat basement, working hard at failing to reach an accommodation with life. And with the irritating sample of teenage youth before him.

Charlie was barely over thirty, but this was one of those days when the age gap … no, it wasn't about the age gap … it was just one of those days when he found himself totally incapable of trying to negotiate a meeting of minds. In his opinion, an individual who couldn't even manage a small nod in the direction of practice should never be lucky enough to own a thousand pound Strat. A guitar was not a posing pouch. It was supposed, indeed it demanded, to be played. In addition to which, a set of over indulgent and possibly over optimistic parents were paying him a weekly sum for the express purpose of making that happen.

"So, you don't think the Strat can get me laid if I don't play it?"

1

The smart-mouthed irrepressibility of youth. Yes, maybe he'd once been the same.

Charlie shook his head. "You will play this guitar," he said, tight lipped, "or you will die trying."

Die trying. Of the many careless words that were getting bounced around the damp walls that Saturday afternoon those two suddenly elected, with an unaccountable perversity, to ring like a death knell in the basement room. Though years had passed, Charlie Peterson felt like crying.

People die and other people endeavour to get over their deaths. That's how life works. And the incredible pain this causes us is the price we have paid for a superior level of consciousness and the ability to fly to the moon. Accepting death is what we have to do. It's part of the human condition and nothing can ever change that. And, in the aftermath of the Enlightenment, we are supposed to do it without any religious convictions or any hope for a hereafter. Charlie Peterson's best friends were gone. Ashes to ashes, dust to dust. And there would be no resurrection. Not of his friends, nor of the dream they had shared together.

A foggy Friday afternoon in late February, a busy motorway, moving, not moving, moving again … And a band van containing a drummer, two guitarists and a manager. And Charlie, waiting at the door of a shabby London flat – a flat he shared with a man who drove a garbage truck and a Lithuanian immigrant who worked in the ticket booth of the local cinema. Mostly just nods on the stairs – ships passing in the night as they each went about the business of earning their respective crusts.

Charlie looking around, seeing beyond the peeling wallpaper and the worn carpet. Looking forward to moving on, moving up. Those agonising shifts in telephone sales a thing of the past. Checking his watch. Cold in the hallway but sweat on his back. Checking his watch again. Eyes roaming over the equipment. Gibson SG. Epiphone SG – emergency standby. Leads, spare strings. Pedal board – DS-1, RAT, Cry Baby, Small Clone, chromatic tuner …

Huge gig, buoyant A&R men, enthusiastic record company executives, jostling music journalists and a fantastically healthy number of fans who were starting to send him less than healthy pictures of themselves. Stardom in the making.

Eyeing the equipment again. Waiting for the band van to draw up … Feeling the sweat begin to run … Checking his watch … Biting his lip. Charlie Peterson, waiting, waiting and waiting …

No survivors.

A worthwhile thing to die for? The need to be on time for the dream of fame and fortune? Maybe not. It's hardly the most worthy of dreams, you might think. Ego driven, exhibitionist, frivolous, and something that was surely never designed to bring out the best the human spirit has to offer. But dreams hatched in school lunch breaks by ten-year-old boys kicking their toes in the dirt tend not to be about creating world peace, or reducing civilisation's dependency on fossil fuels, or getting to thoroughly understand why the theory of evolution does not violate the second law of thermodynamics. Yet, a dream that has been carried, and worked on, and fought over, and cried over, through youth and adolescence, and the separations involved in getting tertiary education and paid work, plus the unpaid embarrassments of playing in empty bars and echoing village

3

halls through useless sound systems - surely a dream like this, by virtue of its sheer durability and the expenditure of love and energy that went into it, has to have had something of merit.

It's a truism that great music and great art can only come from real suffering. And, at least according to Thomas Mann, real suffering must then be followed by a degree of emotional detachment before it can be fastidiously expressed and finely honed into a thing called art. But maybe life was to deliver its lessons to Charlie Peterson the other way around – first the great music (people thought so, maybe not you, but people) then the real suffering and the emotional detachment.

The guitars in their cases and the pedal board had gathered dust in the hallway until, finally, the driver of the garbage truck threatened to take them to the tip. Also, he'd pointed out, Charlie needed to come up with six months' worth of rent and more than a gesture in the direction of council tax. The landlord and the council were not interested in his particular misery – misery was offered to them on a daily basis and they preferred currency. Charlie's parents cleared his debts and, their own emotional ministrations having been ostensibly unhelpful, they provided extra cash for professional grief counselling. Charlie spent it on beer and takeaway curries.

The Gibson made it as far as his bedroom. The Epiphone and the pedals went in order to pay the electric bill. The leads and the spare guitar strings had already been purloined for the purpose of strapping discarded fluffy toys to the radiator of the garbage truck. Floppy ears and helpless little arms flapped in the wind as the toys, dirty but wide-eyed, travelled the streets of London. Children laughed and pointed or burst into tears, according to their sensibilities. The garbage truck driver smiled. Such are the ways that we sublimate our dark sides as we labour through the mundane drudgery to which life can so frequently sentence us.

But nobody could find a way of helping Charlie out of his darkness. The friends and acquaintances and fans who had made their presence so prominently felt around the time of the funerals began to drift away. Nobody knew what to say any more. What could they do to make him wide-eyed again? Strap him to the radiator of a garbage truck? Then one of Charlie's brothers, continuing in dutiful persistence, arrived one day with a telephone number. "Ring it," he said. "It's a job. You don't need any training. Do it *now*. Somebody in the office knows a guy who knows the guy."

More was said, of course, enough so that Charlie finally took himself and his darkness down into a windowless basement twenty feet beneath street level - the underworld of a music shop in Camden. There was a stained, pea green carpet, white flaky paint work, and a dankness that played hell with electrical equipment, encouraged strange mushrooms to grow from the walls, and lured musically inclined newts from the canal to go in for long periods of suspended animation under the skirting boards.

So it was there, and then, that Charlie Peterson began to make something of a living - but not really a life - by teaching the guitar. A man with a ponytail sold guitars in the shop above and Charlie, with forced and weary precision, got fumbling fingers to wring from their protesting strings, notes and chords and rudimentary riffs. The muse of music had left him. Only the

5

mechanical remained. The Gibson SG that had come alive in his hands lay dead in its case. On the rare occasions when it came to him that maybe he would play it again, he would see those same hands shaking over the fasteners on the case, and he would have to push them deep into his pockets and turn away. He played any guitar that came to hand when he had to - exigencies of the job and that kind of thing - but his soul never flowed into it. His soul was stretched out on the hard shoulder of the M4.

And therein lay the problem, because Charlie could have gone on alone. The record company had reacted to the accident with a heroic comeback proposal that involved the putting together of a new band. It could all prove, they'd pointed out, to be an incredible springboard to fresh success – *you'd never be able to buy publicity like it* ... Only after a respectable period of mourning, of course ... He'd slammed the door behind him. For him, the dream had been a dream of togetherness. What was fame and fortune without friends? What was the exhilaration of music when it wasn't reflected in the faces of the people you loved?

Had he been in conscious possession of just some of his old self, his old charisma, even some unthinking, evolutionary urge to fight his way back to the surface, he could have been teaching in one of those entrepreneurial music schools in the Square Mile, where young bankers and traders with vintage Fender Jags from Denmark Street have fifty pound an hour lessons so they can burn off stress by playing guitar hero. But he wasn't. Nor was it really the loss of the dream. Those friends who'd died had been part of who he was. They'd been alongside him ever since primary school, growing with him into adulthood, pouring their

6

struggles and their successes into one group anthem. Without them, Charlie felt like a few notes that could never be turned into a song.

In the cold, unchanging fluorescence of the basement his good looks faded. His hair grew, his face went unshaven, and his eyes lacked even a spark of the passion that had driven him for so long. He became, in effect, nothing more than an unkempt assemblage of old jeans and T-shirts. He ate pot noodle and doughnuts and drank black coffee. He tried a few joints, but he'd never found in drugs the release that other people seemed to. The guitar and the music had been his release - the only ones he'd ever needed. But they were unable to help him now. Somebody offered him Ecstasy, but the name alone was unbearable. There was no more ecstasy to be had. Every day was just an exercise in staving off misery. "Clean yourself up," said the man in the shop. "Lose the beard." So Charlie did. There was a cycle.

In due course, he mobilised enough of his former self to acquire a girlfriend – a pretty South Korean who had, at least at one point, been studying stage make-up somewhere in Covent Garden. She came and went at convenient hours, accepting his moods and his emotional unavailability without cavil. Perhaps cavilling girlfriends weren't the cultural norm in South Korea, but so much quiet acceptance made Charlie uncomfortable. "What do you want to do?" she would ask him. "I'll do whatever you want to do." There was nothing that Charlie actually wanted to do, but he was left with enough empathy to realise that a woman deserved more than he had to offer. He was too leaky a vessel to hold anyone else's dreams - particularly if those dreams involved joint living or marriage or children. Or anything else that smacked of serious commitment. So, when the government went through one of those phases when it felt obliged to worry about illegal immigrants, and his girlfriend began to worry about the fact that the government had started worrying about people like her, Charlie found himself helping her to pack and driving her to the airport. He didn't know what else he could do.

After that he worked up a speciality in the area of the forty-eight hour relationship and then, by dint of cutting out restaurant meals and long movies, the twenty-four hour relationship. But mostly, he ceased to bother at all. He just talked to the newts, though they only showed up in the winter. And time crept on, unheeded, unexploited, until Charlie Peterson had notched up seven long winters in the Camden basement, while his family's communications with him ran the complete gamut of what was humanly possible within the boundaries of loving concern. But Mrs. Peterson was finally reaching her limits. A mother can only be as happy as her most miserable child. Even when he's past thirty years old.

The minute the irritating youth put his thousand pound girl-bait guitar back in its case and slouched out into the corridor with it, Charlie's mobile chirruped. Mrs. Peterson was mysteriously attuned to her son's teaching schedule. She seemed to have some psychic talent for waylaying him with telephone calls and texts that popped up with dogged, but largely unfounded hope in gaps and coffee breaks. The calls were ignored nine times out of ten. Now, Charlie took the phone out of his pocket and stared at it. He didn't like what had been running through his head this last half-hour. Not merely running through his head, but taking over his entire being. Memories and miseries unthinkingly triggered by a few careless words. And maybe that was why he chose, this time, to press a different button. "Hello, Ma."

Mrs. Peterson was not feeling conversational. She was feeling concerned. Desperate even. "Charlie," she said, "I can already tell from your voice that things are not good. You cannot go on forever like this. In and out of despair as the mood strikes. You have a right to live. Entombing yourself in that basement will not bring your friends back. Nor will it get you any nearer to them. Music is not all there is to this world and it is not all that you can do. We barely see you anymore. In fact, we haven't seen you since Grandma's funeral. Come home for a few days and talk to us. Come home. *Please.*"

Charlie didn't answer.

"So," Mrs. Peterson was obviously feeling that the moment for tough love was more than upon her, "you force me to employ the proficiency a mother naturally has with emotional blackmail. It's my birthday in a week's time and, for a present, I would like to see you. Come home. There is something we need to talk to you about."

Still, Charlie didn't respond.

"Charlie," said Mrs. Peterson, "this is not a request. I am your mother, and I am demanding this of you in repayment for all the money that we have diverted to you in lieu of saving it. You and your future have been our investment. We made it with love, and without the need for a return, but we can no longer stand by, wringing our hands and watching, while you squander your life away."

Chapter Two

Charlie had to cancel lessons in order to accommodate his mother's birthday. Teaching guitar was a job with working hours that didn't lend themselves to a convenient social life. Weekends were when other people pursued their hobbies. That's when they wanted their lessons. During the week, children came after school and he taught until nine o'clock in the evening. He made money when the sun wasn't shining, and that way he accrued enough money to see him through the school holidays which tended, financially speaking, to be a little on the barren side. Unfortunately, his mother's birthday didn't fall in the school holidays, and this time it fell on a weekend. So yes, the visit was in the nature of a present – quite a big present. His mother was not normally this demanding. Something was up.

So Charlie got in the car and navigated London's clogged streets to reach the M40. Just a couple of years previously, he'd have had to go no farther than Mill Hill but now, in pursuit of retired parents, he had to drive about a hundred miles, crossing the Cotswolds, dropping down from the edge of the escarpment into the Vale of Evesham, and taking a sidestep into

Worcestershire. It was late May and the waysides were white with hawthorn blossom and cow parsley with a pink sprinkling of early wild roses. But Charlie was a creature of neon lights and tarmacadam so these things did not necessarily catch at his heartstrings, and yet he felt a little lighter, a little less burdened. Somewhere between Evesham and Pershore he pulled into a dirt track that led to a brick farmhouse with a fine view of the bard's Avon, a big asparagus field and some disused glasshouses.

He stood for a long moment beside the car, stretching his legs and easing his back, and wondering if, in this rustic backwater, he actually needed to lock it. It was a ten year old Citroën crappy with a hundred and fifty thousand miles on the clock. Even the Fagin's kitchen of thieves in London had shown no interest in it. And as Charlie stretched, vaguely considering the countryside, absently turning the car's keys over in his hand, a mischievous little breeze sprang up from somewhere and lifted the dark fall of hair from his forehead and out of his eyes. Charlie's eyes were an indeterminate shade of blue - which is to say that they were more like a moody grey. Their distinction lay in their ability to convey a great deal of something, or a significant type of nothing, without the rest of him having to do anything much at all. For the first days of his life he'd conveyed such a significant deal of nothing, on a scale so far beyond normal baby nothingness, that his mother had become alarmed. The old midwife who had done the post-natal visits was unconcerned.

"He was born backwards," she said. "It puts them about for a while."

"Right," said Mrs. Peterson.

11

"This backwards business is all about the artistic temperament. Musical people are often born backwards."

"Really?" said Mrs. Peterson. "Is that so?"

"Probably an old soul too. They're often not suited at first. He'll come into himself soon. You'll see." The old midwife was losing credibility by this point but she was right, as old midwives so often are.

And now, as he stood by the car, letting the breeze cool his skin on what was a rather hot day, after what had been a rather hot drive, Charlie Peterson came, for the second time in his life, back into himself. And there, just for a few moments, was the old Charlie. Six feet and more of lean, handsome, directed energy - legs braced, dark hair blown back by the noise coming from the amplifiers, eyes full of passionate intensity. And a smile - when suddenly it flashed - a smile that could break hearts from London to Los Angeles to Shanghai.

Shanghai? A big music market in Asia, the record company had said. Fans called Wing and Wang and God knows what. They might not be the target audience but they had money to spend and we, the record company beat its big chest, are here to take it.

"We don't really have a target audience," Charlie had pointed out. "The stuff Joe and I write is because we feel it, we care about it, that's why it's different, idiosyncratic."

"Idiosyncratic? *Jesus!*"

Charlie had opened his mouth to explain exactly what he was trying to get across, but the record company waved its giant hand. "Yeah, yeah, yeah. Keep that kind of stuff for sweetening up women journalists, will you? Now, look at this piece here, this is the kind of coverage we want:

Charlie Peterson, songwriter, guitarist and brilliant front man of the post-indie band 'Endgame', has an incredible live presence. He bestrides the stage with a drop dead, visceral authority that just oozes from the raw power of his voice and the casual insolence with which he delivers the sort of virtuoso guitar work that can be derailed by just one bum note. This guy could never have been in a boy band, singing in harmony and clicking his fingers during carefully choreographed dance moves. Mothers are not going to coo over him. He's Sabbath and Zeppelin and Nirvana. Nothing sweeter than that. In fact Peterson, now 22, was probably born too late. But some sounds never die, and with the powerful, gut curling music of Endgame, he could put a distinctive and genuine rock band back on top - where Peterson himself no doubt always ends up. So, if you prefer something gentler, girls, then bass guitarist and co-writer Joe Beck looks like the sweet one ..."

"Bit purple prose, isn't it?" Charlie had commented. He'd liked to have read less about him and something more specific about the music - the unconventional tunings, say, the risky time signature changes, the quick fire triplet riffs, the synchronised arpeggios ... All the things that some days had come so easily and yet, other days, had demanded that he sweat blood in order to drag them, sulky and swearing, from unknown wells and dark, untapped seams. Also, he wasn't remotely averse to being on the bottom. He was only partly this guy in the review. Once he put the guitar down, he was not his publicity. The Gibson SG was his animus - it inspired him, drove him, spoke to him. It took him to rainbow worlds and it took him to hell. And while they were in hell together it exorcised some of his demons - so that when he put it down, Charlie Peterson could be the boy next door. Mostly. Though never the boy band next door.

"*Purple be damned!*" A&R had roared at him with one voice.

13

"This is the colour of money. Big money. Not to mention how often a man with drop dead, visceral authority can get laid …"

But now it was nine or ten years on, and Charlie Peterson was standing in the gentle Worcestershire countryside where drop dead, visceral authority didn't seem to be the order of the day. The mysterious time-travelling little breeze had subsided just as quickly as it had arisen, and the twenty-two year old Charlie was no longer in evidence. The current Charlie, for whom that sudden, whimsical moment of enlivenment had wafted through virtually unrecognised, decided against locking the car and went on into the house.

The parental Petersons, now country people, had stone flag floors. A recent garnish of lawn clippings added a casual, carefree ambience to the large square entrance hall. A feeling of timelessness seemed to pervade the home, some new sense of life having to be lived by the seasons rather than the clock. In retirement, of course, decisions do not have to be rushed, the family executive can take its time, so the fallout from the Petersons' move and the revision of household possessions that it precipitated were still being worked through. A state of affairs that had been in no way lubricated by the death of the last remaining grandparent. Around the hallway's skirting boards, there'd been a build-up of dusty things that looked as if they could be headed somewhere. Maybe. One day. A charity shop perhaps, or a fete. Or even the local tip.

Charlie, glancing round at what was comparatively new territory for him, paused to scan the spines of some old paperbacks. It gave him a start to see that his Terry Pratchetts and his Dan Browns had been tied up in a death bundle with

Grandma Peterson's Jane Austens and Barbara Taylor Bradfords. He wasn't aware of any profound or coherent feelings about this, other than his sorrow at the passing of Grandma Peterson, but somewhere in his mind the idea that his life was like a book that might never be enjoyed again if he didn't reach in there and somehow turn a page, took enough of a hold to make him suddenly bend down and rescue Discworld and The Doors. A black house beetle popped out from beneath one of them and pottered encouragingly around his feet. Charlie put the selected books safely to one side, stepped carefully over the beetle and moved on into the rest of the house.

The Petersons' huge kitchen was two rooms knocked together, and there was an electric range in one fireplace and a wood burner in the other. The space was dominated by a large table made of old pine which was surrounded by gimpy chairs and covered in piles of newspapers, invitations to private views, a half-finished game of chess, some fruit and a few shiny screws that were probably desperate for the call to hold things together. Around the walls there were variously painted wooden cupboards plus a couple of racks that had probably been meant as storage for apples. Charlie's parents now lived a sort of artistic laissez-faire and their ideas on country ambience did not embrace the congruity of design exemplified by the built-in kitchen. They had put together this, their most important living space, with well-loved pieces of this and that like Harlequin's coat. In some nod towards coherence, they had strewn the floor with rush matting which worked to pull together areas of pammets, smatterings of quarry tiles, and a rather fine run of old slate slabs which lay, entirely fortuitously, in front of some French windows.

Charlie's father, seated at the table, deep in the Times crossword, had not heard his son come in. He scraped his chair back now, beaming with enthusiasm, and reached out to take Charlie in his arms. "Mother's out in the garden," he said, clapping his son heartily on the back. "Making a ten-foot rabbit."

Lottie Peterson spent an inordinate amount of time in garden and studio. Understandably so. Sculpture, indeed creativity in general, is a jealous lady who does not like being courted by halves.

"Huh," said Charlie. Released from the bear hug he crossed to the fridge, opened the door and looked in. It was full of interesting-looking meals lovingly created by the chefs at Tesco and Sainsbury's. Elaborate cooking had never seized Lottie Peterson - possibly it was considered too transient an art form. Peter Peterson had declined to take up the slack. In retirement, he preferred to develop his creative side by planting fruit trees at distances dictated by the Fibonacci sequence, and laying out vegetable beds in accordance with the golden proportion. Also, he had taken up the plotting of hugely complex 'whodunnits'. He had no burning ambition to get these published but the timetable accuracy required in their planning entertained him.

"Big," said Charlie, picking up a carton of orange juice. "This new sculpture. Will it actually look like a rabbit?"

"It could do. Or not. Your mother sees a rabbit same as the rest of us do, but she doesn't sculpt a rabbit. She sculpts what makes a rabbit, a rabbit."

"A ten-foot blueprint for a rabbit," said Charlie. "I guess that's something you don't see every day."

"In general, this upscaling thing is an artistic statement," said his father. "So I understand. And, cynically, I would have to say that, for the fiscally attuned artist, it has its advantages. You take something like a garden spade to a place with laser measuring equipment and they blow it up in size, creating a perfectly proportioned replica in polystyrene, then they send it to a Chinese foundry to get it cast in bronze and, voilà, the artist has a giant work of art worth thousands of pounds for pretty much no effort at all. It's all about the idea these days, not the execution. Like Tracy Emin's unmade bed or that pile of sweets. Any artist could've done it, they just didn't think of it. Marvellous what people will pay for an idea. I wish I could have one."

"But Mother is making the idea of a rabbit from scratch, isn't she?" asked Charlie.

"She is, but it's time she started tuning in to something smaller. These things have to be got to exhibitions, and I'm not getting any younger or any stronger. I suppose I should just be grateful she's not carving it out of stone."

Charlie crossed to the French windows and surveyed the environs as he drank orange juice straight from the carton. He could see his mother, a tiny wren of a woman in torn jeans and a checked shirt, augmenting her height with a set of steps here and a kitchen stool there, while she manhandled yards of galvanised netting onto a ten-foot armature. He looked round at his father, a great hairy badger of a man with enormous hands like moles' paws, who liked crosswords and sudoko and writing murder mysteries in note form - and wondered how on earth these things worked. A tiny female art student meets a six-foot-four maths student at a swinging sixties party somewhere in London, and the north and south poles of the human genome come together and battle on side-by-side for the next forty odd years without the continuing support of strong reefers. They have four sons and then the female, though not a particularly rampant feminist, finally declares: 'I give up. There's a limit to how many of these I can inflict upon the world in my desire for a girl child'. Peter and Lottie raise their sons and pay their way through life by, respectively, teaching maths in inner city schools and working in art galleries and auction houses. The boys leave home, one by one, and eventually the Petersons retire and move to a place where lebensraum can be purchased for an affordable sum at the same time as allowing them to be within convenient distances of their offspring who are now distributed between Birmingham, Oxford and London. They hope for visits from a covey of grandchildren who will be lured by a pond, a treehouse, and a small orchard with a neighbour's donkey in it. A donkey that can be ridden, or at least sat upon, as long as it is led around on a halter rope because otherwise it has no predisposition whatsoever towards forward motion.

So far there are only two grandchildren, but Lottie is an optimist. And she encourages. Subtly. The donkey won't live forever, she points out. In the meantime, she expends her supply of energy – which is apparently limitless – in the creation of sculptures. A talent that, once given space and time to really develop, has helped to pad out the pensions. It has, of course, endlessly postponed the fate of the flotsam in the hall.

"Well, it's nice to have you home, son," said Peter Peterson. "Anything new with you?"

"No," said Charlie.

"Not to worry." His father smiled. "Your mother's got a plan to sort that out for you."

For someone with an artistic, even bohemian, temperament Lottie Peterson had produced a few plans in her time. She came in presently, accepted sixty-sixth birthday wishes and a bunch of flowers with a smile for the flowers and a grimace for the age. When Charlie gave her a hug he could feel the ribs on her back, so thin was she. And yet she glowed with health - bright blue eyes in a face as brown as a nut from beavering away out in the sunshine. And she looked youthful - in spite of the sixty-six years and a grey grandma bun. And maybe that illusion of youth was due to a certain childish exuberance that seemed to flow, at least for periods of time, from the creation of ten-foot rabbits.

Charlie needed to find a ten-foot rabbit of his own. It wasn't that he didn't understand this, it was just that he'd had his ten-foot idea of a rabbit and lost it. And that kind of joy was hard to come by twice in a lifetime. Something of this must have flickered across his mind because his shoulders seemed to sag and his hair fell over his face again and, as he stood there in his jeans and T-shirt, he looked to his mother like a broken child and not the thirty-two year old man he really was.

Lottie Peterson felt a sudden and tremendous pain. 'For is there not a pity beyond all telling, hid in the heart of love', as Yeats W. B. put it. This was Lottie's youngest son. She had a lawyer, a doctor and one in the City and they had given her cause for nothing more than a normal quota of maternal anxiety. They pursued lives of carefully financed and well thought out advancement. But this, her baby, and the only one to express any of her genes at all, was standing before her with his own fiery brand of creativity cruelly and prematurely doused.

Lottie put two Sainsbury's lasagnes in the oven and laid the table while her husband assembled a salad and mixed in a dressing with his dutifully washed mole's paws. "Son," she said, as she moved newspapers and mail and a carefully considered rook on the chess board (she was trying hard to appear casual) "We have a suggestion for you. An opportunity."

"Oh?" Charlie was wary. It was something about the word *opportunity*. It had an uncomfortable ring of worthiness about it. An unspoken invitation to take a look at something that had to be considered but would lack the capacity to charm.

"Teaching," said his father, with a broad and encouraging smile. He put a lot into the word but even so, it failed entirely to take Charlie by storm.

"I *am* teaching," he pointed out.

"Proper teaching," said his mother, in a catastrophic choice of words that held the potential to scupper her wonderful plan before it had even got an airing. "In a school, I mean," she added hastily, wanting to bang her forehead on the table. This was what could come from being involved with essence of rabbit all day. Loss of the cynical necessity for verbal screening.

"Teaching chemistry," added his father. As a rescue measure it wasn't guaranteed to help.

"Why would I want to do that?" asked Charlie. "And why would anybody want me to? I got a third or something."

"You got a 2:2," said his father. "But it was from *Imperial*. And your tutors said you could have done really well, if only you'd had the foresight to turn up for the lectures."

"You'll get some paid holiday a year," said Lottie. "And it has to be a step up in terms of atmosphere." She shuddered. "That basement … It's hardly a life affirming place. And, yes, I realise that you don't actually want your life affirmed. That you are undergoing some sort of unconscious penance. Survivor's guilt or something. But that basement, Charlie … It's a tomb. The psychologist said it was a tomb and that's why you insist on staying there. He also said that such an excessive prolongation of grief can be pathological." She held up a hand. "Yes, I have talked to people about it, seeing as how you didn't want to."

Charlie chose to let all of this pass without comment. He didn't want to get bogged down in second-hand psychoanalysis. But neither did he want to be difficult as it was his mother's birthday and his father had produced a chocolate cake with candles. He sighed. His parents had been as benign a set of parents - perhaps even more benign - than he'd had any right to expect. The 'parents they fuck you up' line could barely be applied to them. His personality had not had to be constructed in some sort of opposition to his upbringing. True, he hadn't really wanted to go to university and now, suddenly, the chemistry degree was starting to look like a bit of a liability. He decided to employ some diversionary tactics. "Wouldn't I have to do teacher training or something?"

"Not when it's a private sort of school."

"Sort of private or sort of school?"

"Bit of both, I think," said his father, and received a sharp dig in the ribs. He looked indignant. "Come on, Lottie. It's a soya bean and goats' milk place. One of those pay and pray schools where you send the academically challenged and the frankly weird in the hope they'll come out with a nice manner, a light coating of education and a new talent for something like enamelling that will enable them to make a living other than being on the till at Tesco."

21

"It's called an *ethos*," said Lottie. "The place has an ethos. And what's wrong with enamelling? Or being on the till at Tesco, for that matter? So the place is a little bit Steiner." She turned to Charlie. "Your father's not remotely spiritual, even in the broadest sense. It's always been the greatest obstacle in our relationship."

"That's a lie," said Peter Peterson. "I am bursting with spirit. It animates me. It drives me." He flung out an arm. "I am a monument to spirit."

"You're a bloody poster boy for scientific materialism and you're perverting the discussion," said Lottie, in warning tones. "We've talked about this. Charlie is looking round for the second half of his life and this could be it. If you don't like the idea, just say so."

"I'm not looking round for the second half of my life," Charlie protested. "But I'm prepared to hear a bit more about it, if somebody is finally prepared to feed me." He sat silently for a moment while his mother put a plate in front of him, and then he said: "Who's Steiner?"

That was a question that Lottie wasn't entirely sure she wanted answered in full.

"There's the laptop," said Peter. "We could learn more about Rudolf Steiner than we'd probably ever want to know, in less time than it takes to repeat the question."

It occurred to Lottie that letting people who were even slightly acquainted with scientific method loose amongst some of Steiner's most radical ideas might not be a good plan. The two words 'spiritual science' alone added up to a potentially insurmountable oxymoron that could kill the idea of an interview stone dead. She glanced at her husband. It was possible that he'd looked up more on that computer than he was allowing. And she needn't even have mentioned Steiner in front of Charlie. More verbal indiscretion. She should have made a greater effort to change hats before coming indoors. The concept of sculpture as a process of relinquished control in which one gave birth to that which already existed but could not be seen, was not one to extend to the negotiating table.

"It's not a Steiner school," she said doggedly. "Steiner schools have an extra curriculum that runs alongside the standard one. So things take longer and the children are there until they are nineteen. This school isn't like that. It's just vaguely alternative. Encompasses a wider breadth of opinion, perhaps. I thought it was nice." She tailed off, a shade wistfully. "They seemed nice people. I thought maybe Charlie could be happy again there. It seemed somehow like fate …"

"Sounds like some sort of cult," said Charlie. "I have reservations about cults. Also about Fate. The last time she visited it didn't work out particularly well, especially for my friends, but if you think she's finally come up with something by way of apology then, again, I'm prepared to listen." His mother's birthday was proving an enormously extenuating circumstance. As she had, of course, clearly understood.

So this school, it turned out, this definitely-not-Steiner school that wasn't a cult of any sort, was merely a short step away in Herefordshire, and around Easter time it had held an art exhibition.

"Enamelling," said Peter, "like I said."

"Not just enamelling," said Lottie. "Don't listen to him,

Charlie. He wants you to apply for the job but he just can't resist a dig or two. If it's not because it's a bit Steiner, it will be because it's a private boarding school. He likes to be thought of as a fully paid up member of the proletariat, that's why he reads the Times."

"I only get it for the crossword," Peter Peterson insisted, but his wife was already sweeping onwards. There had been an exhibition and she, amongst a few other local sculptors and artists had, for the purpose of broadening the appeal of the thing to visitors, been invited to show some pieces alongside the pupils. It had been, Lottie said, thoroughly nice and well curated by a very elegant Frenchified lady who was the art teacher and a big, burly northerner who taught woodwork and metal work. Big, burly and chatty. At the private view, under the influence of some palate tickling canapés and too much white wine, he'd become quite voluble - happening to mention, amongst other things, that the school was about to lose a chemistry master.

"Well, you know how conversations go at these things," said Lottie. "You have to seize on something that could have mileage in it otherwise there are these awful silences while everyone searches for a polite excuse to move on."

The burly man, as it happened, hadn't seemed particularly proficient at moving on and the Petersons, possibly as a result of their recent rustication, had allowed themselves to get cornered. "I had no ulterior motive at the time," Lottie said. "It was just that bit of mileage in the word chemistry … You know."

Charlie didn't know. He didn't know why, in the middle of an art exhibition, his mother would have needed to find mileage in the word chemistry. Also, as far as he was concerned, chemistry had never had any mileage in it. It was just one of those things that he'd been able to do. And his parents, being of the middle-class opinion that tertiary education was virtually compulsory, especially in a country where the government was still at the point of paying for most of it, had suggested very strongly that he continue to do it. As insurance, they'd said. Lest the music industry turn out to be a crock.

"So," said Lottie, a shade sheepishly, "I rattled on a bit, and probably the burly man found out a lot more about you than he really wanted to know. However …"

There was a pause for chewing. The homegrown salad was a complex mixture of varied leaves and edible flowers, and it was delivering flavours worthy of some passing consideration. Charlie cleared his mouth. "This doesn't sound like much, so far. A serious degree of over-sharing, obviously, but not exactly a great intervention by Fate."

"I haven't got to the fate bit yet," said Lottie.

And the follow up had been, perhaps, a shade unusual. Three or four days later, the headmaster of the school, a Dr. Carlyle, had rung Lottie up. He had thanked her sincerely for supporting the exhibition, but the purpose of the call had been really to do with Charlie. Not only the requirement for a chemistry master, but the requirement for a chemistry master who had experience of things other than chemistry. A chemistry master who had been out in the world and done things unchemical, as it were. A young man - and some degree of youth was clearly important - who had operated beyond the fume cupboard and the test tube. A young man who had been handled by life. "Send us your son, Mrs. Peterson," Dr. Carlyle had finished. "We deal well with great losses here."

"Great losses or great losers?" asked Charlie.

"I'm not sure," said Lottie, "now you come to mention it."

There was silence for some time, then Lottie added: "Don't either of you think anything about this? Was that not an odd thing to say, whichever way you take it? Is this not," she paused, looking from her son to her husband and back again, "*something*?"

Chapter Three

In the end, Charlie went to an interview at the definitely-not-Steiner school mostly out of guilt. Probably not the survivor's guilt that his mother had spoken of, more the guilt that comes from having had his parents stand without a word of discouragement at his degree ceremony (which he had so very nearly deprived them of) and listen to how he thought that chemistry was nothing more than a pile of offal, and how he was off to seek his fortune in the world of rock music - a world which had thus far stimulated in him nothing more apparently advantageous than the urge to skip lectures and borrow endless amounts of money for bigger and better amplifiers. So, yes, he probably felt obliged to do this one belated thing for them out of some sort of guilt. Which just goes to show that guilt isn't always the pointless, destructive emotion that everybody thinks it is.

Puckrup Hall school was set in a wide valley amidst the green and gently rolling hills of Herefordshire. The entrance to its driveway was flanked by two tall brick gateposts, each capped with a large long-eared owl carved from stone. And owls, except possibly by those most expert on them, are commonly understood to be harbingers …

The driveway was long, at least quarter of a mile, and it was lined by imposing lime trees which gave some impression of structure and formality to the twin rivers of neglected knee high grass which flowed around them and on towards the school. The drive terminated in a very large gravel forecourt in front of a grand house the size of a minor stately home. It was extremely tall with a great many windows, and its medieval origins were only revealed in its beautifully panelled central hall - a fine place for assemblies with a wooden floor that creaked in sympathy with fidgeting children. From the outside, the place looked essentially Georgian, with wings that looked Victorian, and annexes that looked Edwardian, and new brick outcroppings and satellite clutches of prefabrications that seemed pretty much up-to-date. Through gaps in this complicated assortment of buildings, Charlie caught the distant radiance of a lake. Or possibly, it was just more glasshouses. He had never seen as many glasshouses and polytunnels in his entire life as were scattered round here and over his parents' adopted countryside.

The entrance to the main house was protected by a grand portico supported by six Doric columns. Beneath the portico stood a tall, thin man with gold-rimmed spectacles, a bow tie and a smartly trimmed beard. Beside him sat one of those small, trembly terriers, white with a black patch over one eye. It shook as if it were freezing cold but, as the day was fine and sunny, it was probably just excited about the coming interview. The man waved to Charlie and signalled that he should come and park near to him.

Charlie got out of the car thinking: jacket and jeans, jacket and jeans, was that a good move? His mother had said 'suit', but he didn't have one. He was wearing one of his father's shirts which was frankly baggy round the neck, and a navy blue tie with faint white spots. He'd combed back his hair and fixed it with hopeful fingers and a dollop of ancient gel found in the bathroom cupboard, but he was still conscious that it hung over his ears and his jacket collar. He understood that there was an ambivalence in his dress that had to be interpreted as an ambivalence in his attitude to the interview. He wasn't sure why he was suddenly so conscious of this.

The man under the portico didn't appear to be affected by it one way or the other. He stepped forward with a broad smile and held out a hand, introducing himself as Dr. Arne Carlyle, the headmaster. Dr. Carlyle was wearing a biscuit-coloured linen suit that had a well-worn drape to it. His shirt was dark blue and his bow-tie of red silk paisley. On his feet he wore a pair of nut brown veldschoens. The overall effect, with his head of grey hair and his trimmed beard, was surprisingly natty. And maybe slightly German. Or maybe Scandinavian. Yet there was also the impression of a peculiarly English eccentricity. A complicated man, obviously. "So what did you think of our wildflower meadow, Mr. Peterson?" he asked.

Wildflower meadow? What wildflower meadow? Charlie looked around.

"The driveway, Mr. Peterson. Alongside the driveway."

Apparently, he meant all that rank grass on the way in with its nettles and thistles and the sort of flowers that Charlie had seen his father yanking from the vegetable patch with something akin to hysteria. "I'm sorry," he said. "I'm not, you know …"

"Of course not," said Dr. Carlyle. "You're from London. What was I thinking? Should we go in?"

The entrance hall was huge with a floor of Bath stone, an impressive Adams fireplace directly facing the door, and a magnificent staircase curving away from one side up to a galleried landing above.

"Puckrup Hall," said Charlie. "That's a very unusual name, isn't it?"

"It's old English," said Dr. Carlyle. "It means 'haunt of goblins'. Though I don't think we have any goblins. Fairies and gnomes, I'm told, and a boggart, but then it's probably just a question of semantics."

At this point, he turned right and led Charlie a short way down a panelled corridor beset with endless photographs of grinning schoolboys holding up cups, then left down another panelled corridor, and finally into an airy and beautiful room with highly ornate plaster coving that was obviously his study. The wall immediately to the right of the door was covered in bookshelves. At a glance Charlie saw Aristotle, Plato, Kant, Hegel, (Dr. Carlyle's background was in philosophy?) plus Shakespeare, Chaucer, Dickens and the rather jolting inclusion of Virginia Woolf, who was Charlie's mother's least favourite Englishwoman, dead or alive. At the far end of the room, on the opposing wall, there was yet another grand fireplace, and on the rug in front of it sat a small boy, around seven years old, with tousled blonde hair and moody blue eyes. He was playing with a remote-controlled car which he was repeatedly banging into the leg of an enormous partners desk. The desk, a splendid piece of furniture standing in front of paired French windows, was obviously unmoved by these assaults but the trembly terrier, clearly upset by them, immediately seized the car in its jaws and made off with it.

"Goodness me!" exclaimed Dr. Carlyle. "Tempest min, what are you doing here? Why aren't you with your brothers? Your mother is coming to pick you up."

"She's late, sir," said Tempest min. "She's always late, and she should have been here yesterday."

"True, yesterday was the day when we should have been divested of you all, but your mother's flight was delayed."

"She's late today. It's almost lunchtime. And I'm hungry. And when she comes, it's never her."

"That doesn't explain why you aren't waiting with your brothers."

"My brothers don't like me hanging around with them."

"Why not?"

"They don't like me."

"Of course they do. You're their brother."

"Not all of me," said Tempest min.

Dr. Carlyle shook his head. "Come on. Let's go and see if Mrs. Carlyle can rustle you up a sandwich. Then you'd better go and find Blake and Paul, whether they like you or not. Somebody will be here soon, I'm quite certain of it." He excused himself, still shaking his head, and took the small boy off somewhere.

Charlie, who at the onset of this headmaster/pupil conversation had immediately withdrawn to the bookshelves and begun a further perusal of their contents, could still hear snatches of talk as it faded away. 'Why can't I go and stay with somebody else?' … 'Because your mother would be upset.' … 'No she wouldn't.' … 'I'm sure she would.' … 'I did it before.' … 'That was only an exeat, Tempest min, this is the entire summer holidays' …

As the contretemps faded into the distance, Charlie turned to look again at the room and was quickly transfixed by a large picture hanging above the fireplace. It was an oleograph of a portrait of the Emperor Rudolph II as Vertumnus. And Vertumnus appeared to be a man made entirely of vegetables with apple cheeks, ears of corn, a pumpkin chest and a small gourd in the middle of his forehead. That was pretty much the limit of Charlie's ability to identify vegetables in unadulterated form: sprouting green things, in particular, were pretty much just sprouting green things to him. Except he thought he could see grapes in the hair now, and possibly a carrot or two. He leaned forward to read the name of the artist again. Giuseppe Arcimboldo. He was still none the wiser.

Dr. Carlyle reappeared. "Sorry about that. Sad, very sad. The Vane Tempest boys all have different fathers and for some reason, mostly to do with the particular father I suspect, or possibly the lack of him, the two older boys don't really like the youngest one." He looked thoughtfully down at his feet for a moment or two. "One would hesitate to predict that having three children each by a different father would be the way to promote peace and harmony at the tea table, but there we are. People seem to think that this is an inevitable advance in social structure so we must make it come out as best we can. He's such a lovely little boy." He paused thoughtfully. "Strange in some ways, though. Dreamy. He hums a lot."

"Hums?"

"Yes. Gets distracted en route from one lesson to the next, and then we find him in a corner. Humming. Not in some absent, self-consoling way but in earnest."

"He *hums?*" asked Charlie again, wondering if this was some sort of euphemism that he hadn't come across before.

"Yes … you know. Tunes. He hums tunes." Dr. Carlyle began to hum a few lines from something unidentifiable, beating time with one hand.

"Oh, right, *humming*. Got it."

"And he does it so beautifully." The headmaster started to look disappointed. "We keep asking him if he wants to join the choir. It's not a grand Westminster Abbey, panis angelicus sort of choir, but we do encourage singing here. All sorts of singing. But you know what he says?"

This was obviously rhetorical so Charlie merely shook his head.

"He says: 'I don't think I'm supposed to sing'." Dr. Carlyle joined in the head shaking. "We've never got to the bottom of that. A most mysterious child. And always the same tune - a beautiful tune - elegant, poignant, but pitched in a minor key with such agonisingly beautiful dissonances here and there, I couldn't even begin to give you an idea of it. Nobody seems to know what it is. And when we ask him …" He gave a great sigh and shook his head some more. "I can't help worrying about Tempest min."

Charlie gave him a few moments to recover and then asked: "Why do you call him Tempest min?"

"It's traditional. For the younger ones. We don't shy entirely from tradition here, and we feel it helps a little with discipline at the start. Min is short for minimus. Tempest major - oldest. Tempest minor - next oldest. Tempest minimus - youngest. Ma, mi and min. We've never needed more than that. We once had triplets, it was a tremendously useful system then. When they hit Common Entrance age we call them by their first names, of course."

Dr. Carlyle stared absently out of one of the large French windows for a moment or two. The windows gave the view from the rear elevation of the house. There was a terrace immediately outside, flagged in York stone, with steps down onto a vast but rather ragged lawn. Not satisfactory for croquet, obviously, or even for the averagely fastidious gardener. Something was evidently being nurtured in it, but Charlie forbore to ask what. Beyond the lawn there was a ha-ha so that the lawn appeared to flow seamlessly into a bona fide hayfield with woods flanking it on either side.

"Is that a lake in the distance?" Charlie asked.

"An agricultural water reservoir surrounded by a mixture of polytunnels and polythene sheeting. It's a big growing area here. We rather pride ourselves on it." Dr. Carlyle swung round, suddenly beaming, and studied Charlie for a moment or two.

Charlie found this beaming scrutiny a little disconcerting so he said, "It's quite a mix of children you have here, is it?"

"Most definitely," said Dr. Carlyle. "A great mix of children, boys that is, all brought together by their parents' ability to pay. We give scholarships, of course, but the scholars are not a large percentage of the mix, though we do as much as we can. The ability to pay, however, is a much broader church than you might imagine."

"Do you have any selection procedures at all? Entrance requirements, that is?" Charlie asked, after a moment or two. Dr. Carlyle didn't seem in any hurry to take a formal grip on the proceedings, and he was obviously a man greatly at ease with silence, but Charlie felt conscious of some sort of gap that needed filling, so he filled it.

"We find we don't need any. Our ethos is our selection procedure. Because we nurture the spirit, and try to find in every child a character and a métier that is the very best he has to offer, we tend to attract the tender plants. Of course, these are occasionally bonded to less tender plants because parents with more than one child don't always want to be driving off to all points of the compass. But that's by the by." He nodded to himself. "Yes, I would say that we are very successful in bringing out the best in our boys because, by the time they are well into their teens, they appear not to be tender plants at all. In fact, the more the world rolls on and the more they spend hours in the holidays surfing the world wide web, the less and less tender they are becoming. And the farther into the twenty-first century we get, the more I fear that our school must be starting to look like some lost outpost - some sad Noah's ark of attitudes and outmoded beliefs, completely at sea in a world of sophisticated and patronising secularism, recreational drugs and naked women. And I'm sure that Dr. Boswell, for instance – senior English and junior History – has never seen a naked woman. Or a naked man, for that matter. He's very keen on the medieval and in the medieval church marriage was always viewed as inferior to celibacy and virginity. He's a very clever man and a brilliant teacher - we would never want to lose him - but this sort

35

of thing puts you at a disadvantage when it comes to raising up teenage boys in the twenty-first century. You see where I'm going with this?"

Charlie had no idea. The conversation seemed to have taken a very peculiar turn.

"We are not the sort of people who are naturally au fait with the preponderant features of the modern zeitgeist," Dr. Carlyle went on. "We try, of course, but our extramural knowledge encompasses things like planting by the moon, and the habits of processionary moths, and how to nurture spiritual development. But teenage boys want to do things and know about things that are not quite as spiritual as we would like, and nothing to do with moths at all. That's where you could come in."

Charlie wasn't quite following. "I'm not quite following," he said.

"Well," responded Dr. Carlyle, watching him carefully, "in addition to chemistry and maths …"

"*Maths?*" interjected Charlie, experiencing a sudden unpleasant frisson.

"To a level, to a level," Dr. Carlyle spoke soothingly. "Your father taught maths, didn't he?"

"He did," said Charlie. "But I'm not at all sure it's hereditary."

"But you have A-level maths, do you not?"

"I do but …" But he had never seen a system glowing with pure reason as his father had. Something fundamentally enmeshed with the universe. It had merely been sums with solutions. He endeavoured to explain this in style, so as to emphasise his inadequacies in this area.

"We don't need maths to glow," said Dr. Carlyle firmly. "At

this point, we just need the little ones to be able to add up and so on, and the slightly older ones to be introduced to the gist of algebra and geometry. As much gist as you have left will be more or less sufficient for eleven-year-olds, I'm sure. After that, Mr. Hutchinson will get things to glow. It'll all be very easy, you'll see. So, to get back to what I was saying, in addition to junior maths and middle and senior chemistry, we'd like you to take on the very special area of sex education."

Charlie had never really wanted this job, and this astonishing pronouncement of Dr. Carlyle's had the effect of removing even the faintest attraction it might have held for him. He could have left there and then but, out of respect for his mother and the fact that she might be interested, in the future, in becoming further involved with the school's artistic endeavours, he thought he ought to continue to the end of the interview in as intelligent and cooperative a fashion as he could muster. "Isn't sex biology?" he asked.

"Reproduction," said Dr. Carlyle. "Reproduction is biology. Sex is chemistry."

"Aren't you being just a little ... ingenuous?" Charlie asked.

"More than a little," said Dr. Carlyle, smiling broadly. "Let me explain. Our senior biology teacher, Mrs. Gargery, is divorced now. And glad of it, I suspect. Though we continue to call her Mrs. Gargery out of sheer habit ..." (This was a point that seemed to have just struck him.) "She doesn't seem to mind. Clearly, her sense of self is not bound up in the way she is addressed. Anyway, she bore six children - God knows how she ever found time to teach - so she's obviously an expert on reproduction, but her inclinations these days run more along the lines of ladybird counts and great crested newts. She has made it abundantly clear to me, and she's quite happy for me to say so, that she has no interest whatsoever in becoming involved in the school sideshow that is the sex life of the teenage boy. Or the sub-teenage boy for that matter. Any boy, in short. Reproduction she will cover in a scientific, zoological way as per the syllabus. How *not* to get the female of the species pregnant is *not*, she says, her department."

Charlie couldn't deny a sympathy with that point of view but he thought it was a bit steep to expect some unsuspecting chemistry master to take up the slack.

"And I do think the boys need a man for man-to-man moments," said Dr. Carlyle. "Don't you?"

"I can't tell you," said Charlie, "how many man-to-man moments I have tried desperately not to have with my father."

"But you aren't these boys' father, are you? Which is exactly the point. You've been in the music industry, you must have covered a fair bit of ground. As the face of rock 'n' roll, or as near to it as we're ever going to get out here, you're the one who could give them readings from the big book of 'dos' and 'don'ts' without sounding like a prudish, killjoy, stick-in-the-mud."

Charlie hadn't actually rehearsed this interview at all and, if he had, he certainly wouldn't have rehearsed this, but it struck him now that if he *had* been going to come to the school he would most certainly not have wanted his past to come with him. The position would have been in the way of a new start. One didn't make new starts by dragging the past along. One made a clean surgical break so that in time, perhaps, the relationship with the past, with music in his case and with himself, could be adjusted and accepted without the misery it carried with it. That was the only way the situation could have served him. Yet, even as he thought these things, Charlie felt again the acuteness of his original pain. For a moment or two he couldn't speak. The effort he had to make to overcome his feelings was plainly visible.

"But I wouldn't want to come here as the person I was," he said finally and carefully. "I would prefer to allow what is gone to *be* gone. In which case, I wouldn't be the person you need me to be. I couldn't present as what you are looking for."

"Hmm …" Dr. Carlyle studied him thoughtfully for a few moments. "I see … The total divestment of accumulated regrets."

"I didn't quite say that," said Charlie. "I can never stop regretting the death of my friends. That's not possible. Anywhere. Ever. But, maybe, I could stop regretting the loss of what we shared if I was in a circumstance where it never needed to come up."

"Schopenhauer," said Dr. Carlyle slowly, "was of the opinion that music is a primary expression of the essence of everything."

"It is, or rather *was*, to me," said Charlie, "but I suspect that most people would doubt that Schopenhauer was talking about rock music." He had no idea who Schopenhauer was.

"Schopenhauer," said Dr. Carlyle, "was an eighteenth century German with a pessimistic, if iconoclastic, soul, and he felt that we were constantly driven by wants and desires that could never deliver fulfilment. In the absence of a God, he felt the answer lay in art, in aesthetic experience. Aesthetic perception as a mode of transcendence. And he rated music as the most metaphysical of the art forms. The one most likely to transport us beyond ourselves into some sort of wondrous experience that lay beyond our individual gripes and greeds. A younger contemporary of his, Nietzsche, yet another thunderously gloomy German looking for something better than he could find in himself or anybody else, took up with this idea of ecstatic collective transcendence and went off to listen to Wagner. And let us not forget that Wagner was the rock music of the age."

He paused then, and studied Charlie (who'd sort of expected, in so far as he had done any expecting, to be talking about chemistry). "Unfortunately," Dr. Carlyle went on after a moment or two, "Wagner in concert was listened to by an audience of stuffed shirts so it did not deliver quite the group experience Nietzsche was hoping for. Had Nietzsche been able to time travel to Woodstock or Glastonbury - well, who knows? His work might not have become such that it could be so perversely exploited by Herr Hitler."

"Right," said Charlie. He knew more about Wagner - something about a Ring cycle that went on for four days involving a big brass section, a lot of Norse Gods and a magic ring - than he did about Schopenhauer and Nietzsche. But that wasn't really saying a lot. So he wasn't at one with what was really being spoken of, or where it was supposed to be leading. If anywhere. Keeping up with this man, let alone assembling appropriate responses, was like trying to follow a grasshopper.

Dr. Carlyle had now taken to surveying the ceiling. "Music has always been irrevocably entwined with man and his place in the universe," he said finally. "Pythagoras could hear the stars singing and the sun playing flute. The music of the cosmos cleared his spirit. And the Pythagoreans were convinced that

40

numbers and numerical proportions described the structure of the cosmos as well as the structure of music. One was part and parcel of the other. Which brings me back to the surprising situation that you are not more appreciative of maths."

"I understand the maths and music thing," said Charlie, "but maths on its own doesn't really sing to me. It never did."

"Maths doesn't seem to sing to many people," said Dr. Carlyle, coming back to earth with every evidence of regret. "Which is a constant source of irritation to those who teach it. But the point I'm really trying to make," he went on, with a sudden and sympathetic smile, "amongst all of these disparate ramblings, is that music has touched you powerfully because music is powerful. Of all the arts it is the least obviously derived from the visible world and, just as Schopenhauer believed, it's the one with the most mysterious access to our inner spirits. And for you, it's obviously part of who you are. So, wherever you are, it will have its time with you again. One way or another."

Charlie said nothing.

"The Eternal Recurrence," remarked Dr. Carlyle, watching him carefully. "That was another idea of Nietzsche's, spawned by more gloomy efforts to come to terms with the human condition. But let's not get caught up in Eternal Recurrences just now. Back to the situation in hand. I think the job here could be done without the need to tout your credentials. We might not have to pin you down quite so specifically as a modern totem of virility and cool. One only has to look at you to know that you have not spent your particular genius assiduously balancing chemical equations these past years. I doubt the boys will categorise you with Dr. Boswell. I still think we could, with profit, have you deliver the ABC of STDs and so on …"

"I don't know anything about STDs," said Charlie firmly. "I took good care not to catch them."

"And isn't that just the point!" Dr. Carlyle was triumphant. "You are obviously the right man to teach the boys that prudence must be exercised in seizing the moment. Everything must be considered. Life cannot be lived in raging torrents – it doesn't work out well that way."

Was this the actual interview? Charlie wondered. He hadn't had many interviews in his life. One at Imperial, which he could barely pick out now from subsequent viva voces and other unfortunate conversations with his tutors. Another one for the job at telephone sales, but that had been something of an ongoing, practical selection procedure – a sort of 'last man standing' business. The only other, at the guitar shop in Camden, had been more in the nature of a briefing: "Sorry about the band, bro'. Fucking good music. Be nice to the kiddies and don't hit on the mothers." And that had been it, more or less. But this current interlude seemed to be progressing very oddly. It hadn't got off to a clear-cut start, what with Tempest min sitting on the rug and so forth, so consequently he felt as if he were really just chatting, and the headmaster was just chatting, and yet it seemed as if, in the midst of all this … well … frankly surprising chatter, propositions were being put and decisions made. Not that it really mattered … but he was curious.

Surely, he thought, there must be nicely dressed, well recommended and enthusiastic people applying for this position. Chemistry teachers, in fact. Wouldn't they expect a process commensurate with their effort? "Don't you have a panel for interviews?" he asked. "A board or something ...?"

"We have lunch," said Dr. Carlyle. "It's a nice summer's day so we will have some salad on the terrace, courtesy of my wife. Our chief benefactor and head of the board of governors, Lady Keeble Parker, will come if she's not distracted by any rare orchids en route, plus such members of staff as happen to be still in the vicinity and feeling inclined to join in. We like to be informal here. Do our assessments incidentally, as it were. Not fans at all of the good cop, bad cop regime or something based on the FBI's five point interrogation methods. We like catching people off-guard with a mouthful of tomato."

"I see," said Charlie, who could take tomatoes or leave them.

"But to get back to the matter in hand, what else do you think would be pertinent to discuss with our boys? We keep them free of STDs and ...?"

Charlie had no idea. His mind, helpfully or otherwise, shot him back to his own teenage years at school. What had he wanted to know? He remembered wanting to know how to get his brain and fingers to master the solo in Lynryd Skynryd's Freebird. And to work out why it was more difficult than you might have thought to play like Hendrix, instead of somebody trying to play like Hendrix. And to wonder if he could ever get to be as good as Van Halen. He didn't remember being too concerned about much else. The fact that being the singer and lead guitarist in the school's rock band was the nearest thing to a love potion that actually existed had gone mostly to waste. A waste that had been pointed out to him frequently and rudely by the less fortunate. The guys with acne, and those without the talent to perform in any popular public forum, had been

43

understandably peeved at the injustice of it all. The stars of track and field had seemed able to juggle girls and pole vaulting at the same time, but for him the guitar and his nascent song-writing urges had been powerful mistresses. They'd burned most of the fuel he'd had. Plus, girlfriends didn't like just sitting watching while he picked away at singing lines on the guitar. It might have seemed romantic enough at first, but then when he got an eight-track for a birthday present and he and the entire band spent every weekend in the garage, recording, girlfriends developed sulky expressions and occasionally kicked things around. There'd been no breasts anywhere attractive enough to compensate for having his new wah-wah pedal sent flying across the garage floor, so that had been that.

But, while he'd been busy testing the limits of wah-wah pedals, other people had been pushing the envelope of recreational sex. In university and the world beyond, everyone appeared to be embracing (or at least hoping for the opportunity to embrace) the principle of complete sexual liberation. And it seemed, if you were careful, that the whole business could go along much like a game of squash. You followed a broadly accepted protocol, got a workout and tried not to look too disengaged, or disappointed, or desperate, afterwards.

"So," Dr. Carlyle interrupted Charlie's flashbacks, "have you any thoughts on these things? The philosopher Peter Singer, for instance, writes that 'sex raises no unique moral issues at all' and public opinion together with various government policies and legislation seem to reflect this. Where would you stand? What would you say to the older boys, for instance?"

"It's a casual world out there, so avoid casualties," said

44

Charlie. "Consenting adults only. Always the belt and braces approach to STDs and pregnancy. Doubly certain. Always. No means no and a lot of other things mean no as well. And have some boundaries, for Chrissakes. Don't behave like a pig."

There was a silence. A silence that Charlie found impossible to read. He had no idea what the headmaster was looking for and his response, even to his own ears, had been rather blunt. But, honestly, it was a prospective conversation that he was planning on never having. He couldn't believe that his mother had dropped him in for this. Not that she could have known.

"Brief and to the point," said Dr. Carlyle suddenly. "You'd have to elucidate for the boys, of course. The belt and braces principle would need stating in plain terms, and I imagine they'd want more detail on matters porcine. But I'm quite sure that you'd be able to work it all up into some thoroughly enjoyable talks."

Charlie failed to respond, but Dr. Carlyle seemed not to interpret his silence in a discouraging way. "And what sort of things would we say to the younger boys?" he continued brightly. "How do we make these things age appropriate?"

Charlie sighed. "Don't these children have mothers?" he asked, in desperation. "I guess I'd think of something appropriate to say if I was asked a one-off question, but it's not something for which I'm going to volunteer on any organised basis. I thought schools like this had matrons." Truthfully, he was running out of steam. This was so clearly not the job for him and there was a limit to the charade he was prepared to put up in the speculative interests of his mother's future artistry. "You know," he said, "I really don't think I could fill this position for you."

"LAFFAS," said Dr. Carlyle. "The lady from LAFFAS fills it."

Who was that and why wasn't she the one getting interviewed?

"Laying appropriate foundations for appropriate sex," said Dr. Carlyle. "LAFFAS. It's a charity. We give a donation and a nice peripatetic lady comes and acquaints the boys with what they need to know, when they need to know it. She's very large and very jolly and the whole thing goes along swimmingly."

Charlie looked at him.

"Obviously you're confused," said Dr. Carlyle.

One of us is.

"The FBI isn't the only organisation with methods, you know. We do a CRB check, of course, and we probe unstintingly into your past, because in a place like this we cannot be too careful. That Mr. Delaney in the guitar shop is an interesting chap, isn't he?" Dr. Carlyle held up a hand. "Don't worry, we are not crass enough to reveal to your current employer that you are looking to leave him."

That came as something of a relief to Charlie, because he wasn't.

"We masqueraded, Mr. Peterson. Masqueraded most successfully," said Dr. Carlyle in satisfied tones.

Charlie didn't bother to ask how. He'd heard nothing about it so it must have been successful, more successful than he would frankly have credited.

"And we got what we wanted from our masquerade," went on Dr. Carlyle. "In seven years, the guitar man told us, he'd never had one complaint about anything you'd done. Possibly a few too many about things you hadn't done. And also about your appearance. He used very succinct wording there. I remember it distinctly because it was open to misinterpretation. 'Scruffy fucker', that was it. 'He can be a scruffy fucker.' We took it literally at first, which was a bit alarming, but it turns out that the word fucker is almost a term of endearment these days. It's wonderful how the English language moves on, isn't it? No wonder they need to keep compiling new dictionaries."

Was this man an intentional or an unintentional humourist? Charlie wondered. It was hard to tell one way or the other with the light from the big French windows flickering over those gold-rimmed spectacles. The thing Charlie could see, however, was that he was being played with. In the politest possible way, of course. He gave a mental shrug. Charlie Peterson wasn't the defensive sort. Which indicates, perhaps, that despite his current difficulties with life, he still had some confidence left in Charlie Peterson.

"You understand that these things have to be done of course, don't you?" said Dr. Carlyle. "You listen to the news, presumably. The Catholic church, children's homes, public schools and no less a place than the BBC riddled with dreadful goings on. Parents place their trust in us, Mr. Peterson, and pay handsomely for it, so we cannot unwittingly allow a wolf to set up house amongst our lambs. In a boarding school situation a man's character is crucial. So, we like to throw out a few curve balls, as the Americans say, and then watch how you react. It's not necessarily about what you say, it's just another effort to try and read between your lines. It was noticeable, I might add, that you didn't appear to have any."

"Maths but no sex education then," said Charlie, after a pause.

"That's about the price of it," nodded Dr. Carlyle. "But not

47

the whole price. We would like to think of you as someone the boys could turn to about certain things. I think they will recognise in you a man more in tune with the age, as it were. Youngsters are astute that way. Could you tolerate that? You could always have just a little chat with the lady from LAFFAS. That would be fun, wouldn't it?" He gave a mischievous smile.

Charlie sighed. This seemed a nice man, if an odd one. He felt he was going to have to come clean in this matter. He didn't really want the position. It was pointless going on. He took a deep breath and opened his mouth, but Dr. Carlyle had already turned away and was wrenching open one set of French windows in a determined way. "Lunch," he said over his shoulder. "Come along."

It seemed churlish to turn down something that had been specially prepared, so Charlie followed him. As it happened, attending to Tempest min had slowed Mrs. Carlyle down somewhat. Lunch was not in evidence.

"Let's take a walk," suggested Dr. Carlyle. "Let's take a walk."

Chapter Four

They went down the terrace steps onto the hairy lawn and across its mole and moss infested turf to the ha-ha ditch. The trembly terrier, reappearing from somewhere, trotted ahead of them still carrying Tempest min's car in its jaws. At the edge of the ha-ha, Dr. Carlyle turned round and looked back at the buildings. Puckrup Hall had, he explained, been turned into a school in Victorian times by Lady Keeble Parker's grandfather, a great industrialist and philanthropist, who'd got himself a hereditary peerage for services to pretty much everything. He'd been a very Christian gentleman, and also very interested in science. The science wing, which was in one of the Edwardian extensions, had been dedicated to him after his death. The huge wooden benches with their set-in sinks and gas taps for Bunsen burners were still used today. Boys could perch on stools as well as they had ever done, Dr. Carlyle pointed out with some satisfaction. Not everything about them was subject to change by internet . The equipment, he added quickly, was more up to date than the benches, though the fume cupboard was original.

Charlie found that this discussion of chemistry labs wasn't

inducing in him quite the narcosis he'd imagined it would. A few memorable moments associated with them came back to him: ridiculous schoolboy jollity set off by Gay-Lussac's law, the risky pleasure of purloining lumps of sodium and throwing them into puddles in the playground on November 5th ... the subsequent interview with the headmaster. Meanwhile Dr. Carlyle was continuing, with much energetic arm waving, to expand on the school's layout: the library was in the main house as were the kitchens, the dining hall, the sanatorium, Matron's flat, the dormitories for boys up to the age of twelve, the junior common room and the main staff room. The extensive prefabricated buildings housed art and design, the technical side of things and the junior classrooms.

After the age of twelve the boys lived in one of the three houses: Worcester, Gloucester and Hereford, which were located in the various modern brick buildings. The boys lived in these houses in shared bedrooms and each house had its own common room and TV room and was supervised by a resident housemaster. The latest of the new brick edifices contained a theatre with a stage, a movie screen and tiered seating. It was built back to back with a new gymnasium.

"We have some very generous alumni," said Dr. Carlyle. "Some people leave here with both a sense of gratitude and the skills to make big money. It's a happy combination for us when it comes about."

At this point, he descended the steps into the ha-ha ditch and, in a sprightly fashion, scrambled up the opposing slope. Straightening up after a much less efficient scramble, Charlie could see that here and there amongst the knee high grass in the waving, thistle and dock ridden meadowland stretching before them was scattered evidence of derelict and primitive camping - collapsing ex-army bell tents, metal tripods dangling blackened cooking pots, dead fires encircled with stones in evocative boy scout fashion.

Out here, Dr. Carlyle explained, the younger boys lived their personalised versions of Swallows and Amazons. "They stalk tigers," he said. "And fight orcs and build booby traps for the comparatively helpless fauna of England to fall into."

"Humane traps, I must point out," he added quickly. "Somebody actually caught a wood mouse once and everybody in the school had to view it. I hadn't the heart to point out that, come winter, we would be hard put to keep from treading on them in the kitchens. Probably a relief there are no tigers," he finished, thoughtfully. "We'd have to step up the supervision a bit."

Charlie wondered if health and safety ever had its name whispered out here. Dr. Carlyle obviously didn't believe in bush fires and broken bones and terminal asthmatic attacks. Charlie thought of his little niece and nephew kept in padded, if gilded, cages by his sister-in-law who could spot a whole shopping list of disasters in her own back garden. Adders, biting spiders, killer bees come across from Mexico, ticks, plants that give rise to rashes and blisters and kill you if you dig them up and eat the roots, listed and classified zoonoses from every creature under the sun, especially next door's cat which kept sneaking in through the fence. His sister-in-law had been a nurse but instead of making her comforting it had made her neurotic. Chances in a million her husband, the doctor, kept assuring her. But she knew better. She knew that something called Lyme disease was headed their way with that muntjac deer a neighbour had spotted in his garden one winter night. Charlie shook his head. Connie Peterson was a nightmare but, nevertheless, the matron in this place had to be kept pretty busy.

"Do you ever play football or anything?" he asked.

"All kinds of anything," said Dr. Carlyle. "Football, rugby, cricket, tennis, squash, orienteering, tai chi … Everyone is catered for. You'll see."

They were now heading for the edge of the field, moving single file through the long grass. Dr. Carlyle stopped when they reached the trees.

"And here is our forest garden," he said. "The boys come out here and give themselves tummy ache. Some things you do in life give you tummy ache. It's a lesson you need to learn. You can't just grab the low-hanging fruit and gobble it down without thinking. You must ask yourself: 'What sort of fruit is this and is it the sort of fruit I should be eating?'"

Charlie bent and brushed off grass seeds that had adhered in their hundreds to the legs of his corduroy jeans. He wondered, having worked up an uncomfortable sweat in his jacket and tie, what the hell a forest garden was. Wasn't that a contradiction in terms? And what was he doing out here anyway, in a shirt and tie belonging his father, talking forest gardens with a frankly eccentric man in a dickie bow? How had this happened? He was putting his best foot forward in this interview - at least he was doing his best to put forward what his entire family now considered to be his only salvageable foot - but what did that mean exactly? What was happening here? Where was the guy with the guitar? The guy who'd once made music that you could feel, that, when you played it, people screamed with delight and half covered their ears because the human body couldn't withstand the power of the message. Music that those gloomy German philosophers could obviously have done with in their search for a quick touch of group transcendence. But where was the guy who used to play it? This morning he'd insisted that he be allowed to finally die. Not alluded to or resurrected in any way. So who was Charlie Peterson now? Who could he ever possibly be? And what the hell was a forest garden? There were forests and there were gardens. Weren't there?

As if he had heard him, Dr. Carlyle obligingly explained. A forest garden was a woodland in which the large trees were productive trees such as apples, pears, mulberries, and cherries. The understorey, or shrub layer, was gooseberry and currant bushes and so on, whilst the ground cover consisted of wild strawberries and mints and other herbs of culinary and medicinal value.

"It's a naturalistic system of production," he finished. "But what we really hope the boys will cultivate out here," he gestured expansively all around, "indeed, what we encourage them to cultivate, is a feeling of veneration. It was Rudolf Steiner's first recommended step on the path to spiritual enlightenment - the cultivation of the ability to venerate. Veneration coupled with a sense of wonder and a ..." He stopped. "But we don't like to proselytise. We are not, after all, a Steiner school or a faith school. These things can be inspired subtly, however. Veneration is a big thing but it is just a step up from respect. And if the boys develop a respect for the natural world and everything in that world, then that will serve us and them very well. Respect is vital, Charlie, don't you agree?"

Charlie nodded. It was probably the main reason he was stood out here, covered in grass seeds, enduring attack from biting insects, and uncomfortably hot from the sustained effort of trying to look like a chemistry teacher.

Dr. Carlyle watched him bat away at midges for a moment or two and then said, "But above all, of course, there is respect for one's self. We must not abuse our souls, Charlie. Self-destruction is not a path we encourage here." Then he stood there, thoughtful for a moment or two longer, before saying brightly, "Lunch."

"There," he concluded a few minutes later as they climbed the ha-ha steps and re-crossed the lawn to reach the terrace. "That was a nice walk, wasn't it? Exercise always brings a pleasant respite from the existential terrors of existence."

*****

Scattered persons that could have been interpreted as an interview panel were seated round a heftily loaded lunch table covered in health-giving vegetation and fruits from the school garden. Maybe even the forest garden. Anyone unacquainted with the proficiency of the forebrains filling these random heads might have seen an unimpressive and thoroughly motley crew. And Dr. Boswell, Eric, it has to be said, was mostly there for the food. He lived locally with his widowed sister and her several cats which, almost as one animal (not including his sister, though she seemed to positively encourage them into his study) conspired to disrupt his efforts to download thoughts on

Chaucer by storming about on the computer keys. It was the sort of thing that drove him out for lunch, even when lunch would involve one of Arne Carlyle's hair-raising interviews.

Dr. Boswell didn't like sex being mentioned when he was trying to eat. Indeed, since the media's modern mania for explicit reporting he'd had to give up listening to the news or reading the newspaper at mealtimes. In fact, very little of what the media had to offer was likely to bring along his analysis of the development of Chaucer, through the study of four of his love vision poems, in any way at all. Dr. Boswell was short and fat and celibate, and his ideas on love were of a quality that raised it to the level of sacred mystery where it was discussed in terms of lyrical intensity through symbolic figures. He was not, however, as naive and potty as this makes him sound. A man of profound thoughts, he was nevertheless a swift and reliable judge of character.

Dr. Carlyle took a seat at one end of the table with his wife who must, when young, with her ash blonde hair loosely flowing and her vivid blue eyes still innocently clear, have been in possession of an exceptional and ethereal beauty. At that point, she would have fitted nicely into one of Dr. Boswell's love visions. Being married to the headmaster of a boy's boarding school, however, even a headmaster like Arne Carlyle and a school like Puckrup Hall, requires a deal of things that are considerably less than ethereal and Vanessa Carlyle had, accordingly, developed these things - including the talent to be charmingly 'front of house'. She had welcomed Charlie with just the right amount of enthusiasm, offering her own slim hand and then introducing him first to, arguably, the weightiest opinion around the table - Lady Keeble Parker.

Lady KP as she was known (because she was nuts, some unkind person had once remarked) had attended a Steiner school in her far distant youth, developing powerful views on anthroposophy and biodynamic agriculture and being profoundly affected by Rachel Carson's Silent Spring - a book which promises us a sterile life without birdsong and a great many other things if we do not stop drenching the earth in chemicals. Lady KP was now a formidable old lady with a Witch of the West profile and the sharp brown eyes of a bird of prey. A fluffy halo of silvery hair did little to mitigate her air of incidental ferocity but, when suddenly she smiled, her face was suffused with mischief and humour - and big teeth which spoke strongly to the benefits of a sugar free diet.

"Time we had more young blood," she said, pumping Charlie's hand enthusiastically. Her own hands, their joints enlarged with age, had the grimy, cracked look of the committed gardener. Ingrained dirt with diamond rings, that was the essence of Lady KP. "As a group," she added, "we are getting well past the grand climacteric. That may not predispose forward thinking parents to sign on with us. They may think of our ideas as worn out dogma or early dementia, rather than illimitable truths. Are you hungry? Young people are supposed to be hungry, and you'll need a great volume of this stuff to keep you going. It's like being a panda. So you'd best get started. You should sit opposite Mrs. Gargery here. Marjorie has always known how to eat, haven't you, Marjorie?"

"Oh, yes," said Marjorie Gargery amiably.

Marjorie Gargery's relationship with Lady KP was close enough and long-standing enough to withstand this kind of comment. There were days, during the heat of the chase, when the comments flowed both ways. That morning, at dawn, they'd been out on a joint slug hunt. Slug hunting is a slow business so this was probably best classified as a survey rather than a hunt. A count in fact. Slugs had to be counted and photographed and identified from a slug website. Charlie, being made privy to this information as he took his seat opposite Mrs. Gargery passed comment to the effect that there were obviously things of great importance in this world with which he had never been previously acquainted.

"The relevance of slugs to the world," said Mrs. Gargery, "is more than amply revealed by the number of holes in the lettuce leaves." As she said this, she dumped an enormous pile of greenery onto Charlie's plate. "Know the enemy," she added. "First rule of combat. What you refuse to poison, you have to live with, and slugs are stealth fighters. The territory of the lettuce leaf is a hard one to win."

Lettuce leaves full of holes were obviously not all that Marjorie Gargery ate. She looked healthily hefty - apple-cheeked and stout-limbed with muscular calves that tapered miraculously into something that approximated to ankles and then spread out into sturdy feet in brown lace-up shoes. With her Junoesque build and her close-cropped hair she could have presented as masculine, but she didn't. She was the biology mistress of whom Dr. Carlyle had spoken. She of the six children - a great mother, motherhood flowing from her every pore. She had clearly been very fecund, and had always (on her own telling) given birth with no trouble at all. Perhaps as a consequence of that, or maybe for some other reason less self-referential, she was noticeably partisan about the word womb. In Mrs. Gargery's world, women had wombs. The word uterus was reserved for rabbits and the like. Women had wombs, and they didn't have lovers or hop from man to man in hopes of putting meaning into their lives. A woman's life *had* meaning. She *was* life and she joined to a male of the species with the intention of continuing it. If he subsequently left her for a younger model then that was of no consequence. Nature probably dictated it. Nothing in Mrs. Gargery's life had made her either a man-hater or noticeably feminist - any more than it would have made Mother Earth a man-hater or a feminist. On the other hand, it didn't entirely make her someone a boy would come to with a sex-related query. Charlie could see that.

Not that it seemed likely that the subject of sex would be introduced over this thoroughly wholesome meal. For what seemed like a considerable period of time, no subject was introduced at all. Charlie, having expected a bombardment of questions, chewed doggedly on his lettuce leaves. Piles of green stuff seemed to be an inevitable consequence of trips to the country. Finally, he began to wonder if he was expected to show some signs of initiative by asking more questions himself. Eventually, he decided that it seemed surly not to. And also preferable to the consumption of yet more greenery. He turned to Mrs. Gargery. "You'll forgive me for asking this, but Puckrup Hall is a very unusual school and so I can't help wondering, do you teach the theory of evolution in the accepted, scientific way?" (Charlie's father had finally invoked the computer in the corner on the subject of Steiner and he had read out , in order to tease his wife, the odd startling passage.)

"Science is science," replied Mrs. Gargery firmly. "I prefer not to qualify it with whimsy when I teach. Though some of us would have it otherwise." She gave Lady KP a look which was acknowledged in a spirit of amiable combat.

"We are largely post-Darwinian here, I think," said Eric Boswell benignly. "We accept the science but, like Tennyson, we continue to feel the need for a larger hope the more we are assured that there isn't one."

"You must understand the need for a larger hope, Charlie," said Lady KP kindly. "We know of your loss. We know that, indirectly, it is what brought you here. And sometimes, you know, we are brought to things by the unconscious expedient of understanding that there is nowhere else to go." She paused before adding, with apparent randomness: "You seem a very mannerly young man, for a product of the rock music industry."

"Maybe I wasn't in it long enough," said Charlie, with a shrug.

"And handsome." Lady KP nodded thoughtfully. "In accordance with the modern idiom, that is. Have you a partner?"

"No."

"And how comes that, do you think? In truth?"

Charlie sat silently for a few moments, then he said, "I guess I feel that I have nothing to give."

"It can be," observed Dr. Carlyle, "that when we lose or suppress one thing, other things go with it. We don't intend them to, but they do."

"Have you ever been in love?" asked Dr. Boswell.

Charlie's mind flitted briefly to his South Korean ex-girlfriend. "I don't know," he said. "I don't think so."

"I think a man would know something like that," said Dr. Boswell.

"You must forgive Eric," said Dr. Carlyle, "for getting quite so personal. He's deeply involved with Chaucer's love visions. Producing a paper on them is his project for the summer."

"Are you heterosexual?" asked Lady KP.

Dr. Carlyle shot her a warning look.

"I ask merely for personal interest," said Lady KP egregiously.

"I am," said Charlie.

"He isn't going to date you," said Marjorie Gargery. "I can tell."

Lady KP snorted magnificently.

"Is there a bathroom anywhere handy?" asked Charlie. Somebody, introduced with respectful gratitude as Mrs. Batt, had emerged from the house and was clearing plates. It seemed an appropriate moment for him to clear his head.

In a lavatory tiled in bottle green like the conveniences in a Newcastle pub (Endgame had done a big gig in Newcastle – a very successful gig with a memorable fight afterwards) Charlie splashed his face in an ancient wash basin with a name. It said: 'A. Emanuel of Marylebone' above the plughole. He sighed. The collar and tie were killing him. He didn't know why he was starting to find this interview so stressful. Compared to a rumble with a pile of drunken Geordies it should have felt like a walk in the park. It didn't occur to him that life changing decisions, even those being made subconsciously, have to feel like something. He lifted his jacket and laid his back momentarily against the cool tiled wall, then he ran damp hands a couple of times through his hair and returned to the lunch table.

Everyone was drinking coffee. Charlie accepted a cup gratefully. With the meal it had been spring water leavened with home-made elderberry cordial. The conversation had somehow drifted to sport and the chances of an ex-pupil who was competing in the coming Commonwealth Games in Glasgow. Charlie was emptying his coffee cup and enjoying the respite from mental effort when Dr. Carlyle came and touched him on the elbow, suggesting that the pair of them should finish up inside.

"I expect to see you next term," said Lady KP firmly, as Charlie took his leave.

*****

In Dr. Carlyle's study the trembly terrier was snoring on the rug.

"I wondered where he'd got to," said Charlie. "I thought he'd got lost in the hay field."

"I think he abandoned us at the initial descent into the ha-ha," said Dr. Carlyle. "I expect Tempest min's car was too heavy for old jaws but he wouldn't want to give it up."

The car lay on the rug with a line of dents in its roof.

"Maybe, we should get him a new toy of some sort." Dr. Carlyle looked thoughtful. Then he turned to Charlie. "We've seen enough of you to want to offer you the job. I realise that you'll need to think about it, of course. Would a week be long enough?"

"A week? Yes." Charlie felt suddenly dropped on. He hadn't expected to be offered the job on the spot. In fact, he hadn't expected to be offered the job at all - Lady KP's comment notwithstanding. He stood, indecisive for a moment or two, reviewing the fact that chemistry had barely featured in the discussions, then he said, "It's a long time since I did that chemistry degree, you know."

"Memory is one of our moodiest faculties," said Dr. Carlyle. "But one thing about it is constant – it has a great sense of place. Here and now you may think you know nothing, but back in a lab with the hiss of the Bunsen burner and the smell of hydrogen sulphide, you'll find that you know more than enough. And if you don't, then I expect you are conscientious enough to look it up."

Charlie nodded. "Of course, I have no qualification to teach it."

"I'm sure you can hold an audience. I should say that the skills are transferable. And I would be surprised if you can be disconcerted by a room full of teenage boys. Lesson plans are the thing, but we can cover that kind of detail after you've said 'yes'."

"Well, let me think about it …" said Charlie, hesitantly. "But, really, the truth is …" The truth was that he was about to decline the offer but, at this point, the telephone rang and Dr. Carlyle, with an apologetic gesture, picked it up, listened for a few moments and gave a slightly exasperated sigh.

"I can go," said Charlie in a low voice. "Really. There is no need to see me out. I remember the way. I'll be in touch." It would, after all, be easier to send a 'Dear John' letter.

"Goodbye," said Dr. Carlyle, hand over the mouthpiece. "Think on it. Make the right decision. Come."

*****

As Charlie crossed the stone floor of the echoing entrance hall, his leather soled boots noisy in the church-like silence, he was suddenly given pause. He looked around. Tempest min was sitting on the bottom step of the grand staircase staring at him. "I know you," he said.

"You saw me in the headmaster's study this morning," replied Charlie. "Has no one arrived to collect you, yet?"

"Before that," said Tempest min. "I know you."

Charlie shook his head. "I doubt it. Where do you live?"

"Here."

"When you're not here."

"London. And California."

"What part of London?"

"Primrose Hill."

Geographically speaking, Primrose Hill wasn't far from Camden. Charlie took a mental inventory of his past guitar pupils and their various siblings who had sometimes been forced to endure the tedium of waiting in the corridor, plus or minus some attendant adult. "I don't think we've crossed paths," he said, finally.

"I feel as if we have," said Tempest min. "I get a lot of feelings."

"We all do," said Charlie. "Fortunately, most of them turn out to be nothing more than feelings." At this point, he could have continued his progress to the door but, for some reason, he didn't. On the other hand, he didn't want to get into a discussion of all these feelings that Tempest min apparently got. "What's your name?" he asked.

"Tempest min," said Tempest min.

"Your first name."

"Joey."

"And what's that short for? Joseph? Jonathan? Joshua? Jonah?"

"Christopher."

"Joey is short for Christopher?"

"No, silly. I'm called Christopher but I'm always called Joey. Mother brought me back from Australia. Inside her. Like a disease, you know. That's what my brother Blake says. She went there to be in a movie. Not much of a movie. I don't think mother's much of an actress, really, but she's very beautiful so she keeps getting parts. And rich men. Except she didn't get a man with me, so I don't have a father. Blake and Paul say she probably doesn't know who he was. She was just being a great big slut as usual and got herself knocked up by some jackaroo under a eucalyptus tree, which makes me no better than a baby kangaroo. So they've always called me the Joey. Blake and Paul were very cross. I think mother's stopped having babies on account of it."

Jeez, thought Charlie, taken aback. Fortunately, before he actually had to say anything, a tall boy of seventeen or eighteen, darkly handsome, lavishly stubbled and obviously feeling moody to the point of bloody, strode in through the main door. "Come on, Joey," he snapped. "What the fuck are you doing back in here?"

Tempest min stood up. "Has somebody come for us?"

"Somebody's come for Paul and me. We're just taking you along out of pity."

"Hey," said Charlie, sharply. "Don't talk to him like that."

"And who are you, exactly?" Blake Vane Tempest turned to Charlie with a rock 'n' roll sullenness that Charlie immediately recognised and inwardly acknowledged. Most people who knew Charlie Peterson, and this specifically applied to his mother with whom he was capable of being remarkably sunny, would have said that his temperament was fairly amenable. But creative people often have their downside – darkness following the brilliance of inspiration as reliably as night follows day. And darkness can take many forms. Charlie Peterson, provoked when the darkness was upon him, was capable of being … well … a bit like Blake Vane Tempest. "You harness that," Grandma Peterson had repeatedly warned him, "or the devil will." His grandmother had been a fund of folksy threats and moral tales, most of them replete with gruesome comeuppance, some of them capable, on occasion, of having a lasting psychological impact. She'd seen the darker side of Charlie, even if his mother hadn't. But, as Charlie's creativity had come more under his control, so had his difficult streak. But that had all been before life's fateful turn, and now the emptiness was mostly in charge. Indeed, Blake Vane Tempest's question could have been viewed as oddly appropriate. A point that was not entirely lost on Charlie as he contemplated this version of his teenage self. "I could be the replacement chemistry teacher," he said evenly.

"I don't do chemistry." Blake Vane Tempest grabbed his little brother by the arm and bundled him out onto the forecourt towards a new-looking black Range Rover with a personalised number plate. A good-looking man, with a perceptible air of unpopularity hanging over him, was loading luggage into the back. There was no sign of Mrs. Vane Tempest. Halfway across the forecourt Tempest min suddenly shook himself free and ran back to Charlie. He took hold of Charlie's hand and looked earnestly up at him. "You need to come here," he said. "You have to come here."

"I do?"

"Yes."

Charlie looked down into the little, seven year old face. It was screwed up with conviction. "They're calling for you," he said after a moment or two. "You'd better go." But he remained in the doorway, watching the little face watching him, until the big, black car disappeared from view.

Chapter Five

Charlie took up accommodations at Puckrup Hall school just before the start of the new academic year. The practicalities involved in this consisted of two major steps: the emptying of his room in the London flat into his parents' front hall, and the refinement of the resulting jumble into a pile of necessaries that would suit a school chemistry master and fit into a large holdall and two medium-sized cardboard boxes. The initial decision-making process had probably gone along in much the same way - the final emptying out of a pile of redundant hopes and dreams, and the salvaging and buffing up of those that were small enough to fit into a life that was real, that had to be faced, that wasn't hiding in a basement. The sort of life, in fact, that most of us have to live. It's the moment when we finally accept that there's going to be no building of a bridge to the moon and we just buckle down and use whatever we have left to make a woodshed.

But, there are woodsheds and there are woodsheds, and the mental metaphysics that makes us finally settle for one particular woodshed cannot be so handily summarised. What really brought Charlie Peterson to Puckrup Hall school? In truth, he barely understood that himself. Feelings often don't condense themselves sufficiently for the conscious mind to really grasp. Maybe the decision hadn't even been his. Maybe Fate had just moved another piece on her chessboard. But, however it had come about, there he stood at the beginning of a new life, in a space that had, historically, been occupied by a lot of hay but was now a two-bedroomed flat above a space that had been occupied by a lot of horses but was now stuffed with the paraphernalia of sports days and open days and the accoutrements needed for not very convincing productions of A Midsummer Night's Dream.

Puckrup Hall's stables and their associated buildings had been constructed on the heroic scale that once pertained to the landed gentry in such matters, and the eventual conversion of a hayloft to living accommodation had not been a mean one. There was, in addition to two generous bedrooms, a long galley kitchen with a breakfast bar at one end, a shower room with a bath, and a spacious sitting room with three futons, planking bookshelves, a rather nice cricket table and a huge flat-screen television set. It also had a pre-existing incumbent - Rory McEwan, the teacher who had been so garrulous with Charlie's mother at the private view and who was, therefore, partially responsible for Charlie's ending up as his flat-mate. That Rory had somehow brought this on himself didn't prevent Charlie from feeling a bit awkward. The previous chemistry master had been married and had his own house in a nearby village, but now there could be overcrowding of some personal space that was needed for solitary introspection. Or deep academic thought. Or, since Rory was an unattached male much of an age with Charlie himself, romantic seduction scenarios.

Rory McEwan, however, was prone to none of these things. They crossed his mind a lot - at least the romantic seduction scenarios did - but he was less a man of thoughts and more a man of instincts. None of which, it might be pertinent to point out here, seemed to run along the lines of vacuuming or dusting or the wiping of kitchen surfaces. So this was going to be another new experience for Charlie because the garbage truck driver had been helpfully, if surprisingly, fastidious in those areas. Probably because he'd been married. And then divorced - which had conveniently taken care of the seduction scenario side of things because he'd replaced women with a subscription to Sky Sports, which he'd watched, endlessly and at very close quarters, in the kitchen. The Lithuanian ticket seller had never become fluent enough in English to stage romantic seduction scenarios and he hadn't been good-looking enough to get anywhere without them, so he'd had to rely on bumping into female Lithuanians who were prepared to show some interest in him - which happened so infrequently that it had had minimal impact within the flat. The odd, strange woman coming out of the bathroom, maybe. And it was only once that Charlie had got one confused with his own strange women, so that had never been anything of a problem.

But Rory McEwan looked a larger than life sort of guy so it would be reasonable to be assume, Charlie thought, that any problems with him would be of a similar magnitude to himself. Rory stood up now, to shake hands, and he had very large hands which he took the precaution of wiping on the seat of his corduroy trousers before holding one of them out. He was heftily muscled with a headful of auburn curls and a scorching of reddy stubble that built up from Friday night onwards and was allowed to flame and flourish until Wednesday, when it was removed in a welter of bloody nicks and blue language in preparation for the weekly staff meeting. He was the undisputed laird of the practical block where he taught woodwork and metalwork to boys for whom the academic was a business conducted in a foreign language. It could all have been drearily vocational – a lot of sawing and sanding and welding but in Rory McEwan's big red hands, wood and iron became sublime substances that could transcend the mundane destiny of becoming mug racks and fire grates and enter the realm of art. Even magic. He talked about how, to be at their most powerful, staffs and divining rods should be cut from the hazel tree on Midsummer's Eve, how poplar was used by the Celts to make protective shields, and how the yew tree could live for thousands of years, drawing immortality from every corpse in the graveyard.

Rory was descended from what had been a diffuse and notorious family of border reivers, so he was probably genetically programmed to be at ease with the idea of corpses, but there was obviously a weird and wild romance in his soul and when it wasn't focused on coaxing wood and iron to reveal their beauty and their secret magic it was focused across a rear yard onto Christina LeBlanc, the delightful, Frenchified lady who taught art and design but showed absolutely no inclination at all to reveal her own secret magic to some great hairy man from the thereabouts of Hadrian's wall. After all, un-reconstituted men like him were the reason the damned thing had been built in the first place.

"Nice to meet you," said Charlie.

"Turrible about the band," said Rory. It wasn't as much a definable accent he had, as a sort of deep throated Scottish/Northumbrian brogue. He wasn't a gabbler so, in fact, it fell quite easily on the ear. Rory McEwan could do or think a thing with mercurial dash if the occasion demanded, but normally he went about life with a steady stride. Unless there was a woman in the way, and then it was as if he were in an overcrowded room and didn't know quite where to step to do the least damage.

Charlie shrugged. "It was a long time ago."

"Bloody good band tho', wasn't it?"

"Well," Charlie shrugged again, "bloody good friends, at any rate. As a band we weren't really well known or anything." This was just the kind of conversation he'd come here to avoid.

"Och, come on, you were a wee bit really well known. Getting your contract bought out by the big boys, Radio One playlist, Jules Holland, Rough Trade CD of the year ..." The formal list went on, enumerated with dedicated emphasis on Rory's thick fingers.

Silently, Charlie took his mother's name in vain. Had she said all of this?

"I looked you up," supplied Rory helpfully. "Nowt dies on the internet."

"I'd rather it did," said Charlie. He found it hard to talk about wanting to put that part of his life aside without sounding excruciatingly Californian, especially to someone like Rory - as opposed to Dr. Carlyle, who could clearly handle Californian as effortlessly as he seemed to handle so many other things - but he managed something that Rory took up with a dutiful and sympathetic gravitas.

"Well, I haven't spoken aboot it to a soul," he said earnestly, "other than mentioning it to Dr. Carlyle. At the outset, y'know. In fact, I've been in Kielder Forest all summer. It's where I go to …"

"Clear your own head?" suggested Charlie, after a moment or two, because Rory seemed to be having difficulty remembering why he'd gone there.

"Och no, I got nowt to clear ma head of because there was never over much got built up in there. I haven't had a life of publicised tragedy and missed opportunities because I was always shite at everything. Now the McEwans are not allowed to rape and pillage and steal other people's sheep, we're an evolutionary dead-end. We manage nowt and go nowhere, except occasionally to jail. Tho' that's mostly ma cousins." He added the last with an enormous grin that was probably intended as reassurance but, in other circumstances, could have been interpreted as ferocious.

"You must be good at something," pointed out Charlie, unable to avoid grinning with him, "or you wouldn't be here."

How Rory had ended up at Puckrup Hall made something of a tale. Rory's father - a colourful individual whom Rory referred to, with rather strained affection, as 'me da'- was a blacksmith. A blacksmith as opposed to a farrier, although Mr. McEwan senior had shod horses in his time - the time before the farriers act of 1975, a piece of legislation to which he never subscribed. In truth, Mr. McEwan still shod horses if they turned up at his door because he was one of those McEwans who were still disposed to regard the law of the land as more in the nature of guidelines. Rory, however, had never learned to shoe horses which he felt, quite justifiably, to be a bit of a deprivation because horses, as anyone who has had anything to do with them will readily attest, are the most compelling of creatures. Unfortunately, by the year 2000 which was when Rory left school and went into the forge, they had been replaced in the western world by automobiles - even on the border with Scotland. In addition to which their recreational use was under threat from the rising debate on hunting with hounds. All in all, the shoeing of horses had never been included in Rory's work. The McEwans had got along, largely, on blacksmithing - fancy ironwork, not so fancy ironwork and really boring industrial items. And then, with the economic downturn, there had come to be insufficient of any of it. There were other factors of course, as there inevitably are with complicated families like the McEwans, and these Rory hastened over, but the eventual outcome was that he'd ended up squatting in Kielder Forest eking out what he called 'the social' with hurdle making and a new found flair for carpentry and woodcarving. Which he really enjoyed - wood being one of those things, rather like horses, that has intrinsic appeal.

"The wood thing just came to me," he explained with evident pleasure. "There amongst the trees, it just came to me. Wood has more to say than metal, you know. More expressive, like. Lady KP says it's the difference between the plant kingdom and the mineral, the difference between undines and gnomes. You can sort of get that, can't you?"

Charlie wasn't sure he could, but he decided to go with the nod and smile principle that worked with his mother and her ten-foot rabbits. "So how was it you came here, exactly?" he asked, after a moment or two.

Naturally, Dr. Carlyle had been at the root of it. One summer evening, he had just walked out of the trees. With a little knapsack on his back. And then, for some reason best known to himself, he had settled down beside Rory's smoky little fire.

"And then he hangs about for a couple of days," said Rory, in evident bafflement. "God knows why - watching me work, talking up a storm and sharing m' boiled rabbit ..."

Charlie made an involuntary noise.

"It's not half bad," said Rory. "Especially if you put an onion in there and a bit of curry powder. I got to quite like it." He paused. "They'd have likely thrown me off m' patch if I'd killed one of the red deer, but as it was they let me have honorary foresters' rights and were relieved to be shot of some rabbits." He glanced around the room – a shade wistfully, Charlie thought. "I'm better at the curries now," he added. "You'll see."

*****

Charlie did see. About a month later he was eating one with something that approached enjoyment. "The worst bit," he said, "the getting started, is over."

"W'still talking about the job, are we?" asked Rory. There was a lot more perspicacity about him than had been noticeable at first meeting.

Charlie was. Getting started had been less of a culture shock - any kind of shock - than it could have been. And he'd had an oddly rapturous welcome from that little blonde boy, Tempest min, who'd run up to him at some point on the first day and

74

greeted him like a long lost friend. "You've come. I knew you would. You had to come."

"And why would that be?"

But Tempest min was between lessons and being prevailed upon to hurry up. Still, the greeting had been gratifying, if a little obscure.

Otherwise, things had seemed remarkably normal. That Puckrup Hall school was a somewhat unusual place, staffed by unusual people, did not mean that natural laws were entirely suspended there. The boys were as noisy as other boys, as ebullient at the start of term and as potentially moody and inattentive once things got underway as boys could be anywhere. Though their personal and spiritual welfare was always viewed as of paramount importance, this did not mean that their personal and spiritual outlooks were always in sweet and perfect tune. Blake Vane Tempest was not entirely an anomaly.

But Charlie had faced a lot worse audiences. Audiences that were drunk, fluent in profanity and spoiling for a fight. The band, starting out, had performed on some pretty rigorous testing grounds. This audience, on the other hand, stood up when he entered the room, called him 'Sir' and wore ties. Gold and black striped ties for Gloucester House, scarlet and black for Worcester and silver and black for Hereford - worn with white shirts, fawn needlecord jackets for middles and seniors, fawn jumpers for juniors, and black trousers for all. The top buttons of the shirts were not always done up and there were days when the black trousers on the 'cool kids' looked remarkably like black jeans and the shirts hung out over them, but basically the boys, especially the senior ones, seemed mostly amenable. By and large they needed chemistry for a career in medicine or such like, so they were not operating on some uncooperative default setting as he had once been. The music makers and the dreamers of dreams had obviously chosen more free-thinking routes to A-level success. A-level chemistry was a lot of things but it wasn't much open to creativity or poetic interpretation. It was full of facts and rules which continued to hold true at Puckrup, gnomes notwithstanding. Neither had they changed much since Charlie had learnt them - though for the word 'fact' one could occasionally insert the word 'hypothesis', thus creating the breathing space for science to be ultimately right. In the event, however, it all proved to be less about what Charlie knew, than how he went about transplanting it into other heads.

Not that being a chemistry teacher wasn't hard for him. It would have been so far down his 'things to do before you die' list that he would have needed several lifetimes to get to it. There were points, at the blackboard or whilst helping pupils to set up experiments, when he was suddenly overtaken by such intense moments of unreality, almost panic, that he felt as bewildered as if he were in an episode of Quantum Leap. On the other hand, he knew he ought to be grateful. It was a better job than he deserved, bearing in mind his attitude to the interview, and there were surely better people it could have gone to. Just try and do it right, he told himself. Like Dr. Carlyle believed you would. But whilst he never quite forgot that he could so easily have been dead like his friends, somewhere inside he *was* dead. And though he was past those awful days when he'd kept making lists of reasons to stay alive, he was still having to prod himself into an appreciation of life. He had not succeeded in recapturing any capacity for spontaneous joy. But the boys at Puckrup, cooperative beings that they mostly seemed, sometimes tried to do that for him:

"Sir?"

"Yes, Connelly?"

"Porteus is setting fire to the filter paper, again."

"You know Porteus, a more suspicious teacher might think you were doing this on purpose. I applied for a special line in patience in order to come here and help you lot grasp a few scientific principles, but like any other line of credit it will get abruptly cut off if it is abused. Now, get the filter papers away from the Bunsen burner."

No real cause for alarm. Porteus wasn't a serious pyromaniac. He just seemed to like kindling in those around him the odd spark of spontaneous joy. And in addition to outgoing spirits like Porteus, there was yet another thing to be grateful for. Due to the last minute recruitment of a genial primary school teacher returning to work after a couple of babies, the mathematical component of Charlie's duties had diminished. He'd now got just the odd maths lesson a day, tinkering about at the basic levels of geometry and the simple end of algebraic equations. Academically speaking it wasn't anything of a challenge. And, true to his word, Dr. Carlyle had come up with copies of the syllabuses, notes as to what each individual class had already covered, and a pile of lesson plans that had been provided both for current guidance and historical interest. In fact as far as chemistry went, there were lesson plans that dated back to times when sections of the periodic table of elements had been largely a matter of intellectual conjecture. The school seemed to have an enormous sense of self, and to operate along the lines of those aristocrats who never throw away any details of their lives or their demesnes, including the head gardener's plant order from a couple of centuries ago. Furthermore, as an institution, it was persistent and assiduous in its purpose.

On Sundays, Wednesdays and Fridays, after breakfast, all the boys gathered in the medieval hall in the centre of main building. The younger boys occupied the front rows, cross-legged on the wood block floor, and the older boys sat in lines on tubular steel stacking chairs which they unstacked and restacked with such practised proficiency that, were their future lives to consist of nothing but arranging other people's chairs, they would be assured of making a mark in the world.

These assemblies were not of any particular religious persuasion, hymns were not sung nor prayers offered up, but days special to the main religions and the turning of the year were acknowledged in short talks given by a Ms. O'Grady who taught comparative religion and also functioned much like a school counsellor. As a rule, things began with Dr. Carlyle - dispensing reminders and comment regarding current school activities and, on occasion, some stern observation on the latest in behavioural transgression. At least once a week, his remarks were followed by what he liked to call 'inspirational talks'. The aim of these talks – a high aim Charlie felt, in view of the ones he'd heard so far - was that they would strike a chord in the breast of some boy whose breast was not being struck as effectively as it should have been by the school's regular fare. They were given by highly individual enthusiasts who were capable of going on and on about the incredible nature of their subject without ever getting to a predicate. Sometimes they brought props - which were very welcome at times, a way of lending structure to mania.

Dr. Carlyle seemed have a real knack for finding people, much the same way as he had found Rory in Kielder forest, presumably. One of his more successful finds, possibly inspired by Rory, was a very muscular farrier who kept the boys' attention enviously rapt by virtue of his incredible biceps and the pectoral muscles that were helpfully outlined by his T-shirt. He talked about the skills and satisfaction involved in shoeing horses and how, in baby horses, which were called foals, and in young horses of one or two years old called colts and fillies, depending on their sex, it was possible, indeed important, to straighten up their legs and correct serious deviations in gait pattern by filing their hooves in a carefully considered way that gave them balance. And, therefore, the correct base from which to move forward in a straight and true fashion. The accidental metaphor in all of this was not for one minute lost on the staff, who began beaming around at each other and the boys with heartfelt satisfaction and powerful feelings of vindication.

And sometimes a philosophy for life didn't have to be extracted from a homily on shoeing – it was laid onto the boys straight from the horse's mouth. Thoughts for the day poured from the podium. Enjoy the small things. Life is what you make it. Hormones are not a personal experience. Everybody has them, so don't turn them into a drama. The spots will go. Focus your attention elsewhere. On butterflies for instance. Butterflies are a compelling and economical way of giving meaning to life, and they can lead you into a world that can be so much more satisfying than a rich man experiences with his house in Belgravia and his yacht in Monte Carlo … and so it went on … red admirals, peacocks, tortoiseshells, large whites, small whites, green-veined whites … A boy with a butterfly net can become a man with a butterfly net …. God, thought Charlie, where *was* this going? His thoughts had floated from butterflies to his Gibson.

They were doing that more than he'd hoped - and living with Rory wasn't helping. Having Rory complicit with his past meant that he wasn't policing himself as effectively as he ought. Also, it was the first time in something like twenty years that he'd been without a guitar in his life in any way at all. Some days he felt as if he'd lost an arm.

Curry nights were a particular weak spot. Although Rory was prepared to eat curry anywhere and at any given moment, Friday nights were when he liked to cook one to show how his skills had moved on from the days of the blackened pot and the rabbit carcasses full of lead shot. He had now progressed beyond curry powder to a stage he called 'advanced spices'. For him and Charlie, 'advanced spices' had already become something of a Friday night ritual. Charlie supplied the beer. But the trouble with advanced spices was that the amount of beer that was occasionally needed to balance them out was capable of introducing a maudlin aspect to the proceedings. Rory could get introspective about Christina Leblanc, about what could be if only she'd look at him, and Charlie could get introspective about things he was trying hard not to get introspective about. The exchange of speech was meagre but an atmosphere of vague and swirly gloom would permeate the flat, settling over everything like dead autumn leaves, until it was forcibly dissipated by the gusts of a new day.

"I didn't get on here as well as you, at first," said Rory now, unscrewing some home-made mango chutney donated by Lady KP for the enhancement of his efforts. "Such a radical change. Not my world at all. 'Twasn't the boys that were the particular problem, or even having to organise what I could do into something that could be made into a syllabus with a qualification at the end of it, though the world's gone mad for bits of paper in my opinion. Dr. Carlyle helped me with all of that stuff. But life was just so different, y'know. I'd have left before the end of the first year but then Christina came as a replacement art and design teacher. I saw her the length of a corridor away and that was it. I was stuck like a fly on sticky paper with m'gob open. Y' see?" He spread mango chutney all over his curry.

Charlie, declining the chutney, which was now mostly gone in any case, did see. And it wasn't a pretty mental picture. He couldn't visualise any way in which Rory with his mouth open was going to appeal to Christina LeBlanc. The science block and the practical and arts blocks were in close proximity and shared a staff room, so Charlie had seen enough of Christina LeBlanc to form one or two impressions. The first and most important one being that, during their brief meetings, neither he nor she had experienced, nor were likely to experience, frissons of any sort. The second and less reassuring impression was that Christina LeBlanc was not experiencing, nor looking likely to experience, frissons of any sort on account of Rory, either. Though that wasn't strictly true. Occasionally, Charlie thought he saw frissons of irritation. Primarily, when Rory took up space and scattered sugar at the coffee station. Neither of which he could help. Rory was a big man and the little packets of sugar were incredibly uncooperative. And he needed so many of them. Christina LeBlanc didn't take sugar, of course. It was a weakness that she would never have allowed herself.

She was a slim, energetic woman, nearer thirty than forty, who wore artistically draped clothes in shimmering materials and tied up her gypsy dark hair with silken scarves. She did not, however, have a gypsy temperament. She was in possession of a cool, if alluring, Parisian style inherited from her French grandmother and consistently cultivated. Her elegantly manicured hands swooped like birds as she talked, and she moved with the grace and the elusiveness of a ballerina. There was no way, Charlie thought, that she was going to allow herself to fall into the clutches of a burly borderer who wore checked shirts with moleskin waistcoats and arsehole-brown boots.

But Rory seemed to be still in the unfounded hope phase. Satisfaction endlessly deferred was making him heartsick but not defeatist. Spending Friday nights alone, cooking and eating curry, and Saturday nights alone, eating reheated curry, had not, apparently, beaten him down. And now he had Charlie to feel alone with.

This Friday evening, 'advanced spices' had achieved an unusual level of subtlety that Charlie was rather enjoying but which Rory pronounced as bland. Even Lady KP's special chutney, hot with ginger, had not improved matters. He had been eating with his attention half elsewhere. The window was open and occasional yells of merriment and then just plain yells were floating in. "Och, it's noisy out there," he said suddenly, turning his head to listen. "We should go and mebbes take a walk around." He re-employed his fork to despatch the rest of his curry in quick mouthfuls. "They're at the point now where they've got over being pleased to see each other and are starting to flare up a bit …" He took his empty plate into the kitchen, ran a big finger along a work surface to scoop up some dribbles of curry, dropped plate and utensils into the sink and went back into the sitting room. "Julius just started as a housemaster and he hasn't quite got the grip of them yet," he said, looming over Charlie and giving his hair a ruffle with curried fingers. "We'll just drift by, casual like … Coming?"

Julius Harvey had been at the school for a couple of years, teaching English and history alongside Dr. Boswell while his wife taught junior French part-time. But, moving into a residential position in charge of Hereford House was a new step, and boys were harder to police in their living quarters than they were during the academic transactions of the classroom. Nevertheless, the Harveys were gradually gaining the right and necessary level of parental ascendency. Housemasters' positions at Puckrup were always filled by married couples. Having both partners teaching at the school was a bonus. One of those happy coincidences that Dr. Carlyle found so satisfying.

Julius Harvey signalled cheerfully to Rory and Charlie from an upstairs window. Whatever uproar had been in process was over now. They waved back. Nothing lost. The short walk to Hereford House had been no great hardship. It was a balmy autumn night and, the school playing fields having just been mown, there was a pleasant scent of freshly cut grass in the air. The autumn equinox had not long passed, acknowledged as such things always were by a mention in assembly, and a big harvest moon was rising over the hills – a stunning golden orb in a Prussian blue sky.

"Beautiful, isn't it?" said Rory. "I love the sky. We used to get the aurora occasionally up north. Amazin'."

Charlie gazed up with him. The moon was beautiful. He felt suddenly peaceful. It was a feeling that he hadn't experienced in a long time. Maybe he'd made the right decision. Maybe he'd found a place where his chest wasn't going to be permanently weighted with misery ...

And then it came ... G - B flat - C, G - B flat - C sharp - C, G - B flat - C, B flat – G, G - B flat - C, G - B flat - C sharp - C ... Repeating power chords, ad infinitum.

Simple, so simple. But primal. So primal that Charlie knew that at any given moment, at some place on earth, a boy with a guitar would be playing the riff to Deep Purple's Smoke On The Water. Yet, for some reason, he hadn't expected it to be here. Or now. But he knew that, like the sound of Pythagoras's celestial spheres, a riff was a form of irrepressible and enduring magic - melodically compelling, instantly internalised, the repeating and repetitive simplicity upon which everything is built. From the first moment he'd picked up a guitar, the riff had entwined its double helix with his own and relived its endless musical journey of invention and reinvention in him, ontogeny recapitulating phylogeny, as he sat for hour after hour playing the Gibson. And he could feel now, in endless echoes in his chest, how the riff had made its evolutionary leap from the grandeur and majesty of the classical symphony into the street genius of boogie piano and blues guitar. How it had been endlessly propagated and refined until with Chuck Berry's Johnny B. Goode it had kick-started an era. The electric guitar had become the voice of youth and the riff carried the message.

Clean and optimistic with a nice vibrato from the Stratocaster of Hank Marvin, distorted and venomous from the slashed speakers of Dave Davies, dark and satanic from the damaged fingers of Tony Iommi as Black Sabbath gave pain-filled birth to heavy metal with the devil's chord, the riff was on a never ending journey of rebirth. It survived progressive rock to open the era of the killer riff with Deep Purple's Smoke on the Water. It squeezed into soul, cranked up disco, emerged undaunted from the Rickenbacker jangle of the new indie bands and got up from the floor after a pasting from My Bloody Valentine, to become more primal and more powerful than ever, in Nirvana's Smells Like Teen Spirit. Then finally, from The White Stripes' Seven Nation Army, it made a leap into the human voice as a war chant that rang implacably from football terraces everywhere.

And, just as a lifetime is supposed to flash through at the moment of death, all of this reverberated through Charlie now, as he listened to the notes of Deep Purple pouring across the playing fields. And they were, like those of all the greatest riffs, the music of the Pied Piper. Notes scored onto the ledger lines of dark matter, sounds that called from stardust, vibrating irresistibly and eternally in the human soul. And though Charlie was no Pythagoras, he understood all of this. Felt in his bones that the great riff was the key to unlocking the mysteries of the universe.

And, as he stood there transfixed, the moon suddenly seemed dazzling, less a moon than a spotlight. He felt the earth creak a little beneath his feet. A lead snaked over his foot. Reflexly, he kicked it away. He could feel the weight of the Gibson in his hands, its strings under his fingers. Ready? He turned. There, as clear as day, sat Tom behind the drums, the muscles of his shoulders taut, the light bouncing off the shining steel trim of the Ludwigs. 'One, two, three, four ...' Across the stage stood Craig, poised beside the stack of Marshalls. And Joe, dear Joe, his great friend Joe, with that old Fender P-Bass he'd got for Christmas when he was just ten years old, working his fingers and adjusting the leather strapping on his wrist that helped with the RSI: 'We're ready Charlie. What's wrong?'

Rory put a hand on his shoulder. "What's wrong, Charlie? You look as if you've seen a ghost."

Jesus. Charlie shook his head. Jesus. He looked up. The moon was a moon again, the ground had stopped creaking. "Did you put something in that curry?" he asked finally. "Was it a cannabis curry?"

"Och, no," Rory seemed offended. "Only a few spices that people normally eat."

"People where?"

"In Tenbury Wells," said Rory.

Charlie shook his head again. He'd dared to think that it was actually happening, that he was not merely suppressing the past, but sublimating it, having it slip slowly from him like a bad dream that fades by lunchtime, leaving only a manageable memory that is without the pain and sweat of the dark. But here it was, rising up more vivid and powerful than ever, bidden by nothing but a few notes that he'd heard a million times before. He ran a hand through his hair. Shit.

"Maybe you need another beer," suggested Rory.

Charlie shook his head. "Probably better not." He made an excuse about checking out some chemistry. It wasn't entirely a lie and he needed to be alone. And yet he knew, even as he walked across to the main building, that he would never be alone. We never bury the dead. We always carry them with us. It's the price of living. The ghosts of his friends, the ghost of the dream, would always be there.

Unseeingly, he fumbled with the big doors. The library was just along from the medieval assembly hall. It was pure Victorian Gothic. Maybe Lady Keeble Parker's ancestor, being a very Christian gentleman as Dr. Carlyle put it, had been a fan of Pugin with his admiration for the whole medieval ethos and his belief that Gothic architecture was the product of a purer society. However it had come about, the library was a very ornate space with lancet windows in its internal partitions, a plethora of scallops and finials and little carved grotesques grinning down from the ceiling. The atmosphere was pronouncedly collegiate. Though Charlie had treated his own college years with an ungracious level of disregard, he had nevertheless come to view this library as something of a sanctum. He sat down, a little shaky still, at one of the huge mahogany tables and opened an organic chemistry book, desperate for a grounding dose of scientific reality. The moon, having lost its golden glow, was now shining in on him through one of the windows with a pure and innocent, silvery light.

As, glancing up from the chemistry, he chanced another look at its gleaming roundness, he thought suddenly of August Kekule and how he'd claimed that his breakthrough ideas on molecular structure - his sudden understanding of the carbon to carbon bonding in the benzene ring - had come to him during a waking vision of a snake with its tail in its mouth, forming a circle. The ouroboros. It had been oneiric inspiration - inspiration that comes from a dream or a vision. Charlie had picked up the concept of oneiric inspiration at one of those student parties where everybody has had a bit of something, and stopped chatting or discussing and started experiencing instead. Words coming out like puffs of smoke – not organised into subject and predicate or any recognisable pattern of speech at all. But he'd gathered, probably because there had seemed to be rather a lot of them about, that visions, whether from dreams or intoxication, were supposed to be the best raw material available to the artist and represented the highest creative potential. It occurred to him now that some of his own songs had come to him in ways that were perhaps odd – as if the song had already been out there fully formed, in the aether or some far flung corner of his unconscious, just waiting for the door to be opened. But it was a door that had closed with the death of his friends. Nothing had knocked on it since.

"*Jesus!*" He almost fell off his chair. Right at his elbow, silent as a spirit, stood Tempest min.

"What on earth are you doing here?" Charlie managed to find his teacher's voice, sounding, both in tone and content, disturbingly like Dr. Carlyle.

Tempest min looked flushed and damp as from troubled sleep. He was wearing red striped pyjamas and checked slippers with bunnies' ears on them. Fair curls stuck to his forehead. "What are you doing here?" he asked in return.

"I'm reading a chemistry book," said Charlie - adding firmly, before this could turn into one of those Tempest min type conversations, "but you're supposed to be in bed."

"I had dreams," said Tempest min. "And I don't think you're a chemistry master. You look like somebody I used to know who wasn't a chemistry master."

"Well that somebody wasn't me," said Charlie. "Now, I think you should go back to bed."

"They weren't nice dreams," said Tempest min. "And I don't like that new car of ours. It gives me bad feelings."

"Car sickness, probably," said Charlie. "That's why you don't like it. Some cars do that to you more than others. You'd feel better if you got to sit in the front."

"I was in the front."

"Maybe you have a temperature," Charlie suggested vaguely. "That can give you bad dreams. I'll take you up to see Matron."

"But can't I stay here with you for a while, until the dreams go away? I want to stay with you."

Charlie sighed. He couldn't quite understand why a child would want to stay with him, but he could see no particular objection to it. And he could certainly sympathise with the bad dream business. "You can sit beside me for a while as long as you are very, very quiet," he said.

Tempest min pushed a chair right up close, climbed up on it and settled down with two of his fingers in his mouth and his head on Charlie's shoulder. Though the sensation was obviously intended to work the other way around, Charlie felt oddly comforted. Without saying anything, he started to read about organic acids. By the time he'd checked something he wanted to clarify, Tempest min had fallen asleep. He didn't wake up when Charlie closed the book so it seemed most expedient just to pick him up and carry him upstairs to the dormitory. At the top of the house, in some sort of Peter Pan world of linen cupboards, red linoleum, giant wicker baskets and lines of iron bedsteads containing small boys and teddy bears, Charlie knocked on Matron's door.

Matron opened it with her tufty grey hair on end and her bifocals halfway down her nose. She was nearing retirement age and, in her time, she'd been a theatre nurse, a ward sister and a volunteer with Médecins Sans Frontières. At age fifty, never having married (for reasons undisclosed) she'd taken up residence in the top of Puckrup Hall, and after that she was going to live with her sister in Bournemouth. In the meantime, she was the expert on the handling and rearing up of small boys. She knew when they were sick and when they were really sorry, and she knew when they needed a firm hand and when they needed a good cry. She also knew that good-looking young men with overlong hair were probably a handful on the side, however polite their manner, and so they needed to be treated firmly all of the time. And, if *they* felt sick or in need of a good cry, then they'd best go away and do that on their own because they'd no doubt brought it on themselves. She counted herself fortunate that her pretty niece had just gone back to Bournemouth.

Charlie explained what had happened.

"He wanted to stay with you?" Matron viewed him with blunt incredulity. "I can't imagine why that would be. Can you?"

"No," said Charlie.

"You should have sent him straight back up at once. We can't have them all wandering around looking for succour in unsuitable places. It's a recipe for disaster when you have rooms full of them. They have to stay in bed. If they have nightmares or heebie-jeebies of one sort or another, then they know to come to me. That's how it works. It's the only way it *can* work."

"Of course," said Charlie. "I'll be more strict another time. I promise."

"There won't be another time. Roaming about at night incurs too many risks for a young child," said Matron sternly. "I will remind him of the rules and he won't do it again. Now, you give him to me." She held out her arms. She was a very strong woman and she'd learned what burdens she could and couldn't bear.

Very carefully, Charlie handed Tempest min over.

Matron took him, gently brushing back the damp curls from his forehead. "Is there any way he could have been sleepwalking?"

"No," said Charlie. "Though I'm no expert, of course," he added hastily.

At this point, Tempest min stirred and murmured. "Charlie?"

Matron raised her eyebrows and, looking at Charlie, said with careful emphasis: "You mean Mr. Peterson."

Tempest min was coming slowly awake. "Mother's boyfriends always say to call them by their first names," he said.

"But this is not one of your mother's boyfriends," pointed out Matron as she stood him carefully on his feet. "Is it?" She looked sharply at Charlie.

"No, no," he said hastily. "Of course not."

"This is Mr. Peterson, the chemistry master." It was delivered with the clearest of enunciations. "And he is going back to the library now, so you go along to bed and I'll be there in a minute."

But Tempest min seemed to think that it was appropriate to give Charlie a hug. Charlie patted him diffidently on the head. "You run along now. Do as you are told." He turned to Matron, half appealing, half apologetic. "He's still mostly asleep."

"But I'm not," said Matron with conviction. "Are you sure you're not acquainted in any way with Mrs. Vane Tempest? You do hail from London after all, and it works better for everybody if we know these things."

"I'm certain," said Charlie.

"And you can remember every detail of the past few years, can you?"

"Not every detail," protested Charlie. "But …"

"But we must ask ourselves why this child obviously feels such an odd affinity with you," interrupted Matron. "Mustn't we?"

"Must we?" It seemed obvious to Charlie that Tempest min was just a tired and possibly unhappy little boy who was looking for … something. Someone.

"He was just unsettled," he said. "I told you, he said he'd had dreams."

"Didn't we all?" said Matron, mordantly.

Chapter Six

"I want labels," said Charlie firmly. "I don't want things that come in scruffy paper bags."

"But that's how they come," protested Rory. "You buy them loose. That's why they're advanced spices - it's not a commercial curry mix."

"I want typewritten labels with encouraging remarks from the department of health on them. I don't like borderline hallucinogenic."

"You're a wee bit timid for a rock musician, aren't you?"

"I'm not a rock musician. I'm a chemistry teacher. Which tends to make you slightly cautious about putting stuff in your mouth when you don't know what it is."

"But I do know what it is," Rory pointed out. "The wee Indian man tells me what it is. They eat these things all the time in Delhi."

"Well, maybe they're like poison. With repeated small doses you get resistant to them. Go to Tesco. *Please.*" Charlie scrutinised his breakfast. "I don't enjoy visuals of dead friends. They're not remotely comforting."

"My Aunt Bertha used to see dead people. Sundays mostly. Made money at it." If this was intended as either encouragement or commiseration it didn't work.

"She was really a great aunt," Rory added, as if that would help.

Charlie snorted. They ate in silence for a few minutes.

"I'm helping out on the sports field today." Rory got up to make more toast. "You?"

It was Saturday morning, but a boarding school is a throbbing ecosystem that cannot be put into stasis at weekends. Charlie had two lessons to give then an appointment to meet Dr. Carlyle in his study at 11 a.m.. He had no idea why, but it was serving the useful purpose of focusing his mind right here, in this world, at a solidly pragmatic level. It was helping to make his experience of the night before, his vision as it were, much easier to blame on Rory's curry. He ate his bacon and egg wondering if he ought to take over the shopping. But then, Rory actually seemed to like shopping … "I have to see Dr. Carlyle," he said.

"What've you done?"

"I don't know. I don't think Matron likes me, though."

"She disna like any of us once we start growing hair on our faces."

Like all of Rory's reassurances it wasn't that reassuring. Thoughtfully, Charlie watched him making more coffee. The concept of facial hair, however, had obviously set off some chain reaction in Rory, putting him in mind of Christina LeBlanc and her fastidiousness to such an extent that he just had to give the matter an airing. The woman was, he said suddenly and with feeling, a bit of a princess. She referred to his art pieces as craft.

She had to have a china mug. She had to have filtered coffee and Earl Grey tea. And she didn't like stubble. Or hairy chests. Or hairy backsides. Without having heard a specific pronouncement on backsides (as opposed to, but in addition to, backs) Rory was sure that that would be the case. And he seemed to find it particularly exasperating.

"I expect she thinks we should all be like those bare-arsed men on the television," he said. "They're the only backsides you see, aren't they? Bare ones like babies' bottoms. I mean, what sort of a man is it that doesn't have hair on his arse?"

"So, are you going to have this out with her then?" asked Charlie, picking a piece of shell out of his fried egg. "The hairy arse principle."

Rory snorted. "Don't be bloody daft. And mostly, y'know, all these remarks are just aimed at the air around her."

It sounded to Charlie as if Ms. LeBlanc was merely giving off verbal flak in order to discourage Rory from any attempt at a strike. And thinking about it now, he found it hard to imagine how Rory would go about a strike.

"What do you think I could do?" Rory asked him presently, his indignation having run its course. "You must have been round the block a few times. What could I do to ... You know ..."

"Get her to like you?"

"Yes," said Rory. There was a painful depth to the word as if he had suddenly found himself looking into one of those moorland tarns where the hills descend in one fell swoop into still, peaty brown waters. No foothold, no space to linger, just one long slide. A quick gurgle and you're gone.

"So what's your normal approach with women?" Charlie asked him.

This seemed to be an alien concept to Rory. "Approach?"

"Approach."

Rory had to give this some serious consideration. "It was mostly about those porridge dances, y'know."

"No idea," said Charlie. "What's a porridge dance?"

Careful to emphasise that he was going back some years to before his monk-like existence in the forest and his ensuing monk-like existence at the school, Rory explained that a porridge dance was a term that had originated with country dancing and, though the imagery hardly worked as well, it had, in his teens and early twenties, been applied to discos. Basically, it was three times round the floor and then outside for your oats.

"I sometimes wonder," he added, "looking back y'know, if the lasses were all that thrilled with the business. Not that I was any use at it. I mostly stood on the sidelines and drank. I had a good-looking cousin who seemed to have the thing mastered - though there was something about it that you could call, if you weren't a McEwan, a certain lack of refinement."

Charlie looked up from his breakfast. There'd been the odd occasion in his own life when he hadn't been over fussy about things like appropriate location and extended, romance-filled preambles - less Mr. Right than Mr. Right Now - but the McEwans sounded as if they had a long and riotous history of not paying attention to anything as quaint as consensus before doing exactly as they liked.

"And if you *were* a McEwan," he asked, "is there any way that this certain lack of refinement could have been the sort of lack of refinement that could have landed you in jail?"

"Och, no," Rory was genuinely offended. His cousins had gone to jail for the most innocent of offences - trivialities to do with excess alcohol and shoplifting and what he called 'a wee fight or two'. "Nothing bad," he finished earnestly. "Just kids havin' fun. Newcastle on a Saturday night. Y'know."

"I do know," said Charlie. "I was once in Newcastle on a Saturday night."

"Eventful, isn't it?" said Rory, with something that could have been nostalgia.

"But probably more enjoyable looking back," said Charlie. "We broke a perfectly good Strat and somebody put a foot through a five hundred quid amplifier."

"I think," Rory went on presently, in reflective tones, "that it would probably have worked out better for the lasses if there'd been somewhere nice to lie down. Proper like. Sometimes they were back at the bar in ten minutes. It seems awful quick, I mean …" he tailed off thoughtfully. "It's not what you could call romance, is it? And aren't women supposed to like a bit of romancing? What d'ye think?"

"Job to know what to think," said Charlie, wondering if Dr. Carlyle had ever solicited Rory's views on sex education.

"So?" Rory looked expectant.

"Forget about her."

Rory was indignant. Obviously, he felt that his emotions were being badly underestimated. He was unable to forget about her. He was in this 'balls deep' - which was evidently the most evocative expression of lovelorn helplessness that he could conjure.

"Well, for starters, I should avoid expressions like 'balls deep'," suggested Charlie. "I might be wrong, but it seems to me that expressions like that could greatly reduce your chances of ever getting …" he was going to say 'balls deep' but, over the past month, he'd come to realise that Rory seemed to want a lot more than that from Christina LeBlanc. He didn't bother to finish the sentence.

Rory grunted. "That's a given for Chrissakes, what else?"

"Those men on the television probably have their body hair taken off. You could do that if you think it would help. It's called a back, sack and crack."

Rory looked puzzled. "A what?"

"A back, sack and crack."

"Who does that for them for Chrissakes? And what with?" He'd got it.

"Somebody with a strong stomach and some wax. I don't know. Could be they use depilatory creams … or a laser."

"Wax? A laser? Hell's teeth …" Rory's eyes were watering. "I never realised it could be so hard to be on television." He stared into space for a few moments. It didn't look as if body hair removal was an approach he was likely to take.

"What would you do if you left here?" Charlie asked, when all the blinking had passed.

"Have you been listening to me at all? I said I couldn't leave."

"Humour me."

"I suppose I'd go home. Back to the business. Me da's gettin' on a bit now. Mebbes I'd have a bit of a studio on the side to supplement the bread and butter work. Try and get into some local exhibitions. There must be some around up there."

"Sounds like a very sensible plan," said Charlie.

"Which I just can't seem to follow," Rory pointed out.

"You might have to," said Charlie. "Think about it. If you insist on pursuing this Christina LeBlanc business there could well come a point when, if things go wrong, you can't bear to face her in the staff room. Or even the corridors. Some people can laugh things off or brazen them out but, at least where women are concerned, you could be more of a sensitive soul than you look. Much more in fact because, I mean, you look like a big, bloody barbarian who doesn't even have a soul. But, if you're determined to give this a go, then start by letting Christina see who you really are."

"Let her see a real McEwan?" Rory was horrified. "You're kiddin'."

"Not a McEwan. Let her see the man who talks about gnomes and undines."

"Yes, you are kiddin'," said Rory.

*****

On the way to his appointment with Dr. Carlyle, Charlie came across him faster than expected. The headmaster was in the entrance hall of the main building attending to a small boy who appeared to be screaming for no better reason than having dropped his sports kit.

"Don't scream like that," said Dr. Carlyle, when the boy finally stopped. "It's Woodward, isn't it? Imagine if everybody did that, Woodward. What then? This is a social space. We have to behave reasonably when we are in it. If you want to indulge in some primal scream therapy then go and do it in the field. I'll come with you. We'll scream together and you can tell me why you feel like screaming, and I'll tell you why I feel like screaming, and maybe that way we could do each other some good."

Woodward evidently decided against this course of action because he picked up his kit and scurried off down the corridor with it.

"Some other time then," Dr. Carlyle called after him. "Strange boy," he said, turning to Charlie. "Difficult to tell if he's genuinely troubled or just doesn't like physical exercise. We'll find out." He nodded thoughtfully to himself. "We'll find out. Now, I take it you were looking for me?"

"You sent me a text," said Charlie, "requesting my presence in your office."

"Then we'd better go there," said Dr. Carlyle, but he didn't move. "Are you fond of physical exercise, Charlie?" he asked. "The gym and so on? All the young men in the movies seem to go to the gym. I think it can be the only reason my wife watches movies because she swears they're all rubbish."

"I used to go," said Charlie. "A bit of a six pack and some biceps were never going to do a rock career any harm."

"And is there anything left of this six pack?"

Charlie shrugged. "No. It's been years."

"Lift up your shirt."

"Excuse me?"

"Lift up your shirt. Let's assess the state of the psyche through the state of the body."

"Can you do that?"

"I can. Lift up your shirt."

Somewhat bemused, Charlie lifted up his shirt. Dr. Carlyle

looked thoughtfully at his abdomen. One would have to say that, as male abdomens go, it was a pretty respectable one. A person susceptible to abdomens might have considered it a deal more than respectable.

"So you haven't given up," said Dr. Carlyle. "Not really. Not deep down. Where the somatic and the psyche confer together, the dream is still dreaming itself."

And, with that, he started off down the corridor. Charlie followed behind, hastily stuffing in his shirt. He had shirts now. Shirts that were designed to be worn with ties. And trousers that weren't made of denim and held together with studs. And jackets that were just plain boring. It was a look that really hadn't really come together for him. In fact he'd made no effort with it - hadn't tried to personalise it or make it representative of him in any way. Dr. Carlyle liked bow ties, and Eric Boswell was fond of old fashioned sports jackets with elbow patches, and Rory had his moleskin and his brown boots, but he had nothing except what was bland and unobjectionable and being sold off at a knock-down price. He wondered if that meant he wasn't wholeheartedly embracing this new life. Was he really still dreaming the dream at some unconscious level?

"The lady from LAFFAS is here," Dr. Carlyle said, over his shoulder.

Charlie, still reflecting upon the symbolic nature of his stomach and his terrible trousers, didn't quite catch it. Had Dr. Carlyle said 'laugh us?' Or maybe it was Lammas. Lammas being one of those weird days that these people seemed so fond of - days once associated with the turning of the agricultural year. They'd just had Michaelmas Day. That, apparently, was originally something to do with the Archangel Michael and the ending and beginning of the husbandman's year - and the naming of those big daisies which were now arranged so lavishly in front of various fireplaces. There was a great fondness at Puckrup for bringing the outside in. At times, the entire place resembled a giant nature table. Deserted birds' nests, dead bats, all manner of found objects - animal, vegetable and mineral - posing in still-life tableaux on every available surface.

Or maybe, Dr. Carlyle had said llamas. Charlie had seen llamas in the countryside. He'd thought he was passing a zoo. These people were just sort of people who might be going in for llamas ….

Once they were in the study (the Michaelmas daisies in the fireplace were a glowing pink) Dr. Carlyle turned round. "I thought there'd be tattoos," he said.

"Tattoos?"

"You. Tattoos."

"On the back."

"Ah." Dr. Carlyle smiled. "There we are, then. A man of the moment, exactly as I expected."

"There's just the one. Not big."

"Nevertheless, men of the moment must have chats with the lady from LAFFAS. It seems that some of the boys are already developing an affinity with you. Your response has to be suitably honed. Men of the moment must submit to honing when they find themselves in loco parentis. So it's time for the lady from LAFFAS to have her say. She's in the library. You must at least read the leaflets."

Charlie, finally in tune with the conversation, wondered if Dr.

Carlyle with his talk of affinities was actually making oblique reference to the incident with Tempest min. But, if he was, he clearly didn't intend to dally there.

"And then after lunch," he went on, "I would like you to go to the walled garden and talk to Lady KP."

"About anything in particular?"

"Hydronium ions."

"Oh," said Charlie.

"Lady KP went to a lecture last night at Pershore horticultural college. It was about environmental soil chemistry and, apparently, there were words and references in it that she didn't quite understand. And Lady KP doesn't like anything going on that she isn't fully commensurate with. She believes that scientists and engineers involved with environmental remediation will do things behind her back without having thought through the consequences. So, obviously, she needs to know what all the words mean. She thought you could have tea together."

"I see," said Charlie.

"Good," Dr. Carlyle studied him thoughtfully.

Charlie wondered if this was the end of the interview. He waited politely to be dismissed. But Dr. Carlyle hadn't quite finished.

"I know you are still haunted, Charlie," he said finally. "One gets to see these things after years of searching children's faces for a clue to their troubles. But things have a way of working out. Patience, Charlie. Just have patience. This is not the endgame."

If Dr. Carlyle was at all conscious of his choice of words, he gave no indication of it. Instead he beamed broadly and continued, "So, first the lady from LAFFAS, then an edifying chat with Lady KP. Sounds like the makings of a really good Saturday to me."

That seemed to be the end of the interview but just as Charlie was going out of the door, the headmaster called, "What's the tattoo?"

"Just a bird."

"What sort of bird?"

"A raven."

"Goodness me." Dr. Carlyle sat down at his desk. "A bird of portent. Such a choice. And to further choose the mythical mediator between life and death. What made you pick that one, Charlie?"

"I just liked the picture." Charlie shook his head as he closed the door behind him. Really, these were the oddest people.

*****

It seemed a God-given gift that the lady from LAFFAS was behind schedule with her talking. She was a big, blonde lady with bouffant curls, a flowing dress like a large tent or a small marquee, and huge jewellery that rattled as she waved her pudgy hands around. She was with a gaggle of boys who looked as if they'd rather be doing something else – fighting on the floor seemed to be the preferred alternative. Which they promptly took up the minute Charlie's arrival provided them with a window of opportunity. Ms. LAFFAS, however, wielded an authority that was slightly at odds with her appearance. She restored instant law and order in tones that carried the power of unknown and unknowable retribution.

"Now, you will be quiet," she finished, "while I take five minutes to talk to …"

"Mr. Peterson," supplied Charlie. "Charlie."

"Mr. Peterson," repeated Ms. LAFFAS, drawing him to one side. Her voice lowered then as she skipped anything in the nature of chatty preamble and plunged into business. "We have a responsibility for the psychological development of these boys." She glanced furtively in their direction. "Unfortunately, in exercising this responsibility, we find ourselves in head on collision with all manner things that are very far from working in our favour. Internet porn sites filled with outrageous content, this regrettable trend for sexting … and … and … and God knows what else. We want these boys to grow up to be decent husbands, partners and fathers with a respect for, and an understanding of, girls and women. But, in the meantime, they have to get through susceptible teenage years beset by things that could warp them forever. So *you*, Mr. Peterson, must work to our advantage. You must be firmly on our side …" At this point she produced a pile of literature.

"It can, initially, be very much about the choice of words." She proceeded to add to the pile, rummaging energetically inside a capacious bag the size of a haversack. "We need to use words appropriate for the age group. And for the more junior ones, like these," she gestured with a clatter of bracelets, "our responsibility is to supply the facts suitable for their level. Frankly and honestly. Without resort to storks or gooseberry bushes. And, Mr. Peterson, when you deal with the older boys, whatever your outlook has been in the past, it must now accord with what is written here." She tapped firmly on the growing heap of paper. "*Outlook*, Mr. Peterson. The direct delivery of the information is my responsibility - in conjunction with Matron. But as you, like Matron, are here all the time, yours will be the continued influence and also the problems. So, you must maintain the appropriate *outlook*."

Jeez, Charlie thought, looking at his pile of leaflets with carefully assumed gravitas while Ms. LAFFAS studied his face for signs of protest.

"Dr. Carlyle liked your parents," she said finally. "He told me that with a mother like yours, you shouldn't have gone too far astray. He said I wouldn't need to lecture you too much."

"That's nice," said Charlie meekly.

"I hope he was right," said Ms. LAFFAS. "I hear you spent a portion of your life in a very dubious world. Matron and I are not as convinced as Dr. Carlyle that this necessarily makes you an asset."

Charlie had also spent what Ms. LAFFAS would no doubt have considered a developmentally undesirable period amongst gooseberry bushes. Grandma Peterson (an industrious minder of grandchildren) had been a great fan of them. In her day, they'd obviously been very productive plants. It was the one area in which her homilies had lacked conviction. In the end, he'd come to realise that something was up with those gooseberries. It had been his mother, the product of the swinging sixties, who'd eventually read sequential sexual riot acts to him in a freshly minted and thoroughly emancipated form. Dr. Carlyle had got her about right. On the whole, however, Charlie felt that the interlude with Ms. LAFFAS had fallen somewhat short of being amiably collegial.

After taking his leave, he pushed the leaflets into various pockets with barely a glance. It was almost lunchtime, and today he had to spend it in a supervisory role in the dining hall. This meant ensuring that the boys used their cutlery properly and ate up their tapioca pudding without flicking it at each other. Once the dining hall had emptied, he forked up the cooling remains of his shepherds' pie whilst listening to a high pitched lament coming from the kitchens. Something about the lack of a piece of equipment called a swill tub. For the waste food, apparently. 'Time was, we used to save it for a farmer to give to his pigs.' A satisfying frugality now apparently forbidden. 'So why can't we do that now?' 'In case it's diseased.' '*Diseased?* But we've been feeding it to the *children*.' 'It's a pig disease.' 'What pig disease?' 'Foot and mouth,' supplied the chief cook and bottle washer who seemed omniscient in the matter. 'Never been a recorded case in children.' At this point, Charlie pretended that he'd forgotten there was tapioca for afters, pushed back his chair with a sigh and set off for his meeting with Lady KP.

Being a tidy walk away, the walled garden was a destination in itself. Charlie had already grasped the fact that this state of affairs had been decreed by the landscape movement with its insistence that the artifices of gardening had to give way to sweeping naturalism in accordance with the new idyll that was being rolled out over the country estates of England in the wake of Capability Brown. The quaintness of knot gardens and the contrivances of flowers and vegetables had been uprooted in favour of acres of green sward which had to stretch from the very foundations of the house to some obelisk on a far distant hill by way of lakes, bridges, cunningly arranged trees and the odd folly. But, the owners of grand houses still wanted to eat, and as they had to eat better than everybody else, most especially their peers, carefully hidden walled gardens had come into being - complete with glasshouses, potting sheds and fiercely accomplished head gardeners with ranks of quailing underlings.

So now Charlie was taking a walk and, as he had never been to the walled garden before, he took the scenic route. This went by way of a couple of football pitches and he paused for a while on a touchline to watch Mr. Horton the games master, energetically circling a heaving rugby scrum with much arm waving and furious blowing on an ancient Acme Thunderer whistle. Deliberately dawdling to fill in time before tea, Charlie paused yet again by an adjacent and much smaller pitch, to watch much smaller boys stumbling up and down it after a football. Rory was on the other side of the pitch, red faced with exasperation. "Come on, kick it! For God's sake, Crammond, kick the damned thing! It's there to be kicked! It's no' a kitten. Try t'other foot if that one disna work!" His brogue was getting thicker and thicker by the minute. It was entirely possible that poor Crammond had no idea what he was being told to do.

Charlie was just about to move on when a small fist, thoroughly encased in bandaging, was waved in front of his face.

"I've been injured again!"

Charlie looked down at a mud covered child. "The game is football, Tempest min. You're supposed to use your feet."

"I didn't do it playing football. I was wrestling with Braddock. I have weak wrists, Matron says."

"Then don't wrestle," suggested Charlie. "Especially not with Braddock." In spite of the school's best efforts, Braddock was a hefty boy.

"Tempest min!" bawled Rory. "Wa still playing in case y' hadna' noticed! Get back on the field ya wee scrote!"

"What's he saying?" asked Tempest min.

Charlie turned him round, gave him an encouraging shove and watched with a sigh as he re-entered the game on disorganised legs like Bambi getting to his feet for the first time.

*****

Pursuance of the scenic route eventually fetched Charlie up against an arched wooden door in a towering brick wall. If anything substantial in the way of machinery operated within the garden it obviously used some other entrance. The latch was stiff and the door was heavy and as it creaked open Charlie, wiping wet rust from his fingers, was suddenly aware of a whiff of cliché in the air - an atmosphere of secret gardens and sleeping beauties. But there was certainly nothing of sleep proceeding within. Shrill, schoolboy voices led him to a beleaguered patch of earth where Lady KP, wearing a purple shawl clasped at the neck with a diamond brooch that flashed rainbow fire in the autumn sun, and lace-up rubber boots with fake fur tops spotted like ermine, was supervising the digging of potatoes with all the enthusiasm of a Dickensian headmaster.

In all, it was an energetic business. For the boys, it was an activity quite equal in calorific output to the games they had probably been trying to avoid. Or maybe, they just liked gardening. People did. As did hens, apparently. A dozen or so sturdy Cotswold Legbars and some determined little bantams with pompoms on their heads were scrummaging enthusiastically for worms and centipedes in the disturbed soil.

Lady KP, silver hair hectically on end, waved the stout hazel stick that she was using for a mixture of support and poking and called out to him: "We are late lifting this year but it's been a good crop!" She then picked her way through boys, hens and potatoes to the nearest path.

Charlie concurred agreeably about the high production levels though he was, of course, nothing of a judge.

"Take a look around," suggested Lady KP, stamping soil from her boots, "while I find the boys some sacks."

The garden was a magnificent space - at once sumptuously feminine in the fruitfulness of its autumn bounty, yet rigidly masculine in the linear regularity of its crops and the geometric cross hatching of its paths. It was a secluded three acre realm of laden fruit trees in meadows of grass, fruit bushes in ornamental cages, arches festooned with late-flowering clematis and dangling gourds, hazel wigwams with sweet peas still at their endless labour, a cutting garden with chrysanthemums and dahlias and Michaelmas daisies, immaculate vegetable beds lined out with all the wonders of red kale, multi-coloured chards, savoy cabbages and an evocative, glowing sprawl of huge Cinderella pumpkins.

Charlie's assessment of all of this was botanically vague but emotionally satisfying. He wouldn't have become over excited at the thought of joining the potato lifting gang, but to wander in here on a summer evening when everything was at a pitch of perfection and to have a glass of wine in one hand and a beautiful woman holding the other would be … yes … the next best thing to happiness. As it was, he had to make do with a puffing Lady KP who caught up presently and led him past further highlights of the season whilst inundating him with information about carrot fly, gooseberry sawfly and the making of compost. Magical gardens clearly didn't come easy. A homily on the benefits of leaf mould and the useful fungi therein was cut short when they arrived at a rather lovely brick cottage set into the north wall of the garden. It had always been, Lady KP explained, the head gardener's accommodation but now, as her granddaughter was essentially head gardener, it had come back into the family as it were. Lady KP herself lived in the dower house which was a somewhat grander residence about half a mile away down a private road which Charlie had never bothered to investigate. (As he had never even tried to consider the complicated endowments and leasings and quid pro quo arrangements that evidently comprised the basis of the school's very existence.)

In front of the gardener's cottage, on a small lawn that caught the afternoon sun, a rustic table was being laid up for tea by the ubiquitous Mrs. Batt. Mrs. Batt was wearing a flowery coverall and a pink felt hat with a faded rose pinned to it in the general area of one of her ears. She was a sturdy country woman, well on the far side of sixty, with a face that showed its age through a mild, evenly spread crumpling like a Cox's orange pippin that's been sitting in the fruit bowl for too long. Not that Mrs. Batt appeared to sit anywhere. The exact nature of her employment was hard to state, but she was always wherever she was needed at just the right moment so she was obviously indispensable.

"Cakes!" exclaimed Lady KP with every evidence of delight. "I don't eat cake, of course – the sugar you know. And the gluten. But most of us like to keep one eye on the temptation that we pray not to be led into – that's Oscar Wilde I expect, but then I misremember a little these days. Which brings me to the point – do sit down by the way – I did some chemistry at school and I've tried to keep in touch with pertinent aspects of it, but why don't I remember the word hydronium?"

"I don't know," said Charlie.

"But you know the word?"

"Yes."

"And understand it?"

"Yes."

"Then you can have cake. I shall have cucumber on sprouted wheat bread. You may prefer wholemeal. But do start with a sandwich. Always bread before cake, my mother used to tell me."

Charlie took a thin slice of wholemeal bread spread with chopped hard-boiled egg in mayonnaise and sprinkled with cress. There was something of an Indian summer in process so eating outside in the garden felt not only redolent of a more civilised and leisured lifestyle but comfortably warm. There was a steady background hum of busy bees making the most of flowers that were being seduced into prolonged performance by the very late autumn.

"I know hydronium is something to do with pH," said Lady KP when she had emptied her mouth of sandwich. "And in soil chemistry pH is the master variable, you know. It affects plant nutrient availability by controlling the chemical forms of the nutrients. But, between the lecturer making rash assumptions about the scientific calibre of his audience and some wretched woman eating crisps, I failed entirely to come away with all the details straight."

"It's pretty straightforward," said Charlie. "A hydrogen ion, which as you no doubt know, is the essence of pH, does not exist as a free species in aqueous solution. Its presence causes the protonation of water and the creation of the hydronium ion which is, put simply ..." He pulled out a paper and pencil – the need for which he had anticipated - and drew some pictures, going further into the nature of oxonium ions and hydroxonium and other things that could come up in the same ball park, as it were, and provoke further confusion. In between times, having eschewed the school cook's tapioca pudding, he ate a lot of cake while Lady KP asked questions and grumbled copiously about soil contamination and the ensuing ecological and environmental health risks. A fat brown hen had flown up onto her lap and it ate a lot of cake too – crumbled for it in gnarled and diamond-clad fingers.

Mrs. Batt, camouflaged amongst a stand of giant sunflowers which had been left with their seedheads for the benefit of the birds, supervised the progression of the tea with the scrupulous eye of a family butler. If Lady KP as much as tweaked her napkin, the sunflowers began to rustle with concerned enquiry. When Charlie glanced across he got the strange impression, some trick of the afternoon light no doubt, that the sunflowers and Mrs. Batt were actually blending. He shook his head. Though the subject of soil pollution and remediation was a thoroughly modern and practical topic, he couldn't help feeling that some alternate reality had crept up on him. It wasn't just the Frances Hodgson Burnett atmosphere of the walled garden, or the mistress and faithful retainer relationship between Lady KP and Mrs. Batt, or the visual jokes being played upon him by the sunflowers, it was to do with the entire school. Puckrup Hall felt as far removed from the life he'd once planned in the music industry, or even the life he had lived in the Camden basement, as it was possible to be. It wasn't even that the place was a private boarding school or that, as such, it bore some of the hallmarks of another age. It was that there seemed to have been some sort of slippage. Though there was - from newspapers and television and so on - every evidence of the progression of life in 2015, it was as if Puckrup had slipped a little out of synch with reality.

"I detect a flagging on the cake front," said Lady KP suddenly. "And I suspect that I have plumbed the depths of your interest in soil chemistry … No … No need to protest. You have been admirably compliant up to now." She paused to stuff the paper bearing Charlie's notes and drawings of molecules into a pocket. "But before you go, I would like to introduce you to my granddaughter. I thought she might come and have tea with us, but evidently she's found something more congenial to attend to in the potting shed."

The potting shed, in essence the garden's HQ, was a prominent brick building against the west wall and it was positioned authoritatively between two very long and substantial lean-to glasshouses of ornate Victorian origin. It contained, in common with most potting sheds, flowerpots, sacks of compost, horticultural sand, potting soils and fertilisers of varied provenance, plant labels, gardener's string, canes, half empty seed packets, gardening implements in variety and much more besides. It was a place that spoke of serious down-to-earth workings and frank dirt, yet the air in it was filled with fairy dust - golden motes floating in the slanting rays of the low autumn sun that was pouring its final afternoon light through the windows. And there, in the glitter of the fairy dust but ghoulishly set around with piles of cow horns and animal skulls and something that looked suspiciously like a dish of intestines, stood Lady KP's granddaughter. Maybe it was on account of this unholy jumble – this astonishing juxtaposition of the sacred and the profane, the beauty of the young woman versus the charnel house mess on the bench before her - that Charlie became seized with the odd notion that she had to be something beyond the human, a creature of celestial provenance. A charmed light seemed to shine on everything around her, even the gruesome task she had at hand. Her gestures, as she stuffed what appeared to be crumbling bark into a fresh looking skull that still carried the shine of viable looking membranes on its inner surface, were so smooth and gentle as to give him a reflex sensation that he didn't care to even acknowledge.

No doubt about it, Ianthe Keeble Parker could lay claim to unusual beauty. She was slim and golden, hair and skin sun-drenched from a life lived in the open air. Her bare arms and shoulders, set off as they were by nothing but a pair of grubby bib-overalls, seemed to Charlie to be the most erotic thing he'd ever seen.

Her smile of greeting was so unconsciously seductive that it was actually hard to look at. "I hope you don't find this too disconcerting," she said. "But I'm afraid it's actually Grandmama's favourite way to present me. Sort of like her debutante ball in reverse. I won't shake hands. I'm sure you'll appreciate that."

Charlie said, "Er …"

"You must be wondering what, exactly, I'm at."

Partly. Mostly he was overcome with her. He could have wondered to himself why he wasn't wondering one or two other things - things that it probably wouldn't have been appropriate to wonder about in front of Grandmama. Or at all. But he wasn't wondering about those either. He was just struck - like the poor, pale knight found wandering in the weeds in La Belle Dame Sans Merci.

"We're biodynamic," said Ianthe.

It didn't help. Biodynamic didn't compute. Charlie's eyes wandered helplessly back to the hands that were almost caressing the skull. Was stuffing skulls the natural province of head gardeners? And how could a mundane title like 'head gardener' be applied to a divine-looking being such as this? Even the word woman seemed too basic. And then there was the skull. Still. Also those revolting, slippery innards in the bowl. And no advanced spices to account for any of it.

She looked up at him. "Do you find it too awful?"

Lady KP had been having an altercation in the doorway with the brown hen. It wanted to come in and interfere with the skull stuffing and Lady KP said it couldn't. It tried a couple more feints but Lady KP won out on account of her hazel stick. The door was closed firmly in the face of indignant clucking, and the situation inside the potting shed was taken in hand. There were to be no struck young men palely loitering, or granddaughters stimulating admiration but disregarding the niceties of introductions and proper explanations. And what was needed, after the naming of names and the putting of people in context, was for the gruesome scene itself to be given a context. And for

Charlie to understand this context, he needed some understanding of biodynamics as they applied to horticulture. First of all, Lady KP explained, things had to be planted and harvested according to the phases of the moon and other celestial bodies. Things grew better and kept better like that. It was probably a sap thing. By and large. That was the scientific stretch that made the principle vaguely acceptable. But then one had to realise that the earth was a living being and that it was in the process of dying. Even organic agriculture, infinitely preferable as it was to chemical, could not re-enliven an exhausted earth. The administration of special biodynamic preparations, used in consonance with certain celestial rhythms and relationships, was necessary to reawaken earth's energies and feed the forces of nature. Ianthe was making just such special preparations. The fresh skull for instance, that of a domestic animal, was being packed with ground oak bark and it would then be buried for the winter in a swamp before having its contents scattered on the earth. This was the sort of thing that comprised the unacceptable part.

"You can readily see," finished Lady KP, "how difficult it would be to get these ideas to take at a general level. They are almost impossible to discuss in any public forum."

"No doubt," agreed Charlie, a shade weakly. It was certainly a very far cry from hydronium ions. "And the intestines?"

"To be stuffed with chamomile blossoms and buried in the earth for the winter."

"Right."

Lady KP was obviously expecting more. Charlie shook his head. "I'm lost for words."

"So, you're not likely to be asking my granddaughter to dinner any time soon." It was a statement rather than a question. An odd one perhaps, but a statement nevertheless.

"I would have no idea what to feed her," said Charlie, because he felt he had to make a response of sorts and he was suffering some significant mental impairment.

"Oh, the feeding would be no trouble," Lady KP opened the potting shed door and began jousting with the brown hen to clear a path for their exit. Evidently she'd achieved whatever it was she'd wanted to achieve from the interlude. "My granddaughter only eats leaves and flowers and the odd egg. If the hen doesn't object and is prepared to swear that it hasn't been fertilised."

Following her, Charlie took his leave, muttering some uninspiring stuff about its having been all very interesting.

"Come again," said Ianthe Keeble Parker. She was clearly unperturbed at being talked about as if she weren't there. Indeed, she had a serenity that seemed to distance her from the minutiae of minor human interaction. "We haven't got on to stags' bladders yet," she added. "You may find those more interesting."

"It would be what could come after the feeding that I would be worried about," observed Lady KP when they were finally outside.

Charlie said nothing.

He left the walled garden in something of a daze. Lady KP, who escorted him as far as the door in the wall, did not broach the subject of her granddaughter again, which was perhaps a little surprising, but Charlie was thankful for her reticence whatever the reason for it. He was left with an impression of Ianthe Keeble Parker that was half wondrous, half horrific, and for the time being he was happy to preserve it exactly as it had struck him. Further inspection might cause something that felt extraordinary to dissolve into the ordinary, or worse. So he'd been content, as they'd walked slowly along still harassed by a reproachfully chuntering hen, to have no reference to what had just passed and to nurse his impression of some earthbound angel practising arcane magics while he listened with half an ear to a Lady KP monologue on heritage varieties of apple.

*****

Re-crossing the now empty playing fields in the gloaming of late afternoon, he saw a stooped figure silhouetted against a lavender sky. Dr. Boswell, bulky in tweed and wellington boots, was creeping round the edges looking for mushrooms for his tea. A busy little body that quickly revealed itself as the trembly terrier was in attendance, though it hardly looked to be an asset. With the last of the light glinting off his round spectacles, Eric Boswell raised his basket and called out, "Blewits?"

Charlie had no idea what a blewit was, nor was he inspired by a look in the basket. What was being proffered bore only a passing resemblance to the things labelled 'mushrooms' in Sainsburys. He might, just, have taken Mrs. Gargery's word as to their edibility, but recent experiences with advanced spices had made him wary.

"You keep them," he said. "I'm completely full of cake. I've just had tea with Lady KP."

"A great privilege," nodded Dr. Boswell, picking pieces of

grass out of his basket. "And one rarely extended. Did she want something?"

"She wanted to know about hydronium ions."

"And were you able to satisfy her in the matter?"

"I think so," said Charlie. "Look, there's some."

"Hydronium ions?"

"Mushrooms."

Dr. Boswell shuffled forward with the speed and concentration of a questing hedgehog. Helpfully, Charlie walked to the spot and bent down to pick. He was dallying in the gloaming with the lavender sky because he felt that in some mysterious way it would help him stay connected to that extraordinary magic that still seemed to be hanging in the air like the faint smell of a lost love's perfume.

"You seem preoccupied, Charlie," said Dr. Boswell, taking a squashed blewit from his fingers with a little frown. "Rapt."

"We had tea in the walled garden," said Charlie. "I've never been there before. It kind of catches at you, doesn't it?"

"Indeed," said Dr. Boswell. "If you've the soul to register that sort of thing. Cast a spell on you, has it?"

"There certainly seemed to be spells," said Charlie. "Lady KP's granddaughter was brewing up potions in the potting shed with some quite gruesome materials."

"Hard stuff for a chemistry master to swallow?" Dr. Boswell gave him a sharp sidelong glance.

"I guess," said Charlie who had, in truth, made no serious mental efforts to either reconcile or refute what he'd seen and heard.

The fact that some image of Ianthe Keeble Parker had

infused itself into Charlie's faculties and disarmed most of his critical and intellectual processes was not lost upon Dr. Boswell. "She's very beautiful, isn't she," he remarked. He left the comment hanging as he considered Charlie for a moment or two more, but Charlie didn't respond so Dr. Boswell busied himself, poking in his mushroom basket again. When he'd arranged the mushrooms to his satisfaction, he said, "Unusual name, Ianthe. Taken from a poem, you know ..."

"A poem?"

"A Bysshe Shelley poem. Ianthe was the beautiful girl who was, and here I quote: 'judged alone worthy of the envied boon that awaits the good and the sincere'."

"What boon?"

"The boon of spiritual knowledge. While she's asleep, Ianthe has her soul taken by the queen of the fairies, Queen Mab, to celestial regions where it is shown that man could be perfected by the evolution of nature and the virtuosity of those who saw a better way of doing things."

"Of course it wasn't just a simple fairy story," Dr. Boswell added. "Though one should never really say 'just' or 'simple' when it comes to fairy stories. The poem had its angles."

"Right," said Charlie. Grandma Peterson had read him an awful lot of fairy stories. Where bad things happened to bad people. And even to good people if they weren't paying enough attention.

"It's all quite interesting really," Dr. Boswell seemed to be getting caught up in it. "Shelley was one of the Romantics, you know, and they had a number of notions regarding the relation of life and nature to a transcendent reality - including the idea that the poetic imagination could function as a gateway to some unifying and controlling spirit of the universe. All rather counter the Enlightenment, and indeed, Shelley's poem appears to have been written in a mood of some disenchantment with a world that was now bent on replacing mystery with mastery. The Romantics, you see, preferred the unbounded and the indefinable. They understood that the human being is a creature of truly formidable yearnings and perhaps they saw their consolation for the misery of living being taken away from them." Dr. Boswell gave Charlie a sharp look at this point. "Oddly perhaps," he added, "Shelley was also a professed atheist, but he did believe in a living power that resides in nature, and he published the poem at one point under the title The Daemon Of The World. The word 'daemon' being used in the sense of spirit or life force - not something out of The Exorcist. Nevertheless, it didn't go down at all well. Especially not with the Church."

Dr. Boswell went back to his mushrooms at this point, muttering under his breath about the perfectibility of human nature and the difficulties one inevitably encountered in pursuing the principle in a boys' boarding school.

"It's getting too dark to see," said Charlie, when it looked as if the old man's attention had been reabsorbed into the world of edible fungi. "Have you enough, do you think?"

"I have," said Dr. Boswell. "Did you see where that dog went?"

"I didn't notice," Charlie glanced around.

"Strange little beast." Dr. Boswell shook his head. "Seems erratic and unfocused in its comings and goings but it manages to get into everybody's business all the same. Sometimes, I think it's a spy for Dr. Carlyle. My sister's cats are spies, I'm convinced of it. Though heaven knows what she thinks I'm hiding from her."

Charlie laughed.

"It's nice to hear you laugh," said Dr. Boswell. "Have you settled well here, do you think? Has the change been worth the effort?"

"I think so."

"Good, good." Eric Boswell nodded. "Most of us had dreams, you know, Charlie. These days, however, I'm inclined to agree with Tennyson: 'Show me the heart unfettered by foolish dreams, and I'll show you a happy man' ..." He gave a little chuckle. "Tennyson is so quotable, isn't he? Such a knack for the epigrammatic."

"So there we are ..." He added contentedly after a moment or two. "Blewits for tea. There's a dream that can readily be realised."

Chapter Seven

Back in the flat, Charlie found Rory looking as if all of his dreams had turned into nightmares. He was sitting on the floor in the half dark staring fixedly at a computer that was perched on the coffee table. In the blueish glow emanating from the screen his normally ruddy face was putty pale. Charlie turned on the lights.

"Jeez," he said. "You look terrible."

"It's the stuff on this computer," said Rory, weakly.

"What stuff?"

"Sex stuff. I was looking for pointers."

"Well, I should stop it," advised Charlie. "Only this morning the lady from LAFFAS told me how bad it was for unformed minds. And she must have been right because it looks as if it's making you ill."

"I *feel* ill." Rory sounded aggrieved. "There's some nasty things on here."

"You're a very sensitive man, aren't you?" Charlie patted him on the head.

"Ah'm supposed to be a rough diamond," Rory pointed out. "At best. Which makes you wonder what those people on there are." He gestured indignantly at the screen of his laptop.

"Hopefully," Charlie took a squint, "most of them are professional porn stars. It's a multimillion pound business, all carefully choreographed and almost totally without body hair. No wonder it infuriated you."

"Infuriating is not the word for some of it," said Rory. "The McEwans have never been owt special – rogues and swindlers to a man most of 'em - but even at the blackest spots in our history, I think we most likely stole the animals and raped the women, and not the other way around."

"Well there you are," said Charlie, flinging himself on the nearest futon. "It hasn't been a complete downer because now you've developed a fine new sense of family pride, which I feel sure will make you extremely attractive to members of the opposite sex."

"Och," Rory snorted indignantly. "Y'no help at all. Y'know that? You had a three-year, state-sponsored education in sex, drugs and rock 'n' roll, and all you do is mock those of us who've had nowt but the porridge dance as a primer."

Charlie sat up. "So what were you looking for, exactly?"

"Just nice hints about how to go on with women," said Rory. "Approaches that would appeal to an art and design teacher." He looked up accusingly. "You said I had to have an approach. But it doesn't matter what you punch into this thing, you seem to be just two clicks away from stuff that could get you arrested."

"You'd be heartbreaking if you didn't look like such a bruiser," said Charlie. "So this is all about Christina LeBlanc again. You haven't got to try the 'gnomes and undines are me' approach yet, have you?"

125

"I'll try it," said Rory with a sigh. "But I'll just sound stupid. Isn't there any chance of her just accepting me as I really am?"

"But that *is* who you really are," said Charlie. "At times. We've all got layers. And you're not the only man whose most obvious persona hasn't immediately brought the house down."

This put Charlie inconveniently in mind of the first A&R man he'd ever met. It had been at one of Endgame's very early gigs in a popular London pub where, in order to play its own songs, an unknown band had to perform for nothing and bring most of the audience. And induce said audience, which was inevitably composed of friends and relations, and friends of friends and relations, to spend more at the bar than most of them could afford. And maybe because the entire thing then felt like a family gathering, with well over half of the family probably wondering how all of this could possibly lead anywhere good, the band had played as if it were at a dinner party. With napkins. And so the first thing this A&R man had said was: 'What's the story?' Average middle class boys from polite suburbia didn't have much crowd appeal, he'd gone on to point out. One Chris Martin was apparently enough for the world to take. People liked to see the struggle and the fight - the music they would eventually get for free from this new fucking file sharing thing, but they'd pay to see a tortured soul. That's where most of the money was going to lie in the future. Live performance. He could hear some fucker getting tortured in the music but he couldn't see him. And then he'd poked Charlie in the chest. 'Get your dark side on parade, son. Really play it. Get it out there - on the stage for mass consumption - or you'll go nowhere in this business.'

"Okay," Charlie said to Rory after a moment or two, "so

you've got the rough bit of the diamond on the outside. Fine, but you need to let Christina see the twenty-two carat heart."

"Aye, well, it's easy enough to say," said Rory sourly. "But what can I do apart from babble unconvincingly about gnomes?"

Charlie shook his head. "Perhaps you could become a part-time fireman and rescue kittens from trees."

Rory got to his feet snorting. "It's lucky you'd be too frit to eat what's left of last night's curry because there's not much and you're not getting any of it." And he stumped off into the kitchen.

"I'm full of cake, as it happens." Charlie felt vaguely annoyed. He put his legs back up on the futon, stretched his length and closed his eyes. Between Rory sickening himself with porn and him taking an ill-advised trip down memory lane with A&R men, a few demons had been invoked and now he could no longer feel the magic of the walled garden or the golden other worldliness of its enchanted chatelaine. He felt quite painfully dispossessed. He realised now that those moments in the potting shed hadn't been just about a beautiful woman. They'd been about the place she'd taken him to. A place where his heart had suddenly felt bigger and fuller. A place of rightness and joy that lurked just at the edge of consciousness. A place no more than a breath away that he'd totally lost contact with.

Rory came back out of the kitchen carrying a bowl of microwaved curry. Charlie sat up, put his feet to the floor again, and said with a sigh: "Do you think lady KP's granddaughter is very beautiful? Do you know her?"

"Ianthe? Oh aye, beautiful. Nae doubt about that. But touched, y'know. Definitely touched."

"How do you mean, touched?"

"Fey. Her mother was very young, died in childbirth. And the fairies can take babies then. If they want them, y'know ..."

Charlie gave an exasperated snort - mostly because he felt he had to. In truth, a small part of him was ready to believe it.

"Ah'm just telling you what Aunt Bertha would have told you," said Rory. "She'd have known the minute she seen her. She was very familiar with the little people, Aunt Bertha was. Caught them once down by the beck, dancin' and carryin' on, and every one of them with little green caps on their heads."

Hard not to think that Aunt Bertha was seeing gin goblins but Rory was adamant that his aunt took 'the weeniest drop of the hard stuff on occasion but nothing to signify'. Charlie shook his head. Where else in the land could a conversation like this actually get itself going between two grown men?

"And Ianthe's father?" he asked, leaving the subject of Aunt Bertha before he created offence.

"Nobody knows," said Rory. "Except mebbes Lady KP and she's not telling. She brought her up and she's very protective of her. Be warned."

"Did Dr. Boswell tell you about the poem?"

"What poem?"

"The poem about the fairies with a woman called Ianthe in it."

"Nah - nobody's ever mentioned any poem tae me. This curry's better than it was last night, by the way. Shame you're not havin' any."

*****

128

On Monday morning, Rory emerged from his bedroom looking as if he'd had a man makeover.

"Loafers," said Charlie, almost choking on his toast. "This is a new look for you, isn't it?"

"And is this how you were treated when you got out o' the ripped jeans and studded boots?" Rory protested. "Ah've seen the pictures."

"Everyone was thrilled," said Charlie sadly. "My brothers said it was about time I finally grew up."

"Aye well, maybe it's time I stopped dressing like a bodger."

"What's a bodger?"

"I was a bodger. On my patch in the forest."

"You look good," Charlie subjected the outfit to further scrutiny. He was none the wiser about bodgers but he was keen to be encouraging. "Really."

Rory looked as if he'd come into possession of a Charles Tyrwhitt catalogue. In response to Charlie's seemingly genuine opinion, he turned redder than his normal ruddy - a colour change that was easy to spot because he was scrupulously clean shaven. He was wearing maroon moleskin trousers with a navy blue needle cord jacket, a pale blue shirt and a tie with tiny ladybirds all over it. He hadn't abandoned the materials he was comfortable with, he'd just selected them in slicker form. Done his ordering quite well, in fact. Running a hand through his damp auburn curls and getting them all tidily flattened to his head, he gave an embarrassed grin - revealing very effective teeth that years of masticating half-raw rabbit, including the odd bone, seemed to have rendered invincible to all that sugar could do to them. "Think she'll notice the change?"

"If you keep it up and remember the gnomes. You're a fine figure of a man, Rory McEwan, and if she doesn't appreciate you it's her loss."

"Fuck off," said Rory, but he looked pleased.

"See you at break?"

"If she hasna' run awa' wi' me in the meantime."

*****

For Charlie, that Monday morning turned into one of those times when getting boys to grasp some principle – any principle - of chemistry, felt about as easy as getting a non-believer to buy into the transubstantiation. The comparison came into his head - actually it didn't, but it would have been a particularly apt one because, arriving in the staff room for a much needed cup of coffee, he saw that he had been deprived of the opportunity to slump into his favourite chair by Myra O'Grady, the comparative religion teacher. To be exact, Myra O'Grady was actually in the process of contesting the territory of the chair with a very large ginger cat. The cat was probably of the opinion, as was Charlie, that Ms. O'Grady had strayed rather inconveniently from her normal beat. In fact she was entirely legitimate, having been in the art and design block for the past two hours, engaging in joint discussions with Christina LeBlanc and an averagely interested class of A-level students about the cataphatic art of Christianity and the apophatic art of Islam.

Myra O'Grady was a handsome woman of temperament, and she had grown up on the coast of Ireland where the mountains of Mourne dip down to the sea. Her sandy hair, on the cusp of greying (but not quite yet) was confined by a random assemblage of clips and tortoiseshell slides because its springy waves still seemed to be under the influence of an onshore breeze. But though her hair, and her eyes, continued to carry the moods of the ocean, Myra had travelled a long road from Mourne. She'd been a nun, Charlie understood, until disenchanted by the concept of God as presented to her by the Catholic Church, she'd gone in search of a better paradigm. It was rumoured that the man she'd eventually travelled the road with had proved as disastrous, in the spiritual and romantic sense, as a paedophile priest. Whatever the truth of that, Myra had, on her own telling, continued alone, through the Middle East and Asia to China, through Islam and Judaism and Zoroastrianism to Hinduism and Buddhism and Taoism. God, however, seemed to have kept just ahead of her, and somehow she'd ended up at Puckrup Hall - still doggedly on his trail, probably knowing more about him in his various versions and incarnations than almost anyone else, and possibly feeling him less and less as she kept at her exhaustive efforts to beat him into shape.

So, for all her search for the ultimate peace, Myra O'Grady was still possessed by the spirit of the fighting Irish, and after she and the ginger cat had surveyed each other for a few moments with eyes of a similar green (though the cat's were cooler with the pupils pinched into slit-like defiance, or possibly that was just the sun coming through the window) she leaned in and hauled him off the chair without so much as a by-your-leave. With a twisting panther-like leap he promptly took up residence in the middle of the coffee table and proceeded to lick her fingerprints off his fur with insulting thoroughness.

He was an unusual cat and his popularity waxed and waned.

Marjorie Gargery, the biology mistress, complained that cats killed songbirds and were explicitly implicated in the reduction of their numbers, and the school's chief cook and bottle washer agreed that certainly this one was never in the kitchens catching mice, which was supposed to be its job, and not the job of the trembly terrier whose incursions were unproductive and disruptive and deaf to all entreaty.

In truth, the ginger cat was not much predisposed to catch anything – avian or rodent. He was a tomcat, though neutered now, and as any farmer would have clearly stated had anyone thought to ask, if you want a cat to catch things on any basis other than the purely whimsical, you have to have a queen. But the ginger cat had not been a researched choice. A few years previously he had simply appeared one day in the middle of the entrance hall, possibly in response to the usual winter wails about mice in the pantries. A situation that, once he'd got to examine it in close up, had failed to hold his interest.

But none of that was the cause of Myra O'Grady's irritation. "I think I'd better get moving," she said suddenly. Having fought for the chair, she now vacated it. "I don't know why I came in here. I never really like it across this side of the school. Too much opportunity for bumping into that fool Maccabee. I don't know why they let these mad old physicists out of their various institutions. Once they can't keep their crazy ideas one step ahead of the crazy ideas of younger men, they should be put in some special sort of home. Sent back to head office as it were – not allowed out into the world to torment the rest of us." And with that she went across to the sink, poured out the coffee she'd virtually just made, washed the mug carefully, dried it, put it in the cupboard, picked up her handbag and left.

She'd only just gone when Albert Maccabee put his head round the door and expressed his disappointment at catching nothing but a tantalising glimpse of her bottom as it exited the building. "And the cat was here too," he said with increasing regret. "What an opportunity missed. He's called Schrödinger, you know. Opens the way for lively discussions about the relevance of human consciousness to the fundamentals of matter and the nature of the universe and whether God's always around in the quad and all of that stuff. Course, Myra and I aren't actually speaking at the moment," he added confidentially. "I persuaded her that the movie Vanilla Sky was playing with the ideas of the Gnostics. So she got herself the DVD and, needless to say, she couldn't make head nor tail of it. She was furious with me."

And with that Dr. Maccabee evidently decided against coming in for some coffee, withdrew his head and continued cheerfully on his way. He was a sixty-year-old bachelor, a silver fox with the grin of a six-year-old boy, and the provoking of Myra O'Grady brightened his day like the sticking of pigtails in inkwells.

Charlie had a free period so, since there was no one else around, he reclaimed his chair, put his boots on the coffee table, which the cat didn't seem to mind, and opened a packet of biscuits that he'd found in the cupboard and mentally promised to replace. Within two minutes he'd closed his eyes and his mind had drifted to the walled garden. And it was just a short step from there to getting right into the potting shed where he eventually - though the details of 'eventually' were a bit vague because somehow he knew it wasn't going to be as straightforward as those off-the-cuff 'games of squash' he'd played with relative ease … In fact the fantasy got stuck there for quite awhile – mired in the complications of what exactly would be the right way to make up to a Botticelli earth angel. And, re-presented to him in various forms, the answer kept coming - there wasn't one. It was the sort of thing that got you smited. The hand that touched her would begin to wizen and shrivel. But he was a man, and the hand was still working fine, so yes, eventually he got to take a gentle hold of the beautiful Ianthe and … and before he could feel her in his arms she'd disappeared in a puff of phosphorescence. And the more he tried to hold her, the more dazzlingly she slipped through his fingers, until even the idea of her was impossible to hang on to … He came to and shot bolt upright in his chair with such a jolt that one of his feet fell off the table, waking up the ginger cat which promptly disappeared in a huff.

"What's the matter with you?" Rory scrutinised him suspiciously.

"Nothing. I must have drifted off to sleep."

"There's drool," said Rory.

Charlie ran a hand over his mouth with a snort. "When did you come in?"

"Just now. And you've eaten all the biscuits, have you?"

"There's a few left." Charlie held out the packet.

"Do you want coffee? Or is this a biscuits only day?"

"Coffee please, since you're offering."

Rory opened one of the cupboards and reached in for the Nescafé. "I think this room must've been a gun room at one

134

time," he said, looking round. "You can tell by the insides of these cupboards and the bars on the window."

"I wondered why there were bars," said Charlie. "It struck me as ominous. As if, come break-time, the staff might feel the need to skip out the back way."

"Well, certainly there are some people one wouldn't like to be trapped in here with," observed Christina LeBlanc, sweeping elegantly into the room on a lively breeze of Dior.

"Present company excepted, I hope," said Charlie, taking his other foot off the coffee table.

Christina made a non-committal noise, went to a different cupboard from Rory, and produced a cafetière and a packet of ground coffee. There was no doubt that she raised the tone. She was wearing a softly flowing wool skirt in a fetching caramel, a filmy peach blouse in shot silk and a long cardigan of cream cashmere. Her dark hair was looped back with a chocolate coloured scarf, and the rather nice curve of her lips was enhanced with a lipstick as soft as the blush on apricots. She was, in fact, all round edible - which struck Rory so strongly in the gut that he promptly began to fumble the sugar packets again.

"You've spilt some," said Christina pointedly, looking at his new loafers which were now dusted with shiny crystals.

Rory stamped his foot and the sugar bounced off onto the floor.

"Now, that'll get sticky, won't it?" Christina spoke in the tones she used for children at the dimmer end of the spectrum.

Rory obviously had to pretend that he was amused to have spilt sugar all over his new shoes, that he didn't mind being spoken to like a child, and that he didn't feel stupid on account of his carefully selected outfit having blown its mission with such instant efficiency. That's a lot of pretending to have to do and he wasn't very good at it.

"I've got a free period, so I can afford to be generous," said Charlie, with an overt affability that was meant to turn the irritated Christina in his direction. "I'll clean it up when you've both gone."

He could see the problem Rory was going to have in trying to work a conversation round to gnomes and undines. Gliding imperceptibly into Christina's good graces through casual, but heartfelt, references to the magical qualities of wood and iron was going to be difficult for him. As long as he kept losing control of his motor functions whenever she came into a room, it was never going to happen.

The minute Christina had filled her cafetière with grounds and boiling water she picked it up, collected her special china mug from the cupboard and left the room. Obviously, she preferred to drink her coffee elsewhere.

Charlie, watching her go, felt a ripple of annoyance on Rory's behalf. "I don't think she'd like us even if we went in for artificial sweeteners."

"And she didna' appreciate m'new look at all," said Rory. "Why don't I hate her?"

"Because she's lissom," said Charlie. "And cool. And you're bulky and tend to the heated. It's the attraction of opposites except she doesn't seem to be following the rules."

*****

But Halloween was bearing down on them all and so the 'new

look' got a chance for an outing under what Charlie, at any rate, thought would be more propitious circumstances. Rory, on the other hand, was of the opinion that escorting thirty or so of the older boys to a Halloween dance at a girls' boarding school in Malvern would be a poisoned chalice of monstrous proportions. He boarded the coach, still chuntering his misgivings. Through the windows Charlie could see the other allotted chaperones, Julius Harvey and his wife, sitting together and, across the aisle, Christina LeBlanc sitting in splendid isolation. Rory had to sit beside her because there was nowhere else to sit and Charlie, with a sudden spurt of ungenerous mirth, could see him being very careful not to over occupy the seat on account of being at least one and a half times her size. He was holding himself scrupulously together with his eyes averted, like a naughty puppy. Then the driver started the engine, and Charlie had to get off the coach steps and retake possession of his turnip lantern.

His allotted task for the evening was to help supervise a boggart hunt. As he had absolutely no idea what a boggart was, he was managing to sustain a level of mild interest. Beside him stood Marjorie Gargery dressed as a witch - which was pretty interesting of itself. Dr. Boswell with a false nose, stick-on warts and green corduroys stuffed into a set of gaiters was supposed to be a goblin and Myra O'Grady, determined not to be lured to the dark side, was dressed as a white and glittering angel. "At least she's going to be visible," pointed out Albert Maccabee who had just come out of the main doors.

"You can't come," complained Myra. "You're not in fancy dress."

"I am, as it happens," said Dr. Maccabee, turning round to

reveal a long fluffy tail pinned to the back of his trousers. "I'm the big bad wolf. Besides, Charlie's not in fancy dress."

"I would have thought that you'd have gone to the movie," retorted Ms. O'Grady, ignoring his efforts to shift the censure on to Charlie. "It's bound to be interpretable as a metaphor for the second coming or something. You really ought not to miss it."

More fortunate members of staff, having drawn longer straws, were headed for the movie theatre. The boys who were too young for a dance, including those who considered themselves too old or too cool for a boggart hunt, had been given the choice of Monsters University or extended prep. As one animal they had elected to watch Monsters University. A previous mass vote for Lesbian Vampire Hunters had been deemed an illegal ballot. As Dr. Carlyle had explained on more than one occasion, a school is not a democracy. So it was decreed that after the animated wholesomeness of Monsters University, with its accent on integrity and self-belief, the boys would come together with the returning boggart hunters for a Halloween supper in the dining room.

"What's a boggart?" Charlie asked Dr. Carlyle, who was now standing near the main doors benignly surveying a milling crowd of costumed small boys brandishing glow sticks, turnip lanterns and the odd sparkler. (Powerful electric torches were the prerogative of the staff - to be used only in the case of emergency - a disappearance, a brushfire or an attack by the boggart.)

"It's a mythic creature in English folklore," said Dr. Carlyle. "A sort of genius loci - insofar as it attaches itself to a place. Often a house but sometimes, as here, a patch of countryside.

138

Generally regarded as unfriendly, even mischievous, and not particularly good-looking, according to those who've seen one. But the one we have in the forest garden is quite amenable – he shares the fruits of our planting with us and in return he tolerates this annual abuse of his domain and disrespect to his character."

"But he's pretend, isn't he?" Charlie felt prompted to confirm this because Dr. Carlyle's tone and attitude had seemed seriously informative.

"Only in the way that folklore is pretend. In other words it's based on something. That the place has a presiding spirit or energy, I wouldn't doubt for a moment."

"Doesn't Myra regard that as rather pagan?"

"Myra's viewpoint has become more pluralistic since she left the convent. And she knows that, at one time, people were more predisposed to the idea of God being all pervasive, and present in every aspect of nature." Dr. Carlyle smiled genially. "Personally speaking, I find that quite a persuasive perspective, don't you? Spinoza did. Though he may, I sometimes suspect, have preferred to rule God right out and have nature as his prime force. Now come along, people." He raised his voice. "This boggart isn't going to catch itself, is it, Mr. Peterson?"

And so the glowing crocodile of boggart hunters set off round the outside of the house to the hairy lawn, across the ha-ha and into the forest garden. The expedition wasn't intended to be a free-for-all, it was to proceed along the lines of a treasure hunt. There were teams and each team leader had a sheet with the clues as to where the boggart might be found. As with all elementals, he was fond of riddles and misdirection so there were frights and squeals as boys thrust their hands into tree boles and undergrowth to encounter horrid clammy jellies and clinging sticky cobwebs and rattling bones. It had all taken some members of staff an entire day to construct and the boggart had contributed a few surprises of his own - a big toad, a prickly hedgehog and a dead bird. He was finally found in the form of a monstrous effigy, courtesy of a senior design class, and carried triumphantly back to the dining hall where he was hung up and beaten with sticks like a Mexican piñata until all the sweets fell out. It doesn't seem a very glorious end, or a humane one, for a benign boggart but then these were small boys and they still had energy and excitement to dissipate. Also, they knew what was just papier mâché and what was flesh and blood. "You think?" observed the games master, as the sticks swished through the air and candy flew everywhere.

The pumpkins from the walled garden had been carved into lanterns and set along the centre of the big tables in the dining hall, and now the boys scrambled onto chairs and benches for a supper of pumpkin soup with potato eyeballs floating in it. As Charlie watched to see that none of them managed to choke on one, he caught, through one of the doorways, a fleeting figure in the adjacent corridor. His heart knew before his head who this was, and he fell over the bulky Braddock in his effort to catch her. Precisely what he was going to say when he did was quite another proposition, as he suddenly realised when she swung round and transfixed him with a lightning blue gaze that brought colour to his face. He'd given himself away, and he knew it. He found the fact unusually disconcerting.

"Charlie, isn't it?" she said. "Charlie Peterson."

"Yes."

It was disappointing that she'd had to ask. And yet there was something, some slight something, in her manner that relayed the fact that she hadn't needed to. She was wearing a white smock dress and a red cloak, both of which reached the floor. Her sun blonde hair was braided into a plait which hung thick and long over one shoulder. Though there were no golden motes of dust in the air around her, she still seemed to have stepped out of a fairy story. Certainly more so than Dr. Maccabee with his fake fur wolf's tail bobbing along behind him.

"Red Riding Hood, I presume," said Charlie, when he recovered his voice.

"And you appear to be dressed up like the chemistry master of some boys' boarding school."

"I couldn't think of anything else I wanted to be." Charlie was well aware of the irony. He was also aware that his boring grey trousers and charcoal coloured jacket and white shirt were hardly helping him to impress - even if his tie (red with polka dots) and shirt collar had been irritably yanked into what could be generously viewed as raffish looseness during the exigencies of the boggart hunt. But, time was, he would never have felt quite this wrong-footed whatever the circumstances. The chemistry master had somehow seeped deeply into him and, though that seeping had, maybe, begun to fill up the emptiness left by the death of the Charlie Peterson of Endgame, it was an unfortunate truth that just at that particular moment Charlie Peterson the chemistry master would have liked a little more access to the guy with the 'drop dead visceral authority'.

"You could have been Thomas the Rhymer," she said.

"Possibly, if I'd had the first idea who he was."

Ianthe smiled. She had attractive dimples, just a few little

141

stitches here and there round her mouth. They had a mischievous, almost childlike quality that made her, for a moment or two, seem more accessible.

"It's mostly held that he was something of a musician and troubadour," she said. "A man who made rhyme and music so fine that the Queen of Elfland herself came to listen to him. She was so beautiful that he promptly fell in love with her and, because he was handsome, she took him to be her servant in Elfland. After seven years of good and faithful labour in the fairy kingdom, he was released and rewarded for his service with the gift of truth and the gift of prophecy. Both of which gifts can, as can all gifts of course, be either a great boon or a great burden. How they work out is up to you. Some say Thomas eventually went mad and some say he became a great soothsayer. They are tricky things, fairies, you see. One has to be very, very careful with them. I tell you all of this in case you ever meet one."

Charlie was aware that throughout the latter part of this recitation she'd been mostly looking past him. The story might have begun for his benefit but as it progressed it had had to include someone else. He turned round to find Tempest min standing behind him in a Spiderman costume. "Why aren't you in the dining hall eating your soup?" he asked, a shade irritably.

"Braddock pushed me off the bench." Tempest min was wearing black goggles so it was difficult to tell how upset he was.

"I've told you before, you shouldn't keep coming up against Braddock. He's far too big."

"It's hurt my wrist again," Tempest min held up his bandaged wrist.

"Then you go on up to Matron and she'll give you something

for the pain and make it feel better."

"I don't want to go on up to Matron."

"So where were you going?"

"I was coming to see you."

"Why?

"Because *you* have to make me feel better."

"Matron is the one with the bandages and the tablets and the know-how," said Charlie firmly. He still remembered, with startling distinctness, the previous time he'd been called upon to make Tempest min feel better.

"But you have to make my *heart* feel better."

Why hearts should be a body part that fell outside of Matron's bailiwick and into his own was beyond Charlie's comprehension. And he said so.

"He doesn't mean that," said Ianthe.

"Then what does he mean?"

As well as not wanting to reinvoke the disapproval of Matron, Charlie was conscious, and rather churlishly so, of precious time with this beautiful and elusive woman being pointlessly pilfered without his having made anything of an impression. Much as he liked Tempest min, he still longed to drag the boy back into the dining hall, sit him down on the bench alongside a thoroughly chastened Braddock, and tie him there with one of his own webs.

"He means that he wants you to make him feel happier."

"And how does he want me to do that?"

"I think he just wants to be in your company," she said quietly. "You should be flattered. The heart of a child is a very special gift and, though it will no doubt bring its pains, it's a much safer thing to accept than the heart of the Queen of Elfland. Especially on a night such as this." And she smiled at Tempest min who was now holding on to the hem of Charlie's jacket with one hand.

Charlie looked down at the little boy and sighed. "You're tired," he said in gentler tones. "Let me take you up to Matron and she'll help you to get ready for bed."

"I want to stay with you for a little bit."

Charlie looked helplessly at him.

The Queen of Elfland, however, held as much sway over small boys as she did over boys who were full grown. "You go and sit on the bottom of the main stairs with Mr. Peterson," she said to Tempest min, "and I'll bring both of you a helping of pudding. You can eat together and hearts will be mended but, after that, it has to be straight up to Matron."

"I don't usually have to go up to Matron at bedtime," said Charlie.

"Then you may be excused as long as you eat up."

"We'll eat up if you join us."

So the three of them ate together on the bottom steps of Puckrup Hall's grand staircase - green blancmange with chewy jelly frogs. It wasn't exactly Charlie's idea of a romantic tryst but, oddly enough, it made his heart feel better.

He went back to the flat whistling. He might have whistled louder had he got to walk Ianthe Keeble Parker home but she slipped away, as he knew she would, in the minute or two it took him to get Tempest min up the stairs and reliably aimed at Matron's door. He could, of course, have said: "If you would wait, I could walk you back to the garden." But he didn't.

Though offering to walk her home could have been viewed as a mere politeness, it felt to him as preposterous as it would have been to ask the Queen of Elfland if she needed walking home. Nevertheless, he had to pause in his whistling for a moment in order to make way for a bit of enforced mental clarity. This was a flesh and blood woman; she had, before his very eyes, eaten at least a spoonful or two of the school's blancmange, which had to be as far from the ambrosia of fairyland as it was possible to get. So she stuffed skulls and intestines with an awful familiarity and an unconscious, if disturbing, eroticism - but she was neither Bysshe Shelley's imagination made manifest nor was she the Queen of Elfland. She was a woman who might refuse an invitation to dinner because she had a stag's bladder to fill with something highly unpleasant, or because she'd already warned him off through the confusing subtext of some weird fairy story but, if he was ever going to find out (and he was well aware, as he had warned Rory, that the wisdom of doing this in the workplace was, at best, debatable) he was going to have to disabuse himself of the ridiculous idea that she was in some way uncanny.

*****

And at breakfast the following morning, he discovered that you can get disabused of certain ideas in the most surprising of ways. In the kitchen, he found Rory cooking eggs for them both.

"So how did the dance go?"

"Och," Rory put down his spatula and reached for a tea towel. "I think you'll find the general view of it is going to be pretty dim. Especially among the powers that be."

145

"Any particular reason?"

"There was a fight."

"*A fight?* At a private girls' school in a place like Malvern? Surely not!"

Charlie had had a mental image of a school of wholesome girlhood where cat fights and colourful language and getting drunk on Malibu would never have been contemplated. A school full of sweet, unsullied, country girls dedicated to pleasing the headmistress and wiping the floor with the male of the species when it came to examinations.

"It was us, I'm afraid. Some of the lads." Rory, having removed egg from his fingers, threw the tea towel in a heap. Then suddenly, he picked it up again, shook it out, and hung it carefully on a hook.

Charlie, watching this unexpected and oddly timed emergence of a wholly new type of domesticity, said, "Will you stop fiddling and tell me what happened?"

"Well, Vane Tempest, Blake not Paul of course, was naturally at the hub of it. On account of what may possibly come to be viewed as our negligence, he and a few other lads managed to smuggle in some vodka, do some shots in a corner and then have a falling out."

Blake Vane Tempest evidently made for a bad-tempered inebriate. The buffet table had shed a considerable portion of its contents and a lot of pumpkin lanterns had been knocked over. Also Julius Harvey.

"*Julius?* Oh, my God! Is he okay?" Charlie was half horrified, half entertained.

"Physically, yes. He looked a bit shocked, mind. He was

nearest when the pumpkin lanterns suddenly went for a purler so he tried to interfere, but he's no size, is he? I don't think the lads really intended to knock him over. He just got in the way."

"Dr. Carlyle is going to be furious," said Charlie, although he found the concept of a furious Arne Carlyle a difficult one to visualise. "Letters will surely be written, won't they? Parents summoned? Does he do expulsions?"

"A've never heard a' one. But then, in my time, we've never had another Blake Vane Tempest to deal with. I doubt you could expel him though, without expelling the others."

"So what happened after Julius got knocked over? Did they stop?"

"Like hell they did."

"So?"

"So now we get to the silver lining part."

"*There's a silver lining?* How can that possibly be?"

"It's a highly personalised one. Bespoke, as you might say." Rory suddenly gave a great grin.

"Will you stop with the dramatic pauses! It's irritating".

"Okay. So - how much time do you think could pass at this school before something come along that I could do better than anybody else? Over and above working iron and wood, that is?"

"Aeons," said Charlie, without hesitation. "At least."

"See what I mean about the silver lining? Something specially for me?"

"Hurry up," said Charlie. "Just get on with it!"

"Fights, m'friend. Fights are me. More so than gnomes. A melee of flailing arms and legs is ma birthright. I was born to it. Forged in the fire of physical conflict. When it comes to clashing antlers, you can't beat a McEwan. They're bigger, they're stronger and they have centuries of naked ferocity and bad blood behind them. I just picked Vane Tempest up by his belt – he's heavier than you'd think, by the way – so his legs and arms were waving in the air and I pushed the others apart with my other hand and a bit of roaring. Then I set Vane Tempest down again and told them all how it was going to be. I'd won, so now this was my herd, and they were all going up to the school sanatorium to be checked over by the Matron. And they were going to sit there quietly for her till the rest of us decided whether they were to be killed outright or just ostracised. Plus, the one whose nose had bled everywhere was going to get his father to buy me a new shirt." He paused. "It cost good money, that shirt. Supposed to be non-iron an' everythin' …"

"I can't believe it," said Charlie.

"No, honestly, the appearance of quality cotton it said, but non-iron and extra-long sleeves."

"The fight!" said Charlie irritably. "The fight for Chrissakes! So what happened then?"

"Well, Radley had an attack of nervous giggles because he was mixing ostracised up with circumcised, and the other teachers were all for calling it a day. Have everyone go home."

But terminating a dance or a party because of bit of pushing and shoving and a few badly aimed blows had struck Rory as positively ludicrous. He was adamant that where he came from, if you adopted this kind of peremptory attitude, you would find yourself presiding over social occasions so brief they would be barely worth the planning. Of course he hadn't said that. He'd merely, he explained to Charlie, pointed out that the coach

148

wasn't returning until 10 o'clock, and then gone on to suggest that it would be better for the youngsters if they learned that this sort of thing could be dealt with in an adult fashion without any great upset. It was over now, the miscreants would be dealt with in due course, but the show should go on.

"That's how life works, isn't it?" he finished cheerfully. Y'deal and move on. Y'dinna cancel it."

"And they agreed?"

"They did. There was a live band and it struck up with some bouncie golden oldie. I think it was Michael Jackson's Beat It. And everybody leapt back on the dance floor. In fact, I think the furore added some spice to the evening. They can do that, you know."

"Amazing." Charlie shook his head.

"I haven't got to the amazin' part yet." Rory looked suddenly confidential. "Here's the real silver lining – Christina comes up to me and says: 'Well, if we have to continue with this thing to the bitter end we might at least have a dance out of it, don't you think?'"

"*She asked you to dance?*" Charlie was doubly stunned. He tried to imagine it but couldn't. Last thing he'd seen, Christina had looked as if she didn't even want to drink coffee alongside them. Then he tried to imagine Rory dancing and still came up with nothing. In fact it felt rather cruel - like the kind of thing people used to do to bears. Poking enormous wild creatures onto their hind legs. But the porridge dance discos must have afforded him some basis to build on because he'd obviously managed it. Or was about to … "Go on. What then?"

"Well the band was loud, y'know, so it was hard to say much, but she mebbes used the phrase, 'your natural milieu'."

"You're *that* good a dancer?" Charlie was incredulous.

"Och, no. I'm just a shuffler." Rory did an effective dancing bear impersonation. "She was talking about the fight."

"Oh."

"Bad?"

"Hard to tell with Christina, isn't it?"

"Couldn't have bin too bad," Rory went on, "because w'had a bite from what was left on the buffet table then. And some fruit punch and another dance. Then a slow one comes while w'still on the floor and so I says: 'You won't want to do this, I'm none too clean' and I pointed to the blood on my shirt. I thought it would give her an easy out, y'know, but blow me, if she didn't say: 'I don't mind, if you don't'."

"I can't believe it." Charlie shook his head. "Actual physical contact."

"Aye," said Rory. "And not a bloody gnome or undine in sight. Don't that beat all?"

"It certainly does." There was a reflective silence then, but after a moment or two Charlie said, "It's probably a bit late to be asking this, but what's an undine?"

"A sort of water sprite," Rory spoke with the matter-of-factness of someone answering a perfectly reasonable academic question. "Vaporous you could say. I've never seen one meself. But then I haven't got the sight. That's Aunt Bertha's side of the family."

"Unbelievable," said Charlie. "So how did the slow dance go?"

"Awkwardly," Rory looked suddenly downcast.

"Why?"

Rory hadn't known quite how to hold her. He'd picked up a little bird once, he said, a fledgling that had fallen from the nest. Its mother hadn't come and fed it on the ground, like she was supposed to do. He knew that, because he'd watched patiently, all day. And now it was getting cold and dark and something was going to come along and eat it, so he'd picked it up to take back to his camp with him. He'd carried it through Kielder forest, holding it out before him in cupped hands like a precious offering, trying desperately not to stumble in the dark. But anxiety made him clumsy and though, when he fell, he'd put out his elbows to save himself not his hands, the baby bird was dead. He'd accidentally broken its neck. That's what it felt like to be holding Christina, he explained. Miraculous, like holding that little bird. But he was scared he would somehow do something clumsy and crass and kill it by accident. Kill the one and only opportunity he'd been given.

"Right," said Charlie, slowly. "But could you pick up any signals? When you actually had hold of her? Have you any idea what she was feeling or thinking?"

"Not really," said Rory, sadly. "I've never had a flair for picking up that sort of thing. And last night m'sensors just shut down entirely, outta fright."

Charlie shook his head. Rory McEwan was certainly a man of many parts - not all of them obviously reconcilable. "You're a strange and complicated man, aren't you?" he said. "Did you sit with her on the coach back?"

"Yes."

"And was she still alive? Did she speak?"

"She did. Though it was all about how we we were going to explain everything to Dr. Carlyle. Julius thought we should just cut our losses and make a run for it … but probably that was the bump on the head talking."

"Are you worried about what Dr. Carlyle will say?"

"Possibly, as regards the booze. But I have no idea how they got hold of it. We're miles from anywhere, here. One of them must've smuggled it from home at some point. We could have checked but, I mean, it's not normally that sort of school. As for the fight – I did what I had to do with the minimum of roughness. And somebody had to do something. Julius had broken his glasses and Mary was helping him, and some tiny little woman on the Malvern side had a hold of Christina, squeaking at her to get them to use their words. *Why weren't they using their words? Tell them to use their words.* Well, Jeez, it was a bit late for that."

"It makes you wonder, doesn't it?" Charlie shook his head. "If some of these teachers have ever been out in the real world. But Dr. Carlyle is a very reasonable man. He seems to view all shades of disaster with remarkable tolerance. I doubt there's anything to worry about."

They ate cold and rubbery eggs then, and presently Rory asked: "So, how did your evening go?"

Charlie gave a non-committal shrug. "I got to hear a lot of Halloween-type folklore and eat green blancmange with Tempest min."

"Och," Rory grinned. "Those Vane Tempest boys. Just bad to the bone aren't they?"

Chapter Eight

No expulsions resulted from the investigations into the fracas at the Halloween dance. As Rory explained to Charlie after the exhaustive interviews were over, it seemed that Dr. Carlyle regarded expulsions as an admission of defeat. Blake Vane Tempest was a hard nut to crack, but they had over two terms before he had to be inflicted upon an unsuspecting world, and it shouldn't be beyond a school that prided itself on bringing out the best in boys to finagle some psychological improvement in that time. A high aim, it seemed, in view of the previous years, but Dr. Carlyle was ever the optimist.

"Mebbes he was hoping I would take a personal interest in the lad as a result of that bit of male bonding we managed amongst the squashed pumpkins and the remains of the buffet," Rory said. "But I'm nae good at deep, dark waters like Vane Tempest."

McEwans, he assured Charlie, could be dark but never deep. They did not pile up morbidity in their heads. They were not, nor did they have any aspiration to be, complicated psychological creatures. They expressed themselves through the physicality of iron, beating on it, or something else convenient, until the direness of introspection was driven from them. They were simple folk. Even primitive. Fed up or bad tempered was the pinnacle of what a McEwan could manage in the area of despair. Getting deeper and moodier than that smacked too much of serious intellectual effort.

"You don't believe any of that, do you?" said Charlie, shaking his head in disbelief. "You can't possibly." As exemplified by Rory, the McEwans seemed to be anything but simple. More like some bewildering mix of sublimated savagery, strange superstitions and surprising sweetness. "You've just got this creation myth riff working for you," he went on, "and now it's become an everlasting excuse for everything. You insist that you've never developed any handle on women, and so you miss all the signals which means you're romantically incompetent and sexually inept and you can never think of anything to say. Moreover, you can't even get points for enthusiasm because it goes all to hell while you're opening packets of sugar. It's a load of bollocks and its time you changed the narrative. I was told that by the English teacher when I was fifteen. 'The human animal is a narrative creature Peterson, it's how we understand the world, and I have to tell you that your story is defeating me … you seem pigheadedly determined to end up as a shelf stacker in the Co-op.'"

"But you didn't," said Rory. "End up as a shelf stacker."

"No." But that hadn't been the real narrative. The real one was the one he and his friends had made up when they were barely ten years old. And now, on his own, he trying to write a happy ending to an entirely different story.

"I scraped by academically," he said. "Which was the point of the teacher's remarks. But it was more by good luck than good management."

"So what is it I'm supposed to do, again?"

"Think of yourself as a self-improver, a man who was disenchanted with the way things had always gone in his family. A man who retreated to the woods and then, through his love and understanding of the power of trees and their individual natures, came to find his own."

"That's just embarrassing." Rory was aghast. "All that about coming to understand myself through the power of trees. It's … it's …" Words failed him. He probably didn't know the word pseudery but he could obviously recognise it when it was out there making him feel nauseous.

Rory McEwan might have had a weird and wild romance in his soul, but he just couldn't get it working for him in the way he needed. He had more than the makings of a romantic - even of the sort that could fall within Dr. Boswell's definition of the word - but he never seemed able to convert those makings into a product, except through the medium of wood or iron. He looked permanently uncomfortable when called upon to reveal himself, even to himself, in a way that didn't involve a chisel or an arc welder.

"I fell into the hands of publicity people," said Charlie. "And they get very focused on hook-lines and creation myths. And yes, it can be embarrassing stuff. Pretty well the first thing the label's chief publicity guy said to me was: *This inner city school then … you say your Dad was a maths teacher. Couldn't we make him a janitor? Maths teachers … Not really a story there. Doesn't speak to the struggle.*

Y'know?'" He looked at Rory. "But your story is true, isn't it? You just start it at the point where you decided to go into the forest and you don't focus too much on what you were, or think you were, before that. Just put my cheesy book jacket speak into your own words before you start trying to get yourself across to Christina. That's what you do."

"It was pretty uninspiring woodland," said Rory, after a few brow knotting moments. "It's mostly just Sitka spruce and the like in Kielder, y'know. Coniferous forest. Man made. More broadleaves than there used to be, though …"

"It doesn't matter what the bloody forest was like," said Charlie, suddenly exasperated. "It doesn't have to have been full of Ents and Whomping Willows. It just matters that you went there and then your life changed and so did you. That's what you talk about in the part of the process where you exchange life histories. No need to get carried away with the tree thing. Don't end up saying nothing but 'I am Groot' for God's sake."

"We could watch that again sometime," said Rory. "I really liked that movie. Especially the racoon."

"How about we watch it now." Charlie went across to a pile of DVDs and ruffled through them.

"I think I really might be sexually inept," said Rory reflectively, as Star Lord's spaceship manoeuvred through a barrage of blasters and a tousled, forgotten female of a one night stand emerged from the bowels of the machine looking totally fed up. She was also an angry shade of red but, in all fairness, she was probably red before the date.

"I should avoid any allusions to ineptitude," said Charlie. "It's more the kind of conversation you have afterwards. Try walking up and down several times a day, saying 'I am adequate, I am adequate'."

In truth, he felt guiltily aware that whilst he was mercilessly goading Rory into action he was failing abysmally himself. The fact that the walled garden and its unusual châtelaine called to him was indisputable. He felt its pull, her pull, every time he was in the vicinity of the sports fields. It was an undertow that was almost physical. Yet he did nothing. Planned nothing. But, all the while, thoughts of her kept creeping up on him, stealthy and unbidden, and when they managed to reach out and really grab him, the world around was immediately rendered more significant and more lovely.

*****

It was December now and Christmas was in sight. Music and carols were being practised for the end of term concert. Somebody, whose voice sounded on the edge of breaking, seemed to be eternally and precariously rehearsing 'Three Kings from Per … er … er … sian lands afaaaar …' in a distant corridor. A huge Norwegian spruce had been set up in the grand entrance hall and its evocative smell filled the space and stimulated the more junior boys into excessive giddiness. It was a happy time at the school.

Charlie sat on a bench by one of the sports fields and watched the afternoon sky deepen into unfathomable blueness. A heron flew over, huge and prehistoric-looking in dark silhouette. Charlie's eyes followed its flight. It was Saturday but there were no sports to watch. The school teams had away matches and the concert was occupying not only the prospective performers but also the arty types who were involved with backdrops and props. That was naturally Christina LeBlanc territory, and Rory was lurking in the wings to help with aspects of construction.

Charlie had no idea why he was sitting on this bench feeling cold. He might have been thinking of walking to the walled garden, or he might not. Having no allotted task, he had wandered outside in a state of irritable listlessness. He might have been going to sneak a peek at Rory's efforts with Ms. LeBlanc and her scenery, or he might not. The sports field's benches were an indecisive halfway house. That wasn't true. They were in the opposite direction to the theatre.

"Aren't you cold?"

"I am, as it happens," Charlie conceded.

"That's because it's cold. I'm cold."

"Then why are you out here?"

"Because I'm supposed to be."

Charlie was getting used to these conversations because he kept having to have them. It was by no means clear to him *why* he kept having to have them. It was possible that Tempest min patrolled the school having them with everyone. It just didn't look that way. It looked as if Charlie was being peculiarly blessed.

"Why are you supposed to be?"

"I'm taking a message."

"A message to whom?"

"Miss Keeble Parker."

"A message about what?"

"To make sure she's bringing the holly and stuff tomorrow. For the decorations."

"I see."

"Do you want to come with me?"

"Maybe I'd better. It's getting dark."

"No it's not."

"It comes upon you quickly in December." Charlie got up off the bench. Sometimes, life is obliging enough to take a decision out of your hands.

"I have to go to the garden because Miss Keeble Parker never answers the telephone," said Tempest min.

"She doesn't?"

"My mother never answers the telephone either. She checks who's rung her first. She says men ought to have the decency to look you in the eye."

"Does she answer texts?"

"Miss Keeble Parker?"

"Yes."

"I don't know. My mother doesn't like them. They get to be too many."

"They do that."

"Texts?"

"Yes."

"Do you like Miss Keeble Parker?" Tempest min asked after a short pause.

"She seems very nice," replied Charlie guardedly.

"I like her. Did she like those jelly frogs, do you think? On Halloween?"

"She looked as if she did."

"Sometimes it's a job to tell with women. My mother always says, 'oh yes, how lovely,' and then drops things in the bin."

As they walked, Tempest min kept on chattering. Ingenuous, small boy chatter about the school's Christmas tree and then about the concert, which was mostly for the benefit of parents except: "Mother never comes, Blake says, because she always has some big party to go to which is important for her career." He looked up at Charlie in evident expectation of some response.

"Parents have careers," said Charlie carefully. "And they need these careers to be successful in order to provide for their families. It isn't always convenient but that's how it is."

"It seems to be convenient for other people's parents."

Fortunately, by this point, they had arrived at the arched entrance in the big wall. Charlie paused. He was still hesitant, cautious of actively fostering something that could complicate his life more than was desirable, and this moment and this spot were somehow presenting as the point of no return. Tempest min was struggling manfully with the rusty latch and the weight of the old wooden door. Charlie watched him thoughtfully for a few moments and then leaned in and contributed a purposeful shove.

The air was getting colder as the afternoon wore on. It seemed to be holding itself sharp and taut, ready for the formation of frost. And it was transmitting sound across its chilly stillness with a bell-like clarity which meant that Ianthe Keeble Parker was easy to find. She was on a rough patch of ground at the opposite end of the garden to her cottage, tending a small, unenthusiastic bonfire. Curls of sulky smoke rose reluctantly into the wintry air. They obscured Charlie's view like dry ice hides an onstage magician's trick, so Ianthe seemed to materialise gradually before his eyes - a vision of spun, tumbling hair, golden, ash-smudged skin and lithe limbs, all coming effortlessly together to make a graceful and lovely woman. Yet not quite a woman - more some wayward nature spirit with the elusive glow of the will-o'-the-wisp or the flickering incandescence of Saint Elmo's fire. A creature that has been ritually invoked in order to produce flames for the benefit of some cloddish woodsmen. "There are things," she said, by way of greeting, "that just refuse to turn into anything better than they are. Sometimes they need to be burnt first."

Charlie was not remotely enlightened by the statement but it didn't matter because he was deriving a great deal of pleasure from simply looking at her. Just at that moment he felt no particular urgency to understand her as well. Her otherness felt enormously attractive.

"Mrs. Carlyle wants holly," said Tempest min, plunging into the practicalities of the visit.

Ianthe looked up from the fire with a smile. "I have holly," she said.

Tempest min picked up a stick and began poking at the beginnings of a flame with it. "I have to remind you to bring it to the school," he said, "because you never answer your telephone."

"You know, Tempest min," said Ianthe, "one of this country's greatest gardeners wrote that he would like his gardens to enable everybody to experience life at a much deeper level than that of the visible world. He did not say that he wanted the spaces he created to be comfortable spots for people to take telephone calls."

"The holly," said Tempest min doggedly, "for Mrs. Carlyle."

In spite of the reluctance of the flame, he'd managed to set his stick on fire. Charlie took it off him.

"I'll bring the holly tomorrow, after lunch," said Ianthe. "As I said I would. If there could be someone around to help me unload ..." She left the statement hanging.

Charlie, throwing the stick into the middle of the bonfire, wondered if he were grasping at straws to interpret the remark as an invitation. He was still caught up in the sensation of being in the presence of some enchanted creature. But maybe that was how chemistry teachers always felt around women. Maybe they simply watched them from a point of confused helplessness and then ran back to their laboratories and ached.

"Would I do?" he asked. "For the unloading?"

"I'm sure you would. After lunch? By the side door to the kitchens in the main building? Around two o'clock?"

"It's a date," said Charlie with a smile.

Tempest min looked up at him. "It's not a date. You have to have a restaurant for a date."

"I stand corrected," said Charlie. "It's not a date. Obviously, I have no idea how these things work."

"I'm fairly sure you do," said Tempest min. A preternaturally aware comment that turned out to be the final words of the meeting.

*****

At two o'clock the following day, Charlie found Tempest min standing at the aforementioned side door bundled up against the cold in a bright red anorak. "What are you doing out here?" he asked.

"Miss Keeble Parker said to be out here, after lunch."

"I don't think she meant you."

"I think she did. It's our job, isn't it? Yours and mine. Together."

"Fine," said Charlie, giving up. "Just as long as there isn't anything else you're supposed to be doing."

An old Ferguson tractor, pulling a flat-bed trailer loaded up with piles of holly and mistletoe and various other greeneries, chugged into view. Tempest min waved. Ianthe Keeble Parker waved back. She brought the tractor to a halt beside them, climbed down and handed Charlie a pair of work gloves. "The holly is very prickly. Tempest min, you will have to carry other things. But handle them with care. We've already deprived the birds of all these berries, we might as well preserve the decorative effect as best we can. Half of it is for here and half we take on down to the theatre."

Charlie felt more at ease with this side of the Queen of Elfland. There had to be something reassuringly earthbound about a woman who could drive a tractor.

"Give the birds some other stuff", suggested Tempest min pragmatically, as he tugged determinedly at a huge bundle of mistletoe.

"Herefordshire is famous for its mistletoe, you know." Ianthe tried to guide him into a less destructive way of doing things. "This is cider country and mistletoe grows well on apple trees. And we actually have druidical mistletoe here at Puckrup. On our ancient oaks," she paused and looked at Charlie. "I don't know if you've noticed it in those woods around the sports fields and the walled garden?"

163

"No," Charlie confessed, not knowing one tree from another and never feeling prompted to look up into any of them.

Ianthe explained that that particular piece of woodland was one of the very few remaining in the country which could be described as primordial. She counted it fortunate that the various enthusiastic landscapers who'd been at work at Puckrup over the centuries, had had the good sense to preserve it. There were some yews in there , certainly never planted by the hand of man, that still grew as they'd done when they were being pollarded for long bows.

Charlie had no concept of the lifespan of trees but he managed to identify with druids and longbows sufficiently to look impressed. And he was prepared to spin out such scant knowledge as he had to keep her talking. It occurred to him that it would have been a lot more convenient if he'd fallen for Christina LeBlanc and Rory had fallen for Ianthe.

"What's druidy mistletoe?" asked Tempest min, who never seemed to have any problems keeping conversations in the air.

"It's very special and it has to grow on an oak tree. And if you were to cut it under a full moon using a golden sickle it would heal whatever it is that ails you." Ianthe gave him a considering look.

"What's a sickle?"

I know this one, Charlie thought, but the conversation had already left him behind. As the greenery was transferred into what Ianthe called a 'flower room', the talk moved further and further into the outfield of horticultural folklore and Charlie lost even the vague grip he'd had on it. All he really registered was the lovely, lilting effervescence of Ianthe's voice. Variously interpreted and reinterpreted by Tempest min the exchanges seemed to add up, in arrestingly fantastic detail, to some sort of holly hagiography. The holly tree was apparently a guardian tree that was the protector and guide of the energies of life. And when its branches were brought inside, they provided shelter for elves and fairies who could, at Christmas, join with mortals without injuring them. Charlie gave an involuntary start.

"Could you hand me down those jugs, please?" Ianthe pointed to the top of a cupboard. She filled them with water and then with green bits and pieces that smelt vaguely of Christmas dinner. "Mrs. Carlyle likes making seasonal tussie-mussies with herbs," she said.

Charlie smiled and nodded. Tussie-mussies. Don't even ask. Just enjoy the way the winter air has brought that lovely flush to her skin. Dragging his eyes away from the delicate line of her jaw - just where it blended into the soft curve of her neck - he glanced down to where Tempest min was now tugging at his jacket. Unbelievably, the child had yet more to report on the subject of holly trees. They had to have sex apparently. Because there were man trees and woman trees. Amazing, Charlie shook his head. Even the trees were doing better than he was. Though Golden King was apparently a woman tree and Silver Queen was a man tree. Which was silly, wasn't it? Tempest min held up a branch of golden variegated holly with berries and a branch of silver variegated without berries, looking from one to the other in disapproval. Ianthe took them from him with a smile. "When these plants were given their names," she said, "gardeners weren't quite as clear about which were male trees and which were female trees."

"He was asking," she explained to Charlie, "why some of the holly had berries and some of it didn't." She turned back to Tempest min. "It's sexual reproduction but it's not precisely what you would understand as sex. It's pollination. The pollen from the male tree is carried to the female tree which, as a consequence, bears the berries which contain the seeds which can grow into a new tree."

"Have you been talking to the lady from LAFFAS?" Charlie asked her. He wished she would talk more to him on some subject that he could at least take a stab at.

"People are supposed to kiss under mistletoe," said Tempest min. "Which means that if you held some up you could kiss Miss Keeble Parker."

"I suspect that teachers kissing other members of staff in school is frowned upon," said Charlie.

Mrs. Batt appeared then, with an expression on her face that pretty much confirmed this. She proffered up mugs of tea and gingerbread men with a careful correctness that was obviously intended to be contagious. "Lovely foliage," she said to Ianthe. "Mrs. Carlyle will be very pleased. Now, if you'd just put the mugs back on here when you're finished …" She put a galleried silver tray down on the wooden draining board.

"She is everywhere. All the time," said Charlie, when Mrs. Batt had gone. "Does she never need to rest? Is she secretly some sort of guardian tree?"

"You could say that," laughed Ianthe. "She's always been more or less a nanny to me and she still thinks I need looking after. Yet while I've grown older, she hasn't changed at all. She's still exactly the same as when I was small enough to hug her round the knees." She gave an affectionate sigh. "But that's Mrs. Batt, of course. Purposeful, timeless and indestructible."

*****

Tempest min seemed to lose inspiration when it came to unloading the greenery at the theatre. During the hundred yard ride on the trailer he had become somehow deflated – which is surprising as riding on trailers behind tractors is normally an inflating experience for small boys. Nevertheless, he did not get down but remained disconsolately seated amongst a debris of dropped leaves and fallen berries while Charlie and Ianthe unloaded around him.

"Don't you want to go in and see how the rehearsals are going?" Charlie asked.

Evidently not.

The greenery was being piled up at the back door to the theatre so that it could be carried in, as and when required by set dressers.

"I must remind them to reserve some particularly nice pieces for the table in the foyer," said Ianthe. "Grandmama and Vanessa Carlyle are enthusiastic conscripts to the idea that an initial impression is the only one you ever get to make."

She reappeared five minutes later followed by the drama teacher whose attention alighted on the greenery for only a split second before flying to Tempest min who was still sitting on the trailer. Being a drama teacher (drama and junior English to be precise) Madeleine Lowry had naturally developed the type of attention that always settled on whatever was failing to provide satisfaction. Herself, she invariably performed at peak, her innate theatricality emphasised by flowing silver hair, dramatic eye make-up, dangling earrings and an insistence upon always wearing black like some super-cool sixties fashion designer. "There you are," she exclaimed, as if she had just found Banquo's ghost hiding in the curtains. "You were supposed to be *here*, Tempest min. Being Tiny Tim in a skit."

"I don't want to be Tiny Tim in a skit," said Tempest min.

"And would you like to tell me why not?"

"It's too sad."

"It's just a skit, Tempest min. And he only has one line."

"But it's a sad line."

"No it isn't. He says 'God bless us every one'. That isn't sad."

"But he doesn't, does he?" And with that Tempest min jumped down from the trailer and ran in the direction of the main building.

Ianthe went immediately after him.

"That child is getting stranger and stranger," said Madeleine Lowry crossly. "He seemed perfectly happy to be Tiny Tim last week." She looked at Charlie with something that could have been suspicion.

"Well, if he doesn't want to do it, I should find someone else," he suggested. "There must be enough boys to choose from."

"Mrs. Vane Tempest has made it known that she would like at least one of her sons to become interested in drama."

"Mrs. Vane Tempest sounds to me as if she can create quite enough drama by herself," said Charlie. He said it perfectly equably, though for some reason the thought of Mrs. Vane Tempest never made him feel equable.

Madeleine Lowry pursed her lips (almost white lipstick, very retro). "Since you are new here," she said, "I'll take the liberty of reminding you that this is a private school and it behoves us to cooperate with the people who pay the bills."

"It seems to me that the only price being paid in the Vane Tempest household is by the boys themselves," said Charlie, much less equably. He turned away and walked quickly towards the main building. His dark side had been given a little poke and for the first time in many years it had turned over in the deep grave it shared with his creativity and given a little growl.

Back in the main building, he stood in the entrance hall wondering where Ianthe and Tempest min had gone. He felt vaguely annoyed for some reason he made no particular effort to define, but his mood immediately softened as Ianthe came running down the stairs. She'd taken Tempest min up to Matron, she explained, as he'd been a little tearful. And Matron had taken charge with her usual briskness although Tempest min had wanted to talk to Charlie.

"Something about the stage," Ianthe said. "He knew that you would understand, he said. Matron, however, was of the opinion that you would be able to understand nowhere near as well she could."

In fact, Charlie doubted that. He could empathise quite strongly on the subject of stages equating to misery. "I'm sure she's right," he said. He looked thoughtfully up the stairs.

"He'll be fine," said Ianthe quietly. "For now."

There was a silence then that neither of them seemed to know how to fill, and during it Charlie felt a change. The more graspable version of Ianthe that had presented at points during

169

the afternoon was fading. The woman who drove a tractor and wore work boots was withdrawing with the afternoon light, being reclaimed, as it were, by the estranging other. With the mutability of Hermes, Ianthe Keeble Parker seemed able to shift from one world to another. So fairies really do wear boots, thought Charlie. Ozzy Osbourne had it right all along.

"I have to go now," she said.

Charlie nodded. In his pocket he had a piece of mistletoe. He had stowed it there with no particular design. Most likely he'd intended to slip it to Rory in the theatre but the opportunity had not come along. He knew he would not be using it himself. And then, to his surprise, Ianthe pulled a sprig of mistletoe from her own pocket, stood on tiptoe and kissed him lightly on the lips – oh so lightly, just the brush of a cobweb.

"Take care of Tempest min, Charlie Peterson," she whispered. "It's important. What goes around comes around, as they say."

Before he could recover himself, she was gone. He thought about running after her but then Mrs. Batt appeared at his elbow, knotting her headscarf, buttoning up her coat. "The theatre crowd will be along for tea and talk soon," she said. "You'd do better to get involved in that sort of thing."

Then the hall lights with their automatic timers suddenly flicked on and before Charlie had stopped blinking Rory came in through the big doors in the vanguard of said theatre crowd looking like a giant puppy with two tails. "I got to hold her legs," he whispered. "She was wearing trousers but there were legs – her legs – in them."

"And this was necessary because?"

Because Christina LeBlanc was a perfectionist and she liked to go about adding tweaks of perfection - a dot of light here, an enhanced shadow there - to any less than perfect effort from the scene painters. But the backdrops and pieces of scenery were tall, so the pursuit of perfection necessarily involved stools and sets of steps and occasionally planks running between sets of steps. The boys were happy to climb and scramble and jump but Ms. LeBlanc was not a climber or a scrambler or a jumper. For all her ballerina elegance she was not at ease with stools and sets of steps and planks running between sets of steps, so they contrived to continually diminish the pleasure she was able to take from the school's various theatre performances. But having Rory there to hold her legs, or her ankles, or to lift her down when she got somehow frozen in position, had elevated the scene painting to the level of pleasure that it was capable of providing for an art and design teacher. And then to be lifted about so casually and easily that the boys didn't even notice enough to giggle, and to be told that she weighed next to nothing had been, judging by Ms. LeBlanc's face at any rate, an extremely satisfying experience.

"She was afraid of falling," explained Rory. "So I said, 'I won't let you, and if you somehow manage it, I'll catch you.' And she said, 'Are you sure?'. And I said, 'Of course I'm sure'. And she said, 'You won't crumple to the ground?' And I said, 'You're kiddin', right?'"

"Very smooth," said Charlie.

"I think I was quite smooth," said Rory, reflectively.

"Well, aren't you just getting to be a rascal."

Chapter Nine

On the whole, the Christmas concert seemed to repay the great variety of effort that went into it. The choir was more than competent, the boy soloists particularly so. The real live donkey in the nativity was at its most cooperative, and the new Tiny Tim in the hugely condensed version of Dickens' A Christmas Carol delivered the closing line with brio.

Afterwards, the parents filed up to the main building for some refreshments. Members of staff, in the role of hosts, were kept busy. This was intended to be a social evening rather than an occasion filled with parent/teacher type consultation – or confrontation – but inevitably there were those moments when parents 'just wanted to have a quick word'. Charlie felt as if he were in receipt of more than his fair share of quick words. Of course he had the curiosity value, not to mention the vulnerability, of the new. And his pupils, in senior chemistry at least, tended to the more academic. Predictably perhaps, they seemed to have more academically minded, or at any rate more motivational, parents. On the other hand, these 'trials by parent' served the greater purpose of distracting him from his personal disappointment of the evening – the fact that Ianthe had not put in an appearance. He hadn't seen her since the unloading of the greenery ten days previously, though he'd mulled over their last couple of minutes together ad nauseam, trying unsuccessfully to wrest some significant encouragement from what she'd said and done. The kiss had been the subject of extensive analysis, as had her last words - which had had a ring about them of … well … last words. It was as if she hadn't expected, or hadn't intended, any further communication with him.

And Tempest min, who had been the subject of the last words, was another of the evening's absentees. Matron had diagnosed him with some sort of fever aggravated by anxiety and suggested that, as the term was drawing to a close, he would be better off going home early. The big black Range Rover, piloted once again by the unpopular man, had come and taken him away. For a few days after this, and including this evening, Charlie felt that in some indefinable way the school was a much emptier place.

But, of the various trials of the evening, Rory's was the most acute. Christina LeBlanc had produced a man. A man with self-consciously swept hair, a pink polo shirt and a black velvet jacket. He transpired as someone prominent and arty from the University of Gloucester. And though the University of Gloucester was hardly Oxford or Cambridge, or even Bristol, it was to Rory a place unassailably superior to his wood and metalwork shops in the practical block at Puckrup. And the type of men who came from the University of Gloucester obviously felt themselves too unassailably superior to be thrilled by mere ankle holding or leg steadying. They had more than a natural helping of suavity and pressed themselves upon people, whispering intimately and with no obvious expectation of being rebuffed. It was unbearable.

"He's giving her lascivious looks," said Rory, in aggrieved tones.

"And you don't give her lascivious looks?"

Charlie studied the pink polo shirt briefly in the moment he had between Mr. Porteus getting concerned about whether or not his elder son's capabilities in the area of chemistry would get him into medical school, and Mrs. Leadbetter wondering if it was really necessary for her son to learn all those confusing chemical symbols.

"Can't these things just have names? Like in history, you know, kings and battles have names. Aren't we just making it unnecessarily difficult for the children?"

"Actually they do have names, Mrs. Leadbetter. The symbols are abbreviations for those names and they are much more convenient to use in chemical equations."

"And do there have to be equations?"

"I'm afraid so."

There was a pause here in which Mrs. Leadbetter radiated a degree of dissatisfaction and Charlie stole yet another look at the pink polo shirt. He gave an inward sigh.

"The thing is, Mrs. Leadbetter," he said, finally, "chemistry appears to hold insufficient scope for Cornelius. He's a boy with very original ideas and chemistry doesn't really lend itself to originality until you are a lot further along in the subject. It's possible that Cornelius will want to leave it behind long before that moment arrives but, in the meantime, there is very little to be done apart from help him to learn the chemical symbols and get him to appreciate that we have to string them together in very particular ways. Otherwise, it's just plain wrong."

Cornelius Leadbetter was just twelve years old and his future had not yet declared itself, but Charlie seriously doubted that he was incubating the start of anything scientific.

"I do not give her lascivious looks," hissed Rory. "I give her adoring looks. And never when she's facing me. The man is blatant."

"He's a university lecturer," said Charlie. "They always end up with an inflated idea of themselves. Especially the men. It's to do with the power and influence thing. Because the whole bloody academic sphere revolves around them, they look a lot more attractive than they really are. It's the intellectual version of celebrity."

"I'm stricken," said Rory.

Charlie could produce even less consolation for Rory than he'd done for Mrs. Leadbetter. The pink polo shirt was in possession of supreme confidence and smooth moves. He slid easily into Christina's parent/teacher chats – welcomed and deferred to because of some perceived academic superiority, which Charlie felt sure he drew attention to at every available opportunity. Plus, he was casually and lazily familiar with Christina herself - worryingly so. He guided her by the elbow and apparently produced excuses for her to move on if she seemed to be getting bogged down. He looked adept in so very many ways that it put Rory's bumbling, if attractive, modesty at what seemed to be an insurmountable disadvantage.

At the end of the evening, Charlie and Rory sat together in

the flat nursing a beer apiece in a build up of Stygian gloom.

"I'm going to go home for Christmas," said Rory. "You?"

"I guess," said Charlie.

"Is there any hope, do you think?"

Charlie racked his brains but came up with nothing.

*****

Rory packed a bag and left immediately after the official end of term. Charlie was intending to leave but somehow he didn't manage it for a few more days. He hung around, sleeping late, watching too much television and taking moody walks around Puckrup's grounds. No doubt he was hoping to bump into Ianthe but he just couldn't make the specific detour that would take him to the walled garden and the almost certainty of a meeting. He did, however, get to know the trembly terrier a lot better. It accompanied him cheerily on these walks until it almost appeared to be lying in wait. They spent periods of time on the seats by the sports fields sharing thoughtful silences, both of them secretly hopeful, though probably for entirely different reasons, and each given to glancing optimistically around whenever there was a noise. It was quiet without the boys and Charlie and the terrier had become supersensitive to sound. They were approached from the rear one day by Dr. Boswell, and in their few moments of ignorance each had an incredible feeling of glorious, yearning anticipation - though it was unclear what the trembly terrier was yearning for. Maybe he was simply being empathetic.

"I recognised that split second look, Charlie," Eric Boswell said. "I recognised that look."

"What look?"

"I suspect you had hopes of my footsteps turning out to be Ianthe's so I imagine it was something similar to the look Dante had on his face when Beatrice first greeted him and … well … To tell you the truth, he was so overcome he had to run away. Of course that was back in the fourteenth century. I imagine young men are a little braver today. More forward, at any rate."

"I'm not quite following you," said Charlie.

"He only saw her three times," said Dr. Boswell. "Dante, you know. And yet she was the love of his life. She inspired the Divine Comedy and that was even after she was dead. Romantic love's a funny thing, isn't it? Dante didn't invent it but he certainly he brought it to everybody's attention in fine style."

And Eric Boswell wandered off in the direction of the library.

*****

"Tell me more about the young woman," said Lottie Peterson.

"What young woman?" Peter Peterson looked up from the immense pile of potatoes he was peeling. It was Christmas Eve and ten Petersons and a Buchanan had gathered together at the Worcestershire farmhouse for the festivities. The big pine kitchen table was heaped up with the necessary provender for the following day's lunch, and between all the chopping and slicing and grating various discussions were circulating. Charlie's report on his new job was the discussion that was trending. At first, his descriptions of life at Puckrup were treated like an excerpt from Enid Blyton's Malory Towers - something infinitely old fashioned and picturesque. In-depth questioning, however, was beginning to lead to a level of audience dissatisfaction.

"The gardener," said Lottie, who was chopping a heap of home grown parsley. "I want to hear more about the gardener."

"And why do we want to hear more about the gardener of all people?" asked her husband, wonderingly.

"One would imagine," said Lottie, "that I would have become used to being the only person round here who has any sense of inflection, or timbre, or subtext. Or anything, in fact, other than actual words."

"What's wrong with words?" asked Nick. He was the son who had become a lawyer so words naturally served him very well. "People do better to say what they mean."

"It seems to me," said Lottie, "although it hasn't been explicitly stated, that Charlie is rather sweet on this young woman gardener."

"*Oh God,*" Nick paused in some frustrating attempts to peel a chestnut. "I can't believe this. Didn't he say she was the granddaughter of the head of the school's governors, who just happens to be the queen of all financial benefactors? The first time in his life he's had anything approaching a decent job and he has to try and nail some odd-sounding woman who could get him sacked. Is he never going to develop any sense at all?"

"Since you've recently been dumped," said Charlie loftily, "and as a direct result, it seems, of saying what you mean, I'm going to overlook those remarks and hope you manage to acquire a little subtlety before you try to get yourself hooked up again."

Nick Peterson did divorce law in a large firm in Birmingham and, financially beneficial as the whole business was, it had not predisposed him in favour of marriage. He had been on the point of sharing his house with a woman called Marie but, in the interests of transparency, he had felt obliged to point out to her that a common law wife had no legal rights. This was not taken in the spirit in which it had been intended. Marie was a modern woman but she was not that modern, and Nick was not such a magnificent specimen that he could not be replaced. He was now, at forty years old and in the absence any outstanding romantic flair, having to come round to the idea of computer dating. It was making him grumpy. "Some of us were working at careers," he said under his breath, "while others of us were playing the guitar and getting laid."

Charlie was at the far end of the table decorating gingerbread men with his niece and nephew. The children were professing to enjoy this practical involvement with Christmas but, though the piped icing and the various sprinkles were being laid on with a will, Charlie thought he could detect a subdued hankering for computer games and another screening of Frozen.

The children's mother's was, as usual, focused on germs. Connie Peterson's brief nursing career seemed to have yielded up little of advantage apart from her husband, Ben, who was asleep in an armchair in front of the wood burner. As an exhausted medical student he had learned to sleep anywhere at anytime, and now, as an exhausted consultant at the Radcliffe in Oxford, he was planning to spend the few precious days of holiday he'd been miraculously granted (unless the phone rang) revelling in untrammelled sleep. That's why he'd promoted the idea of spending Christmas with his parents.

"Should he really be that tired?" Lottie had asked. "Is he terribly run down?"

179

She'd meant this to sound sympathetic but her daughter-in-law had regarded it as undiplomatic. An imputation on her husband's home life rather than on his job.

"Are you sure you washed that parsley properly, Lottie?" Connie asked now. "All that donkey manure spread on the vegetable patches can't be hygienic. Have you none of that dried parsley that comes in a jar?"

"It's going to be cooked for hours in the oven," said Lottie.

"But not in the body cavity of the turkey, I hope."

"No. At the other end. So, tell us about this young woman, Charlie."

"Oh for God's sake," said Connie. "She's obviously weird and Charlie's been weird for so many years himself, he needs somebody a bit in touch with the realities of life. We've all finally been able to stop giving him financial bungs, so please don't encourage him to take up with some crazy, new age hippy."

"She's not entirely crazy," said Lottie peaceably. "There's an actual society, the Anthroposophical Society and the headquarters are just across in Stroud. And planting by the moon has become almost mainstream. There's even a calendar for it. I'm thinking of trying it myself next year."

Connie snorted. "She had skulls for heaven's sake. And cows' intestines. That is not normal behaviour."

"I agree with Connie," said Nick.

"Demeter Foods," said Lottie. "They're biodynamic and they're in health food shops everywhere. I'm sure you must have seen them. You're forever in health food shops, Connie, you must surely have noticed Demeter Foods."

"I go in to buy vitamins. Not crazy stuff."

"Thinking of odd women, where's Marcus?" asked Peter Peterson.

Marcus, the brother before Charlie, chronologically speaking, had been head-hunted into a City bank that made a lot of money. He was good at women but his latest in lady friends, one Clarissa Buchanan, was a long-standing but unfathomable choice. She was something in a bank as well, and had a reputation for extreme cleverness that might not have been the sort of cleverness much appreciated by taxpayers. And it was proving quite difficult for most of the Petersons to pin down. Clarissa barely spoke and was an indifferent listener. She'd quickly confounded any hopes that her cleverness might be used contribute something in the way of sociable entertainment. Or even to deliver any monologues on the new improved face of banking - which could have been such a source of secret pleasurable horror for everyone. Connie said she probably had a touch of Asperger's. Nobody disagreed. Possibly because they didn't know what it was.

Marcus was outside, in fact, taking the carrot scrapings to the donkey. A task he'd performed without fanfare because the children weren't allowed near it on account of its new and hotly disputed affliction with ringworm. Donkeys plus ringworm was the latest in exhaustive internet searches. Clarissa Buchanan was not interested in donkeys, or their skin diseases, and noticeably not in the lemons she had been zesting with such pronounced carelessness that Connie had mouthed 'dyspraxia' at Nick, who'd mouthed back: 'What?' Clarissa had left the kitchen after that. Maybe she was extremely clever at lip reading.

This was all so terribly normal, Charlie thought. Similar

scenes of family life, each with its own frustrations and quirky tics, would be in process the country over. He owned to himself that, once he'd outgrown Santa Claus, he'd mostly dodged Christmas gatherings. In his teenage years he'd been prone to escaping to the bedroom with his guitar, and in the years succeeding that it had been a similar situation but even more pressing - always some song to lay down or something new, but as yet indefinite, to coax from the aether before it stopped calling to him. And the basement years had just been lost time. A homogenised, painful blur. If he'd been at his parents for Christmas lunch, which he assumed he had most years, he could barely recall a single specific occasion. So this fresh crystallisation of normal family life around him was ... yes ... kind of a new thing. And it was pleasant enough. But he knew that he only had a few days' worth of it in him. He wished his heart lay there, and in the paradigm it represented, but it didn't. He wished he wanted a farmhouse in the country and two children. He wished he wanted something. Anything that would make his heart beat a bit faster. But the heart wants what the heart wants and who can really understand it? His thoughts flitted helplessly to Ianthe Keeble Parker.

On New Year's Day he stood in the bedroom that had been allotted to him and looked at the Gibson propped in the corner amongst other possessions that had been deselected in the transfer to Puckrup. On a sudden unfathomable impulse he almost picked it up to take back to the school with him. But he didn't. So his heart merely laboured on - just a lump of muscle beating in dutiful, leaden montony.

Chapter Ten

Rory came back to Puckrup just after New Year with tales of an indifferent Christmas and the remains of a black eye from going up to celebrate Hogmanay with some cousins who lived in Edinburgh. Almost immediately after his arrival, he took to holing up in the practical block to apply balm to his 'wounded soul and aching heart', as he put it, by losing himself in some woodcarving. He was referring, of course, to his upset over Christina LeBlanc - he held the black eye and the disappointing Christmas in no particular regard.

"I should have known it could never be anything," he said bitterly. "A woman like her and a bloke like me. Stupid."

But the wood carving seemed to work out less a pain transcending art form and more a day devouring compulsion. Rory kept coming back to the flat in the dark, covered in dust and leaving behind chunks of savagely chiselled wood which greeted him reproachfully each morning. Staring at their thoughtlessly inflicted wounds he'd seen himself, his own soul, crouched on the bench leaking sap.

"I thought you said you were supposed to let it season a bit before you carved it," said Charlie.

"Never mind the bloody sap," said Rory. "Dinna' be so literal. There was no drippin' sap. It just felt like there was."

"Ah," said Charlie. "Finally tapping into the romancing McEwan."

"Too fucking late, as usual," snorted Rory. "Always got left with the one in the boiler suit with the piglet under her arm. I mean, honestly, where would you start?"

"I'm sure she was a very nice person," said Charlie egregiously.

"She wasn't."

"He'll move on." Charlie returned to Christina LeBlanc's university lecturer. "That sort of guy always does."

"She was singing in the corridor yesterday."

"He'll move on," Charlie gave it more emphasis, "because he won't be able to resist a fresh opportunity to prove he's still got it. He's surrounded by female students hanging on his every word. The temptation will be just too great."

"But if he does move on, it may not help me," said Rory despairingly. "I'm not smooth."

"But you're a decent bloke. Appearances occasionally to the contrary." Charlie took a look at the black eye which was now fading to an unbecoming shade of yellow. "You're kind and you're strong and you're not as stupid as you think you are."

"And when did being a decent bloke get to be a criterion? And what would have happened if it had worked out even a little bit, and then she'd found out that I can only do it stood up with her sat on the bonnet of a Land Rover?"

Charlie shook his head. "I don't know," he said. "Frankly,

I'm still a bit boggled from the last time you said that. And now I've got to work a baby pig into the picture. But Christina apart, Rory, there are always other women, so you've got to stop this catastrophising. Stop thinking of yourself as 'a bloke like me'."

Rory snorted. "Do the words 'sealed in fate' mean *nothing* to you? It's the story of my life. Them local discos, in fact nothing we ever seemed to do, was set up for romance, y'know. Or love. I dinna' think any of us ever advanced our understanding of life worth a damn on a Saturday night. Or at any other time for that matter. If there was great thought given to anything other than siphoning off farmers' diesel, I never heard of it."

There hadn't been much romance at the foot of Cheviot, Charlie gathered. Mostly weather. Nobody of note seemed to have invested the place with magic, or illuminated it with poetry. No Wordsworths or Housemans or Walter Scotts or Brontës had been around to channel the power of the landscape into a story that would fire the imagination. Just tough farmers who could walk the hills in a foot of snow with a ewe across their shoulders and a lamb in each hand dangling by its legs.

"And great louts like me," Rory went on, "no earthly use at any sort of dancing or nifty conversation openers. We just hung around talking about the price of four-wheeled drives, and listening to Thomsy Kerr tell us that pretty soon worm drenches wouldn't kill worms any more. If we went into Newcastle to a club for the night, it never worked out any better. We were hopeless. I guess the city blokes with soft hands were getting all the girls. They'd probably written an algorithm for it. They seemed pretty slick. I just got to be grateful when the local rough element came in with a few pints on board and started a fight.

Those city slickers could certainly run. Gym membership, I suppose. Gyms don't hold much attraction for you when you beat iron all day, y' know. Couldn't have afforded one in any case. Barely had enough spare to take a woman out for a decent meal. We all still lived at home because we hadn't the money to do anything else. And what d'you say? Let's go back to my place and lie on a pile of coke in the forge? I didn't even have a comfortable car. I drove a pick-up with two seats, one of them with the stuffin' hangin' out. And a back full of scrap iron and small bits off tractors that needed weldin'. The Land Rover was Thomsy's. It was impossible to find anywhere for canoodlin'."

Rory took a deep reflective breath here. The sound of a hefty emotional refuel. "On a double date with Thomsy and his girlfriend," he finally went on, "me with a girl I'd known at school called Sandra, who wasn't exactly what y'would call the love of my life - well, we ended up in Thomsy's hay barn one Saturday night. A roll in the hay sounds a fine thing, better than the coke pile anyway, but believe me it's a marginal gain. Especially when the stuff's been baled from a field with every type of thistle in it. Nobody wants to lie there any longer than they have to. And then Thomsy's da' lets the terriers out for a last run before bed - he had six that he used to take with the North Northumberland - and they soon cottoned on to us in the barn and come runnin' in barking and carryin' on. Then one of them puts up a rat, right by where this Sandra girl I'm with has stowed her handbag, and she screams, 'Y'dirty brute get outta that ...' And Thomsy's da' comes rushin' in and thinks she's yellin' at me, and he knows her da' from the hunt, so he grabs me before I can get my pants up, and fetches me such a swipe round the ear that I can hear nothing in it but ringin' for days afterwards."

"Never tell Christina any of this," said Charlie firmly. "I can't imagine how it could possibly come out at this point, but now it's reared its head don't, on pain of death, let it escape by accident. Just in case."

"I might," said Rory, with a degree of anxiety. "Sometimes I get flustered. She flusters me. If a moment somehow ever came, I could babble."

"Go to a hypnotist then," said Charlie. "Have your memory erased. And maybe replaced with selected readings from Cosmopolitan or Marie Claire."

"*What?*"

"And stay away from hay barns and Land Rover bonnets. The lady from LAFFAS gave me a fistful of leaflets a bit back and last night, looking for something in my other jacket, I came across them and thought I should take a look. See where the boundaries lie." He stopped. "Have you ever read them? The ones for the seventh formers?"

"No."

"Well, you should. It's surprising what's in there. Serious stuff intended to promote good relationships."

"Like what?"

"Like the average time it takes a woman to reach orgasm is fifteen to twenty minutes - and that's when they're not lying on prickly hay."

"Twenty minutes," said Rory aghast. "And what exactly am I supposed to be doing in the meantime? Does it say?"

*****

With Rory carving wood like a dervish, Charlie began to wonder: had he brought the Gibson back with him, would it have delivered balm, or merely brought back memories that were showing some signs of closing? Could he have even opened its case? He didn't know. He just knew that there was only one thing available to him that would, to use the words of Tempest min, make his heart feel better. He set out for the walled garden.

It was mid-morning but cabbages and brussels sprouts, in fact all the vegetative inhabitants of the garden's beds, were still sheathed in glittering frost - the earth and all its produce rigid in the constraining cold. Far distant sounds came thin and ghostly through the chilled air. Everything seemed only half alive, except Charlie's heart which had suddenly shaken off its lethargy and introduced a bass drum boom into its performance. Knocking on the door of the cottage seemed a rather intrusive approach that required an exceptional excuse that he didn't have, so he went instead to the potting shed in hopes of finding Ianthe there. And Fate was on his side. Ianthe was engaged in the typical work of frost-bound gardeners everywhere, i.e., the cleaning up of indoor work stations. Dark corners and storage places underneath benches were being subjected to vigorous exhumations and fumigations in preparation for a new year.

"Just passing," Charlie said, any consciousness of the absurdity of this remark totally lost in the rapture of finding her. He wondered how come she bloomed so beautifully in the dusty gloom. How her hair managed to look as if it were reflecting sunshine. How it was that she could so miraculously transcend the mundanity of her task. How soft her lips looked …

"And just in time for coffee," she said, with a smile that made his heart suddenly strike the high hat.

"Rory has immersed himself in the …" he paused for a moment "… the creative process. I was looking for company."

"Then come in and take a seat." She pushed towards him a wooden stool that was wreathed in cobwebs and liberally dusted with potting soil. After a second or two, she handed him a piece of sacking. "To wipe the stool," she explained, as he stared vaguely at it. Obediently, Charlie wiped. The results weren't encouraging, but he'd certainly sat in worse places. The stool wobbled so he sat with his legs braced for a minute or two while Ianthe attended to the kettle, and then he decided that he would be better off stood up. In spite of his initial rapture, or maybe because of it, he didn't feel at ease. And the stool wasn't helping. Having come here, he thought, he must have some sort of intentions. But his compelling desire to see Ianthe hadn't yet narrowed itself down to a graspable point. Was he really looking for a date? His opinion on whether or not a date would be a good idea changed as rapidly as the sun's position in the sky. Plus, in practical terms, it was oddly unclear to him as to how he would set about getting one. Did they ever get dates, chemistry teachers? Once again, he pined for a touch of the old Charlie Peterson … But he seemed to have been sentenced to a sequence of personality deaths. Before he knew it, he would be near as dammit Eric Boswell.

Ianthe was putting coffee into a couple of mugs. Dandelion coffee? She sought his approval. Why not? It was a comfortable humdrum scene with just that hint of domesticity that could have provided an easy way in for an invitation to dinner. Charlie said nothing. He couldn't believe he was actually giving advice to Rory about this stuff.

But, with a woman like this, what exactly had he to offer in terms of a date? The best restaurant in the world would be nothing to someone who ate only leaves and unfertilised eggs. He could hardly hope that he would be so fascinating that the circumstances of a date would be rendered irrelevant.

She looked up at him. "Milk?"

"Please."

"Sugar?"

"A small one."

"Biscuits?"

"Always." Charlie paused. "No skulls on offer?"

"Not today." Ianthe gave him a considering look as she handed across a mug.

They exchanged a few innocuous remarks about Christmas then. Ianthe had shared hers with Lady KP and Mrs. Batt. Charlie tried hard to hide just how completely he was unable to comprehend that she could apparently find pleasure in the middle of nowhere with two old ladies.

"Was there ever anybody else special?" he asked, hesitantly. "For you … You know …"

"No," replied Ianthe after a pause. "Not a man, if that's what you mean."

"A woman?"

"No." She laughed.

"Don't you ever get lonely?"

"No. I was born here. I was born to *be* here. I'm not a restless person, Charlie. There are no far horizons calling to me. Maybe the time will come when I'll have work to do elsewhere ... but in the meantime, I'm in the service of Puckrup."

She seemed so completely at home. Totally in harmony with time, with place, with ... He envied her this rootedness. He felt, in comparison, somehow disinherited. Exiled. Permanently homesick.

She smiled. Sometimes, like right now, she was hard to look at. Her eyes were shifting shades of blue, every mood of the sky in there, changing, reflecting, clouding over. And the shimmer of the other was in there too. Charlie felt sure he could see it. Watching him. Not looking. Watching. He didn't know quite how to hang on to the part that he could grasp - the part that made coffee and drove tractors and cleaned out sheds. And yet, somehow, he couldn't leave. And perhaps she didn't want him to. Could he actually feel that, or was it just foolish hope? Unfortunately, the nurturing of foolish hope wasn't making for fluent conversation. The songwriter in him might have made something of it, but the songwriter wasn't there. He took a silent swig of coffee. Terrible stuff. He tried not to wince. He tried to think of things to say. Things that in an earlier incarnation, with other women, had come to him relatively easily.

"The preparations bother you, don't they," Ianthe said. It wasn't a question.

"The coffee or the skulls and intestines business?"

She smiled faintly. "As you say, the skulls and intestines business."

"No ..." It was a bit of a lie. "Maybe a little." Charlie wanted to explain, but he couldn't. His concept of what she had been

191

doing the first time he saw her was too mixed up with his conception of her.

She nodded, apparently unperturbed, exhibiting no need of either approval or justification. "Maybe you have to be born to it."

"Possibly." Charlie had spent some time over Christmas doing a computer search, and the rationale of skulls and intestines hadn't turned out to be any easier to accept on second acquaintance. Biodynamic agriculture was esoteric. Alchemical. It got written about by contemporary folk as if it were not, but in the original concept the preparations which were integral to it were viewed as growth stimulants extremely extraordinaire. They were not, in any reasonable measure, about physical properties or chemical constituents - their ritualistic production supposedly enabled the creation of something that had an irrational power. They were believed to act as forces or energies, something that had the ability to redeem and heal and transform. Something that was capable of sustaining the spiritual elements of nature, but which a dying earth could no longer create for herself. Something that had to be provided now by the free deed of man. By any other name it was witchcraft - yet spoken of at Puckrup in the same breath as soil pH and hydronium ions. It was a lot to take on board. But not, apparently, for the Keeble Parkers. Ianthe was obviously dedicated to something, lit by something even, that it was impossible for Charlie to comprehend.

"It must be nice," he said after a long pause. "To be so committed. To believe in something so absolutely."

He'd had that once. In a much more earthbound way, of course. Yet, it had kept his spirit airborne. Again, he envied her.

She was standing in dirt, surrounded by spades and garden forks and a piece of equipment that looked ready for a chainsaw massacre, but when she spoke of what she did it was in a voice that carried the magic of moonlight. In one person the mystical and the mundane seemed to live alongside one another. And the result was obviously a life infused. Illuminated. A life really worth living. Whereas he, dragging his own soul through the dust these past years, had shut out the music of the spheres.

"That willing suspension of disbelief thing," she said with a smile. "If you tried hard enough, could you get it to work for you?"

Charlie smiled in return. The truth was, he thought, most men would probably be able to suspend almost anything for a woman who looked like Ianthe Keeble Parker. Though not, maybe, for an indefinite length of time. Maybe only until they were asked to spend a Saturday night by a swamp while she waded in and buried the skulls of a few domestic animals. It was a whole lot more than taking up with someone who was simply intending to campaign for the green party.

"You don't have to believe, Charlie." Ianthe took the coffee mug from him. "Just accept that this place is different. And it's my job to help keep it that way, so that people who come here can be helped to find what it is they need."

Charlie took the space of a semibreve rest to let that turn over in his mind, and then he said, "And Puckrup has been able to give you everything you need?"

It wasn't really a question. Ianthe smiled. "I have no personal needs. My purpose is of the place. I am, as I said, just a custodian. But come and take a walk through the glasshouses with me.

They're a lovely place to be on a frosty morning."

Charlie had never been in such intimate contact with plants as he found himself in Puckrup's seemingly endless glasshouses. The benches - before, behind, stretching ahead to some Land of Oz vanishing point, were laden with seedlings, cuttings, sprouting bulbs, resting houseplants, winter salads … plants for all conceivable purposes arranged in sequential batches according to their requirements. Glass doors, which Ianthe carefully opened and closed as they progressed, divided up sections kept at different temperatures. Anybody with any horticultural nous whatsoever would have been deeply impressed. Charlie was less impressed than bemused. Because for him, the significant thing about these plants was not their numbers, or their variety, or their evident health - all of which he pretty much took in as a green coloured vagueness, like looking at grass, but the startling fact that they were listening to music.

Plants thrived on music, apparently. They were responsive to sound waves. They responded to the human voice. Certain vibrations enhanced their growth rates. This was science, Ianthe assured him. Proven science. Did that make him feel better? Did it compensate in any way for the more disturbing aspects of her witchery? She smiled up at him. He was over six feet. She was nowhere near it. He looked down at her. He had to. The space between the benches was tight so their bodies were almost touching, emphasising the height difference. It was nicely warm where they were, and the most romantic compositions of Tchaikovsky, Mozart and Beethoven were chasing each other in the air around them. Things suddenly felt intimate, encouraging. He thought about kissing her. Just kissing her. No verbal

194

preamble. Just bend his head a little more … look into her eyes … search for the 'yes' … and then kiss her. He did nothing.

"We try to avoid the impromptu," she said. "Lettuces in particular are not fond of too much that's exploratory or experimental."

Half a tone astray was more than enough for them, apparently. They liked functional harmony. Staying in the same key, knowing what was coming next. Sorties into the accidentals made them anxious. The unexpected could be an agonising sweetness when you had a practised ear for it, she said. Lettuces didn't.

"Really," said Charlie. He was stuck far away in the purple haze of a kiss in E seven flat nine that hadn't happened.

"Of course," she said, "not all plants are lettuces."

She stepped away from him then and opened a seemingly heavy door into a cold, chilling world. And a saturated monster of a guitar riff, slow and dissonant, one note rubbing painfully against the next and a deliberate split second behind the beat, blasted the well worn comforts of Tchaikovsky and Mozart and Beethoven to the four winds.

"Really," said Charlie again, except more heavily.

"Yes really," said Ianthe. "These are Grandmama's hellebores. She breeds them. Hybridises them. Their musical taste, discovered entirely by accident through the medium of a work experience student, fills her on the one hand with horror, and on the other with the knowledge that there are, in this life, no coincidences. We knew you, Charlie, long before you ever came to us."

And she opened the final door that led them back out into the frozen world of the garden.

As Charlie walked slowly back to the school, his path joined that of Marjorie Gargery, the biology mistress, who was heading in from the direction of Lady KP's. Mrs. Gargery was tightly encased in a green Barbour, straining Hunter wellies and a beanie that was working itself down over one eye. She greeted him cheerfully with the breathless information that she had just seen a wonderful flock of redwings in a tree. She indicated her bird watching binoculars which hung around her neck. "Never leave home without them," she confided. "You should get a pair."

As they progressed in tandem towards the school, they moved on from the spontaneity of the redwing conversation to the polite follow ups: 'Good Christmas?' 'Yes, thanks.' 'You?' 'Yes.' Mrs. Gargery with her six children – adult children now and some with children of their own - had obviously been heavily embroiled over the festive season. She was, she said, quite looking forward to the comparative peace of a few hundred boys. After these routine exchanges there was a silence. They were nearing the point where Mrs. Gargery, who lived a couple of miles away, would peel off towards her car. But just before they got there, she said casually, "Been to see Ianthe?"

"Yes." Brief, but Charlie was not inclined to be forthcoming. The visit had not settled out in his mind in any satisfactory way. And the finale - the curious insertion of Endgame into the situation - had dislocated him entirely. His leave taking had been awkward. Even curt.

Marjorie Gargery gave him a searching glance as she ostensibly began to pay attention to the problem of finding her car keys in a pocket that was stuffed with pencils, paper handkerchieves and bits of string. "You don't find her ideas at violent odds with your scientific principles?"

"Not violent, no." Charlie was not emotionally involved with scientific principles, nor was he deeply concerned with the protection of them. Certainly, Ianthe had some beliefs that were difficult to handle, but had she given him any signals of a recognisably romantic nature, had the concept of a kiss, for instance, rung in her head in the same key as it had rung in his ….
And yet there'd been a moment … he was sure there'd been a moment … and had he been able turn it into something before being presented so disconcertingly with his former self, he would have swept away science and all its fact based certainties without any compunctions whatsoever. Mrs. Gargery on the other hand had, at his interview, made a prominent remark about not tainting science with whimsy. He wondered how she managed her close relationship with the Keeble Parkers. "And you?" he asked.

Mrs. Gargery was of the opinion that human beings, in which category she took pains to include herself, were capable of quite a remarkable degree of cognitive dissonance. By which she seemed to mean that they could carry apparently conflicting ideas at the same time without developing any marked schizophrenia.

"Did you know, for instance," she went on, warming to the theme, "that whilst he was commanding the Prussian army with every evidence of competence, Blücher was under the impression that he was pregnant with an elephant?" She paused, searching for effect. There wasn't a visible one.

"Probably that was an extreme example that isn't likely to help my case at all," she added hastily, "but the principle just fascinates me, you know."

"What would make somebody imagine they're pregnant with an elephant?"

"Frenchmen," said Mrs. Gargery firmly. "But this isn't helping, is it?"

"No."

"Forget Blücher. Look, the fact is that I can teach within the rigorous scientific paradigm of 'what you see is what you get', yet also make room for the idea that what we see might be very far from the whole story. Maybe what we see is nothing more than what our eyes have evolved to pick up and what our brains have developed to present to us. It's possible that the brain, or perhaps our consciousness, is geared to provide us with the director's cut, as it were – an acceptable and largely consistent version of model dependent reality that we can function within, and which obligingly stands up to the repeated onslaught of scientific process. That's all we can honestly swear to, isn't it?"

"I guess." He was now wondering what would have happened if he had seized that fancied moment and gone ahead with the kiss. If he'd bravely left the comfort of the tonal to things like lettuces, and introduced the type of dissonance that could have totally changed the mood music ... In short, instead of listening to Marjorie Gargery, he was busy expanding a few seconds of failed action into an inattentive, irritable reverie.

"Even Einstein said that reality is an illusion," said Mrs. Gargery, "although a very persistent one."

"Yes." Frankly, in asking about the nature of matings

between science and whimsy, he'd expected an answer more instantly assimilable. And a lot shorter.

But Mrs. Gargery obviously thought she hadn't done enough. "Scientists", she went on, "even with all their instrumentation, have to operate at the level of the brain and the senses. Unable to abstain from complicity with the reality they perceive, they are essentially operating at the level of what could be termed naive realism. As a purveyor of ultimate truth, the human animal may well have its limitations. Don't you think?"

"Em ... I ... er ..."

Like the rest of it, the concept of naive realism needed more attention than he was capable of giving it at the moment. Mrs. Gargery had gone in for some pretty elaborate remarks considering that she'd barely paused in the conquest of her pocket. Plus, she'd found a fluff-covered fruit pastille which she now popped into her mouth with an apologetic shrug. "So Lady KP's plan of presenting Ianthe to you in gruesome tableau didn't put you off, then?" Sucking on the pastille with every evidence of satisfaction, she was changing tack.

"Was it meant to?"

"I think the jury is still out on that. Lady KP considers young men very carefully and takes a solidly binary approach. She's both for them and against them. Torn between having Ianthe live – what shall we say – the normal life due a lovely young woman, and the feeling that she might be ill equipped to deal with it."

"How so?" This he would give his full attention.

Mrs. Gargery explained that Ianthe had been brought up in a way that was, at once, both free and restricted. She'd had the freedom of fields and woodlands and the extensive farms that lay within in the widely distributed estates of the Keeble Parker family, but she'd never been to school or college, or even to a city of any size. Moreover, she'd betrayed no interest in doing any of those things. And maybe she had it right, Mrs. Gargery suggested. Sometimes the outside world looked like somewhere you took your heart and your hopes for no greater purpose than to return with them in need of serious refurbishment. A pointless trip in other words. And here she gave Charlie a searching look. Anyway, for better or worse, Ianthe had been home educated – very effectively so, with the entire staff of Puckrup Hall to call upon - but nothing she'd learned had tempted her to the bright lights. She remained nature's own exceptional child. Beyond her grandmother and Mrs.Batt, her focus and her emotions did not lie in the world of men. And using the word men in the more specific sense – i.e., as men, in other words people like Charlie … well, here Charlie was left to assume that men, as men, had never featured in Ianthe's life at all.

There was a sudden jingle of car keys then, and Mrs. Gargery produced a set with evident relief. "Sometimes I lose things," she announced cheerfully. She turned the keys over in her hand, studying them carefully as if they could be impostors - the keys to somebody's Maserati or a Harley Davidson motorbike instead of a Renault people carrier kitted out with seats for grandchildren. "Ianthe," she said, looking up suddenly, "lives on levels that the rest of us don't. Call it expanded consciousness, call it the sight, call it by some fancy medical terminology that means she's not neurotypical. Call it what you will, but the fact remains that, unlike the scientists, she doesn't see, or perceive perhaps, the world as the rest of us do. She has a greatly enhanced ability to experience what a metaphysician might call 'the thing in itself'."

Yet another pronouncement that Charlie didn't entirely get, but he took the time to mentally concede that though these people might present as bizarre, their bizarreness often had a thought-through ring to it. It was an informed sort of bizarreness. You could never quite settle for nodding agreeably and walking away with your fingers crossed.

"Don't get me wrong," said Mrs. Gargery. "Ianthe behaves perfectly normally, but it seems to me that she has to perform a balancing act between the world as we experience it, and another one that lies behind. And the world of 'what lies behind' seems to carry the most weight with her. I understand that that's how it is but, to tell the truth, I doubt it's ultimately beneficial to the health of a young woman. She is human after all."

Before he could stop himself, Charlie gave a sort of curious grunt.

Mrs. Gargery smiled faintly. "And it's my opinion," she went on, "that it would be rather better for her if a little more freight was added to this world. Course, it would have to be the right sort of freight, wouldn't it?" She took another suspicious look at the keys and then a more contemplative one at Charlie, and finally made a harrumphing noise of her own and set off for her car.

Charlie stared thoughtfully after her as she paused again to watch rooks rising and falling over the nearby trees. "We shouldn't let them settle there," she said over her shoulder.

"They're noisy things, rookeries. And messy. We should get old Jed from the village to chase them away with a few pops and bangs before they start nesting in earnest."

*****

Back in the flat, Rory was in the kitchen wrestling with elastoplasts. He'd taken a lump out of one finger with a chisel. It was atypically clumsy of him. Blood had now superseded sap. Trying to help him out, Charlie looked into the scarlet sink with some alarm. "You're sure you don't want me to drive you into A&E for some stitches?"

"Christ, no. It's a flap. It'll stick down."

"That's a lot of blood."

"It's a sign," said Rory. "A sign that it's time to get over it."

"Over Christina, you mean?"

"I don't think I'll ever get over Christina," said Rory. "But I'll get over the part of it that makes me moon about the place and take lumps out of meself with chisels."

Charlie ran the cold tap and a sanguinous swirl of water got sucked down the plughole. "Are you sure you'll be alright?" he asked.

"Yes," said Rory.

The certainty in that 'yes' was the dubious gift of the McEwans. The only family jewels that had ever got passed down their generations consisted of a high pain threshold and a high pain burden. It was the sort of inheritance that meant, for those who survived it, there was pretty well nothing that anybody could ever do to them that they wouldn't be able to stand.

Chapter Eleven

The new term finally began with a flurry of snow and an avalanche of boys. For a few days there was the buoyancy of the coming-togethers and the recounting of Christmases. Then came the period of disgruntlement before a final settling in to the routine of lessons and an acceptance of what had to be done. It was, however, the term of bad weather and a greater degree of confinement. Grumpiness and gloom were more prevalent than when the sun shone.

Rory was resolute in his new determination to throw off grumpiness and gloom. Yet slumped in front of Strictly Come Dancing, which he'd once watched with what Charlie regarded as unaccountable glee, he was keeping up a monotonous rumble of discontent. "Would you look at this great goon now? Nae idea. Nae bloody idea at all. I could do better meself. Look …"

"No," said Charlie, getting up. "I can't stand the programme. I think I'll go across to the library and try to find a decent book to read."

He felt less sunk in gloom than moody and restless. The conversation with Marjorie Gargery had not helped him towards any conclusions whatsoever. He felt trapped in a frustrating limbo where something he was unable to resolve pulled continually at him. He had not been back to see Ianthe. All his instincts told him that he ought not to go again. He hadn't handled the last visit well and he had absolutely no idea of how Ianthe had really wanted him to handle it. Or even if she'd thought about it at all. But she had. He was sure she had. And to some purpose. So all those instincts that were telling him not to go were also telling him that, sooner or later, he would go anyway. In this uncertain mood, he was not especially overjoyed to find himself being pursued through the corridors of the main building by Tempest min. He'd been glad to see the little boy back at school and seeming his normal self again - it was just that Tempest min's normal self was an oddity at best. And when he was wearing his school jumper and trousers over his pyjamas it spoke of something that Charlie didn't really feel up to handling at the moment.

He came to a halt without turning round. "Well? What is it now?"

Tempest min had stopped behind him - which Charlie immediately regarded as an irritating thing to do. Most children would have walked round to the front and stood before him. He turned round with a sigh. "Yes?"

Tempest min was obviously involved in some hefty emotional turmoil. It was evident from the intensity of his expression, the pitch of his voice and the confused state of his dress that some big drama was taking place. Charlie braced himself. He didn't enjoy the sort of dramas that seemed to overtake small boys. They demanded a level of logic that he hadn't mastered. Already he was at sea. Tempest min's eyes were screwed up with intensity. His brother Blake had apparently ordered, and received, from undesirable forces operating on the internet, a knife especially designed for doing away with mothers. The fact that there were no mothers, most specifically no Mrs. Vane Tempest, available at hand to be done away with, did not appear to be relevant. Though Charlie carefully reiterated it, the salient fact of Mrs. Vane Tempest's pronounced absence had no damping effect whatsoever on the panic.

The knife would be confiscated, Charlie said. He'd tell the housemaster about it and confiscation would immediately ensue. As would a long and thoroughly chastening conversation. And the murderous moment would be over long before the Easter holidays arrived. People got angry with their parents on occasion. Ridiculous threats and foul tempers were part of growing up. Frequently, they were exaggerated to discomfort little brothers. He knew this because he'd been a little brother. He could see the situation exactly in his head. Blake, the supreme dramatist, with a knife that was little more than cutlery, threatening revenge on mother for some minor injustice that sounded like the end of the world. Little brother listening in horror, marvellously upset. But these things passed, he said again. Everything would be sorted. No need to get panicky.

But there was a guitar ...

How could there not be? Charlie felt suddenly weary. And this guitar was responsible for the entire situation. As they inevitably are, thought Charlie. He shook his head. Its very presence in Blake's bedroom was a time bomb. Understood. Absolutely. The Gibson, sitting in his own bedroom back at the farmhouse, signalled Armageddon every time he glanced in its direction. Interference from Julius Harvey, the housemaster, would almost certainly cause this bomb to explode. There Charlie had to disagree. He did not think that Julius Harvey was the sort of person who provoked explosions. He'd recovered amazingly from being stampeded into a pile of pumpkins. It was the kind of forgiving, balanced resilience that had got him to be a housemaster in the first place. Provocation or not, however, something was destined to go seriously wrong unless Charlie attended to the problem personally. Charlie had no idea how Tempest min had come to this conclusion, but it was being repeatedly aired through labyrinthine logic with all the stubborn conviction of a seven-year-old. It was difficult stuff to outmanoeuvre.

"It has to be you." Tempest min looked as if he were about to be sick. Charlie sighed. He'd been sighing more or less constantly and more or less obviously, for a good ten minutes now. Truthfully, he felt infinitely better equipped to outmanoeuvre the eighteen-year-old Blake and his knife than he did to carry on the conversation he was currently having.

"Come on, you go up to bed and I'll go and see Blake," he said finally. "This is all just one of his terrible moods. You must try not to let them upset you. I do wish you would stay away from him while you're here at school. It would be an easy thing, given the size of the place. Now, let's go and find Matron."

Tempest min didn't move. Charlie turned him round and gently encouraged him to head towards the stairs. Matron was leaning over the bannisters on the middle landing. She was far from amused to find the pair of them once again in some sort of troubled confederacy at an hour that was well past bedtime. Charlie didn't wait to hear about it, though he recognised with a heavy heart that presenting her with a tearful Tempest min would add a fresh flurry of black stripes to his name. He left the building and headed for Hereford House.

He also knew that he wouldn't be the one to talk to Blake. It wasn't his job. There was a well-defined chain of command in this type of situation and the housemaster, Julius Harvey, was the boy's most immediate mentor so he was first up. If it was something really serious, then Julius would report to Dr. Carlyle. Charlie didn't even teach Blake Vane Tempest so there was no reason at all for him to be in the chain except as a purveyor of information.

Unfortunately, Julius had just popped out to consult on a history paper with Eric Boswell.

"I know Blake is in his room," said Mary Harvey looking slightly nonplussed. "It's almost lights out. But I can't say I'm aware of any especial problem with him at the moment. Nothing above the usual, anyway. When did Tempest min see him? When exactly did he have this knife?"

"I don't know," Charlie confessed. "Maybe I should have asked more, but cross questioning Tempest min can be a very frustrating business. Talk about tangents. And half of it could just have been a dream. He's apparently prone to these little fevers. They seem to make for disturbed sleep."

"I'll go up and talk to Blake," said Mary Harvey, suddenly decisive.

"Let me go," suggested Charlie, thinking of the Halloween dance episode. Mary Harvey was a delicate-looking little woman like a Chinese geisha girl - yet she had no trouble keeping law and order in the classroom, so maybe she was really more of a titanium plated tiger mama. And maybe, he thought, he was being a bit sexist. All the same … "Yobs with guitars were my bailiwick for quite a long time," he said carelessly. "I guess I still have something in common with them. Plus there's the mother thing. Maybe he's not feeling too well disposed towards the female of the species just now. Maybe it's time for one of Dr. Carlyle's excruciating man-to-man moments."

"So what do you think this is really about?"

"Who knows?" said Charlie. "Knives, guitars … might as well throw in a Norman Bates or two."

Mary Harvey was starting to look as if she felt that she and her husband had been in some way remiss.

"I'm sure it's nothing." Charlie was pretty certain. He had a confidence in the oddness of Tempest min that far outstripped the possibility that Blake Vane Tempest was fermenting some serious scheme involving matricide.

There were very few single bedrooms in Hereford House but, unsurprisingly, one of them had been allotted to Blake Vane Tempest. He was sitting on the bed taking nicks out of the body of very fine guitar with what looked like a large skinning knife. Something one might have expected a Gurkha to carry. The guitar was a Fender - an American vintage Tele in three colour sunburst - and there was a signature in one corner that Charlie couldn't quite read. Blake, surprised maybe by the knock on the door, had caught one of his fingers slightly with the knife. Charlie watched unsympathetically as the boy stuck the finger in his mouth and sucked it.

"You know," he said finally, "one of the very first things one used to notice about Slash was that he had all of his fingers. It's not essential for a guitarist - look at Django Reinhardt, or Tony Iommi if you want a live one - but believe me, it's a great help."

Blake gave him a filthy look but, if he wondered why some teacher he had virtually nothing to do with was standing in the middle of his room passing remarks, he didn't say anything. He simply took his finger out of his mouth and looked at it. The knife had inflicted little more than a paper cut.

"It's nothing," said Charlie. "Still, it won't help Smoke On The Water come out one whit better."

"I hate it," said Blake.

"Smoke On The Water?" asked Charlie. "I'm getting to feel a bit that way about it myself."

"The guitar."

"It's a very beautiful guitar," said Charlie. "Why would you hate it?"

Blake held it up and pointed to the signature on it. It wasn't a mere piece of product endorsement stamped on by the manufacturers but a genuine signature, and it was that of a famous member of an American heavy metal band. A real hot ticker in every sense of the word.

"Mother had sex with him," said Blake. "That's how come I've got it. It was his. That's why I hate it." It was a raw and angry statement, and it was a measure of Blake Vane Tempest's state of mind that he just had to get it out there.

That this boy was seriously screwed up over his mother wasn't a challenging concept for Charlie, given what he already knew. So it wasn't impossible, he thought, that Blake had put the very worst interpretation on the situation. On the other hand, he could be exactly right. It was difficult to know what to say.

"Your mother is single, isn't she?" he offered finally. "And a responsible adult. And it's 2016. She's allowed to have ... friends ..." He let that hang in the air.

"She has sex with everyone!" It was a fierce response. Blake Vane Tempest's darkly handsome face was twisted with a combination of rage and misery.

"I doubt that," said Charlie mildly. "I doubt that very much."

"She was a porn star, you know, before she fucked her way into proper movies ..." Blake flung the guitar furiously to the floor.

No point in even commenting on the language. It was the least of the problems. But it was becoming increasingly difficult to know how to respond. Charlie took a deep breath.

"Well," he said lightly, "I expect that was a long time ago, and she certainly won't be the only beautiful woman who has the odd centrefold or a few artistic pictures lurking in her past. When we're young, we don't always envisage all the repercussions of what we do before we do it."

"It wasn't just arty pictures," said Blake angrily. "It was movies. I hate her."

Charlie wondered just how colourful Mrs. Vane Tempest's past really was. His knowledge of the woman was pretty scant, but he'd never felt predisposed in her favour. She wasn't the only example of apparently careless parenting that he was aware of but, for some indefinable reason, he found her far and away the most irritating. Yet, at the moment, it seemed that his best course - his only course - was to defend her. He hoped against hope that Blake hadn't been looking at the kind of thing that had made Rory blench - and then imagining his own mother projected before him in lewd and vivid technicolour. And God only knew what had made it onto the web. But wouldn't Mrs. Vane Tempest's career in the porn industry have been quite a time ago?

"Porn was a much milder affair when your mother was young," he said. "Short movies with titles like 'The Milkman Calls'. A man and a fridge and some dairy products. Nothing perverse and all simulated. Even the cream would have been processed."

Charlie had no idea if any of this was the truth because he'd been ruthlessly excluded from the preoccupations of his older brothers and their friends but he was desperate, if not to absolve Mrs. Vane Tempest, then at least to minimise her. But he found the conversation excruciating. He wasn't doing this well, he thought. Somehow, in spite of his weird interview, he'd mostly envisioned this job as one of completing some personal metamorphosis. One-time rock musician to guitar teacher to chemistry teacher. Flying fairy coach, to wheels coming off, to pumpkin. And that had been difficult enough. But this ... There are things that you do in life that you can't fully explain, and Charlie was thinking now that deciding to come to Puckrup was one of them. He was sitting by a boy whose pain was filling the entire room and he had no idea how to deal with it. The way people had had no real idea how to deal with his ...

But he had to do something. His attempts to trivialise Mrs. Vane Tempest's past were cutting no visible ice at all. Probably, there were people who could remain unmoved by the fact that their nearest and dearest were, or had been, porn stars. People who took the pragmatic view that porn is merely well remunerated employment. Non-vocational. Or even vocational, so what? But it was pretty obvious that Blake Vane Tempest wasn't one of them. Nor planning to be. Perhaps, Charlie thought, his mother had been disturbing in too many ways. A maternal maelstrom who'd left him with no comforting bedtime stories whatsoever. Or maybe Blake was just too sensitive. His half-brother Paul seemed to stand on firmer ground. Which immediately begged the question: where were the fathers in all of this?

Desperate for a way to move on, he picked up the guitar. Without the nicks it would have fetched a significant price on eBay. But then money probably wasn't a problem for Blake Vane Tempest. This guitar, on the other hand, obviously was. And it was the only thing he felt competent enough to address. The other stuff was for the analyst's couch. And Blake Vane Tempest was going to be spending a lot of time on one if something didn't change. Charlie wondered why the school's counselling system, as assiduous as it seemed, had apparently broken down so drastically when it came to this particular boy. He turned the chewed up Fender over in his hands.

"You don't have to play it." The back was in a worse state than the front. "You don't even have to have it here."

"I always wanted to play," said Blake dully. "It's all I've ever really wanted. And I've been learning. I wanted to be good. I wanted to be great – like him. And now she's spoilt it. She insisted that this," he made an angry stabbing gesture at the guitar, "would inspire me. I'd already told her I didn't want it.

Told her she was spoiling things forever for me, behaving like a slut, but she said I was just being stupid. Childish. She's ruined everything ..." There were tears in his eyes now. He dashed them angrily away, hot with mortification.

That a boy would call his mother a slut, and had done so to his little brother at least once in the past, struck Charlie as profoundly disturbing. Yet a corrective remark could simply widen a discussion around a subject that still felt well outside his skill set.

"Haven't you a different guitar to play?" He glanced round the room. Smoke on The Water had kept coming from somewhere.

"Not now. She ... I ..." Blake stopped, evidently unable or unwilling to go on. "I wanted to be good ... great..." he repeated, after a choked moment or two. "I really did ... and now just the idea ..." He stopped.

Whether Blake's desires to be great, and maybe by inference famous, were simply a need to be up there with the men who did actually get his mother's attention was yet another psychological situation that Charlie felt ill equipped to address. And the need of people to come out on top had to be driven by all kinds of things. Success was another child with many fathers. Charlie sighed again. He could do nothing about Mrs. Vane Tempest but he was sorry that Blake had lost his pleasure in the guitar. It wasn't, by all accounts, as if he were bursting with genius or inspiration in any other direction. The boy really had to find a way of getting more control over himself, or he was going nowhere good.

Charlie sat down on the bed beside him. "You know, Blake," he spoke with his eyes on the carved up guitar. "Life often dumps us in painful situations that we just can't do anything about. And if we can't change them, then we have to find a way to live with them. And that's why it would be such a shame if you rejected the music. I can claim to know quite a bit about painful situations, and I can also claim to know a fair amount about music. I used to play the guitar - just a hobby - but I played it well enough to know that it can be a great escape. Which means that when you're upset about something you have a place to go to. A place where you can deal. And playing a musical instrument can *be* that place. At first it just feels like hard work, I know, but that alone is therapeutic. It's good for concentration and self-discipline and all the stuff you don't really want me to talk about. But then, with serious practice, it gets easier. And finally the moment comes when the playing can be sheer pleasure. And in this pleasure you can find yourself - realise that you have something, that you've earned something, that you *are* something. And all of this puts you in a better frame of mind, takes you to a better world. Don't let whatever your mother's done deprive you of an opportunity to make your own happiness. Not if you really want to play as much as you say you do."

Charlie wasn't unaware that the gods of irony would be raising their collective eyebrows as he took this 'play out your misery' line with Blake. But, though the boy hadn't shown much in the way of listening, he had put the knife to one side and was looking a little calmer. Finally he spoke, "I could never bring myself to play that … that …" He couldn't even bring himself to name it.

"Understandable," said Charlie. "But sitting here stabbing at it isn't doing you any good at all. I doubt it's in any way cathartic. You're just building up more resentment. It's tantamount to self-harming." He took another glance at the cut finger. "And you're the only one taking the pain - not your mother, or the guitar, or the guy who owned it. Forget about him, in any case. He's not that great. I could name you half a dozen better. I'll tell you what, I still have the guitar that I used to play. It's at home with my parents, but I could pick it up this weekend. How about we get Mr. Harvey to put this one of yours into storage, and you start again? With a guitar that carries no associations for you whatsoever ..."

Blake Vane Tempest looked at him. And maybe there was a flicker of interest in his eyes. He had almost black eyes – difficult windows to see through.

"We could do a swap ..." he said, finally.

"Yes we could," said Charlie, flicking bits off the Tele. "At least for a period."

"You'd bring it this weekend?"

"Sunday evening. I promise. And now ..." he held out his hand. "The knife, please."

Blake picked it up and laid it on Charlie's outstretched palm. Charlie watched him for a moment or two. "So we're good here? We have a plan?"

"I guess."

Charlie picked up the unfortunate guitar by its shaft and headed towards the door but, before he left, he turned round and said slowly, "Your little brother, Blake. He's like this guitar, you know. It isn't his fault. Try not to take things out on him. You could call him Christopher, for instance. Start there. Try, eh?"

Blake said nothing. Charlie thought that maybe he'd tried to push him just a bit too far. He hoped against hope that Mrs. Vane Tempest hadn't given her eldest son the one gift that really *can* keep on giving - irreparability. "Sunday evening then?" he said. "Is that still what you want?"

"Yes."

"Then I will see you here Sunday."

"Yes."

Julius Harvey was heading up the stairs as Charlie was heading down. He looked at the mutilated guitar and the skinning knife with horror.

"Do you want to hear all of it?" asked Charlie with a grimace.

"God, yes. And so will Dr. Carlyle. Is Blake okay?"

"For the moment, I think. Maybe you should sneak your head round the door, in a while."

"Coffee? While you bring me up to speed?"

"Sure."

*****

Saturday teatime and, as Charlie threw a holdall into the back of his car, Eric Boswell paused beside him. "Leaving us so soon in the term?"

"Just for the rest of the weekend," Charlie said. "I have to pick up something that's with my parents."

"No Saturday night date then?"

"No."

"Seems a waste. If I'd looked like you ... well ... Life might have gone very differently." He squinted up at Charlie through his thick spectacle lenses.

Charlie slammed the back door of the car. "How so?"

"It's a long story," said Dr. Boswell. "Maybe some other time." And he pottered off in the direction of his own car.

*****

The Gibson hadn't been out of its case for eight years. Charlie felt as if he was handling deteriorating dynamite, sweating nitroglycerine. So many feelings assailed him that his hands shook slightly as he sorted out new strings. With hot, pricking eyes, he fought off the inevitable compulsion to rerun that final night when he'd stood in the hallway of the London flat, full of hopes and dreams and nervous excitement, holding the guitar in its case as if it were some sort of talisman. An amulet that held the key to everything that could be. An amulet that, in the end, had delivered nothing but death and disaster.

"Going to play it?" asked his mother from the bedroom doorway.

"I'm going to lend it to one of the boys." Why on earth had he suggested that? What a promise. What a can of worms to open. He kept his voice calm and his face averted.

Lottie Peterson settled for casual comment: "I should have thought most of the boys at that school would be in a position to have their own guitars. Is it for one of the scholarship youngsters?"

"No. But it's complicated."

"It must be." Lottie thought of all the pain her son had gone through, and hoped desperately that he wasn't about to revisit an issue that had been ostensibly resolving itself.

"It's just a loan," said Charlie. "No big drama."

"Fine," said Lottie. She'd learned when it was pointless to push. "Food's on the table soon," she added brightly. "And I'd like to hear more about the biodynamic woman."

"That's complicated too."

"Dear God," Lottie shook her head. "The whole point of that job was to make life easier for you."

Charlie spent fifteen minutes re-stringing the Gibson. Time was he could have done it in three or four but his fingers … well, he was just upset. When he finished, he did a quick re-tune, put the guitar back in the case and went downstairs for supper.

Lottie and Peter Peterson wanted their son to stay for Sunday lunch but he just couldn't. He felt moody and unsettled. He looked at his mother's latest sculpture after breakfast, careful to show more than just polite interest, and then left for Puckrup after coffee. He was aware of the Gibson on the back seat of the car as surely if it were the disgruntled eye of some lesser Sauron.

*****

Parking the car at the school, he bumped once again into Dr. Boswell. Eric Boswell was an inveterate potterer. It was as if he had some chronic disease that manifested as forced ambulation. He and the trembly terrier both, lost to aimless wanderings. Dr. Boswell, in fact, wandered around to think. Walking brought his deepest thoughts to the surface. And then he composed and conjugated them aloud, soliloquizing his way around the school grounds, trudging through woodland and across football pitches. In this way he produced lyrical and profound pieces that got published in obscure journals. And though their impact on the world was limited to small correspondences with a few literary eccentrics like himself, they served the very practical end of justifying his repeated escapes from his sister and her cats. Coincidentally, cats were featuring in the agenda of the trembly terrier - which gave him and Dr. Boswell a bond of sorts. The terrier had lately spied Schrödinger. The damned cat had got out of the box alive. Again! What were the odds?

"You're back early," Dr. Boswell said.

"Yes."

"I suppose young men without dates get restless."

Charlie gave something that was half a laugh and half a groan. Obviously, he looked as restless as he felt. And it wasn't only the Gibson nagging at him. He longed to go and see Ianthe. That was probably the real reason he'd come back early. He found her so lovely that just looking at her could be an end in itself. He wouldn't need to say anything in particular. And she would just smile like she always did. And then he'd feel better. But he couldn't constantly be searching for solace in her smile ... without ... without ...

"Have you had lunch?" Eric Boswell was wearing smart cavalry twills and a poaching jacket in West of England cloth. He'd been going to go to church, he explained, but a quick thoughtful walk had somehow got out of control and time had snuck past him and forged ahead unheeded. Which was a pity because churches, if one didn't view them as exclusively about the sermon, were places that carried the deepest of human emotions in their very stones.

Charlie agreed to lunch without giving the matter any real thought. He didn't feel particularly like eating. On the other hand, he felt in need of something.

"I know a good pub," said Eric Boswell. "I'll drive, I don't drink any more. It makes me dyspeptic."

"Does he come?" Charlie looked down at the trembly terrier, who seemed expectant.

"He does not," replied Dr. Boswell, with some asperity. "He pees on the table legs. The landlord doesn't like it."

The Drovers Arms was not on the main road or, indeed, on any thoroughfare that promised a commercial level of footfall. It was standing rather abruptly, as if its construction had been prompted by spur of the moment necessity, on the side of what looked like a track for cloven-hoofed beasts. In fact, it was less a pub than an immaculately preserved artefact. Something well out of its time. The entire cast of Under The Greenwood Tree could have walked in at any minute. It didn't of course – even though it was Sunday lunchtime – which made Charlie think that the landlord had to manage the place as a hobby. Some bloodless alternative to shooting rabbits or hunting foxes.

They ordered two roast dinners, half a pint of real ale and some bottled water. All the tables wobbled on the uneven flagstone floor but Dr. Boswell knew exactly which one was least likely to spill his gravy. It was empty, as indeed were most of them. They proceeded to it past a curved oak settle where a couple of old men, engaged in desultory chat before a log fire, looked up with curt nods of greeting. The target table was next to one of the small cottage style windows, and there was a bowl of snowdrops on the broad sill. They gleamed white and innocently beautiful in the gloom. After sitting down on an ancient gimpy chair that more than compensated for the table's stability, Charlie reached out with a finger and gently lifted one of the shyly drooping heads.

Eric Boswell watched him. "I was in love once, you know," he said. "Like Dante, I had my Beatrice."

Charlie looked up.

"We read English together at Cambridge." Dr. Boswell's voice began to take on a faraway tone. "She had a plan to be a librarian. Foolish as I was, I thought that librarians just issued membership cards and stamped books in and out for county councils. I had no concept of people who collated and curated ancient and irreplaceable manuscripts in fantastic places like Hampton Court Palace. But she had the contacts and the background to understand the nature of such a job and have it come to pass. She had a title too, as it turned out, though she never used it because this was the egalitarian sixties and the upper classes and the aristocracy had yet to re-establish their equilibrium. But some advantages you just can't hide – the natural self-confidence in any and every situation, the unassuming belief that everything will work out just as you want it to ..." Dr. Boswell paused, staring at the snowdrops. "And she had a remarkable beauty," he went on finally, "which she carried with exactly that effortless and unaffected grace, as if it were just another natural thing that she'd been granted by the gods. Yes, she was God's chosen creature alright, and I – well I was a working class, grammar school boy, clever but gauche, and overwhelmed by the type of people she circulated amongst. And I was desperately lacking in the only currency that could really have helped me – good looks. I wasn't even tall. I was totally bankrupt in the things that could ever have made her want me. Unglamorous as I was, I couldn't even style myself the parfait knight of courtly love. But I could still feel what the parfait knight was supposed to feel ..." he gave a deep, reminiscent sigh. "Oddly enough, we became friends after a fashion, she and I ... sitting together in the library ... exchanging notes on medieval romance poetry. Fortunately, she never seemed to notice how my heart turned over every time she looked at me. Or maybe she was just too discreet to let on ..."

The food arrived at this point and Dr. Boswell checked over his swamp of gravy with an absent eye. Charlie felt a sudden and rather sad kinship with him. He had only the vaguest ideas on courtly love and parfait knights himself, but he was prepared to listen to Eric Boswell talk of such things, if that was the old man's inclination.

He looked down at the curiously carved chunks of meat he'd just been presented with. His heaped and swilling plate, delivered by a somewhat incongruous waitress with tattoos and a turquoise streak in her hair, looked fraught with dark possibilities. Charlie had never thought of himself as a gourmet of any sort, but he'd certainly been struck by Rory's predisposition to eat anything that didn't eat him first. But, as this was Dr. Boswell's treat, he didn't want to appear churlish, or interfere with the old man's enjoyment of the meal, so he picked up his knife and fork and prepared to work his way unflinchingly through whatever lay before him.

After a few minutes devoted mostly to taking the edge off his own appetite, Dr. Boswell drifted thoughtfully back on topic. He explained courtly love - using his fork, with something unidentifiable wobbling precariously on it, as an occasional point of emphasis. Courtly love was, he said, the idea of love. The grand poetry of the business. That which makes us yearn and ache and soar and long to pull off heroic deeds. But, and now he ate the wobbling thing (which Charlie finally categorised as a parsnip) it was never physically consummated. At this point he fixed Charlie with a hard stare. Troubadours, he said, sang about it to ladies. Knights whispered it in the ears of medieval beauties as they walked through flowery meads. It was passionate but disciplined. Illicit on occasion because these ladies may have been betrothed or married to somebody else, but it was morally elevating in that nothing was ever allowed to happen. It was, at once, both human and transcendent.

"Right," said Charlie. He was pretty sure he was listening to a lecture given in some university English department long ago. Nevertheless, he felt a vague and oddly uncomfortable shadow pass over him.

"I've written of it in terms of Plato's Forms," Dr. Boswell went on. "The Form, in Plato's use of the word, being a blueprint of perfection. The essence of a thing. We can't point to it or touch it but it's not just of the mind. It's a real absolute, outside of space and time, forever unchanging. Justice, Beauty, Courage, Temperance and Love are all Forms. Unfortunately, we can only experience corruptions of them in this world. They cannot hold up in an earthly reality. And courtly love cannot survive the consummation. Maybe it never really existed outside of literature. And yet, we can all appreciate the concept. The bells on the hill that you can hear ringing, the birds and those wonderful roses, in sweet fragrant meadows of dawn and dew ... I forget the exact words but you've heard the song?"

Charlie nodded. "I think so."

"It ran in my head a lot at that time. From The Music Man I believe, though the Beatles recorded it in their early years. Yes, all of the wondrously new and almost surreal appreciation of the world that comes with falling in love cannot, in the end, withstand the messiness that is human life."

Charlie said nothing.

Dr. Boswell studied him for a moment or two. "On the whole," he said eventually, "I think I'm glad I never got to consummate the love I had for my particular Beatrice. My hunger fed my Ph.D. and a fairly decent academic career after that. And now, well now I'm getting to be an old man, and I'm happy to teach in such a school as we do and, in the autumn time, gather mushrooms for tea. And after I've eaten the mushrooms, I can sit by the fire, and if it's really quiet, I can still hear those bells ringing." He paused and wagged his fork at Charlie. "You can have love in an idealised form, or you can live it in the form we humans most understand. You can't do both. There's romance and there's life. And they serve different ends. It's the poet's dilemma. Inspiration or reality. You must think carefully which it is you want. And which, in the circumstances, you can have."

And he began to search for puddings on the blackboard menu hanging over the bar.

*****

Fortified by beef and gravy and a helping of trifle, Charlie sat down on a much less wobbly chair in Blake Vane Tempest's bedroom. There was a framed retro poster (signed) of Raquel Welch stepping out of the sea in the original version of 2,000

Years. B.C., a Mexican throw on the bed and a pair of designer jeans on the floor. And Blake, with a cool lock of dark hair drifting in a drop dead fashion over one eye, was refusing to take the Gibson. "I want to hear you play, first." There was a strong challenge in his voice - the challenge of the teenager who won't take orders unless they come from the alpha male.

"Go on, sir," chimed a voice from the doorway. "Show us what you're made of." Charlie turned to see one of his A-level chemistry students looking in on them, and one or two more starting to gather. There was a slight atmosphere of a pre-planned chicken run.

He'd half expected something like it - though certainly not the elbowing audience that was rapidly building - and yet he hadn't practised back at home. Restringing the Gibson had been unbelievably hard, but if supper had not intervened? If there'd been no excuse to put the guitar back in its case? If he'd looked steadily into its Sauron's eye? Would his fingers have been driven beyond a re-tune?

But then, this entire thing was not really about him, his past or his ego. It was about Blake's past and Blake's ego. One might have assumed that Blake Vane Tempest would have an enormous ego and yet, somehow, Charlie felt that he didn't. He had temper and surliness and misery because he didn't feel secure in himself. His mother had provided him with everything but the thing he seemed to need most - the certainty that he mattered more to her than a procession of lovers. So the problem, as Charlie now saw it, had turned into this: how could he best make Blake Vane Tempest feel that he mattered? By playing the guitar like an average chemistry master? Or playing the guitar like the Charlie Peterson of Endgame? Who would a teenage boy want taking an interest in him? A well-meaning schoolteacher with a command of some chords and a few popular songs, or someone who'd once touched greatness and could play a guitar like it was part of him? But could he, anymore? Greatness requires practice. Daily practice. Hours of it. Muscle memory was a fine thing but it couldn't work miracles. Thoughtfully, Charlie checked the Gibson's tuning.

"Come on, sir! Can you actually play it?"

"Yes."

"How well?"

The strings on the guitar's shaft suddenly flashed fire in the light of the desk lamp. *Like a motherfucker.*

"Better than you could possibly imagine." He looked up. "I mean, how well would you imagine that the average chemistry teacher can play a guitar?"

"Not very well."

"Exactly. I play better than not very well."

"We'll let's hear you, sir, whatever." There was a chorus of encouragement.

Charlie looked back down at the guitar, and for a moment there was a catch, a tell-tale lack of evenness in his breathing. They'd once travelled a roller coaster of a road together, he and the Gibson. But how should they greet each other after long years? With something recognisable that he'd taught to a hundred students in the Camden basement? Or with something virtually unplayed and maybe half forgotten that was theirs and theirs alone?

And for a moment he was suddenly back in Brick Lane studios:

226

'Look son, you can play it to the world for thirty seconds, or you can play it at home for the rest of your life to nobody but your mother and the paint pots in the garage. We're facing a mess of new music genres and an audience with a terminally shortened attention span. Most people these days want instant gratification with no effort. Nobody's interested in what an instrument can actually do, or how something that's a bit difficult can give a pay off worth the concentration. If there isn't a really cheesy hook-line or some sort of noise that more or less slams their heads in a door after ten seconds, most will just press the button and move on to the next track. It's the fucking internet if you ask me, but what do I know? I'm just the poor schmuck who works for a record company that'll find itself going broke on account of bloody Napster, if it's not very careful. Three minutes, Charlie, there's a reason singles are that long and the maths of a three minute track means you can't fit in a two minute guitar solo, even if it *is* the dog's bollocks. Thirty seconds. Tops.'

'Then honestly, what's the point? If I barely get to play the guitar?'

'You do that on stage. When they get to look at you. Then you seduce them into listening. They feel your passion, the music grabs them, and then they listen. For as long as you want them to. I went to see the Floyd at a student union dance in 1970. Nobody danced. We stood for what seemed like forever, watching some funny bloody oil drop patterns projected on the wall behind them, while they just played. I don't remember a specific song at all. I just remember the sound and the oil drops and the sheer fucking marvellousness of it. But that was then, and this is now. And survival in the now depends upon not putting something like Pink Floyd's unfinished fucking oil drop symphony out on a single that needs to make the Radio One playlist.'

But in the *now* now, Charlie was in the garage surrounded by paint pots, and he could feel that guitar solo coming through him as if he'd just written it yesterday instead of eight or nine years ago. The solo was asking to be played and the guitar wanted to play it. 'And can you remember it?' Charlie whispered, delaying the moment, checking the tuning again. The pegs turned in sulky jerks. *Damned right, and this is all so fucking not before time, if you don't mind my saying so.*

So Charlie stood up, bent over, and plugged the lead into a Blues Junior that was sitting on a low table. And then he put his fingers to the strings. But in the seconds before he started to play he felt something powerful, something spine tingling, something primal yet passionate, with a hint of the diabolical, rising from the soles of his feet and climbing up inside him. A thing that held the death of his friends, the darkness of his pain - and the demiurge that drove his talent.

Once again the guitar's strings flashed brief fire. *It's here, the duende. It's with us. And stronger than ever before. We're beyond memory and fingering and practice now. No rationalising can be done. There's just you and me and the dark muse poised on the rim of Lorca's well. One instrument, one energy, one desire. Acknowledge the duende, Charlie, take what it offers and accept that it will scorch your heart again - or put me back in the case and walk away.*

"PLAY … PLAY … PLAY … PLAY …"

"Come on, sir!"

So Charlie played the Gibson for the first time since his

friends died, and the incredible sound poured out and filled the room and hit the walls and ran down them like pounding surf. And the boys covered their ears and jumped and played air guitar and grinned wildly at each other and Julius Harvey came running up the stairs shouting, 'My God, what on earth is happening?' And Charlie Peterson's soul raised its face from the dust and greeted with tearful recognition that long lost feeling of blood-rocking rightness.

When the last note faded away there was a sudden hush, and then somebody said quietly: "How do you get to be that good?"

Charlie unplugged the guitar in order to be able to hide his face for a moment. "You play until your fingers are raw and you can barely see for tears of frustration," he said. "And then you pull yourself together, and you play some more." Straightening up, he turned to Blake. "People can teach you and they can guide you and I will do both, if you want me to. But the work that really matters, you have to do for yourself. There is no other way. And, in the end, the reason we keep on trying has nothing to do with becoming great or being famous. We keep on for one reason and one reason only - because we can't not."

Then Charlie handed the Gibson over. "This guitar," he said, "is part of me, and I am lending it to you in the hope that you will learn what that means. All musical instruments come out differently, you know, even those that are supposed to be identical. This one has a great heart, and when you go for the big one it won't let you down. It will look after you all the way, so treat it with respect. If I find as much as a nick on it that hasn't come about by pure bloody accident, I will drag you down the stairs by the hair, take you outside, and kill you. You understand me?"

Blake Vane Tempest nodded. He was smiling. They were both smiling, but a line had been drawn. And between them, things had been understood. Charlie turned away. "I'll be back next week," he said. "At the same time. And I want to hear something that isn't Smoke on the Water."

The boys in the doorway parted in a wave of murmured comment to let him pass. As he clattered down the wooden stairs a small voice floated after him: "I remember now. I know who you are."

Charlie paused for a split second. "I'm pleased somebody does," he said quietly. "Because *I* really don't."

Outside, he turned in the direction of the sports fields, made his way through the winter dark to the farthermost bench, sat down and cried. Playing the Gibson had been like a bloodletting. He actually felt weak. But maybe it had been a turning point. A kind of reconciliation. With himself. With his dead friends. With all the terrible feelings he'd had one time and another. He'd come to Puckrup Hall in acceptance. But reconciliation - that was something completely different.

"It was only supposed to last thirty seconds."

Charlie raised his face from his hands, wiping it surreptitiously as he did so. Tempest min, a small muffled figure in the blackness, was studying him gravely.

"What did you say?" Charlie asked.

"I said, that guitar solo was only supposed to last thirty seconds."

"Who told you that?"

"You did."

Charlie thought for a moment or two. He didn't remember

saying anything aloud about the solo. Maybe he had. At the start. Maybe he'd said, 'this guitar solo was only supposed to last thirty seconds'. As a kind of introduction. Had he? He wasn't sure. He certainly hadn't recited the entire flashback aloud but, yes, maybe he'd just said that bit … as he started to play … 'this guitar solo was only meant to last thirty seconds'.

"Why are you always wandering around at bedtime?" he asked. "It's dark, for heaven's sake. And freezing cold. You could catch another fever. And how on earth did you escape Matron again? And why? She's going to to be furious. She's going to start putting you on a leash."

Tempest min's eyes filled with tears and then he held out his hands. "Because I had to tell you about what I remember," he said in a trembling voice. And Charlie, wanting to comfort him and maybe wanting comfort himself, reached out to hold him. But as he did so, Tempest min collapsed to the ground, unconscious.

Chapter Twelve

Matron was summoned. Dr. Carlyle was summoned. Lesser mortals appeared as if by magic. Tempest min lay, as white as if death had already claimed him, on the dusty chaise longue in the entrance hall of the main building. There was an other worldly beauty about his marble stillness. Everyone was shocked. It was a scene from the fall of Icarus. He didn't wake up.

What happened? What had Tempest min been doing out there in the dark? Why was Charlie out there in the dark? What had it all been about?

"It was about nothing," explained Charlie, for the umpteenth time. "Nothing happened but a few spoken sentences. I was just sitting out there, on my own, when he arrived."

"Why? Why were you sitting out there?"

"I was clearing my head."

"Of what?"

Charlie couldn't see his way to telling the whole truth of why he'd sought out the darkness. It was irrelevant, in any case, to the matter in hand. He was merely, he claimed, reviewing what he'd said to Blake Vane Tempest. Wondering whether or not he'd done the right thing in making his offer. That was enough of the truth.

"I'm quite sure you didn't do the right thing," observed Matron, sniffily. She was not in the best frame of mind, her predictions about 'this being just a faint' not having been blessed by Tempest min's prompt return to consciousness. "Blake Vane Tempest has had any number of official guitar lessons here," she added, emphasising the word 'official'. "And they haven't done him any good at all, that I can see. And that was from a *proper* guitar teacher. With qualifications."

Charlie had been questioned endlessly. And he felt sick. "Formal qualifications are not the be all and end all," he said shortly. "You inspire people with your love of the instrument and your own inspiration."

He thought then, suddenly and somewhat tangentially, of all those pupils in the Camden basement. Of how he'd effectively short-changed them. Not through lack of knowledge, or lack of proper qualifications, or even lack of putting in the time. But through a lack of the wherewithal to really inspire them. A lack of joy in the task. A lack a love.

Dr. Carlyle was of the opinion, which he firmly stated, that any genuine interest taken in Blake Vane Tempest should be encouraged. So many of the professionally qualified and the well-disposed had tried and failed to effect a change for the better in the boy, that most of the staff's brains were still in some sort of refractory state when it came to wondering what could be done for him.

Matron sniffed again and worked Tempest min's cold little hands in her own. Somebody brought a blanket which she tucked solicitously around his legs.

"What did he say to you, again?" Julius Harvey asked. "On the stairs?"

"Something about remembering. 'I remember you now. I know who you are.'" Charlie repeated this for what felt like the hundredth time.

"And who is that?"

"I don't know," said Charlie wearily. "He's always had me mixed up with somebody else. Somebody from his past."

"So he was in the crowd when you were playing the guitar?"

"Well he had to be, didn't he? Because of what he said when he was out in the field. But I didn't actually see him. As I went down the stairs, I thought I heard a voice. It could have been his."

"And out in the field he said pretty much the same thing?"

"He said he wanted to tell me about what he remembered."

"About knowing you from before?"

"Presumably. He passed out before he managed it."

"But he doesn't? Know you from somewhere before?"

"No."

"He shouldn't have been in Hereford House," said Matron. "*Or* outside in the dark. He should have been in bed." She gave Charlie a black look.

"Could be bird flu," suggested somebody. "Maybe he's got that bird flu."

There was a perceptible shrinking back of onlookers. The sound of a distant engine triggered a relieved surge towards the door.

"Ambulance," Dr. Carlyle raised his voice. "Finally. Clear the way, people. Somebody go out and signal to the paramedics. Show them where to come."

*****

Worcester Hospital kept Tempest min for a few days while dark imaginings plagued the school. Mrs. Vane Tempest was in California. And difficult to get hold of. Tempest min regained consciousness before she was given the news so the shock she received was not, apparently, great enough to cause her to climb aboard an aeroplane. She conversed by telephone with the doctors at the hospital. The doctors at the hospital conversed by telephone with Dr. Carlyle. Mrs. Vane Tempest conversed by telephone with Dr. Carlyle. Matron went to the hospital and conversed with the doctors directly. Which they didn't enjoy. Dr. Carlyle passed on health bulletins to the school. Paul and Blake Vane Tempest went to the hospital with Matron on her second visit and returned with the news that Tempest min was as healthy as they were. Mrs. Vane Tempest conversed with them by Skype. They assured her that Tempest min was as healthy as they were. The doctors thought they were probably right. Blood tests and scans had proved unrewarding. Maybe Tempest min had some as yet unidentifiable problem with maintaining blood sugar levels. He was not actually diabetic. And he didn't have a brain tumour. Or any other sort of tumour. Nor was he an epileptic. Or a victim of bird flu. That put an effective end to most of the dark imaginings. He came back to the school towards the end of the week and was put in the sanatorium for an extended rest. His eating habits were put under strict review by Matron. He had brief visits from teachers and some light worksheets to encourage him to remember how to read and write and do simple arithmetic. Not that he'd forgotten, but loss of consciousness in a pupil is worrying for teachers. They need to be reassured. Hospital doctors don't know everything.

They didn't, for example, know that Tempest min had had what he thought was a Eureka moment concerning Charlie. And then forgotten it.

Matron and Tempest min conversed with Mrs. Vane Tempest by Skype. The fact that Mrs. Vane Tempest was based mostly in California probably accounts for the way things started to go. Had Mrs. Vane Tempest been in the sort of profession that hasn't taken a double major in lying on analysts' couches, things could well have gone differently. Or maybe not.

Charlie was unaware that Tempest min had forgotten exactly what happened before he lost consciousness and that, in addition, he was only vaguely cognisant of having been in Hereford House to hear Charlie play the guitar - though his presence had been confirmed by one or two of the older boys. None of this vagueness had proved helpful to interested parties in terms of precipitating factors, but it would have been helpful to Charlie in terms of wanting to go to the sanatorium to see him. He didn't go because he didn't know what would happen. He was entangled in Tempest min's mind with someone whose presence in the sanatorium would, perhaps, have been prejudicial. Yet through the tears, Tempest min, just before he blacked out, had seemed sort of happy that he had remembered something. Or had he? Charlie wasn't sure. So all of this rather hung over him when he went, as promised, to hear Blake Vane Tempest play 'something that wasn't Smoke On The Water'. He wondered if the issue of Tempest min would add another difficult dimension to his arrangement with Blake. An arrangement that already came with an inbuilt labyrinth of difficult dimensions.

In the event, Blake seemed unperturbed by his little brother's stay in hospital. And he was obviously not nursing the opinion that Charlie's involvement in the entire business had been in anyway causal. "Always been a feverish little git," was his careless summing up. He added a quick dismissive retrospective as he gave the guitar a final tune: "He ended up with a tutor at one point, being home-schooled, because he was so weird. Then he took it into his head that he had to come here. Paul and me tried to dissuade him, but once he's got something in his head …" He tailed off, apparently losing interest in the matter.

Charlie would have liked to hear more, but he let the subject go because he wanted Blake to feel that he was the focus of attention. "He seems fine now, anyway," he said, closing the matter. "So let's hear what you've got."

So Blake Vane Tempest played the guitar. He was a youth who had consistently failed to stimulate pleasant surprise in any of the school's staff, but he managed it now. Charlie was aware of some inward release of breath. And then a pleasant inrush of relief. Blake Vane Tempest had contrived to pull a musical rabbit out of his hat. The seemingly desultory effort and the endless, lifeless repetition of Smoke on the Water had been evidence of the boy's pain – not his ability. He was at ease with the physicality of the instrument, there was lightness and fluency in his fingering, there was soul and feeling in his playing. In short, there was the seed of something special in Blake Vane Tempest. If only he could maintain the application and the temperament to grow it … Charlie looked at him for a moment or two. "Sing," he said.

So Blake Vane Tempest fired up some more chords and sang.

Damn, thought Charlie, this boy's got it all. "You have talent," he said. "A talent you could really do something with. But it's a hard world out there, so you must never lose sight of the fact that unless you're very lucky, real success is always going to be 10% talent and 90% effort."

"I can do effort," said Blake Vane Tempest.

"Good," said Charlie. "Because according to the ten thousand hour rule you've probably got some ground to make up."

"What rule?"

"The ten thousand hour rule. In a study that just happened to be undertaken on musicians, it was shown that, given an acceptable level of aptitude, the key to acquiring world-class expertise in any skill is mostly a matter of practising in the correct way for approximately ten thousand hours. This came up in a book called Outliers – which I haven't read by the way but which greatly excited one of my brothers because he thinks the ten thousand hour rule explains why none of his girlfriends think he's very good at sex. Anyway, according to the author of this book, Bill Gates is Bill Gates because he worked for ten thousand hours in an after-school computer lab, and The Beatles became The Beatles because, over the course of five trips to Hamburg, they played for ten thousand hours in strip clubs. Sometimes they had to play for hours at a stretch. To play hours at a stretch, night after night, sometimes until two in the morning, and to keep audiences coming, pretty much forces you to develop musically. They had to find a new way of playing.

They mixed up all kinds of influences. Not to mention the stamina and determination it took. Before they had their first hit, they'd played more gigs than most modern bands play in a lifetime. When they started going to Germany they had a level of innate musical talent, sure, but they were nothing more than an average band, called the Quarrymen, playing mostly covers. But by the time they gave up going, they sounded like no one else. They were The Beatles."

"Ten thousand hours?"

"Yes. Shocking, isn't it? That's what it takes to be great. Not good, not in a position to get a whole lot of pleasure out of playing a guitar, but *great*." Charlie paused at this point, waiting for more reaction. The boy's previous focus on being great nagged at him.

"Did you do the ten thousand hours?" Blake asked.

"I started when I was in primary school."

Blake studied his own feet for a while, and then he said: "Well I'll just have to get to be great on less than ten thousand hours, won't I?"

"We could just play, you know," suggested Charlie. "Relax. Have some fun. Enjoy the instrument."

"So I can play Kumbaya at cook outs while everybody holds hands and sings? I don't think so."

Charlie studied Blake for a moment or two more. "Then I need to say something else as well." He kept his eyes on the boy's face. "And I want you to remember it, because I'm never going to say it again. If commercial recognition is the only reason you do this, you will never get from it what you really need. You can neither gain real pleasure, nor free your individual creativity, if

239

you play with only fame and fortune in mind."

"Okay, I get it," said Blake irritably. "First the love, then the fame. Now can we just get started? Those ten thousand hours are slipping away."

*****

Monday morning a week or so later and Charlie was waylaid by Dr. Carlyle.

"A word," said the headmaster. He seemed, as always, relatively buoyant. This was not, Charlie thought with some relief, about to be a recriminatory word of any sort. There was still, in his mind, some unallayed anxiety about Tempest min who, though apparently healthy, was nevertheless condemned to return to the sanatorium for compulsory nap periods each afternoon, as if he were a toddler. Charlie had not yet seen him, and he apparently shared his anxiety about how things were going with Tempest min's mother. Mrs. Vane Tempest was not, Dr. Carlyle explained now, a fan of vague diagnoses. She regarded them as mere suggestions. In California, people and their insurance companies did not pay doctors just to make suggestions. They paid doctors to think that little bit harder, and so she had dispatched to Puckrup Hall a doctor who was paid to think extremely hard indeed. A man who could be described as having his entire raison d'être occupied with thought processes.

"In your free period, this morning," Dr. Carlyle finished, "he would like you to talk to you. About what happened."

Dr. Deshpande had been allotted a room on the first floor of the main building. A room in which to consult, as it were. It had the look of a place that was not much used. The carpet was a barely trodden moss green, the walls were pure clotted cream and there was a small cast-iron fireplace, of the type once installed in bedrooms, which gleamed with the soft graphite glow of Zebra grate polish. On the tiled hearth there was an old china foot-bath planted up with sprouting, budding, optimistic daffodils. Charlie thought suddenly of Ianthe's glasshouses. And of Ianthe. And of the hellebores. Fervently wishing he were elsewhere, he took another glance at the bulbs.

Dr. Deshpande was seated in the watery sunlight that flowed in from an east facing window. He was at a very elegant Georgian desk. He had a notepad and a small tape recorder. "Please sit down, Mr. Peterson." He indicated a wing chair upholstered in the palest green velvet. "Make yourself comfortable."

When he spoke, Dr. Deshpande (pronounced Deshpandy) sounded exquisitely English. But, apart from his perfectly tailored Savile Row suit, and the crisp stripes of his Turnbull and Asser shirt, and the immaculate Windsor knot in his silk tie, he looked exquisitely Indian. He could have been descended from a line of dashing polo playing maharajas. He wasn't – although he'd gone to Eton and Cambridge with one and the pair of them remained close friends. But with no binding responsibilities to an Indian heritage, Dr. Deshpande, unlike his friend, lived entirely in the western world. He had a practice in Los Angeles and a practice in Harley Street. A beach property in Malibu and a mansion flat in Cadogan Square. And all from being the modern answer to Sigmund Freud. Or perhaps he lay a little nearer to Carl Jung because Dr. Deshpande, despite his acquired British nationality and his access to an American one, courtesy of his California born wife, still carried in his heart faint echoes of India's mysticism. He was, of course, fully aware of all the latest developments in neuroscience. He had dinner regularly with one of its most influential proponents. But he was yet to be convinced that the neuroscientists, in spite of all their wonderful flashing pictures, were ever going to fully explain what makes a man. He could not, even after a very good dinner, entirely accept his friend's belief that man and his infinite capabilities and complexities could be fully explained through protoplasm and electro-potentials, however brilliant the imaging. And woman certainly couldn't. He understood the academic consensus that consciousness is simply a product of the brain, a delusion created by a combination of things like intelligence and memory and self-awareness, and so on and so on, and that, in truth, we have less than we would like in the way of free will and nothing at all in the way of a soul. This is the creed of the church of science and it was obviously a deep understanding of this creed that got him all the letters after his name.

But understanding is not sworn commitment - and Dr. Deshpande also knew that the nature of consciousness is, and may well remain, 'the hard question'. Furthermore, he held quietly to the suspicion that the more biologists and medical researchers tried to pin down life itself, the more they reduced it to molecules and atoms, passing the baton on to biochemists and geneticists and physicists for further dissection, the more its true nature would slip through their fingers. In any event, he was widely recognised as being exhaustively informed. One didn't get houses and psychiatric practices on different continents, and open cheques from movie actors, for being anything less. But he was yet to be fully convinced that the 'selfish gene' is God the creator and the only answer to our prayers.

Nothing, however, was allowed to muddy Dr. Deshpande's thinking or interfere with his process. In its execution, psychoanalysis is not an exact science, but nevertheless, like a good scientist, Dr. Deshpande was always prepared to go where the information took him, not where he thought it ought to go. Nor did he waste the money of his clients on endless pleasantries and casual chat. So now there was the briefest exchange of names and courtesies, then: "You know, of course, what we are here to talk about? Why I asked to talk to you?"

Charlie nodded. "Mrs. Vane Tempest is worried about her son – Tempest min … Christopher … Joey…"

"Let's call him Christopher," suggested Dr. Deshpande. "And do you think she's right to be worried?

Charlie was still nurturing rather churlish feelings about Mrs. Vane Tempest, and since this was a psychiatrist he was talking to, and not a parent who had to be treated with diplomacy, he saw no particular reason to hide them. "Maybe if she'd been more concerned at some point, she'd have ended up less worried in the long run."

Dr. Deshpande betrayed not so much as a flicker. "And do you think she has the need to be worried at this point? However she got to it?"

Charlie said something to the effect that he'd probably, in psychological terms, be more worried about Blake than Christopher. And about his influence on Christopher.

"Undoubtedly a factor," said Dr. Deshpande. "But let's just stick to Christopher - and you - for the moment. What do you think about him? In general. Just give me your impression. As a starting point."

"I don't teach Christopher," Charlie pointed out, "so my impressions of him are only what I've been able to form outside the classroom. You realise that?"

Dr. Deshpande nodded. "But would you say that you've had more chances to form these impressions than one would have expected?"

Charlie wasn't sure what he was getting at. "I'm not sure what you're getting at," he said.

"Well, would you say that you have more to do with Christopher than you do with any other boy his age who doesn't feature in your lessons? Could we say that that was true?"

"Probably."

"And, if it is true, then why do you think it is?"

Charlie felt a little as if he were being interviewed by a lawyer. "He seems to think he knows me from somewhere," he said. "I think that has something to do with it."

"And where would he know you from?"

Charlie shook his head. "I don't know. *He* doesn't know. Except just before he had his blackout he said he'd remembered …"

"Now that is extremely interesting, don't you think? He finally remembers where you met before and then he blacks out." Dr. Deshpande watched Charlie with the unrevealing regard of the practised psychiatrist. "Remembering and then blacking out, as you put it," he mused finally. "An unfortunate juxtaposition of events, wouldn't you say?"

That was undeniable. Charlie started to feel uncomfortable. He wanted to explain that his impression of Tempest min's remembering was that it had been tearful but not tragic, though

244

as he had been in tears himself at the time he wasn't confident in stating this as absolute fact. And before he could find quite the right words to state it at all, Dr. Deshpande moved on: "So let's go back to these meetings you keep having with him outside of the classroom. How do these happen?"

Charlie shook his head. "He just keeps popping up."

"*He* pops up? *You* don't pop up?"

Charlie felt that Dr. Deshpande had somehow given a curious and rather disconcerting tweak to the expression 'pop up'. It suddenly sounded less than wholesome. "*He* pops up," he said evenly.

"And can you account more fully for this 'popping up'?"

Charlie cast his mind back. "Well, he wandered into the library one evening complaining about bad dreams, he came to show me his bandaged wrist once on the side of the football field and …"

The psychiatrist interrupted him. "That isn't really accounting for it, is it? It's just describing it. Why, for instance, would he conceivably put you and bad dreams and injured wrists together?"

Charlie thought this was an odd way to phrase things, but before he could formulate an answer, Dr. Deshpande swept on: "It would, in fact, be accurate to say that his development of injuries and ailments and bad dreams seems to have accelerated considerably since you arrived at the school … And, in addition, there is the fact that he has stopped humming. Which was, apparently, a fairly consistent habit of his. And entrenched habits do not normally stop, just like that. Now, if one were asked about humming in the abstract sense, one would say, just off the top

245

of one's head you know, that people who hum are happy. And, if they suddenly begin to hum less, then it's because they are less happy. Wouldn't you agree?"

Charlie gave these questions some prolonged consideration, and he didn't terribly like what he was being forced to consider: the fact that he was doing some carefully unspecified *something* that was making Tempest min significantly less happy and healthy than he had previously been.

"You know," he said finally, "the interview I had for this job seemed extremely strange to me. It was a very curious grilling of the type I'd never had before. In retrospect, it's maybe made me a little - let's just call it aware - in a way I would never have particularly thought of being. And it's not a nice sort of awareness, though I realise that it has its origins in concern and unfortunate necessity."

Dr. Deshpande raised his eyebrows. "So you weren't ... *aware* ... before the interview?"

"When I got my last job," Charlie spoke as levelly as he could manage, "about which I'm sure you already know everything in your very thorough way, the boss said to me: 'Be nice to the kiddies and don't hit on the mothers'. That might sound an odd and very unsophisticated instruction to someone like you. Just two men with long hair and guitars doing things half-assed as usual, but, you know, it pretty much accorded with my view of how the world worked. Indeed, it was more than that. It was how the world *should* work. You're nice to children and you don't try and hit on their mothers. It's not a bad way to view things, is it? Reductionist but oddly normal. And the fact is, although I realise now that we were probably well behind the curve on this, it never occurred to either me, or my boss, that the instruction could conceivably be phrased *the other way around*! But I understand, of course, that during my interview for this place, Dr. Carlyle was only doing what he had to do to in order, as he put it, to read between my lines. He wanted to know if I was fit to be let loose amongst children in a boarding school. So now, unfortunately, I think I recognise this particularly unpleasant ballpark that I'm taking yet another turn in. So let me make myself clear as regards my associations with Tempest min: in all of our meetings it is *he* who has sought me out. I have been both affable with him and faintly irritable with him, according to the situation, but I have never sought *him* out. *For any purpose whatsoever.* And our meetings have had no sinister side *whatsoever.* I won't deny however that, as children go. I find him oddly likeable. The word is *likeable*, Doctor whatever-your-name-is. And I sincerely hope that that isn't against any odd Freudian concepts that I may yet be … *unaware of.* I hope we haven't got to the point where a man can no longer say: 'Yes, I like this child,' without there being some subtext fit to make everyone's hair stand on end."

There was a long silence then, during which the psychiatrist merely stared thoughtfully at him.

Boy, thought Charlie, this guy must be one hell of a poker player.

"So you feel an affinity with Christopher?" Dr. Deshpande asked eventually.

"Yes," agreed Charlie, "I probably do. And so, I think, does Dr. Carlyle."

"I would say that Dr. Carlyle is an exceptional man. He seems to manage an affinity with everyone," Dr. Deshpande remarked.

"Yes, he does," said Charlie. And then he sat back and thought: I'm going to let this guy paddle this canoe on his own.

"I'd like to talk more about this affinity," said the psychiatrist.

"Go on then," said Charlie.

"Correction. I'd like *you* to talk more about this affinity."

"I think the reason one uses the word affinity," said Charlie, "is that the feeling isn't any more accurately definable."

"Let's start this again," said Dr. Deshpande, with a sudden sigh. "The world has, unfortunately, as you have chosen to point out, conspired to make us all suspicious. It's not nice. It's very far from nice and, if there ever was a real age of innocence, I must say I would have infinitely preferred living in it. However … I am trying to help this child. And I am asking you to help me, help this child. A person, especially a child, cannot be understood in isolation. The people near to him have to be taken into consideration."

Charlie sighed. Angry and insulted and, yes, hurt as he felt, he still wanted to help but he didn't see that he could provide anything that hadn't been adequately provided by other people. "I wouldn't say that I was exactly near to him," he began.

"And yet the child speaks as if you are," said Dr. Deshpande. "This is the problem we have, you see. According to his mother, he mentions you a lot more than he does any of his other teachers which, considering that you don't actually teach him, has to be a little surprising. Now, in spite of the fact that he seems to have undergone some sort of deterioration since you came here, he talks about you as if you were his special friend. I'm just trying to get to the bottom of this. Things sometimes start out as so called special friends and then … it's a process. Obviously you've already got it, so I don't have to spell it out for you, do I? But you must understand my position. Like Dr. Carlyle, I can't skate over this."

"But then, Dr. Carlyle is a man of charm and humour," pointed out Charlie. "Which makes it all seem a lot less offensive."

"Help me," said the psychiatrist. "As I said, I can't avoid that I've had to offend you. And may do again. Believe me, I've offended a few other people here too. But I have a feeling that your help may be the help I particularly need. Something is buried – well, only half buried really, in Christopher Vane Tempest's psyche. Something significant enough to be, perhaps, affecting his physical health. And you may be the key, if the unwitting key, to the process of unlocking it. Help me. Please."

"Fine," said Charlie. "I'll tell you, as best I can, every word and every thing in every situation that I have shared with Tempest min - Christopher - and you can make the deductions for yourself. Is that any good?"

"Let's see," suggested Dr. Deshpande.

"Then let me begin by telling you about the first time I met him."

"In Dr. Carlyle's study, at the start of your interview?"

This man had certainly done his homework. "The second time I met him, then," said Charlie. "In the entrance hall of this building. Just as I was leaving the interview - roughly two hours later. There was only the two of us there at first, though his brother Blake arrived within a couple of minutes or so. Christopher was sitting on the bottom step of the staircase. *He*

249

spoke first. And these were his exact words …"

A few sentences later, Dr. Deshpande held up a hand. "Wait! So there was a black car, definitely black, you say, a Range Rover. And there was a man you obviously weren't in a position to recognise loading luggage into the car, and Blake, having first been a little obnoxious, grabbed Christopher and led him towards this car. And then Christopher shook him off, and ran back to you, and took your hand and said: 'You have to come here'?"

"Have to come here, need to come here, I forget which. It could have been both. He was most emphatic."

"I'd like to call Dr. Carlyle," said Dr. Deshpande, taking a mobile from a smart leather briefcase. "To ask if it's possible to have your next lesson covered while we get to the end of this. Would that be acceptable to you?"

"It's up to Dr. Carlyle."

"Plus, I'd like to record everything you say from this point on. Have you any objections to that?"

Charlie shook his head.

*****

Dr. Carlyle caught up with Charlie at lunchtime. "Nice chat?"

"It started civilly enough," said Charlie, "went badly off the rails after that, and ended in something you could call a heavy silence. I really didn't enjoy it. Which is unfortunate, because it seems that we might have to do it again. Dr. Deshpande is processing. I dread to think how that will go. Goodness knows what he will be implying next time we meet."

"Well, this *is* voluntary," said Dr. Carlyle. "We are doing it in

250

the spirit of trying to help. And psychiatrists are always a bit like dogs - worrying away at the bones of a thing, trying to get to the marrow. Unfortunately, they are a lot less interactive than dogs. If they'd lay back their ears occasionally, or wag their tails, we'd all know where we were. Matron came out of her little chat with him looking positively explosive. She said he'd just looked at her as if he didn't believe a word she was saying, and then started asking about her own past – as if that had some bearing on the case. I don't think she's up for a rematch. You must be more tolerant than she." He paused for a moment. "Indispensable of course, Matron. Indispensable to a place like this. She keeps us grounded. Earthed. She's the lightning conductor."

Charlie wasn't in the mood to plumb the metaphorical depths of lightning conductors. "There were some pretty unpleasant implications to deal with," he said irritably. "The fact that none of them are remotely true doesn't, somehow, take as much edge off their impact as you would imagine."

"This is the modern world, Charlie," said Dr. Carlyle sadly. "One long, explicitly and endlessly broadcast reminder that human nature is very far from what we would like it to be. It's a continual sadness to us all. We are allowed no blinkers now, no rose coloured spectacles. We have to face the rawness of everything. We are expected, indeed forced, to be continually aware. And those of us in positions of responsibility have to be exceptionally aware. An awareness that can result in the saving of some, but which can also take on the unpleasant and unwarranted suspicions of the permanent witch hunt. Whichever way we go at these things, somebody innocent can suffer. I don't believe in the devil as such, Charlie, but this devil that doesn't exist, however we try to outwit him, he gets his work done just the same."

Then he slapped Charlie suddenly on the back. "But not here, young man, not at Puckrup. We might look as if we just live lives of helpless whimsy, but we are rewarded with moments of grace. And in a moment of grace, we get a sudden, swift aerial view. A glimpse of the bigger picture. And then we see. We get it. Oh yes, Charlie, I am quite sure that Dr. Deshpande is working solidly towards a moment of grace."

Chapter Thirteen

Rory was not much involved in the goings-on surrounding Tempest min. He'd had a ten minute exchange with Dr. Deshpande in which he'd recounted his contretemps with Blake Vane Tempest at the Halloween dance, but other than that he was not viewed as having a significant impact on the Vane Tempest brothers. A state of affairs which he had no cause to regret. He was happy to be able to focus on his own situation which, almost the minute he'd resolved to shrug away the pain of it, had undergone, a shade perversely one might think, a remarkable transformation.

"You were right!"

Charlie, waiting with some dread for his Dr. Deshpande recall, was glad to have his attention claimed in such a promising fashion. Now at the point where he was consciously avoiding Tempest min as he went about the school, he was desperately hoping that the boy was not in any way aware of this. The very last thing he wanted to do was add upset to upset. Also, he couldn't completely rid himself of the feeling that what had passed between them had been somehow sullied. Their oddly timed meetings, their sometimes bizarre conversations and Tempest min's strange attachment to him now carried a taint. He hoped it would fade. He did not share Dr. Carlyle's faith that it would be dramatically expunged by some moment of illumination but he desperately wanted to feel at ease again. He desperately wanted to feel at ease with Tempest min again. Plus, if he was never going to feel at ease here, then where was there for him?

"I was right?" he asked Rory, hopefully. "What about?"

"That smart ass university lecturer."

"Really?"

"I could kill him," said Rory, with a sudden flash of temper. "She was crying. In the corridor. Christina, almost sobbing. I could enjoy killing him."

"Well let's hold off on that," suggested Charlie. "Let's not go to jail for the man."

A Saturday shopping trip to Gloucester Quays, followed by an impromptu visit to the lecturer's flat, had proved Charlie's theory – the lecturer was exactly the sort who couldn't resist screwing his students. Christina had caught him with his pants down. Had this been all, it would have been terminal but not totally insulting. He'd had, however, more things to say than just 'sorry'. In fact 'sorry' was the one thing he didn't say. He was not, he'd explained, to blame. It was a proven fact that men who work continually with young beautiful girls become less capable of being sexually attracted to older women. They have no control over this. Men naturally go for women who have a lot of sexually active, childbearing years ahead of them. Evolutionary psychology had shown this to be so. And there was, apparently, no way to buck the programming. He'd tried, he'd told Christina, because she was an interesting woman. She had conversation on a par with his own. It wasn't enough. He just wasn't able to keep it up for her. What, exactly, he hadn't been able to keep up had not been reported in depth. And, in addition to being hurt by the incidental insults, Christina was stricken that someone who'd talked so loftily about the importance of art to the human spirit, about how artists could bring to the world transcendent insights into the true essence of things ... how this same person could then invoke biological programming in order to explain his inability to stop indulging in the reproductive act with any female whose ovaries were coming nicely to the boil ... well ... It was just ... well ...

"And she told you all of this?" Charlie was incredulous.

"How else could I know it?" Rory's summary had been in rather more forthright language. "But I've given you the joined up version. I got it in dribs and drabs. In my cubbyhole. I took her in there for privacy. Nobody comes uninvited to my cubbyhole."

"Your *cubbyhole*?"

"My tool cupboard. Where I have my private tools. It's quite big. Not a hole at all, in fact." Rory was reassuring. It was an extremely attractive and remarkably spacious storeroom. With a big skylight. And nicely swept. Everything tidy on hooks. Interesting pieces of wood waiting to be carved (all of them released now, by the blessing of blood, from uncertain futures and sap leakage). A few pieces of found art and a very special workbench he'd made from oak. Chisels and planes all in lovely lines, and a comforting smell about the place. Like being in a pine forest on a hot day. A fine place in which to restore the will to life.

"Not like our kitchen, then," said Charlie, who'd never been invited into the cubbyhole - but probably just in the way that it had never struck him that Rory might want to pay a visit to the reagent cupboard in the chemistry lab.

"Kitchens aren't at all the same," said Rory indignantly. "They don't give me the same urge to hang things on hooks in descending order of size. That's for chefs. People who get really worked up about cooking."

Charlie thought of the neat, satisfying line-up of guitar pedals he used to have. The coils of carefully labelled leads. The way he'd lovingly wiped fingerprints off his mixing desk. Yep. He got it. In fact, Rory had been doing more than taking Christina into the most secluded space he had to offer. He'd been showing her his beating heart.

"And did she appreciate your cupboard?" he asked.

"I gave her a mug of tea," said Rory. "In a china mug. I ran and got it and an Earl Grey tea bag from the staff room."

"That would help, I guess."

There was a pause then, during which Rory raked anxious fingers through his hair, setting it alarmingly on end. Watching him, Charlie found it hard to imagine how he had actually coped with having the woman of his dreams sobbing in his inner sanctum.

"So how did you respond to all of this? Apart from making her a mug of tea?"

"I told her the lecturer was mad," said Rory with feeling. "To have a beautiful woman like her and then go cheating with some student. The man might fancy himself an artist, but in fact he had no discernment at all. He had a classic work of art and threw it away for a string of beads."

"You said that?"

"I did. It's what I was thinking. It was pretty much all I was thinking, so it's what I said. Do you think it was wrong?"

"Not at all," said Charlie. "It could have been bordering on brilliant."

But Rory was still plagued by some anxiety. He wondered if Christina would be uncomfortable the next time they met. If heartfelt outpourings would be subsequently regretted. Certainly, she must never find out that he'd talked about it. But he needed advice ... Was it possible that she might now start avoiding him out of embarrassment? Charlie thought it *was* possible. The situation certainly had the potential to get awkward. They looked gloomily at each other.

"And I said some other stuff ..." Rory confessed after a minute or two. "I dunno what came over me."

"You went ahead and spoiled it, did you?"

"I said she needed a man who would really appreciate her. A man who would realise what he had. A man who would never look elsewhere because there was no elsewhere for him." Rory suddenly looked very self-conscious.

"Go on."

"I said she needed me."

"Jeez, that was brave."

"Could that be the same as disastrous?"

"How did she react?"

"She smiled. A bit. Between tears, y'know. But she didn't say anything. Mebbes she won't even remember." He looked hopeful.

"Fat chance," said Charlie.

*****

Dr. Deshpande had taken himself off back to London. No doubt there were things to attend to in Harley Street. It was early February and snowdrops were blooming in places other than the windowsill of the Drovers Arms. Charlie could see sheets of them under the trees at the edge of the sports field. It was a Saturday morning. He'd given two chemistry lessons and had a tutorial to give later to a Cambridge candidate. He was staring at his usual bench thinking over the times he'd been caught there by Tempest min, and it was having the effect of making him not want to be in the area. A sickening feeling lay heavy in his chest, wavering in intensity, impossible to shake off, impossible to talk about. Even to Rory. The trembly terrier watched him sympathetically. *Is it better sitting? Would a walk help? The cat might show up. There's a brightener. Think about that …* He put a paw on Charlie's knee and gave a concerned whine. Then suddenly he stopped studying Charlie and looked intently in the direction of the walled garden. Within a few seconds Ianthe Keeble Parker appeared, stepping carefully, faun-like, through the trees with a bunch of snowdrops in one hand. She was wearing a longish, loose, brown velvet coat that caught now and then on low hanging branches and springy saplings. It was almost as if they were reaching for it. Her beautiful hair, loose and swinging, caught the few rays of the low February sun as she disentangled herself, smiling and laughing. When she cleared the trees, she walked steadily towards Charlie. When she got to him, she handed over the snowdrops.

"In the language of flowers," she said, "they represent hope and consolation. I can see that you feel in need of both."

"A little," admitted Charlie. "Thank you."

"Dr. Deshpande is a very clever man. He'll come to the right conclusion. Eventually."

"You've got involved in it?" Charlie's heart sank.

"Inevitably. After all, I was the only person who'd been much privy to any of your meetings with Tempest min. He needed to talk to me."

Charlie looked away. He knew that Dr. Deshpande would not have revealed anything of the details of his own interview with him, but somehow it seemed as if she knew. Realised and understood just exactly how unpleasant it had been for him. And still was.

"He obviously thinks that you and Tempest min are connected in some way," she said. "He just hasn't worked out how, as yet. But he will. Try not to be upset about it. Come and see the snowdrops growing. There are thousands of them. They look so wonderful." She held out a hand. Charlie looked at it. His heart should have leapt but, instead, he felt as if the sullying of his relationship with Tempest min had now extended to his association with Ianthe. It was agonising. "There is no connection between me and Tempest min," he said. "I don't see what he can possibly work out."

"I told you before that people come here for a reason," said Ianthe, gentle reproach in her voice. "Have a little faith, Charlie. Come and walk with me amongst the trees. It'll do you good."

She reached across and took his hand. "I insist. And when I insist, I always get my way. Out here, all the gods that matter are on my side. Come …"

Charlie followed her obediently. On a narrowly trodden track through the stretch of woodland that surrounded the playing fields, they paused to look at the snowdrops. Though last year's leaves still lay brown amongst the green of the bulb foliage and the moonlight gleam of the flowers, it was evident that spring was in the ascendency. Palpable life enlivened the wood. The birds were already busy choosing mates, establishing territory. A robin flew to a nearby branch and struck up a song, its little throat swelling and trembling with effort as if it were performing to perfection, just for them. And then it cocked its head, black-eyed and sharp.

"There is more going on out here then you can possibly imagine." Ianthe looked up into the treetops.

"Fairies?" suggested Charlie. He suddenly felt a smile coming on. The warmth of her hand was bringing him back to life. "Gnomes? Boggarts?"

"Let's just call them elementals," she said. "Thomas Hardy - Far from the Madding Crowd I think it was - chose a more classical word and referred to them as 'Dryads' which, he supposed, woke up for what he called the vernal quarter and set off 'bustlings, strainings, united thrusts and pulls-all-together, in comparison with which the powerful tugs of cranes and pulleys in a noisy city are but pygmy efforts'." She looked at Charlie. "Lovely imagery, isn't it? It's always stuck in my mind. I like Hardy." She broke off for a thoughtful moment. "Which is just as well because Grandmama made me read him. And not just for his wonderful understanding of the countryside, I suspect. He deals in a lot of heartbreaking comeuppance which is visited upon women who allow themselves to be romantically misled."

Unsure whether the last remark was meant to apply to Ianthe's unfortunate mother, or be taken as a warning for Ianthe herself, Charlie thought he'd sidestep that feature of the conversation. "And these Dryads are supposed to be actual creatures, are they?" he asked.

"They are part of the spiritual body of nature - its energetic framework, if you prefer." Ianthe looked into the treetops again. "A framework of infinite plurality, unimaginable multiformity." She smiled then, a shade mischievously - partly at Charlie and partly at the trembly terrier who, in spite of not having been explicitly invited, was nevertheless seated by them on a piece of sun-warmed stone no bigger than a tea plate, while he listened with shivering concentration, elf-like ears spread wide. "The elementals," Ianthe gestured round them, "are not what is normally implied when we talk about the 'forces of nature', but they are here just the same – in the growing of the trees and the flowering of the flowers and eventually the setting of seed and the swelling of fruit. Vital forces hard at work - dedicated purveyors of the eternal spark, the stuff of life, the very life of life …"

Charlie shook his head. Did all of this seem so attractive - and sane - simply because it was being delivered by somebody so beautiful? "It's an oddly compelling viewpoint," he conceded. "And yet …" He stopped. It was almost as if the entire wood, that primeval place with its druidic mistletoe and ancient yews, had gone silent, pausing on a concerted intake of breath, daring him to deny it. There was something supernatural about the silence, as if all around them lay everything there is to be known, everything there is to be understood, just waiting for the right moment to explain itself. The trembly terrier had even stopped trembling.

"It was Sartre," Ianthe said finally, "who stated that, in emotion, consciousness is degraded and turns the determined world into a magical world. But he also acknowledged that there is a reciprocity - that the world sometimes reveals itself to consciousness as magical. We do not only impose magic upon the world as our emotional frame of mind dictates, but an irruption of magic may come from the world because there is an existential structure to the world that is magical. And when you're out here, involved with it all the time, working with it, working *for* it in fact ..." she studied him silently for a moment or two, "... then it eventually shows itself to you." She paused again. "It's never a good thing to close off our personal connection to the feeling of magic, Charlie," she finished finally. "The inner landscape gets a bit grim then. Our souls, our psyches if you prefer, grope around in the dark getting pinched and thin."

Charlie said nothing. He didn't know anything about Sartre and he knew even less about this noumenal world that apparently lay all around them. But he didn't want to dispute anything, ridicule anything, even discuss anything. He just wanted to be with her. So she saw stuff in trees. And maybe she did. All he knew was that she had the power to lift the gloom off him with just one smile. And having her stand beside him felt like exoneration.

"Don't let this stage in the proceedings get you down," she

squeezed his hand. "People don't come to Puckrup to be made miserable. They come to have the cobwebs swept out. To get a rebore. To get reconnected to the magic of life through whichever conduit it is that works for them. It hurts a little now and then. That's all."

Charlie looked down at her. He couldn't believe the easy way she had at once shrugged off Dr. Deshpande's psychological rummagings. Relegated his critical scrutiny of everybody's unmentionables to the pragmatic purlieu of the process. He'd tried himself, of course, to get things in logical focus. He just hadn't been able to get the perspective. Hadn't been able to feel right about it all. Until now. Until the whole unpleasant situation had been cleansed by her smile. He wondered if Dr. Deshpande had met the Queen of Elfland, or had dealt with the Ianthe Keeble Parker who wore work boots and drove a tractor.

"And did you tell Dr. Deshpande about the magic?" he asked. "About the purveyors of the eternal spark? Did you quote Sartre at him?"

Ianthe laughed. "I told Dr. Deshpande about you," she said. "And about the dear little boy he is trying to help. What he needs to know about the eternal will come to him as and when he's ready."

"You are incredible," said Charlie shaking his head. It was a statement that held space for interpretation. Ianthe responded in kind.

"And I," she said, "find you incomparably grounding."

"Is that a compliment? Or is grounding another word for boring?"

"It was said in some appreciation." She squeezed his hand.

Choosing not to push that point just at the moment, Charlie said, "At Christmas, you told me to look after Tempest min. That it was important. What exactly did you mean?"

"That it was important."

"Yes, but what were you getting at?"

"It was just a feeling," she said lightly. "Something I picked up from the pair of you. But I have to go now." She smiled. "Put the snowdrops in water. Don't forget about them. Give them a chance to live a little. No need to brass the fairies off completely." And she stood on tiptoe and kissed him on the cheek.

Charlie couldn't believe just how effectively she'd made his heart feel better.

*****

"She gave me flowers," he said, putting them on the windowsill arranged in a mug with 'Are We Having Fun Yet?' written on it.

"Could you live with somebody like that?" asked Rory. "Like Ianthe?"

"I live with you and you believe in fairies," Charlie pointed out.

"It's different," said Rory. "You know it is. You know *she* is. Uncle Robbie left Aunt Bertha. Couldn't abide the idea of dead people being summoned in the sitting room."

If Rory McEwan had a mother and obviously, at one point at least, he had, she was never mentioned. Maybe, like Charlie's rock career, she'd been too brief an interlude and become too painful a topic. Great Aunt Bertha as spiritualist and seer was the only female who, for better or worse, seemed to haunt Rory's past. She was, at any rate, the only one he ever spoke of.

"I had a conversation with Eric Boswell about love," Charlie said after a moment or two.

"Get away," said Rory. "Dr. Boswell? When did he get to be an expert?"

"He's a great intellectualiser," said Charlie. "Writes papers on Chaucer mixed up with Plato. And his ideas aren't really a million miles from what you just said. To fall in love with somebody is wonderful, exhilarating. It's romance. The stuff of fantasy. But to live with them, even to have a relationship with them, is quite another matter. Consummation can spell catastrophe."

"Well," said Rory, suddenly phlegmatic. "I'm ready to take my chance - if I'm lucky enough to have it come along. I don't want to be a lonely old man reading Chaucer. I haven't got the brains for it." He shook his head. Rory McEwan just lacked the vanity that makes men want to be smart. "And I'd like a family," he added, watching Charlie take the snowdrops back out of the mug and put them in one with a chicken on the side. "A family like you read about in old-fashioned children's books. Where the parents take the children to the sea for the day and everybody has a lovely time in the sand and the rock pools. I used to long for that when I was little. Somebody who'd take me to Bamburgh beach or Beadnell. And mebbes out to Holy Island. I want a 'Let's take the children to Holy Island sort of family'." He paused for a moment. "I know it sounds corny but, y'know, I'd really like that kind of corny in my life. Wouldn't you?"

"I suppose I kind of had it," said Charlie. "We used to go to Madame Tussauds and the London Dungeon and Windsor Safari Park. I never felt any lack, so I guess I've never focused on family as an ambition." He stood back. "Better in the chicken mug, do you think? The snowdrops?"

"Aye. That's a classier mug altogether." Rory gave something that could have been a derisory snort.

"Well, we haven't got a vase," said Charlie. "But thinking of classy, it's frankly amazing that Christina hasn't, in fact, started to avoid you out of embarrassment. You must be a whole lot better at the emotional ministrations stuff than you've been giving yourself credit for."

"Not really." Rory shook his head. "And, of course, I've never said the 'you need me' thing again. Or tried to make any capital out of something that could be a rebound situation. We've ended up together in the staffroom a few times for coffee, and I found her a nice piece of wood for a plinth for one of her students' pieces. We're … we're …" He gave the matter some consideration, "… amicable."

"And that's quite an accomplishment," said Charlie, "considering. Maybe she's starting to get the 'decent bloke' aspect of you. Coming to appreciate the charm of the ingenuous. The lack of exploitative tendencies. In years to come, a woman could take a trip to Holy Island with a man like that."

Rory gave a huge grin. "You think?"

"I do." But Christina? With Rory?

"Yet you're not looking to take a trip to Holy Island yourself?" Charlie didn't answer.

"I'm not slick," said Rory. "Or clever. Or any sort of hot catch to get into bed with - but if I was you, I'd be thinking seriously about exactly what it was I wanted from a woman like Ianthe before I accepted any more flowers. If it's not anything that could lead to a trip to Holy Island, then what is it?"

Chapter Fourteen

Dr. Deshpande was looking enigmatic. Or was it conspiratorial? Either way it seemed to Charlie to be an improvement. Maybe the trip to London had borne some fruit. He sat down in the chair. Dr. Deshpande remained silent. Still an improvement. Charlie glanced at the daffodils in the china foot bath on the hearth. The buds were opening. Didn't these things need light?

"Genetics," said Dr. Deshpande.

Was he referring to the daffodils? Were they a variety specially bred to flower in the crepuscular gloom of old fireplaces?

"Let's not beat about the bush," Dr. Deshpande went on. "Modern science has, after all, made this an easier one to resolve. Could you be Christopher's father?"

Charlie didn't feel as shocked as he might have done. There had been overtones of this sort in some of Matron's remarks. *'Are you sure you're not acquainted with Mrs. Vane Tempest at all?'* So … had he ranked amongst Mrs. Vane Tempest's boyfriends/lovers in such a way that Tempest min would have been sufficiently aware of him to remember? Absolutely not.

Had he ranked as a one night stand around the time of Tempest min's conception? No. Quite apart from anything else, Mrs. Vane Tempest sounded pretty memorable.

"Christopher was conceived in Australia," he said finally. "We discussed this in the 'I will tell you every word' part of our last interview."

"The human gestation period," said Dr. Deshpande, "is not exactly a NASA countdown. And Mrs. Vane Tempest has a flair for the impromptu coupled with a distinct lack of inclination for digging in old ground. Possibly because there is so much of it. She appears to have a dazzlingly commodious love life. And I assure you that she would have no problem with my stating this - should it become a salience. Which it now does." At this point he looked hard at Charlie before going on. "After Australia, Mrs. Vane Tempest was in London for a while … So you see, there is not only room for manoeuvre in the date of Christopher's conception, but in both the nationality and the identity of his father." He paused here for a moment to glance out of the window before adding, "On which subjects Mrs. Vane Tempest herself remains stubbornly incurious. But yes … I would have to say that there is room for manoeuvre."

"I'm a belt and braces man," interrupted Charlie. "Always have been. Never liked leaving things room to manoeuvre."

"Thoroughly admirable, I'm sure," Dr. Deshpande nodded. "But, 'the best laid schemes o' mice and men gang aft agley' as my prep school English master was prone to say. He was an expat Scot. A veritable claymore of a man and quite a challenging linguistic hurdle for small Indian boys. Not that any school without one or two spectacular eccentrics is worth attending, of course. But that's by the by. I'm sure you take my point. Condoms fail, pills and diaphragms get treated with unconsciously motivated carelessness, and the female physiology can take a very dismissive approach indeed to the rhythm method. In other words, the need of a species to reproduce itself will triumph in the face of any and all obstacles. Unless you're a giant panda, of course … Pity that," he finished, musingly. "Such appealing creatures."

Charlie sighed. Dr. Carlyle was right. Talk about a dog with a bone. "Give me some dates," he said finally. "To stimulate the recall." It was easier to submit than to protest.

"Or we could just have a DNA test," suggested Dr. Deshpande brightly. "In case your memory, like Mrs. Vane Tempest's, isn't quite the well-oiled machine I would like it to be."

Charlie was silent for a few moments and then he asked, "Why have you come to this particular conclusion?"

"It's not a conclusion," said Dr. Deshpande. "It's a ruling out. Or a ruling in. And one thing we can't rule out at this point is genetic recognition. People who don't actually know that they are related can nevertheless feel what we referred to last time as an 'affinity' for one another. Sometimes with unfortunate sequelae."

"Like psychosomatic symptoms of illness?"

"Actually," said Dr. Deshpande, "I was thinking more of brothers having sexual relationships with half-sisters and fathers having sexual relationships with daughters. Unbeknown, that is. But there are a surprising number of unbeknowns circulating in this modern world, and if the unbeknowns somehow become knowns – well, then everybody comes to see me in a high old state of distress."

"My unbeknown doesn't run along those lines," said Charlie warningly.

"I was in no way implying that it did. I have ruled that one out. Definitively. I was just illustrating the reality that is genetic recognition. So now …" Dr. Deshpande produced a slim plastic tube from his briefcase and with a deft unscrewing motion withdrew from it a buccal swab, "… if you would just open your mouth, please."

It was a Sunday teatime and Dr. Deshpande was intending to travel back to London, hand-carrying the swab to the laboratory he routinely dealt with. "Seventy-two hours tops," he said to Charlie. "And we'll know."

"I already know," said Charlie.

*****

He went down to the dining room then, to supervise the boys eating salad and cold cuts, and afterwards he went across to Hereford House for Blake Vane Tempest's guitar lesson. It was the fourth one and something typifying Blake's reputation was probably due. The boy was not being in any way cooperative. If music had anything of a real emotional hold on him, it still lacked the power to overcome everything else he had to wrestle with. Charlie watched, half sympathetic, half despairing as the boy fluffed the chords, and then readjusted his T- shirt and fiddled with his hair and fluffed the chords again. It was like watching a highly strung tennis player preparing industriously to serve and repeatedly slamming every ball into the net. Blake's eyes were starting to develop a dangerous glint - part tears, part temper. The Gibson could end up on the floor.

"Do you want to talk about it?" Charlie asked finally. "There's nothing well served by just losing your temper with the whole business. I'm happy to listen if you need to do a bit of venting about something."

No reply.

Charlie studied him for a few moments. "Just routine stuff, eh?"

Still no reply.

"Miss O'Grady's 'stop-breathe-be' mindfulness sessions not working for you? Dr. Deshpande not got you on his list?"

Blake Vane Tempest made an impatient sound. Probably the boy just refused to try them, Charlie thought. Either of them. He was put in mind, once again, of his younger self. The intensity, the overwhelming but sometimes purblind desire, the tendency to give way to black moods … And he hadn't even had to carry the same family baggage. His parents having been pretty stalwart, he'd had nobody's baggage to carry but his own. Yet that hadn't meant that everything had come easily to him. Sometimes, his greatest problem had been himself.

"When I was fifteen," he said, after an unproductive silence that Blake was obviously not intending to fill, "I travelled right across London to have a guitar lesson with someone who shall remain nameless, but who gave guitar workshops and also individual lessons if you paid him enough. I'd run errands for my older brothers and saved bits of money for months to have one of these private lessons and when I finally got to it I played like shit. I'd missed the tube I should have caught, and on top of that

I was so full of hope and excitement that I just fell apart. I can't, now, remember anything I was told except something along the lines of 'don't give up the day job'."

A flicker of something faintly encouraging passed over Blake Vane Tempest's face, so Charlie went on. "Coming back on the tube, I was still pretty much in tears. Absolutely gutted, you would say. It was getting on for the peak of rush hour and I was squeezed up against an old man I'd barely registered, but suddenly he tapped on my guitar case and said, 'It didn't go so well?' It was obvious from his accent that he wasn't English, plus he was dressed in a stiff black suit and odd felt hat as if he'd been to a funeral. He could have been Russian or something – eastern European at any rate. Frankly, I didn't feel up to the effort of talking to some old boy who had such a heavy accent, but my parents had brought me up to be polite – they'd also warned me not to talk to strangers, but you can't do both of these things at the same time - and so I said, yes, it hadn't gone so well at all. Bloody disastrously, in fact. And then the old man told me that he played the violin and that he had been taught by one of the greatest violin players of all time – not because he'd had the money to pay him, or because he'd drawn his attention through some spectacularly precocious talent, but because his mother had been the great man's maid and his father the great man's gardener. The lessons were sort of a perk - probably an alternative to paying higher wages. I can't honestly say I betrayed a whole lot of interest in this, I was still too upset, but nevertheless, the old man went on to tell me that the most important thing that the great violinist had ever taught him was that playing an instrument begins in the mind. And because it can be hard to consciously put aside the cares and woes of the day and get your concentration in line, you have to do it through a process."

"A process? What process?"

"Well, the great violinist always practised in the same room, standing on the same spot. He always wore the same colour shirt. He always sat in the same chair for a minute or two beforehand and smoked a fresh cigarette - five puffs exactly - before standing up and going across to the violin. It was a ritual, and it spoke to his mind in some way that meant the mental gears began to click into place. The muse, as he called it, would then come upon him without any conscious struggle. But the old man on the train, well he didn't have a special room, or a room of his own at all in fact, so he found a special mat. It had been his grandmother's prayer mat. Just a little thing it was, that he kept rolled up and clean in his drawer. And every day he ran home from the village after his few hours of schooling, washed his hands and face, put on a clean white shirt that his mother ironed specially for him, unrolled his grandmother's prayer mat and stepped onto it with the violin. 'Now we play,' he used to say. 'Now we play'. Of course, I looked at the old man as if he were mad. But he just smiled and nodded. And then the tube pulled into a station and he stood up to get off. But just before he did he put one hand on my shoulder and said, 'I can't tell you how these things work, baba. I'm not a psychologist. But I *am* a great violinist.'"

"I don't believe a word of that," said Blake Vane Tempest. "You've just made it up."

"You may choose not to believe me," said Charlie. "But I *am* a great guitarist. So think about it. Now, should we try again?"

It wasn't a spectacularly successful lesson but maybe, just maybe, something had taken. Charlie was leaving, hand on the doorknob, when Blake asked, "Did you never want to do the music for a living? Have a band? I mean, you could maybe have made it big, if you'd tried."

"It crossed my mind once or twice," said Charlie slowly. "But that's a story for another day."

*****

"So is there any way you could actually be Tempest min's father?"

It was 8 p.m. and Rory was wading through the remains of the Friday night curry - apart from a stiff helping left in the pan which he had saved for Charlie. Perceptible and permanent change had come over him. His new look, having slipped during the period of heartbreak, had been resurrected and enforced. He shaved every day with an electric razor instead of having heroic cut throat efforts a couple of times a week. His hair was never wild man of the hills and his fingernails were conspicuously clean. He had what he thought was a secret bottle of hand cream. And though one could never have really accused him of having an actual gut, he now had less of one. These were incremental changes, and Charlie teased him only mildly about them because at the same time he was worrying that, caught up in a fresh bout of dreamy possibilities, Rory would fall into the same trap twice.

He looked down at the curry. Spooned stickily into a bowl it looked less than appetising. Optimistically, he added some cold rice and put the bowl in the microwave. He came to the kitchen doorway, leaning against the jamb as he forked up the result.

"I'm quite certain I've never even met Mrs Vane Tempest," he said. "And after the accident … well, I was pretty unappealing and useless all round for a considerable period of time. But I didn't want to get into all of that, so I just settled for the DNA test. It was the easiest thing to do. And, by the way, this isn't curry it's stew. It was stew on Friday night, it's had a whole weekend to think about it and it's still stew."

"Aye," agreed Rory. "I'm cutting down on the spices. I don't want to smell." A perceptible wave of pink spread over his face. "Close up, y'know …"

"Stew's good," said Charlie.

"I'm just being precautionary." Rory sounded awkward. "I know it's early days for her."

"Sure," Charlie nodded, stepping aside to let him into the kitchen with his empty dish.

"I've got yours," Rory held up two beers as he headed back to the futon. "How long do you think it takes a woman to get over that kind of thing?"

Charlie walked across and sat opposite him. "Being told by some jerk ten years her senior that she's too old to get it up for, you mean? I don't know. In some ways I'm surprised that someone as attractive and together as Christina has let it bother her this much. The man was obviously a complete waste of time."

Rory sat down with a sigh. "I'd just like to …" he paused, "make her feel better somehow. But I'm just not very … you know …" he tailed off, "… adept at this."

"You seemed to be fairly adept when she was sobbing in your cubbyhole."

"Aye, mebbes," Rory rubbed his chin. "I'm not quite sure how that happened."

"It'll happen again," said Charlie. "When the moment's right."

"Will it? How?"

"These things just develop."

"How?"

"I don't know. They just do."

"Like with you and Ianthe Keeble Parker?" Rory gave him a sidelong glance.

"No," said Charlie. "I was maybe just coming to grips with the oddness of her when you started on about Holy Island. So that gave me real pause. And now the button's got stuck. I'm in a holding pattern. Except without the holding." He sighed and took a gulp of beer. "But I still can't help wanting to see her all the time. She just makes me feel ..." He stopped.

"It's a bugger, isn't it," said Rory, obviously giving up on the expectation of the sentence ever getting finished. There were always a lot of unfinished sentences when they had conversations like this. On whether or not Ironman was a better character than Wolverine, the pair of them were fluently, even belligerently, opinionated.

"She makes everything seem so beautiful," said Charlie.

*****

Dr. Deshpande was looking disconsolate. At least Charlie thought it was disconsolate. It was an expression that hadn't really decided what it wanted to be. The daffodils, on the other hand, were pressing on regardless. In just four days their buds had expanded into outgoing, yellow trumpets.

"You are not a father," said Dr. Deshpande finally. "At least you are not Christopher's father."

"I know," said Charlie. "Not a father and not an abuser of any kind. So where does that leave me?"

"One thing taken with another, I'm beginning to suspect that it leaves *us*," (and Dr. Deshpande attended carefully to the emphasis on the word 'us') "in very strange country indeed."

He stared out of the window then - the hint of disconsolance replaced by a statesman-like absence of expression. There was a smattering of iron grey at his temples that added to the gravitas. His shirt was pale pink, his tie was dark pink. Pink set off both his complexion and his grey suit admirably. Dr. Deshpande was obviously a man very much at home with his masculinity. And himself. Psychiatrists have to be at home with themselves, of course. And these homes have to be built on solid foundations. They cannot afford to be endlessly rocked by other people's cataclysms - or the things that these cataclysms can go on to reveal. That would prejudice the ability to do the job.

Charlie interrupted the meditation. "And are we about to plunge into this strange country?"

Dr. Deshpande turned back to him. "Not today," he said, suddenly decisive. "This is merely a flying visit to deliver the news to you, and have another short session with Christopher. I have to leave again almost at once. It never pays to open cans of worms when there isn't much time."

"Cans of worms?" Charlie felt new alarm. Whatever theory had the man worked up now?

"No need for panic," said Dr. Deshpande. "I probably

choose the wrong expression. It's more as if we were entering a maze where the pathways will constantly change position."

"Okay," said Charlie slowly. "And do *I* have to get into this maze?"

"I'm afraid so. Assuming we want to come out of the other side with some semblance of understanding." If nothing else, Dr. Deshpande was betraying a generous confidence in the imaginative powers of his audience.

"And you can't give me a hint as to what kind of country it's in?" Charlie asked finally, having conjured nothing at all from the remarks. "This maze of yours?"

"No," Dr. Deshpande paused. "You haven't seen Christopher since his episode, have you?"

Charlie, who'd spent a lot of time since 'the episode' sloping around the school in furtive mode, eyes peeled, ready to dodge round a corner at any minute, immediately felt guilty. "I wasn't sure it would be the best thing."

"Understandable." Dr. Deshpande lapsed into thoughtful nods. "But your absence is beginning to upset him. However, I'm of the opinion that it would be better if you could continue to work around the situation until I come back next week. I'd like to be present the first time you see him." He consulted a piece of paper. "I understand that there's an exeat this coming weekend. Perhaps if you went home it would be easier? Christopher is staying with Matron, and his brothers are going to stay with friends. I believe that does away with the responsibility of the Sunday guitar lesson?"

Charlie nodded. "Yes."

"So we are agreed upon a course of action?"

"Such as it is."

"Don't stress over this." Dr. Deshpande got up from his chair and looked around for his briefcase.

"Hard not to," said Charlie, standing up with him, "as I keep getting cast as the villain of the piece."

"Not any more," said Dr. Deshpande. "It's now my turn to get into the hot seat."

*****

Charlie went straight back to the science block after this. In trying to avoid Tempest min, he'd been holding very much to his own territory. And with the additional complication of the Rory/Christina dynamic he'd found himself avoiding the staffroom as well, brewing up lonely cups of coffee in the chemistry lab's reagent cupboard. So now, since the rather cryptic interview with Dr. Deshpande had occupied less of his time than scheduled, he was wondering where exactly he should go to get a relaxing cup of something. He was sick of boiling up water in a beaker but, in spite of the irritations of having to virtually set up an experiment every time he wanted some coffee, he had not yet stirred himself to lay hands on a spare kettle. Maybe nip back to the flat? He was loitering in the block's main corridor, host to a jousting mass of contradictory impulses, not one of them nice enough to really settle on, when he was accosted by Myra O'Grady.

Myra was looking a little flushed. Reflexly, Charlie glanced around for Dr. Maccabee. Usually when one ran into Myra O'Grady in this part of the school, which was neither frequently nor predictably, there was a hint of Bert Maccabee on the loose from the physics lab. Though he hadn't near enough examples to make a real sum of it, Charlie felt there was a significant correlation. But if it classed in any way as sexual harassment, nobody was trying too hard to put a stop to it.

"I hear you're doing a bit of music therapy with Blake Vane Tempest," said Myra, with just that touch of breathlessness which confirmed Charlie's suspicions. "I wish you well of it."

Charlie tried to explain that what he was doing only qualified as music therapy in the very broadest sense, but Myra swept on: "He's a very difficult boy. I've had a hand myself in trying to balance him out but nothing seems to take. I blame his mother."

"He certainly seems to have some complicated feelings about her."

Myra shook her head impatiently. "I have no time for these people who keep giving birth by this one and that one without any clear idea of why they're doing it. Children get reared up, hit and miss, without getting properly rooted at all, and the next thing you know they're a failing crop and being transplanted out to some place like this in the hopes that somebody will find a way to make them flourish. Yes," she proceeded to confirm her own opinion as she cast turbulent green-eyed glances up and down the corridor, "that's about the price of it."

"Paul Vane Tempest seems alright," Charlie supplied, since Myra didn't look quite ready to take flight. "Not that I've really had anything to do with him. He seems a very quiet boy."

"He'll end up the worst of the lot!" exclaimed Myra with spirited and unflinching pessimism. "He's been polishing up his personal sociopathy in silence for that long, it'll be a real humdinger when it finally surfaces."

"Any idea what it's going to be?" Charlie took a glance down the corridor. Myra was up on her toes now.

"Nobody has," she gave him a look. "We'll just have to wait till we find the bodies." And with that she set off at a stirring pace.

About ten seconds later Bert Maccabee came striding past. "Rory's in the staffroom," he called over his shoulder, by way of greeting.

Without making any conscious decision, Charlie headed in that direction. He almost fell over Schrödinger, who was sitting outside the staffroom door, the end of his tail twitching slightly but otherwise coldly statuesque in some form of malign meditation. Charlie bent down apologetically. "Who got thrown out, then?"

The cat looked up at him, stonily inscrutable apart from an almost supernatural glow in its green jewel eyes, and then with a sudden furious flick of its tail it got up and stalked off. However, the brief delay had made Charlie privy to some conversation that was being transmitted through the staffroom door.

"Have you stopped taking sugar?"

"I didn't think it was helping ma waistline much," Rory sounded bashful. "Course, it improved the coffee a lot."

"I think your waistline seems fine."

Whoa. Charlie paused, hand on the knob. Christina's normally egregious tones had taken on a softer, friendlier aspect altogether. Maybe more than friendly. Could crashing in on this be embarrassing? And if that didn't prove embarrassing then could some whiffy three-cornered awareness of sexually incontinent university lecturers suddenly blow in to taint the atmosphere? Wouldn't it be easier to just give Rory and Christina space? But then he seemed to be giving so many people space these days it was becoming difficult to get about the school. He opened the door and walked casually across to the kettle, nodding greetings and projecting an airy sense of oblivion.

"I hear you would have put money on Cliff being an arsehole," said Christina.

Charlie blinked. Twice. Once for Cliff. Once for arsehole.

He turned round. "That lecturer guy, you mean?"

Christina nodded.

"If I'd known he was called Cliff, I'd have staked my life on it," he said.

Christina looked reflective. "He was so charming though ..." There could have been some regret in it.

"Charm's a greatly overestimated asset in a man," Charlie turned back to the kettle. "It so often incorporates such a big slime factor."

"You think he was slimy?"

"Don't you?" Charlie had to admit that she was being amazingly upfront about this. The most he'd expected of 'Cliff' was that he might hang about in a corner like a bad smell. He most certainly hadn't expected him to be flung into the middle of the floor for public inspection. It was so horribly healthy, so very grown up of Christina, you had to be just a bit admiring. Of course, being so very grown-up was what had given her the problem in the first place.

"I do now," she said. "But at the time ..." she paused.

Charlie hoped that this wasn't going to be some great, slurpy backwash of wistful regret that would be a slap in the face for

Rory. He couldn't feel entirely enthusiastic about having break period suddenly take on all the qualities of an encounter group.

"… well at the time I was obviously a complete fool." Christina finished.

"No, no," protested Rory softly. "Don't go thinking that. We thought ourselves what a smart man he looked. He certainly didn't immediately strike Charlie as slimy. Not when he saw him at the concert. He was just generalising about university lecturers, weren't you, Charlie?"

There was a wheedle in there that Charlie chose to ignore. He made non-committal noises as he spooned out some coffee. It was his opinion that Christina should be left to think that she *had* been foolish. It might keep her away from pink polo shirts and velvet jackets in future. But, even though his admittedly churlish feelings were mostly driven by concern for Rory, he had to keep conceding that Christina was still managing to appear astonishingly adult about things. At least in company. After the potential awkwardness he'd imagined, it was something of a relief.

"What's all this business with Tempest min, then?" she asked suddenly.

So that was the relief part over with. Charlie applied himself to his drink. "Who knows? The Vane Tempest boys seem to be attending this school with the express purpose of complicating my life."

"So, you're not the youngest one's father then?" Christina smiled sweetly.

Charlie going down in the balance now, Cliff maybe rising a little.

"No." Charlie aimed a dark look at Rory.

"What's the psychiatrist like?"

"Thorough. A man who covers every possible angle including the one where I impregnate a woman I've never even met." Charlie paused. "But can we not spread this round the entire school, Rory? Not least because it might upset the child. The rest of the pupils are supposed to think that Dr. Deshpande is just a regular doctor." He shook his head. In his desperation to keep the conversational ball in the air, Rory was never going to be up to hiding much from Christina LeBlanc. He might be able to fight like a lion and more than able to survive a heavy emotional bludgeoning but he was totally without guile. Before he knew it, he'd have blurted out every one of his personal inadequacy stories. And if he actually got as far as getting a date with her, he was going to have to go into church and light a candle for himself. And maybe one for Charlie as well.

"Of course he won't tell everybody," said Christina sharply. "You think this is the first time we've all had to operate around psychiatrists or psychologists in this place? I sometimes wonder how a school that doesn't actually bill itself as special needs or some sort of correctional facility manages to amass so many weird people. And I'm not just talking about the pupils."

"So you know he believes in fairies, then?" Charlie nodded at Rory. "And in specific genera thereof - gnomes and undines no less." Not the most helpful of remarks perhaps but maybe, he thought, it was time that some genuine reaction to the real Rory should be elicited from Christina while the encounter group was still in process.

"I do," said Christina, in suddenly indulgent tones. "It

slipped out yesterday over a piece of wood. But after the initial shock of hearing it from someone who looks like he would be really at home in Game of Thrones, I realised that it was just a version …" and here she paused to give Rory a quick smile, "… that it was a way of expressing the stupõre of the artist."

"Stupõre?"

"It's the word the Italians use to express the wonder and amazement that lies in really seeing and understanding the qualities of the material. Cliff would have called it that right off, no talk of plant worlds or mineral energies. He was totally fluent in high-end art speak but, you know, I really doubt he would have known what stupõre actually felt like. I realise now that he was sadly lacking in authenticity. On the other hand, it turns out there's one or two things about Rory that are deeply authentic."

She crossed the room then to look thoughtfully out of the window and Rory edged towards Charlie and whispered. "Are we sure stupõre isn't foreign for stupid?"

"Definitely complimentary," Charlie hissed back, surprised. Yet going on to contemplate the pair of them over the rim of his coffee mug, he wasn't at all sure that stupõre or anything else was going to get Rory a trip to Holy Island with buckets and spades and a couple of children. And he went on to wonder, idly but reasonably perhaps, why an elegant metropolitan, a product of the Slade and the latest in exhibitions at the National Gallery and the Tate Modern, would come to the out of the way, country fastness of a place like Puckrup.

Chapter Fifteen

The school was decanting boys into cars to be whisked away for the long weekend of the exeat. Charlie was walking back to the flat to prepare for his own departure – as suggested by Dr. Deshpande – when he was caught by a panting Blake Vane Tempest. The boy had a pack on his back, a guitar case in each hand, a rolled-up something in ethnic looking weave wedged under one arm and a small book under the other. He handed Charlie one of the guitar cases in a stiff, awkward gesture that ensured he didn't drop anything. "This one's yours," he panted.

Charlie took the case, Blake Vane Tempest took a few deep breaths. He was both puffed and excited. He had a brand new Gibson. He held up the case. The guitar in it was apparently the same colour as Charlie's – 'and everything'. Blake grinned happily between pants. Perhaps a few too many pants. He was a tall boy with a lithe swimmer's build but he was the very devil to drive to exercise. The games master had long since ceased to expect anything of him but a morose wandering on the rugby pitch that would bear little or no relationship to the location of the ball. This new guitar, however, was clearly inspiring him. It had arrived with astonishing speed, courtesy of some efficient shop in London and his mother, after the previous Sunday night's Skype session. (Skype sessions were now routine, having been compulsorily inserted into the boys' weekly schedule since Tempest min's sojourn in the hospital). Forced to talk because his brother Paul was starting to baulk at being the one who always had to paper over the family cracks, Blake had apparently told his mother Charlie's story about the trip across London to the disastrous special guitar lesson and the subsequent encounter with the old man on the tube. And he had, he said, recounted it almost word for word. 'I'm good at remembering word for word – if I want to." He shot Charlie a conspiring smile.

This new bent for fluent communication and detailed storytelling had evidently made an impression on Mrs. Vane Tempest. At this point in his excited tirade, Blake removed the ethnically woven 'something' from under his arm and it promptly unrolled to reveal itself as a small Mexican mat. Then he displayed the book - Zen and the Art of Archery. These had both arrived with the guitar. But, from Charlie's point of view, the most impressive aspect of it all was the fact that the boy had actually used the 'mother' word and remained smiling.

"Well this is all excellent," he said, keeping comment to a minimum in case he somehow broke the spell.

"The email telling me to expect parcels had a P.S.," said Blake.

Something in the tone suddenly induced an 'oh dear' feeling in Charlie.

"It said …" Blake paused.

"Let's have it then," said Charlie finally. "Word for word

would be good, eh? Since you can."

Blake took a breath. "It said," he paused yet again.

"Yes?"

"It said: 'I'm hearing a lot about this Mr. Peterson lately. How come he's inserted himself so dramatically and efficiently into our lives? Tell me why you like him. Who is he, exactly?'"

"And have you replied?" asked Charlie.

"I said: 'The guitar is brill. Thank you. Mr. Peterson is the chemistry teacher.'"

"Very nice," said Charlie, suspecting that Mrs. Vane Tempest already knew that. "Uncontroversial and to the point."

"It won't be enough ..." Blake let that hang in the air before adding: "She'll be investigating you ... She might email you or ring you up. You won't like it."

"I guess I'll survive," said Charlie, wondering how much Dr. Deshpande was sharing with Mrs. Vane Tempest at this point.

"I'm going to Booger's for the weekend," said Blake.

"Booger?"

"David Borgsen."

"Right."

"We were thinking. Booger and me." He stopped. Charlie waited.

"We want a band," said Blake, after a shuffling pause. "There is every kind of music in this school – choirs, orchestras, a string quartet and a jazz band. But no rock band. We want a rock band."

"Oh," said Charlie. He had kept away from the school's musical activities.

"I think it's very behind the times, this place," said Blake.

"I'm only here because I've been expelled three times from other schools and now I'm so far from civilisation that I'm not supposed to be able to get up to anything."

"We certainly live in hope," said Charlie.

"We should make a band." This was obviously an inclusive 'we'. Charlie's heart sank a little.

"Booger and I will find a drummer," Blake went on cheerfully. "Somebody should be able to take a pitch at rock drums. How hard can it be?"

"Harder than all the drummer jokes might lead you to believe," said Charlie. "But the music teachers will help you sort it all out. They'll be pleased to."

There were several music teachers, more or less self-employed and teaching different instruments, who each did a day or so a week at the school. Their comings and goings and progress with the pupils were monitored and orchestrated by the head of department who'd come to Puckrup from more celebrated musical realms, including a famous Cathedral school and the Albert Hall. That was pretty much all Charlie knew about the people he was so thoroughly recommending. That and a rather impressive Christmas concert.

"No." protested Blake. "I meant you."

"I can't tread on their toes any further," said Charlie. "As you explained to your mother, I'm the chemistry teacher. Bands are not my department."

"But you play the guitar like a fucking genius," exclaimed Blake, suddenly angry. "They have to be."

"You're not helping yourself here," warned Charlie.

"I'm sorry, sir. Please ... I'll try to fix it ... with the head of music. You don't have to be in the band if it'll make you feel silly. Just help us pull it together. You have to have been in one at some point - nobody gets that good at the guitar just to play it in his bedroom."

"Blake!" An impatient man shouted across the car park. "We're waiting."

"Booger's dad." Blake pulled a face. "I have to go. Band, Mr. Peterson. And with your help. *Please* …" And picking up his new Gibson he set off at a run.

After looking thoughtfully after him for a moment or two, Charlie picked up his own Gibson and took it on up to the flat. Rory was already preparing for a peaceful weekend – stretched out on one of the futons, he was staring contentedly into space.

"I was feeling a bit guilty about abandoning you," said Charlie, putting the Gibson down. "But you're looking remarkably self-satisfied."

"Looking forward to the quiet," said Rory, hands linked behind his head. "I have things to do. Wood to carve. One or two interestin' ideas have been brewing lately … and I've come by a grand piece of oak. Really looking forward to it." There was a pause. "Christina isna' going away …" He gave Charlie a slightly bashful glance. "And she mentioned something about needing to talk about the Easter art exhibition. Also, she looked at a couple of my latest pieces for a long time. Said they were arte povera."

"Does that mean poor art?"

"No. It's Italian again. Apparently, it means art without the superfluous. Where the material is just encouraged to reveal what it is in itself. Not carved to represent anything else."

"Impressive," said Charlie. "I'm impressed."

"And she said I was that kind of man."

"What kind of man?"

"A man without the superfluous. A man who hasn't tried to present himself as something he really isn't." He paused. "D'you think that's meant to be good? You can't always tell with Christina. She could just be meaning that I've failed to do anything with meself. I was hoping it was good but I didn't like to ask."

"I would say it was good," said Charlie.

"Aye." Rory resumed his contented contemplation of the ceiling. "I was thinking it was."

*****

At his parents' farmhouse Charlie sat on the floor of his bedroom and opened a box. His younger self, spotlit, open-mouthed, looked up at him. Microphone, guitar, no fillings in the teeth ... bloody marvellous. Hultsfred, Sweden. The first festival the band had ever been paid – expenses anyway – to play. Looking at the photograph now, he could feel a powerful echo of the surging excitement of the moment. Remember his hysterical glee at first reading the email invitation. Sighing, he pushed the photo to one side. Underneath, there was a picture of Tom – caught in profile, frozen in space and time at the drums, the muscles of his upper arms standing out as he reached for the high hat. Those incredible muscles of Tom's – their resilience reinforced by work on building sites, their infallible automatic memory honed by hours at the kit. Tom, monolithic, metronomic - the click track a device for the benefit of lesser

291

mortals. Question: 'How can you tell it's a drummer at the door?' Answer: 'The knock speeds up.' But never when it was Tom. He could lay down an unshakeable groove or play The Black Page on a hangover. A strong, talented guy whose greatest regret in life was that you could never get a woman to listen to a drum solo. Charlie glanced at the bottom corner of the photograph: BBC T in the Park.

He eased Tom to one side and looked at Joe. Joe with the quiet smile and the sweetest of natures. No ambition to be the front man or the guitar hero. Joe, happy with his bass, happy to be the co-writer, happy to be there.

After school they'd lived together, Joe, Tom and he. Their lives had had to change, of course. He'd been at Imperial (when the mood took him). Joe, who was never especially academic, went to the Rock School, and Tom worked in the family building firm - learning the trades from the bottom. Together they'd rented the non-too-smart flat that Charlie had eventually vacated to come to Puckrup. It was the base they'd wanted to confirm their togetherness, ensure the continuation of the dream. And the one they could afford. Only Craig had elected to stay living at home. Craig was the practical one, the pragmatist. He'd shared the enthusiasm for the dream but perhaps he'd come up a little short in the belief department. He'd started training to be an accountant – alone amongst them he was prepared to count the cost of failure.

Over the next two or three years things had moved on - for the band but also in the living arrangements. Tom's family firm was no longer just a local London business. The bank crash and its subsequent effect on the housing market had not yet taken place and Tom's father, getting flush, had bought a large property to renovate in Berkshire. The most on board of the parents, possibly because he was the best financed, he'd built the band a studio out there. Drums are noisy things, the flat had thin walls and Tom, becoming progressively frustrated at always having to play on pads or fit in personal time at practice rooms, eventually moved out to live above the studio. And Joe, much as his loyalty lay with Charlie, eventually followed nature and moved in with his girlfriend. He and she – Lucinda she was called – had had an on off relationship since school. It seemed to be part passion, part pain and a huge helping of something that the rest of the band just couldn't understand. Charlie had had to find new flatmates to make the rent but Joe kept turning up and sleeping on the floor when things with Lucinda were rough - which seemed to be most of the time. Fortunately, in some twisted way, the more miserable Joe was, the better he played and the more creative he became. He distilled the essence of his pain into the most resonant of bass lines and the most heart wrenching of melodies. Melodies often too beautiful to be bent to Endgame's sound. 'We could run a Stax beat behind it,' Tom would suggest. 'See if that helps'. But Joe's songs were moody, ethereal creatures, skittish of committing fully to this world, uneasy with the bondage of a beat, unwilling to be upstaged by a chorus or a compelling riff. Some days, Joe channelled the descants of angelic choirs not the subterranean throb of the gods of rock. But, as long as some of what he wrote saw the light of day Joe, sweet soul that he was, never carped about the rest.

Charlie replaced the box lid with a sigh. He suspected that

the school music department would be only too pleased if he got involved with a band. Members of staff did not get protective of their spheres of influence at Puckrup. They were keen to build boys not empires. And Charlie knew that with Blake Vane Tempest they would gladly take any help they could get. With another sigh, he got up off the floor and went downstairs for supper.

*****

He drove back to Puckrup on Sunday night. In the flat Rory and Christina were watching a French movie.

"My God," Charlie said to Christina. "What are you trying to do to him? This is a man of forest and moorland and big skies and Guardians of the Galaxy, and you're trying to to reduce him to subtitles?"

Rory looked up with a grin. "Mostly I don't bother. I just get a vague gist of what's going on from the expressions on their faces. There's no action to speak of."

"That's because you're missing all the nuance with not reading the subtitles," said Christina reprovingly.

Rory grinned. "I'm sitting beside the most beautiful woman in the world and she's expecting me to get worked up about nuances in some art house movie full of foreigners." He shook his head.

"*Foreigners?*" repeated Christina, every bit of Frenchness in her rising indignantly to the surface. Elegant as she was, she delivered a punch to Rory's upper arm that would have induced high dudgeon in a university lecturer.

It worked on Rory like a caress. Like lightning he caught her fist on the rebound and kissed it. If Rory McEwan had to take the punishment due other men then he was big enough to stand it. After all, he'd done it for years. It was what he was used to. And if Christina LeBlanc had some demons to work out, even some with a more deep-rooted hold on her than Cliff, then Rory was tough enough and big-hearted enough to let her do it in his arms.

Charlie shook his head. As foreplay it was all fairly novel, but he could hardly stay and watch. He thought he'd go across to the library. He left them looking into each other's eyes and smiling.

The library was deserted. Charlie sat down at one of the big tables and stared into space. Now that Christina seemed to have become more of a reality and less of a fantasy, the companionship he'd found with Rory, the level of intimacy, would change. That much he'd learned from Joe. He felt suddenly lonely. He resisted the urge to draw parallels between Christina and Lucinda. Rory was not Joe. In spite of his lack of guile and his oft-times surprising innocences, Rory was made of resilient material that had been exhaustively tempered.

There was a shuffling noise on the floor beside him. He looked down. The trembly terrier looked back up at him. "Well, hello there," Charlie bent down to pat him. The dog put his front paws up on Charlie's knee and made a couple of heaving efforts.

"Nowhere else for you to go, either?" Charlie lifted him up onto his lap.

"You're a bit smelly," he added after a moment or two, but he felt reluctant to put the little thing down. It seemed to be getting comfortable. He allowed it to settle itself, and then sat staring into space for a moment or two more before leaning forward to pick up a book that was lying on the table. He looked at the title. Moby Dick. A six hundred page, heavy-going allegory about a man chasing something that finally killed him. He opened the book at the beginning. "Call me Ishmael," he read aloud. The trembly terrier soon fell asleep. Charlie began to nod off himself.

"So there you are!"

Charlie jerked into life but the comment was being addressed to the dog.

As Ianthe came nearer it seemed to Charlie, still not fully in possession of himself, that everything else around him went dark. Her lovely smile and her tantalising, unknowable beauty were all that he could see. The way the golden glow from the desk lamp lit her skin was mesmerising.

"I didn't hear you," he said. "Neither did the dog," he caught up the trembly terrier's front paws in his hands, "which is unusual." Would that she had been looking for me, he thought.

"He's feeling a bit down," said Ianthe. "And getting a bit deaf. Old age is catching up. He knows."

"How old is he?"

"Thirteen, fourteen maybe. Old for a dog,"

"Whose dog is he, anyway? Dr. Carlyle's? He seems to have fairly random loyalties." Was this the most he could manage with her now? The life history of a little dog?

"Originally he was the old head gardener's. Got him to chase the rats away from the compost heaps and the potting shed. When the old man died the dog sort of became communal. School property, as it were …" Ianthe bent down to stroke the terrier's head. Her hair brushed Charlie's face. He tried hard not to breathe her in too obviously. He would talk dogs forever just to keep her near. "Does he have a name?" he asked. "Nobody ever seems to call him anything."

"Guess."

"Patch?"

"No. Guess."

"Shortie?"

"No. Guess."

"Rumplestiltskin," said Charlie finally. "His name is Rumplestiltskin."

Ianthe laughed. "The fairies have told you."

"So he's actually called Rumplestiltskin?"

"No. He's actually called Guess."

"Guess is his name? No wonder nobody uses it."

"It was the old head gardener's joke. He liked to play it on the new boys. The little ones. They enjoyed it. They're only seven or eight, aren't they? Obviously it didn't cheer you up quite as effectively. What's wrong?"

Charlie didn't answer.

"Could you tell me?"

"Tempest min. Dr. Deshpande. Tempest min again. Blake Vane Tempest. Joe and Lucinda."

"Joe and Lucinda?"

"Past life," said Charlie. "Rory's got an insanely hopeful relationship going with Christina LeBlanc and it stirs a few memories for me. As does Blake Vane Tempest's new desire to have me help him form a school rock band. I look at Blake and I see myself. It's all so horribly reminiscent. And selfishly speaking, I didn't come here to do reminiscent. Unselfishly, I think it could all end in tears."

297

"Whose tears?"

"Rory's. Blake's."

"Why Blake's? Any more than usual, that is?"

"I think he has the dream of having a successful band, and it's maybe not the thing for him. It was never easy, but now it's even harder. I'm not even sure the guitar is the voice of youth any more. Youth has so many voices these days, and they're all screaming for attention on YouTube and Facebook. So many voices, so few notes, so hard to stand out ... let alone make a living." He tailed off.

"Does Blake Vane Tempest *need* to make a living?"

Charlie shook his head. He wasn't sure. He explained that he thought that even if Blake Vane Tempest didn't need to make a living he needed to make a life. A life in which he could make his own happiness. And not have it entirely dependent upon the responses of other people. The boy had already spent years competing for the attention of his own mother – it was seriously doubtful that competing for the attention of great swathes of a very fickle public was really what he needed on top.

"I don't want to encourage him," he finished. "It's hard up on that stage. Putting yourself out there. Trying to hit the right note in every possible way. Trying to connect but at the same time risking rejection and humiliation. It's not easy. Even for someone like I used to be. Maybe I did the wrong thing encouraging him with the guitar at all ... It could so easily be the road to nowhere. Or worse. He doesn't seem to be able to look on it as a hobby."

"He needed something," said Ianthe. "Desperately. And nobody else had anything for him. You gave him what you had."

"I should have thought harder. I gave him a Grandma Peterson homily without sufficient thought to the punch line."

"The dream was already there," said Ianthe. "All you can do now is help him with it to the best of your ability."

Charlie thought suddenly of Dr. Boswell, gathering mushrooms and listening to distant bells. 'Show me a heart unfettered by foolish dreams and I'll show you a happy man ...'

"And the thing about dreams Charlie," Ianthe went on, as if she had heard his thought, "is that it sometimes seems as if they have a life of their own. That we have very little control over them. That they are just there, things unto themselves – waiting and wanting to be lived. And if you feel like the right sort of person, then a dream will try and live through you. You can argue with it but ..." She shook her head. Charlie was becoming used to Ianthe's way of looking at things, so he didn't comment on the premise but merely said: "I don't think this is the right dream for Blake Vane Tempest."

"You don't know that, Charlie. And neither do I. But one thing I do know - Blake will handle this dream better with you, than without you. Consider that." After a moment or two of silence, she held out her arms for the trembly terrier. "I'll take him home with me. He needs some supper and some love."

Take me home with you, thought Charlie, as he carefully handed the little dog over. I need some supper and some love.

Chapter Sixteen

The following day, Charlie was still feeling lonely as he climbed the stairs to what he had come to think of as Dr. Deshpande's green room. Rory had been all silence and secret smiles at breakfast, though there had been no evidence of Christina's having spent the night. Finally, Charlie had been unable to bear it any longer. He'd just had to ask. "So?"

"W'a takin' it slow."

"Very sensible," said Charlie. "But how did it happen? How did you finally get it together?"

Rory seemed a little mystified himself. "It just happened, y'know. W'a looking at some students' work in the woodwork room and then …"

"The pretext," said Charlie. "I get it. Go on."

"*She* came to see *me*," Rory protested. "I was in my cubbyhole thinking about m'nice piece of oak."

"Liar."

"Thinking about m'nice piece of oak and her … Then we went across to the benches to look at some of the boys' wood-turning efforts. The Easter exhibition, remember? Then I suddenly said I'd made a curry and maybe ..."

"Aha," said Charlie. "The premeditated spontaneity part of the plot."

"And she said yes," went on Rory, ignoring him. "Yes, she'd like curry for supper and then she turned up with the movie. Which was in French."

"Maybe, she's going to be too French for you ..."

"No," said Rory firmly. "She's just French enough. As was I when I finally kissed her." And after that he'd got up, taken Charlie's unfinished breakfast away from him, scraped what remained on the plate into the bin, and gone off whistling.

*****

Outside the green room, Charlie took a deep breath. He wondered if Dr. Deshpande was currently of the mindset for taking peoples' food away. Hard to tell, of course, what Dr. Deshpande ever had in mind. His previous talk of mazes had declined to go on and elucidate itself in any way.

Charlie went in and sat down. There was a nice smell about the place. The daffodils had had their moment and been replaced by hyacinths.

"Now," said Dr. Deshpande, managing to invest the word with serious portent. "We must play this exactly right ..."

He was wearing a blue shirt which almost matched the hyacinths. His tie was of a darker shade and had tiny hedgehogs all over it. He seemed to do most of his clothes shopping in England. The U.S.A. has a great many wonderful things but hedgehogs are not amongst them. He consulted his watch. "Matron says that four-thirty is a propitious time ... Christopher will have had a little snack so his blood sugar will be just right. Personally, I do not think that blood sugar has anything in particular to do with it, but it would take a braver man than I am to suggest that to Matron after her weeks of policing his diet and his exercise. Your Matron here is a solid devotee of the mechanistic, Charlie. The mind body axis is a closed book to her. She does not like, she tells me with egregious matronliness, stupid theories built on psychoanalytic woolliness. Which is unfortunate, as we could be about to get very woolly indeed … But not, I hope, stupid." He got up from his chair.

"*Please*," said Charlie in desperation, "could you tell me what I'm supposed to be doing in all of this?"

"Just respond," said Dr. Deshpande. "Respond to everything Christopher says as if it's perfectly normal. Don't show surprise, don't quibble, don't make alternative suggestions …"

"To what?" Charlie interrupted him.

"To whatever he says."

Charlie protested. "I'm a bit with Matron here. This seems extremely woolly."

"It has to be," said Dr. Deshpande. "Were I to tell you more, it could prejudice the process. Christopher must not, in any way, be led or prompted or discouraged. Not even by subliminally received micro-expressions. You must accept what he says, perfectly ingenuously and agreeably. Do not betray alarm or surprise, however things sound …" He nodded towards the door. "Ready?"

Charlie did not feel remotely ready. He felt that this crash course on how to be an inscrutable psychiatrist had almost certainly failed to take. Mystification and a level of anxiety accompanied him along the corridor and up some back stairs to the sanatorium.

Tempest min had the eight-bedded room to himself. It was a sparsely furnished place, devoid of homely touches and infinitely swabbable. He was sitting on one of the beds, propped up on pillows and wearing full school uniform except for his shoes which, in deference to the counterpane, had been replaced by the bunny-eared slippers. The counterpane was of light green cotton and tightly applied to the iron framed bed by means of strict hospital corners. Matron did not believe in the difficult-to-launder flouncy comfort of duvets - not for rooms where dust and bacterial counts had to be kept to a minimum.

Tempest min held out his arms with every evidence of pleasure. "Charlie!"

"*Mr. Peterson*," Matron corrected him firmly, removing a glass of milk before it got knocked over.

"Let's just go with Charlie, for now," suggested Dr. Deshpande. "I believe we can take it from here, Matron, thank you very much."

So Matron left them to it, though she would clearly have preferred to stay and supervise. Her initial interview with Dr. Deshpande had not forged a satisfactory relationship between the pair of them and subsequent exchanges had not made it run any more smoothly. "Don't you upset him," she warned them both as she left.

After a surreptitious nod from Dr. Deshpande, Charlie bent over and gave the little boy a hug. Tempest min gripped him tightly saying, "I'm sorry I let you down. I couldn't help it, you know."

"You've never let me down," said Charlie squeezing him in return. "Ever, ever, ever."

Tempest min beamed.

"So," Dr. Deshpande sat on a tubular steel chair by the bed and indicated that Charlie should do the same. "How are we feeling?"

"I think I'm better," said Tempest min.

"Better how?"

"I don't think I need these afternoon rests any more,"

"That's good," said Dr. Deshpande. "Very good. Maybe I could have them instead, and you could do my job?"

Tempest min giggled.

"No?" Dr. Deshpande looked around as if surprised. "Ah well, maybe not, all things considered. So you're feeling better and you're still sure you want to stay at the school?"

"Yes."

"We were worried, you know, that you seemed less happy here."

"I wasn't."

"No," said Dr. Deshpande casually. "But you did stop humming. And the headmaster told me that you used to like to hum."

"I've told you about that before," said Tempest min with a slight 'stupid adult' tone in his voice.

"Tell me again," suggested Dr. Deshpande genially. "Tell Charlie."

"I stopped because you came," said Tempest min to Charlie.

There had obviously been some subtle change of emphasis here which Dr. Deshpande seemed to find very interesting.

"Ah," he said. "You stopped because Charlie *came*. Not because *Charlie* came."

Tempest min looked puzzled.

Dr. Deshpande whispered to Charlie under his breath. "You see how your presence subtly alters things."

He turned back to Tempest min. "So you *wanted* Charlie to come?"

"Yes. Charlie was my friend. I needed my friend to come."

"Before you saw Charlie here at the school, did you have a clear idea of this friend?"

"I knew there was a friend that I needed to see. And then, when I saw him, I started to know him again. I think I've told you this."

"Did you recognise him by what he looked like?" asked Dr. Deshpande.

"First it was by his footsteps. In the hall. The noise of his boots. I remembered footsteps just like that walking round me on the floor. I started to know then."

"Now what floor was *that*, and why exactly were you on the floor?"

"I had to sleep there. When I stayed with him. When I didn't live there anymore. In the ..." Tempest min paused here for a second "...in the place where we used to live together. I used to go back there when I was sad. I think I felt sad a lot. Especially after I left the music school. Not like this ... It wasn't a school like this." He looked around for a moment or two, as if suddenly confused.

Charlie was developing some peculiar lurching feelings in his chest. Obedient to Dr. Deshpande's instructions, he tried hard to not to give way to them in some potentially disruptive way.

"And when you went to stay with Charlie," Dr. Deshpande said gently. "How did that make you feel?"

"Better."

"Better how?"

"Better than I felt before."

Charlie was finding it hard to sit still. And remain silent. He tried to channel his increasing discomfort into an air of actively interested inquiry. Dr. Deshpande shot him a sidelong glance, then asked Tempest min why he thought that humming would bring his friend to him. Tempest min didn't really seem to know. He just knew that the notes were important because his friend would hear them, and he would come. His friend was a musician too, although he didn't go to the music school. Because he was clever. "You're clever, aren't you, Charlie?"

"Averagely," said Charlie.

"Do you want to tell us about the time you were supposed to meet Charlie and didn't turn up?" asked Dr. Deshpande. "You've mentioned it, but you've never talked about it. Could you do that now do you think?"

Tempest min started to look upset.

"Well never mind, let's just leave that, then," Dr. Deshpande spoke in bright and cheering tones . "Why don't you just hum the tune that you wanted Charlie to hear?"

"I've already hummed it for you."

"Yes, but would you hum it for Charlie?"

"Charlie's already heard it. He knows it. That's why he came."

Dr. Deshpande turned expectantly to Charlie and raised his eyebrows. Charlie, sickenly adrift in the tune department but trying desperately to sound casual, said: "Well, perhaps you would run it past me again. Some tunes are hard to get at first hearing."

"Not for you."

"I'd like to hear it again, all the same."

So then Tempest min began to hum. And it was as melodically intoxicating as the Panis Angelicus. Exquisite, as Dr. Carlyle had said. Pitched in an agonising minor key, and replete with unappeasable yearning. And reminiscent. Almost note for note, painfully reminiscent. Charlie felt his guts twisting. It was as if Joe Beck himself were sitting there, boyishly young again, sweet-voiced and fine of face, absently channelling one of those ethereal songs of his that were so difficult to bring fully into realisation. How many of them lay half-recorded in a dusty box somewhere? The essence of Joe's romantic pain, imperfectly rendered, mostly unfinished and largely unsung. Charlie began to sweat now, experience an alarming tightness in his chest, feel really quite sick.

Dr. Deshpande reached out and put a hand on his shoulder, gripping it firmly, smiling encouragingly. "Charlie is overcome with emotion at the very memory of it, aren't you, Charlie?" he said brightly. "Does it have a name, this beautiful song?"

Tempest min began to cry.

Matron arrived at the bedside in full sail with the skull and cross bones flying. "I knew it," she said, with what could have been interpreted as dark satisfaction. "You've upset him again. I knew you would. I think he's had enough of the pair of you for today. Come along."

Tempest min put a hand out and Charlie took it. Matron repeated her demand that he should leave.

"In a minute." Charlie leaned forward and looked into Tempest min's tearful little face. "Hey," he said softly. "I'm here. Whenever you want to make your heart feel better you can come to me. That's how it always was. That's how it'll always be."

And Tempest min started to smile through his tears. His little hand was clammy. Charlie didn't want to let it go.

"Come along," said Matron firmly.

When they were out in the corridor, Dr. Deshpande said, "I think I need a word with Dr. Carlyle. I wasn't about to argue in front of the child, but Matron will have to give way to me in terms of therapeutic judgement. Otherwise, this just won't work."

"And exactly what is it that just won't work?" asked Charlie, considerably disturbed himself. "What is really going on here? Is this some sort of role-playing therapy or what? How does Tempest min know these things? Have you been able to brief him in some way that entirely escapes me? You're a big one for the background work, as I well know."

"Not that big," said Dr. Deshpande. "Let's go back to the office."

*****

"I have to be a bit on Matron's side," said Charlie as he sat down rather heavily in the green velvet chair. "Tempest min was extremely upset. His little hand was sweating and, frankly, I thought it was a bit cold in there."

"Tears are not always a bad thing," said Dr. Deshpande. "They can be a letting go." He looked thoughtfully at Charlie for a few moments more. "Tea and cakes would be a big help about

308

now, wouldn't they? Cups of tea are supposed to be the iron in the blood of the British."

There was a sudden light knock, the door slowly opened and, as there was no protest of any sort from Dr. Deshpande, in came Mrs. Batt bearing tea and fairy cakes on a tray. She set it all down on the desk with the utmost care - no unsolicited slops from milk jug or teapot - and after the briefest of nods she turned away. But, as she did so, she laid a light hand on Charlie's shoulder and looked into his face. Her lips moved briefly and to Charlie it was as if he felt, rather than heard, a couple of words. Mrs. Batt smiled and nodded and then she was gone.

"Did she say something?" asked Dr. Deshpande, looking after her.

"I'm not sure," Charlie shook his head. "She could have said 'accept this'."

"Well it's very welcome, I must say." Dr. Deshpande studied the cakes. "But who is that lady, exactly? She's, she's …"

"She's everywhere," said Charlie. "All the time. And nobody can seem to remember a point when she wasn't."

"She's the only person I've ever seen Matron defer to," said Dr. Deshpande, taking a look in the teapot. "And yet she appears to have only one pinafore."

There was silence for a moment or two as tea was poured carefully into china cups and then Charlie, for whom Mrs. Batt's interruption had proved a handy hiatus, asked in relatively calm tones, "What's going on?"

"I find that things seem to work better if I ask the questions." Dr. Deshpande wielded the tea strainer with aplomb. "Have one of these nice little cakes. A mild sugar high might make you feel more robust, and there are some things I want to show you. But let's enjoy this unexpected treat first."

After they had cleared the desk, Dr. Deshpande produced from his briefcase a sheaf of drawings which he proceeded to lay out, one by one. They were obviously done by a child, and varied quite a bit in detail, but the predominant theme was of a car crash and its accompanying carnage. The number of bodies was constant, the amount of lurid red blood spatter variable - as was the number of vehicles involved. The other notable constant was that the bodies were always associated with a big black van. These drawings, Dr. Deshpande explained, had emerged in recognisable form from the minute that Tempest min had been old enough to wield a crayon properly. A couple of early ones had been kept - in the way that parents will keep a child's drawings – but later ones had been kept because they were starting to bother Mrs. Vane Tempest, accompanied as they frequently were, by panicky, tearful outbursts. At one point, she'd blamed Blake for letting his little brother watch unsuitable movies or unsuitable computer games, though it was evident that Blake's predominant game plan was one of staying as far away from his little brother as possible. The most recent ones, a veritable stack, had been done both at school and at home and represented something of a resurgence.

"I want you to look at this writing," said Dr. Deshpande, indicating the area of the black van in some of the recent drawings. "This is one of the things, other than Grand Theft Auto, that made Mrs. Vane Tempest think of computer games. At a glance you can see that it could be interpreted as 'end of game'. On the other hand, if you were privy to certain information, and looked a little longer and a little harder, you'd notice that in some of the drawings the writing is always more or less on the side of the van. And it reads: 'Endgame'."

"What *exactly* are you saying?" Charlie asked. In spite of the recent cup of tea, his mouth was starting to feel dry again.

"First of all," said Dr. Deshpande, "I'm going to say this: compulsive repetition - in this case of drawings - is a phenomenon often seen in children who have survived or witnessed a major trauma. It's called post-traumatic play. If taken in conjunction with nightmares about the same kind of scene, nightmares which we both know Christopher has, drawings of this nature could suggest very strongly that a child is trying to work through a traumatic event. Yet Christopher has never been in a car crash or seen a real car crash, so possibly ..." he paused here for a moment and took a significant breath before concluding, "... so possibly, taking other things into consideration, we must at least wonder at this point, if he's remembering an event from a past life."

"What?"

"This must have been occurring to you, Charlie."

"No," said Charlie. "No. *For Chrissakes!* It's crazy."

"And yet," said Dr.Deshpande. "I have a very close and eminent friend who worked for many years in the department of psychiatry and behavioural sciences at a prominent university in the U.S.A.. Unlike me by the way, he's American born. Irish descent I think - a tabula rasa in other words, when it comes to past lives. Anyway, he undertook a project to look into exactly this sort of thing in American children - talking to them, talking to their parents, checking out historical facts. Previously, most quotable examples of the phenomenon had been from Asia, of course, and so it was very easy for westerners to write them off as 'cultural and religious leanings'. However, my friend's research in the USA went on over a number of years and yielded up some quite astonishing results. When he talked about these results to informed bodies he was wont to say, 'I cannot tell you how these findings can be possible, I can only tell you that they are genuine'."

Charlie said nothing.

"It seems that these things are variably explicit," went on Dr. Deshpande, calmly conversational. "Children with past life memories vary enormously in how much time they are in character. In other words, how often and to what extent the memories assail them. And how strongly they affect them. The tendency seems to be for the memories to pass by the time the child is six or seven years old. However, some children remember right into their teenage years and live a normal life, apparently quite accepting. In fact, by the time Tempest min came here to Puckrup a lot of his most intense feelings had passed - though Mrs. Vane Tempest remembers his complaints about not living in the right house, not going to the right school, not being taken to see his friends for some very important meeting. Not even having the right parents - though that, well …" He paused for a moment, but before he could go on Charlie leapt to his feet, almost knocking over a side table.

"*No!*" he exclaimed. "*This is not possible! I just cannot countenance this!* First you virtually accuse me of being a paedophile, and now you're trying to tell me that Tempest min is my dead best friend come to life? Just exactly what sort of a psychiatrist are you?"

He slammed the door behind him.

Chapter Seventeen

"You are supposed to be supervising prep," said Dr. Carlyle quietly.

"Sorry." Charlie didn't even look up.

"Aren't you cold?" The headmaster sat down on the bench beside him. It was dark and a sharp wind was blowing. Charlie hadn't noticed. He shrugged.

"I realise this has to be hard for you," said Dr. Carlyle. "But try not to take it like this."

"Like it all wasn't completely insane, you mean?"

"Yes."

Charlie didn't respond.

"You haven't properly processed the loss of your friends, have you?"

"It's been over eight years," said Charlie. "I would think I have."

"I'm older than you," said Dr. Carlyle, "and wiser about this kind of thing. Don't dive back into the basement, Charlie. That phase is over now. And, yes, it was a long one but, to your credit, you got through it without some addiction or overtly destructive behaviour. And one could say that, at least in terms of outward appearances, you've finally moved on. But now it's time to close the door on that basement properly. And forever. Dr. Deshpande is anxious to help you with this. Talk to him. *Please*."

"I never like what he has to say."

"You can handle whatever he has to say. You've already handled much worse. At one point in your interview for this job, you said that you felt you had nothing left to give. But it turned out, didn't it, that you have an awful lot left to give."

"Let's see what the chemistry results are like."

"You were speaking of emotional giving, Charlie, and so am I. Look at Blake Vane Tempest."

"That's just about the guitar."

"As Matron so tactlessly pointed out, Blake Vane Tempest has had any number of good guitar teachers – one or two of the American ones were even great teachers - and whilst they've no doubt made some impression on his guitar playing, they've made absolutely no impression at all on Blake himself. On his outlook, or his behaviour. But what you gave him was not just your expertise, you gave him *you*. And it's working." He held up a hand to stifle protest. "I see these things, Charlie. That's my job. Now, obviously, it was terribly painful for you when your friends were killed, and everything came to nought. And that is still there. And I can quite understand that it's less than fun to be digging it up. But this with Tempest min is something that could prove extraordinary, and so I'm asking you to give of yourself again - even though the idea you have to work with runs against all of your scientific and cultural conditioning. And your pain. But if you can deal with the situation alongside Dr. Deshpande, even for no reason other than to help a little boy, I promise that in so doing, you will finally process your own grief."

He stood up then, and looked down at Charlie for a moment or two before putting a hand on his shoulder and saying, "Some pain can never be completely expunged. I know that. But you must learn to be in charge of it. Owning pain and owning fear is what it takes to be a courageous human being. You can't let either of them run your life. Spinoza would have called them passive emotions, inflicted upon you by circumstance, draining you of energy and freedom. Depriving you of what he called your 'conatus' - the power to persist in your Being. Don't let that happen. Get this thing done."

*****

According to Rory, Aunt Bertha had had disappointingly little to say on the subject of reincarnation. She'd apparently dealt in spirits and spirit guides to the extent of clearing houses of unwelcome forces and contacting the dead, and she'd also had something of a grip on the little people. But reincarnation?

"No real mention of it," said Rory definitely.

None of the McEwans had evidently seen fit to come back in corporeal form. Not to the same locality at any rate - which was probably just as well, given the damage some of them had done during previous visits.

"I saw a movie about reincarnation once," Rory added helpfully. "It could have been Nicole Kidman."

"Great," said Charlie. "Just great."

"It's all very strange," said Rory, "I'll give you that. But this is a strange place and Tempest min is a strange child. But I think

Dr. Carlyle is right. To be honest, he usually is. So if I were you, I'd just go along with it."

"Don't mention this to anybody, will you?" said Charlie. "Not even Christina. *Please.* It could be viewed as a breach of medical confidentiality. But I just had to get it out."

*****

Charlie took his seat in the green room with a sigh. He didn't notice what flowers were in the fireplace, or Dr. Deshpande's sumptuously silky, peach coloured tie. But at least he'd come.

"I'm pleased you decided to go on with this," said Dr. Deshpande. "It could work without you, but barely as well."

Charlie gave a brief nod.

"Could we talk a little about the accident, do you think? At the very least, it would help me understand more of what Christopher is saying."

"I wasn't there."

"So tell me why not," said Dr. Deshpande gently. "I've already looked up details from official sources, accident reports, newspapers and so on. At least my secretary has. But tell me why you weren't in the van. Tell me about that."

Charlie still didn't want to talk about it, but Dr. Deshpande was a very patient man and he just sat there quietly until finally Charlie said in a low, monotonous voice, "The gig was scheduled for a Friday night at an enormous venue in London. It was to be the showcase for the release of our third album which was going out on a really big label. We weren't what you would call famous, but we were pretty well known by that point. And yet, we weren't making enough money to give up the day jobs. Surprising, you might think, but some record labels were already in trouble - including the indie label we'd started out on. Modern technology wasn't running in favour of the music industry - but that's another story. Craig still worried that he might have to be an accountant. None of us had ceased other work entirely. But a month previously I'd finally given notice, and what was to be my last shift ever had fallen on that fateful Friday morning. Much as I hated the job - it was in telephone sales - for some peculiar reason I wanted to do that final shift. It was like a goodbye, almost a rite of passage, and I felt that to do it would be a good preparation for the evening's performance. Everybody prepares for the big moment in their own way. I was the band's front man so virtually everything depended on me, and I thought that the best thing would be to continue in the way things had always worked in the past. Take the gig as it came. Stay calm. Don't disrupt the routine. Do exactly what I would have done had it been any other local, Friday night gig."

He paused, suddenly distracted. "We had a final run through of the set on the Thursday evening, in the studio Tom's father had built for us at their house in Berkshire. We got so much pleasure out of that studio. Did so much together there … jamming and stuff, you know. Musical ideas often come through jamming. When a band just plays together, things develop and progress. We didn't always set out to write, or to arrange something that Joe and I had already written. Some days, we didn't feel like that. We just wanted to play together. We'd say, 'How about we just mess about in E minor and A for an hour or so?' It was … it was …" He stopped and stared off into space. "It was pleasure, it was companionship, it was life. Actually, it was more than life. It was what we lived for …" He stopped.

"So, tell me more about that then." Dr. Deshpande nudged him quietly along. "You're doing fine. Tell me more about the band and the music."

"Look, during the day, my job was to ring people who didn't want to talk to me, and try to persuade them to buy special chairs or something that would help them get to their feet when they couldn't. It didn't feel good and I never liked it, but when I got together with the band … well, then I knew why I was doing it. Why I needed the money it paid, until such time as …" He paused for a moment. "You never really make music alone, you know. There's the other musicians, and the producers, and the sound engineers … In the end, it's a collaboration. Even for a lone folk singer with an acoustic guitar, it can still be a collaboration. With the audience. A kind of reaching out - to those who'll be part of it, to those who might eventually listen to it, but most importantly of all, perhaps, to your own soul. I know that sounds a bit … well … souls and stuff … and I should probably be using the word psyche, shouldn't I? Especially bearing in mind my initial reaction to all of this. But after Joe, Tom and Craig were killed, there was no one I wanted to reach out to any more. Not even myself."

He stopped, suddenly lost. Dr. Deshpande just sat quietly - staying with him emotionally, holding the space, but asking nothing of him. Then finally he said, "You're right about the soul thing, Charlie. Creativity is, at its purest, a form of self-development. A finding, an exposure even, of oneself. And sometimes, perhaps, a reaching towards that which seems beyond oneself. Done for the purest reasons, without any nod to the social significance it could bring, it becomes a form of consecrated action. Whether a person puts a religious or metaphysical spin on that is another matter. As a psychiatrist, I can vouch only for the therapeutic effect it can have on the psyche."

"Sometimes, it can feel like hell," said Charlie.

"So you suck it up, take a deep breath, and start again," said Dr. Deshpande. "And therein lies the lesson. 'What is written without pain is rarely read with pleasure.' Dr. Johnson, I think I was told. Though sometimes I wish our prep school English teacher hadn't been quite such a dour Scot. He believed that happiness was the consequence of struggle, not the avoidance of it. And you had to keep on earning it. It was the pay off, brief but beautiful, that you got for all the blood, sweat and tears. And I can assure you that there were plenty of tears. We were all crouching behind our desks like Rabbie Burns' terrified 'wee mousies'. It's no wonder I ended up as a psychiatrist." He glanced round the room for a moment or two. "But let's get back to the accident, if you feel you can. You say you ran through the set on the Thursday night."

Charlie pulled himself together. "Yes. Yes, that's right. The others had arranged to keep the Friday free so they could stay over at Tom's, spend the morning getting stuff organised, load it up into the van, pick me up from the flat, and get us to the venue in plenty of time for set up and sound check. The problem was the fog, a previous accident that held things up, and the fact that it was Friday afternoon when half the country's population starts tearing along motorways in preparation for the weekend."

Charlie sat silent again after this, head in his hands, tears suddenly filling his eyes - reminded yet again that he and the Gibson were the only tangible remains of that exciting, uproarious Thursday night practice session when he and his friends had played together for the last time. He'd taken the Gibson home with him afterwards because that's what he did. He played it before he went to sleep, he played it at the start of every day. After the accident, the guitar had become a painful touchstone. The strongest remaining connection between him and his friends. Until now. And now there was … what exactly? Tempest min? Or Joe Beck?

"I'm so sorry," Dr. Deshpande finally filled the silence. "So very sorry."

"Thanks," said Charlie. "Me too."

There was further silence, and then Dr. Deshpande said, "Christopher has a very strong feeling that he let you down. One could assume that he was talking about, well, to put it bluntly, the fact that he managed to get himself killed instead of turning up for the most important moment in the band's life."

Charlie looked at him in surprise.

"I know it sounds harsh to put it like that, but it illustrates my point. The situation was obviously beyond Joe Beck's control. He wasn't even the one driving. I believe it was a type of manager?"

Charlie explained that the new record company had sent someone to make sure they didn't forget anything, keep them focused for the performance, and drive the van. A roadie cum 'for Chrissakes hold it together' person.

"So isn't it odd that Christopher should feel quite so guilty? Why would he feel this great sense of having betrayed you? What else was going on?"

Charlie shrugged.

Shrugs that could be an effort to disengage with the process had no deterrent effect whatsoever on Dr. Deshpande. "When we were all in the sanatorium together," he said, "Christopher talked about sleeping on your floor because he didn't live with you anymore. At other times, he's talked about a woman. Quite a difficult woman with whom he seemed to be very close. At first, I thought he was talking about his mother, either the one he has now, or the one he had before. But then I came to realise that she actually sounded more like a girlfriend. Was there some sort of triangle going on between the three of you?"

"No way," said Charlie. "I was never any fan at all of Joe's girlfriend. Joe came back to me whenever she gave him a hard time. It was a stormy relationship."

"And your relationship with Joe was purely friendly? You were just friends?"

Charlie gave him a look. And took exception to the use of the word 'just' - going on to explain that he'd been closer to Joe Beck than to any of his own brothers. Suspicious of Dr. Deshpande's thought processes, however, he took time to emphasise that there had never been anything, nor was there ever likely to have been anything, sexual between Joe and him. That sort of thing hadn't been on the cards. Or in the wind. Or being secretly suppressed in any way. And he wasn't interested in hearing about the Freudian double-bind where 'yes' meant 'yes' and 'no' meant he was in denial. The third part of the triangle, he said, since they obviously had to have one, was not repressed homosexuality but the band. By which he meant the music, the project. He felt, he explained, that Joe, in living with

321

Lucinda - Lucinda being the girlfriend - was going to move farther away from the project.

"Why?" asked Dr. Deshpande. "Because he would be less available to tour or to write? What was it?" He glanced at his notes. "Tom didn't live with you anymore. Craig never did. So what was it?"

"Lucinda was at med school in London," said Charlie. "Barts. By the time Joe moved in with her, he'd finished at the music academy and was just doing whatever convenient odd jobs he could find, in order to keep the wolf from the door. Teaching the guitar here, labouring a bit for Tom's father there. But this never suited Lucinda, who ran with a crowd that wanted to cure cancer or be brain surgeons. And it certainly didn't suit her parents. It wasn't their way of going on at all. And I don't think for a moment that they ever thought the band could make it really big. They viewed the entire thing as some sort of teenage fantasy that was getting well past its sell-by-date. Joe was never particularly academic, but they'd all come to feel that he could, and should, set about upgrading himself in some way. That was the elephant in the room."

"And Joe was starting to think that way too?"

"No. But it put a strain on him. It divided his loyalties and didn't do a whole lot for his self-respect. He felt really hurt that one way and another - including as a musician - he wasn't seen as good enough."

"Do you think he would have left the band?"

"By the time he was killed, the band was pretty well there. The third album was generally voted, by those in the know, as the mother lode. Not that that would have been the end of the pressure on us, far from it, but at least Lucinda should've been about to stop getting at him."

"Why do you think this girl didn't get herself a boyfriend more in keeping with her ideas?"

"The relationship started back in school," said Charlie. "At that point, having a boyfriend in a band was generally viewed as cool."

"But then, in university, she apparently came round to the view that it wasn't quite as cool. So why hang on?"

"Joe was a good looking guy," said Charlie. "And, unlike most good looking guys, he had a very sweet nature. He would certainly never have cheated or messed her around in any way. His parents' divorce probably played heavily into that. Joe had seen, at first hand, how much pain cheating and betrayal could cause. He was an only child, so I was the one he always shared his misery with. And there was a lot of it, believe me. Even when we were still in primary school. By the time he died, he had virtually no contact with his parents. They'd been an emotional train wreck for him. I don't know how he stayed as thoroughly decent and easy tempered as he did. He had every excuse to be robbing supermarkets and shooting-up all day. Maybe the music saved him ... I don't know ... maybe it did. Our dream anyway. The thing he looked to for some wonderful, if hypothetical, future. But to get back to Lucinda, you could say that at one level she understood what a good thing she had – at another level, she just wasn't quite satisfied with it."

Dr. Deshpande studied him thoughtfully for a moment or two. "You know, Charlie," he said finally, "you might have made a halfway decent analyst."

"I'd have made a better rock star," said Charlie. And he gave a flicker of a smile for the first time.

Seeing it, Dr. Deshpande nodded contentedly to himself. He let a contemplative silence reign for a few seconds and then he began to talk, quite impersonally and factually about Christopher. He explained, again, that children who remember past lives often began to lose the memories by the age of six or seven. As far as it was possible to tell, by the time Christopher came to Puckrup, the predominant thing he felt was a compulsion to hum. To call out to somebody - as they now understood it - even though he could no longer visualise exactly who. Previously, of course, he might well have been able to, though according to his mother he never mentioned any names. Or maybe she just didn't register them. Impossible to know.

"But then *you* arrived," Dr. Deshpande leaned back thoughtfully in his chair. "His most enduring, and possibly most powerful, emotional bond from his previous life. And, in addition to that, you represented the great appointment, the great commitment in fact, that he failed to keep the night he died. But perhaps, most tragically of all, that very night also also held what could have been his grand moment of personal vindication. Of validation. No wonder it was such a hard thing to erase … Nevertheless, had you never come here, it might all just have faded. Even the humming."

"Well, let's look at that," said Charlie, slightly sharp again. "I admit that I was surprised at how Tempest min's hummings were so reminiscent of Joe's. I can't deny that listening to him gave me the oddest feelings. But, as I've already pointed out to somebody else lately, there are a limited number of notes.

Sometimes people stumble on very similar tunes. Even to the extent of getting sued for it. And you know what they say about originality being the art of remembering what you heard and forgetting where you heard it. But, that apart, we're not actually saying that the humming brought me here, are we? Because that would be ridiculous. Tempest min might think it did but ... well ... frankly, the limits of possibility are already a long way past breaking point, don't you think?"

Dr. Deshpande didn't seem to have any comment to make on that. He took a look out of the window instead. At which point, the door suddenly opened and Dr. Carlyle came in. He was looking very spruce and chipper in a fawn corduroy jacket, a maroon shirt and a bow tie with Jack Russell terriers and foxes' masks all over it. Which, being a man of many and varied ties himself, Dr. Deshpande noticed and passed comment on, by way of greeting. A present from the trembly terrier, Dr. Carlyle said. And one he felt obliged to wear, even at the risk of looking like a member of a hunt supporters' club. He called it cross-cultural respect. He and the trembly terrier, he explained, obviously had different views about things, and understandably so, because the trembly terrier was only fifteen inches tall and not equipped for reading, or studying ethics, or queuing in an orderly way to get his food at Tescos. So he was obliged, by nature, to lead a different sort of life, with different kinds of values. But, he'd been so touchingly pleased to have found himself depicted on a bow tie that a person just had to wear it now and then.

"Right," said Dr. Deshpande. Possibly as he himself was touting what could be regarded as a somewhat fantastical view just at the moment, he didn't even raise his eyebrows.

Dr. Carlyle put the tray he was carrying down on the desk. "Some discussions are always better for timely interruptions," he said. "Gives the emotional dust time to settle. And, as I persuaded Charlie to be cooperative, I thought I'd find an excuse to come and see for myself how that was working out." He beamed round at them. "Unfortunately, I couldn't find Mrs. Batt to make the tea. I hope she's not up to some mischief. You'd never think it, but sometimes she has little plans that she doesn't share with me." He swirled the teapot round a bit. "Should I be mother? It should be brewed. Could be awful, of course." He gave a slight grimace. "Still, I'd like to have a cup with you, if you don't mind. A hot drink is quite a novelty for me - though it has to be said that cold tea is one of the lesser trials of being the headmaster of such an event-filled establishment."

He pulled up a spare chair, picked up the teapot and beamed brightly again. "So, what were you just talking about?"

"The humming," said Dr. Deshpande, watching suspiciously as a stream of dark brown liquid issued from the teapot spout. "Charlie was baulking at the humming. And even I find it difficult to give credit to Christopher's claims that it was an effective summons. Some sort of musical carrier pigeon."

"Oh, Charlie," Dr. Carlyle pulled a face - whether it was at him or the tea, Charlie couldn't decide. "I believe we've touched on this subject before."

"Being summoned by long distance humming? I don't think so."

It's doubtful if, up to this point, Dr. Deshpande had been fully acquainted with Dr. Carlyle in full expository flow. Though he may have benefited, in the way of advanced warning, from the commentary on the bow tie, what followed had to be a serious test of the elasticity of his scientific opinions. If his boundaries were as near to popping point as they cared to be, all credit, he didn't look overly discommoded. His pupils merely began to dilate a little, as if he'd been given some mind expanding drug. The music of the cosmos was obviously a new concept for him. That the Chinese had once had a high old time with the idea was clearly not last year's news in Malibu or Harley Street.

In ancient Chinese theory, Dr. Carlyle explained, pitches and intervals and modes were set in relation to all conceivable elements of the cosmos. Right down to kinds of animals and body parts. The belief was that music did not only reflect the order of the cosmos but could, itself, influence it. Could influence the cosmic harmony and affect the order of things. "You were called to, Charlie," he finished. "Tempest min called out in just the right tones, and the cosmos responded. It got you here." He took a sip from his cup. "Not bad this tea, is it?"

Charlie and Dr. Deshpande looked at each other.

"But, putting the ancient Chinese aside, why would Tempest min feel prompted to call in that way?" Charlie asked, finally. "Isn't this just so beyond …?" He gave up.

"Puckrup is a place where these things happen," said Dr. Carlyle. "And the staff and I are simply midwives to the process. As mere mortals, we just do the best we can. Provide help for the journey and strength for the way. You were never meant to live out your life in that basement Charlie, you were meant to come here. As was Tempest min. And his coming was in the face of quite some family opposition, I might add. And Dr. Deshpande, good man that he is, was always due his moment of grace. Didn't I tell you? There's a synchronicity bordering on predestination that operates in this place. That's how it is. Stuff happens. We are a quantum phenomenon. I think the Celts might have called Puckrup 'a thin place', meaning that it is one of those rare locales where the distance between the realms collapses. That's all I can tell you. More than that would be mere speculation. Man can ask the great questions, Charlie, but he cannot come up with great answers. So," he stood up suddenly and gulped down the rest of his drink, "sorry to leave you, but it's time I was on my way. Something else is always brewing in the world of the unfathomable. Now," he mused to himself as he headed for the door, "I wonder if I could find Mrs. Batt and sweetheart a piece of cake out of her?"

"A moment of grace ?" asked Dr. Deshpande, when Dr. Carlyle had gone.

"I think he means a helpful glimpse into the great scheme of things. An enhanced understanding," said Charlie, shaking his head. There was no rationalising any of this. It was positively hallucinogenic in its oddness. Puckrup certainly seemed to be stationed under some weird belt of astral influence. There were moments when Dr. Carlyle was a normal, if slightly eccentric, school headmaster but there were other moments when he was well … something way beyond eccentric.

"Quite remarkable," said Dr. Deshpande, leaning back in his chair as if suddenly struck with wonder. "Quite remarkable. However, you did in fact end up here, didn't you? By whatever means." He brought the front legs of his chair back to earth with a jolt, and then went on with his train of thought. "And consequently, Christopher's memories started to resurface. But because Christopher, or Joe as he was then, died a traumatic death in a state of high emotion on what seemed destined to be a life-changing evening - literally a life-changing evening as it worked out - these were very difficult things for him to process. Also difficult to completely expunge. He was left prey to unsettling half-formed feelings and vague recollection. Only in his dreams and the surrendered creativity of his drawings, did his unconscious knowledge come through. But when he heard you playing the guitar that night in Hereford House, it was like a lightning strike. Everything was suddenly and starkly illuminated for him. And it was just too much to cope with. His instinct, as always, was to run to you. And yes, at one level he would have been happy to recognise and be with his friend again, but with that came such a sudden emotional and psychological overload that his brain just switched off. In this life, we must remember, he's just a child."

"I'm categorisable as an adult," said Charlie with a sigh. "And I'm showing signs of psychological overload myself." He paused for a few moments to gather his thoughts. Then he pointed out that it might have been a lot easier on everyone if the 'universe' (for want of a better expression) had done things differently. Simply allowed Tempest min's memories to fade.

"And you had stayed in the Camden basement?" Dr. Deshpande looked thoughtful. "Obviously it wasn't meant, or at any rate it didn't happen, that way. Christopher kept calling and, according to Dr. Carlyle, the universe responded. And in the long run, Christopher will be the happier for it. It seems - from some of my friend's background reading, as opposed to his personal research - that individuals with strong emotional ties, that are suddenly and prematurely disrupted by unexpected death, can return into the same story, as it were - a continuation of life in the same area with the same people. And hopefully, that turns out to be beneficial. Provides some sort of resolution. Psyches never flourish as well in the face of unfinished business, you know. Even if that business is ostensibly forgotten. And, after all, a great and ultimate flourishing would be more or less the point of reincarnation, don't you think? It seems to me that if there is anything in the nature of the Christian God, and if he is really as good and loving as is claimed, then only an insane optimist could honestly reconcile this goodness with a one-shot mortality that is so outrageously unfair in its allotment of experience. In which case, if the paradigm of this paradoxical God is to persist at all, people should maybe allow themselves a revision of the way they look at death. Or perhaps, more pertinently, life."

"I don't know," said Charlie shaking his head. "It all seems so unlikely. So far outside the box, I just don't know how to respond to it."

There was another silence then, until Dr. Deshpande finally said, "Supposing this were true, Charlie. Supposing Christopher were really your friend Joe. Reincarnated. Wouldn't that be something? Really something? Wouldn't it be life-changing? The idea that second chances are infinite? That life is not just a one-off experience that we cram, sometimes very badly, into such years as we have? Freud, of course, taught us that it was. When religion in the western world began its terminal decline, he heralded what the

330

sociologist Reiff came to call the age of therapeutic man. An age in which we are thrown back on nothing but our own psychological resources. Freud once wrote that the minute someone started to question the meaning of his life, and of existence, he was already sick because neither life nor existence had any ultimate meaning. And with particular genius he went ahead and systematised this belief. Nobody was going to save us, except ourselves. And that saving consisted of nothing more than maintaining a balance between the inner man's struggles and the outer man's ability to function in society. A thing that could be achieved by deep analytical self-scrutiny. It was simply a means of preventing our feelings and failings from disrupting our lives. His method had no doctrinal synthesis. He merely intended to create a person who could, in the memorable but much less intellectual words of Winston Churchill, 'just keep buggering on'."

"I know very little about any of this," said Charlie, after a pause. "But didn't Freud at least provide us with some excuses? Aren't most things the fault of our potty training, or some innate desire to kill our fathers?"

"You're quite right," said Dr. Deshpande. "One must never underestimate the salvific value of a really attractive and intellectually propagated excuse."

They sat in silence for what seemed like a prolonged period, and then Dr. Deshpande finally said, "But to actually believe that there could be a time to do things better, to get another chance at happiness, to earn redemption … For me especially, with all the pain and confusion that I have to witness in this world, to come to understand and believe something like that - well, it really *would* constitute a moment of grace."

Chapter Eighteen

Whilst the idea that Tempest min could actually have once been Joe Beck naturally occupied a large part of Charlie's mind, it was prevented from totally disrupting it by the pressing intervention of other things. With the term of important examinations looming nearer there was, primarily, his constant endeavour to transplant chemistry into skulls that occasionally seemed quite barren and dry. And then there was Rory's love life, his own lack of a love life, and the demands he'd inflicted upon himself due to his involvement with Blake Vane Tempest. Fortunately, of all these things, Rory's love life was the only one that actively demanded attention at breakfast.

The progress with Christina Le Blanc was best described as stumbling. It wasn't every day that Rory set out from the flat with a light heart and a cheerful whistle. Charlie dispensed sympathy and advice as best he could, the tone and content fluctuating daily according to the pitch of Rory's confusion and the quality of the coffee. Obviously, Christina came with emotional baggage, he said. Who didn't at thirty-five years old? So what was the baggage? Was it still the git from Gloucester, or was there something else?

Rory didn't know. Speaking generally, Charlie offered, he thought women were hormonally complex and emotionally unfathomable. Some days it was impossible to tell what they really wanted. And in his, Charlie's, experience what they wanted seemed to be influenced by all sorts of random variables … the phase of the moon, the direction of the wind, a toilet seat left up, a pair of underpants with 'abandon hope all ye who enter here' written across the crotch in marker pen by persons unknown … Any number, in fact, of unpredictable environmental events could trigger a mood that would be impossible to suss and extremely dicey to try and mess with. You needed to be a complex systems analyst to deal effectively with the female of the species. Or, better still, a threat analyst. Especially with women like Christina. They could send a day to hell faster than anything else he knew.

And with a stab of pain he saw again his friend Joe, sobbing in a sleeping bag on the floor of the flat.

"I," said Rory, standing up with a savage scraping back of his chair, "am going to punch you in a minute. And as useless and deliberately provoking as you're being as an agony aunt, you can get your own damned coffee." He paused. "Do you always have to be so fucking flippant?"

"Do I begrudge *you* your coping mechanisms?"

The most he'd learned about male/female relationships, Charlie added, looking at the new Nespresso machine which had Christina written all over it, was that he'd never had one he'd been desperately keen to maintain. Plus, the wind didn't seem to blow quite as changeably in South Korea. Mens' foibles seemed to be more readily indulged there. Possibly. Or ignored. One or the other, for sure.

"Well, shouldn't you just be writing the book?" Rory snapped. He'd found himself in possession of a well-thumbed copy of Men are from Mars Women are from Venus, which had been unaccountably pressed into his hand one day by Madeline Lowry, the drama teacher. He didn't like it.

"You keep wanting information," Charlie pointed out to him.

"Aye, but how come Madeline Lowry's got involved?" Rory was seriously irritated.

"Same way I have, I guess." said Charlie. "Has anybody suggested that you should be reading Fifty Shades of Grey?"

"Is it thick?"

*****

And so the month of March came in like a lion, bringing with it fitful sheets of hail. Lady KP and Ianthe seemed to have gone somewhere. A holiday? Some sort of biodynamic retreat? Charlie didn't know. All he knew was that in his hour of need, or one of them at any rate, when he'd wanted to turn over the reincarnation concept with a confidant more beautiful and less otherwise preoccupied than Rory, he'd found an alien youth in the potting shed, mixing up compost with a pronounced disinterest in the whereabouts of the people for whom he was evidently working. In fact, it hadn't even been a youth, exactly. Youth could, perhaps, have excused the total lack of anything remotely useful to say. It had been some strange, ageless creature, sharp of eye but apparently dull of wits. And with the dirtiest hands imaginable. Weird ears too. Large with cavernous holes sprouting wiry hair. Charlie felt gripped by an annoying

334

sense of being deliberately put off. And he felt such a need to talk to Ianthe. Though he was frankly bemused by half the things she said, he always felt better for talking to her. It was like having a confessor who never pressed for a confession, or a psychoanalyst who never accused him of having suppressed sexual urges (though in her case he did) but simply pushed open a window so that some sunshine could come in and illuminate what needed illuminating, and chase away what was merely lurking to no purpose.

In her absence, he found himself walking round the sports field, taking handfuls of hail in the face, and needing somebody to talk to. Three or four weeks had elapsed since the concept of reincarnation had been introduced to him, and Dr. Deshpande was continuing to ply to and fro between London and Herefordshire, possibly neglecting Malibu, but having regular sessions with Tempest min, and calling on Charlie to be present for a portion of the time. More things had emerged. The fact, for instance, that lesions and other bodily defects or injuries were often inherited in a vestigial way from a previous incarnation. Tempest min's propensities to sprain his left wrist could conceivably be correlated with Joe's repetitive strain injury. Moreover, the timing of everything seemed to chime happily with certain statistics drawn up by Dr. Deshpande's friend during his research. The average interval between the death of a previous person and the birth of a child was only sixteen months, the interval being typically short. (Charlie did some quick sums in his head.) The endings of past lives that are remembered tended to be premature, and frequently traumatic in some way. The individuals had usually died whilst quite young. Most of this pragmatic information was, of course, aired for Charlie's benefit. And it was of unquestionable significance to him that it had been gathered during bona fide scientific enquiry, and not from religious myth or 'new age' past life regressions.

In terms of therapy, Dr. Deshpande had explained, problems presenting from past lives could share a lot of symptoms with post-traumatic stress disorder, and so his conversations with Tempest min, on his own, remained mostly private – involving, as they did, the necessity to work through things in a way that would enable a little boy to process trauma.

For Charlie, the situation didn't feel quite so convenient. Unfortunately, certain aspects of it remained difficult to explain in any 'get real' way. Tempest min, however, seemed remarkably philosophical. An amiable and affectionate acceptance of his 'memories' from Charlie was apparently a fundamental need for him and, given that, he appeared to be improving. Even Matron had to admit that he was sleeping a lot better. The only problem was, in certain circumstances, he had to remember that his friend Charlie was actually Mr. Peterson, one of the masters at the school. And he had to respect that. Nevertheless, there were occasions when he seemed unable to suppress the urge to run up to him in corridors and launch into episodes of 'do you remember when?'. And more often than could be comfortably swept under some mental carpet, Charlie *did* remember when. And sometimes very thoroughly. Truthfully, he didn't like it.

He especially didn't like conversations about sleeping on floors. Lucinda was still mostly a closed book to Tempest min, and Charlie didn't think he should be opening it any further without Dr. Deshpande present. And maybe not even then. He had no idea how to talk to a child about an adult sexual relationship that the child was supposed to have had in another life. In compiling her leaflets, the lady from LAFFAS had disobligingly overlooked this problem.

"It was a woman, wasn't it?" Tempest min seemed pretty sure about this. "But I don't remember her as well as I remember you. And she sort of gives me funny feelings."

Charlie interrupted him hastily. "There's always a woman," he said, thinking of himself and Rory - both at least quarter of a century older than Tempest min, and barely more advanced in understanding. "And women can give you quite a variety of funny feelings. Some of them nice, some of them quite painful. And it's been like that for, well, forever. So being confused about a woman is far from a unique experience, whichever lifetime you're in. It's just one of those things we have to accept. You'll realise that as you get older."

"I think I will," said Tempest min. "My mother seems to cause no end of trouble. There's always some man about the place in a terrible sulk. Do you think that's why I don't have a father? Because women are so difficult?"

"It isn't just women who are difficult," said Charlie, hastily. "Men can be extremely difficult. And, given half a chance and a few drinks, they can dig very deep holes for themselves. So, men and women getting along together presents – yes – difficulties. It's something we have to learn to deal with. Like life itself. Maybe that's why we have so many lifetimes. So we can learn from a whole mess of different difficulties."

"It doesn't sound much fun."

"Well, that's why we have to do our best to create as much

fun as we can." Charlie quickly reinvigorated his tone. "We must enjoy the fun in life, and be as sensible and brave as we can about the difficulties."

By this point, they had reached a parting of the ways. In spite of possibly having had numberless lifetimes, Tempest min was currently a child and fortunately, at least for the length of time it took to traverse a corridor or two, he could be verbally parried without getting too deeply into those things that Charlie wasn't certain it would be a good idea to get deeply into.

But, in spite of the airing of so many indisputable facts, and the accumulation of startling coincidences, Charlie persisted in his feeling that the whole business was a nonsense. And then he wondered if he was getting like the awkward character in a science fiction story. The one who's been given too hefty a dose of wilful blindness. The one who refuses to believe in the killer tomatoes even when they're rolling down the street to crush him. The one the reader starts to get really irritated with.

On a practical level, however, and he had to keep reminding himself of this, the reincarnation theory appeared to be working well as a base from which to conduct post-traumatic therapeutics. Plus, he seemed to be the only one deeply disturbed by the actual principle. It was not, apparently, an enormous thing to a small boy who still had the wonder of childhood left to protect him.

Then, as another blast of hail hit him in the face, Charlie found he'd had enough of wandering round the sports field thinking about all of this to no particular end, so he walked down the school drive and a mile or more along a silent country road.

*****

Myra O'Grady's small rented cottage could once have been the gatehouse to somewhere very impressive. It wasn't obvious which somewhere - maybe it was merely a back entrance to the original estates of Puckrup Hall. Charlie just took it in at the level of fleeting observation. This being an impromptu visit, he was more concerned about his reception. But Myra was most welcoming – in a disorganised, hair-on-end sort of way. The cottage was a place of squashy armchairs, cluttered coffee tables and piles of books. The small sitting room had the upended look of a church bazaar or a rummage sale. Green logs were strewn over a quarry tiled hearth, drying out in such heat as their smouldering companions in the grate were prepared to give off. Whatever legacy Myra had brought away from her sojourn in an Irish convent, spare and austere minimalism wasn't part of it. Nor was abstaining from alcohol. There were two glasses of whisky in evidence, and Dr. Maccabee was drinking one of them.

Charlie suggested that, as there was entertaining in progress, he could come back another time.

"I don't entertain him intentionally," said Myra. "It's merely an unfortunate side effect of his infuriatingly persistent visits."

And she added, while Dr. Maccabee continued to smile genially, that she had no desire to be visited by an unmoored old man who was the defunct product of a business that was part maths, part science and part philosophy, whilst managing to serve none of them particularly well. "So please sit down," she concluded. "I was just praying for some sort of divine intervention. Drink?"

"No, thank you," said Charlie, blinking slightly in the face of the fierce energy that Myra always managed to infuse into her verbal onslaughts. "I feel in need of a clear head these days."

"Tempest min?"

Charlie nodded.

"Coffee then? There's some here," Myra laid a hand on a cafetière. "It's still warm."

"Thank you."

"Dr. Carlyle did bring me in on the situation to some extent." Myra poured coffee into a rough pottery mug. "It *is* rather my field, you know. I hope you don't mind. He guessed you might want to talk to me about it at an appropriate moment."

Dr. Maccabee, who had obviously been brought in on it too, had trouble with the idea of reincarnation. The survival of a consciousness which was supposed to exist, and subsequently persist, as an entity separable from the material body was not a box he felt inclined to tick, he said. At least not in the way that Myra would have liked him to tick it.

Obviously, Myra was not best pleased to have the principle disputed outright, and so she leapt in before Charlie had a chance to react. "And wouldn't you have thought," she said, with a deal of irritation, "that as a former particle physicist he would be open to the idea? That he could just envisage this eternal consciousness - or soul to use religious terminology - as some sort of indestructible energy field? But he won't even try. Primarily to irritate me, I suspect."

Dr. Maccabee took a deep breath at this point, but she waved him aside. There didn't seem to be much chance of the pair of them managing a united front in the business of easing Charlie's anxieties. Myra was indelibly committed to the idea that any physicist with a brain had to use it as Niels Bohr had used his, i.e., in acceptance of the principle that consciousness could be a critical factor in the universe - a thing irrevocably entwined with the outcome of quantum events. And she proceeded to cite the famous double-slit experiments in which the transition from the possible to the actual had been shown to take place during the act of observation.

"Over two thousand years ago," she finished, "Epicurus was of the opinion that we don't exist unless someone can see us existing. He was hardly looking at it like a modern physicist of course - it was a philosopher's comment on the nature of our experience. In fact Epicurus, up to his knees in the ideas of 'atomism', believed that the mind was not the brain but still, being atoms, it had to break up as a functional unit when the body gave up, nevertheless … *He*, however," she gestured towards Dr. Maccabee with a snort, "is a denigrator of consciousness. He's determined that we are no more than a brain. And that the brain is just another observational device at the end of the von Neumann chain."

Dr. Maccabee, unperturbed as always by Myra's attacks (and recently and rather strokably bearded in his silver fox way) obligingly went on to explain more about the von Neumann chain. Physics was his business, but he didn't seem to mind Myra telling him how it could work. And how he should think it could work. Albert Maccabee had nothing to prove. He seemed to like himself - not in any adulatory sense, but just in the way that he thought he was good enough. And being at ease with himself seemed to put him at ease with the world. And with women too.

He liked women. Not to the extent that he'd worked up his best ideas on the back of paper napkins in strip clubs like one famous physicist was reputed to have done, but in the sense that he'd as soon have a platonic drink with a woman as with a man. And since his undergraduate days - and especially during his undergraduate days - he'd always wished, at least so he always said, that women in general were more attracted to the magic of maths and the infinities of the cosmos, and less interested in the smooth-tongued, passionate pretensions of poets and other weasels. (Poetry, some colleague on an exchange from MIT had once told him in dark frustration, was most correctly defined as a 'get into her pants' routine that favoured the liberal arts.)

It was a genuine sadness to Dr. Maccabee that the institutions in which he'd gone on to spend most of his working life had been heavily weighted towards the male of the species. If they hadn't, he might even have ended up married. Bert Maccabee was really only a silver fox to look at. He teased Myra because the results were fetchingly pink and because she understood, quite as well as he did, that it was all just … well … very extended foreplay. And what was the rush, after all? He was barely sixty, hell, he had plenty of time.

Quantum phenomena, minus the giant sums at least, weren't entirely incomprehensible to Charlie. As Dr. Maccabee talked, distant bells rang in his head. Things he'd learned himself, and things he'd picked up whilst occasionally sitting around at uni with a bunch of physicists who'd discussed this kind of stuff openly and loudly over coffee. Which they done quite particularly if there'd been a few male sociologists within earshot discussing something like social capital. It had been a form of public dick measuring that didn't get you arrested and which was suddenly turning out to be unexpectedly useful. Charlie might have been surprised to hear just how little such rivalries had changed since Dr. Maccabee's day. Poets and other weasels forever aggravating the geeks who could never quite manage to pull beguiling enough chat-up lines out of the quantum soup.

"Don't stop there," said Myra, when Dr. Maccabee showed signs of slowing down. She wanted Charlie to be given an understanding of the whole von Neumann shebang. The conviction, bolstered by calculations that made even very smart people go cross-eyed, that the end of the observational chain was not the brain acting in the capacity of a mechanical recording instrument, but the observer's abstract ego, 'the intellectual inner life of the individual'. An opinion, expanded in conjunction with Wheeler and Wigner, that came to the final conclusion that thought and consciousness were fundamental causative elements of the cosmos.

"And so we get round to the great pseudo-science of that damned self-help book," said Dr. Maccabee, irritably. "What's it called again?"

"The Secret," said Myra.

"That's it. I once spent an entire parent-teachers meeting hearing about the 'law of attraction', and how thoughts can change the world. Not ideas put into practice, or even talked about. Just thoughts. It was Tucker's mother. Mad as a hatter. I asked her if she was aware that I was the physics master, but she didn't seem to hear. People like that never do, do they?"

"No," said Myra, intent upon a line about committed materialists or 'physicalists' having been so determined that

343

human consciousness must not be critical to the outcome of quantum events that they'd scrabbled to come up with *any* alternative accommodation however gob smacking.

And they had, she said, in tones of bitter triumph. Through some sort of higgledy-piggledy reasoning (her words) they'd come up with the 'many worlds' theory. The 'many worlds' theory was something she'd obviously filed somewhere in a category on the far side of outrageous. Rather than accept that human consciousness could bring about certain outcomes in the quantum world, the materialists (referred to alternatively as 'some subset of lunatics') had postulated that every possible outcome is played out in a parallel universe. The 'we' that are in this universe don't see these outcomes, but they happen. In spite of us, not because of us. So, in effect, for every quantum event that takes place, a new world pops up to accommodate every possible outcome.

"Do you realise how many worlds there would have to be if the many worlds theory was correct?" Myra was getting shriller. Dr. Maccabee was doodling smiley faces on the front of the parish magazine. "An infinite number of worlds raised to an infinite power!" Myra's voice dropped at this point, as if she were delivering the punchline to a horror story. Which she probably thought she was. "And undetectable worlds, I must emphasise," she added. "Nobody's getting up a trip to go to one in the next few hundred years. Not even Richard Branson." Thus, she went on, committed scientific atheists had, by preposterous means, removed human consciousness from the equation, and with it any suggestion of a conscious universe. And the dreaded possibility of such consciousness being in any way divine.

Dr. Maccabee looked up from his expanding menagerie of emojis. "Niels Bohr," he said, "was a pragmatist. He accepted the intelligent-observer paradox, but he never believed there was anything behind the curtain. No deeper reality. He just called it quantum weirdness, put it in a box with things like entanglement and non-locality and didn't get worked up about a 'hidden order' like Einstein and Bohm or the 'many worlds' brigade. 'Just shut up and calculate' was Bohr's attitude. And I guess that was pretty much mine. Quantum mechanics is a useful tool for accomplishing things in the real world, just forget the bollocks behind it."

"But the many worlds theory is beyond all common sense, isn't it?" insisted Myra.

"In quantum physics common sense simply doesn't apply." Dr. Maccabee drew an unruffled face. Or was it smug face? "It's a bit like religion that way," he added, probably wishing he'd never brought up Bohm because pre-space and implicate order would be heading his way before the week was out.

Myra now launched into the history of religion as the history of mankind - the spiritual doggedness of the human species entwined irrevocably with its back story. She believed, she said, that it was the psyche's reach towards the divine that had formed the foundations of culture. In no particular order, homo religiosus, druids, Moses, Mohammed, Celtic Christians, Buddha, the Venerable Bede, the Dalai Lama, Jainism, Taoism, endless 'isms', chunks of quoted text, and fervently expressed notions flowed across the coffee table as densely as if Myra had as many mouths as Shiva had arms. She was a prodigious talker, a hectic non-stop monologuist. And all of it, Dr. Maccabee

345

pointed out when he could get a word in, the entire catalogue of superstition, was predated by the laws of physics and their mathematics.

Smirking face emojis began to embellish a piece in the parish magazine about empty pews and dwindling congregations. Myra eyed them with irritation. The magazine was an old one, but she didn't seem very keen on the underhand way it was being weaponised.

"And since such laws are derived from experiments that can only be performed on what can be materially detected, science can only make statements about the material universe," she exclaimed. "It cannot say anything authoritative about the existence, or non-existence, of purpose and meaning behind the material world. And yet it does. It just cannot keep its material mouth shut. It has anointed itself the lone explanatory apparatus and it too quickly raises what it knows to the status of an absolute. First, it told us there was nothing; we just are; it's just one of those things; now it's speculating that we could be some sort of computer simulation. University physicists actually discussing this in all seriousness at conferences. They'd rather believe that we are the product of some highly advanced computer geek than utter the word 'God'. The truth is that scientists are just inventing for themselves what they consider to be a more acceptable deity."

A computer geek to be von Neumann's conscious observer, she said. To function as some equally insane alternative to the many worlds theory. A different god to turn the possible into the actual when nobody else was there to do the beholding. A geek god for the quad. They were techno-creationists, Myra insisted, and she was extremely cross with them. "And if there wasn't some annoying consensus that they're actually very smart, they'd be in receipt of the intellectual opprobrium that gets heaped upon every other type of creationist." She sank back into the sofa cushions then, obviously in need of a respite in which to parse and reconjugate her next swarm of notions. As much as she had to convey, and as energetically as she needed to convey it, she had to find it challenging on occasion to steer a lucid way through all the sentences. Though she was obviously well qualified for the job on paper, Charlie wondered how on earth she managed to produce anything approaching meditative calm in her stop-breathe-be mindfulness sessions.

"She looks fetching when she's het up," said Dr. Maccabee. "Doesn't she? And if she'd just let me get her into bed, she'd feel a lot better about all of this, I guarantee it."

"Christ Almighty!" Provoked to blasphemy, Myra sprang back to life. "Just listen to the man! He's a primitive when it comes to human relations. I sincerely hope he was a better quality physicist than he is suitor. Nobody says that sort of thing anymore, do they, Charlie? They don't even think it."

Charlie declined to comment.

Dr. Maccabee looked at Myra for a moment or two and then announced, with a far from innocent blandness, that he was pretty certain young men thought a lot worse things. Less patronising in feminist eyes perhaps, but much more explicit and conspicuously lacking in decent feeling. Young men were now exhaustively over informed. He might not believe in God, and he might believe, chauvinistically perhaps, that a few orgasms would be a real mood lightener for her, but, and he put this on

the plus side, he did not fantasise about subjecting women to …
Clear evidence followed then, delivered in crisply scientific
tones, that Dr. Maccabee was not entirely unacquainted with
modern diversions into the more outré aspects of advanced
sexual practice. Charlie was only partly relieved that they got
mostly lost in the high-pitched soundscapes of Myra's horrified
protests.

"Bert!" She snatched Dr. Maccabee's whisky away from him.
"Not in front of the children. You mustn't drink so much."

"Well, this is all very bracing," said Charlie quickly, "but I've
obviously come to the wrong place to reach any sort of
consensus on reincarnation."

"I should point out," said Dr. Maccabee, "that computer
programmes can be stored and run again, so maybe we really *are*
in some ancestor game played by the computer whizz kids of the
future. That would accord exactly with some current theories of
mind … plus we could get to be reincarnated. What do you think
about that?"

"What do you?" asked Charlie. "Honestly, I mean."

"I think it beats the hell out of the Garden of Eden and all
the rest of it."

"Do you really?" Charlie felt it rather lacked for something -
as creation myths go. But, each to his own. And what was the
truth, in any case?

"In the Bhagavad-Gita," said Myra, "which is an ancient
Indian text, and one with which I'm sure Dr. Deshpande is at
least partly familiar, it was written that for the soul there is
neither birth nor death at any time. It 'had not come into being,
does not come into being, and will not come into being. It is

unborn, eternal, ever existing and primeval. It is not slain when the body is slain'. That's a beautiful concept, isn't? Something that inspires. Listen to this:

'I know I am deathless,
We have thus far exhausted
Trillions of winters and summers,
There are trillions ahead, and
Trillions ahead of them.'

Walt Whitman," she finished, "one of the American transcendentalist poets. For him, the question of death was the question of questions. The only one worth answering."

Bert Maccabee snorted again. He found poets irritating not inspirational, he said, finally annoyed enough give his prejudices another airing. They'd always got many more column inches in this world than they ever deserved. They were credited with grand ideas and grand ideals when mostly they were just wife swapping or bedding their sisters. It took great physicists to know what a grand idea really was, and they tried to tell people about things that no one ever knew before in such a way as to be understood by everyone, while poets did the exact opposite. And yet everyone had heard of a whole bunch of poets whereas, apart from Einstein and Stephen Hawking, the names of great physicists and mathematicians remained largely unknown and unsung.

The words of Walt Whitman had stimulated a militant build-up of emojis with bared teeth. 'Poets and other weasels' remained the Achilles' heel of Dr. Maccabee's even tempered and largely benign persona.

"You'll come back as an animal," Myra warned him.

"Something with a very limited consciousness and a total lack of self-awareness that will live for no reason other than to eat and breed."

"Can you come back as an animal?" asked Charlie.

At this point he learned that according to some early Christian oracle called Origen, one could, as a result of outrageous behaviour, come back as a plant.

A hellebore, he thought idly. Rock musicians evidently became hellebores. Ah, well. Maybe he'd die young and come back quickly enough to be in one of Puckrup's glasshouses, getting attended to by Ianthe. He was drifting. Since the discussion had increasingly turned into some adversarial mating ritual, he'd become sceptical about the value of it. As it grew in personal complications, it diminished in interest.

Meanwhile, Myra was still pressing on and Dr. Maccabee was still snorting. In the sixth century the Emperor Justinian had, for mostly doctrinal reasons, put a stop to Christians thinking they had return tickets, but Tibetan Buddhists, Myra said, still believed. And furthermore, a particularity of their belief was that the state of being you are in at the moment of death, almost how you are thinking of yourself and things at that moment, can affect what you come back as. Or even if you come back at all. Basically, as long as you are still concerned with things in the material world, you will always come back. "No prizes," she finished, "for working out why Joe Beck is here."

"Computer game rebooted," mouthed Dr. Maccabee as Myra, with the air of the one who feels she has finally triumphed in the face of persecution, went off to make some more coffee. "What do you think?" he asked Charlie when Myra was out of earshot.

"About reincarnation?"

"No. About Myra and me. Getting it together."

"Well if I were you," said Charlie, "and I was serious about it at all, I'd accept that there's no mileage in telling her she's computer generated. My father had a period when he got caught up in The Singularity stuff - you know, redemption through technology as we become spiritual machines or something, and develop an advanced consciousness that can break through the material framework of time and space."

"Transhumanism and its variants."

"That's it," said Charlie, "and I seem to remember that it coincided with a period of getting to sleep on the sofa."

"But Myra likes academic argument."

"I'm not sure she likes the sort of academic argument that reduces her to a bunch of computer generated algorithms, or promises some future fusion with an artificial intelligence. Just a suggestion, you know."

"I'm talking about us as well," protested Dr. Maccabee. "We'd be computer simulants too."

"And that would be just one more thing that could render us, you in this particular case, infinitely less attractive," Charlie pointed out. "One more reason for women to prefer the poet to the physicist."

"I never get that," said Dr. Maccabee. "I just don't get it."

"Look," said Charlie. "The poet says:

'I have known the most dear that is granted us here,

More supreme than the gods know above,

Like a star I was hurled through the sweet of the world,

And the height and the light of it, Love.'

And the physicist says:

'Cygnus X-3, an X-ray source consisting of an imploding star, is 35,000 light years away. The cosmic ray particles arriving from this object have been shown to be travelling in a straight line, showing no signs of having been deflected off course at any time.'

Get it now? All other things being more or less equal, I would say it's obvious which one of them was going to get the girl."

"That's actually correct," responded Dr. Maccabee in some surprise. "About Cygnus X-3."

"Very probably," agreed Charlie. "And the bit of poetry was probably Rupert Brooke. I have a knack for remembering disconnected irrelevancies and getting confused about big things. Like who I'm supposed to be."

"You're the chemistry master," said Dr. Maccabee. "And as such, you're *supposed* to be on my side."

At this point, Myra came back from the kitchen looking calm. She'd obviously shrugged off the indignity of being a computer simulant, and forged a new line of attack. She produced from her cardigan pocket a piece of paper which she proceeded to unfold with an air of conspiracy.

"'The conservation of information law'," she read out. "There is a postulate in physics which states that information, like energy, can neither be created nor destroyed." She paused and looked up before going on. "Now - and bear with me here - supposing, just supposing, that our consciousness were, as I previously suggested, and as people much smarter than I am have also suggested, a type of information carrying energy field.

Then I quote you this: 'The no-cloning theorem and the no-deleting theorem can provide permanence to quantum information. To create a copy, one must import the information from some part of the universe, and to delete a state, one needs to export it to another part of the universe where it will continue to exist.'"

She paused again here, to allow this to sink in. "Now, I understand that I could be way off beam and need this properly explained to me. I also understand that sex can be a transactional procedure so, in the interests of my fascination with the possible nature of the soul, I am prepared to review the advantages of joining the oldest profession of all. If Albert Maccabee were prepared to go through all of this stuff with me, very nicely and without prejudice, in the sweetest of ways, I would be prepared to go through a lot of stuff with him, very nicely and without prejudice, in the sweetest of ways." And she gave Charlie an enormous wink.

"Pass me the laptop," said Dr. Maccabee. "I always knew you didn't need to be a bloody poet."

Stimulating as this discussion about the 'conservation of information' was obviously going to be, Charlie thought he'd better excuse himself from it, so he took his leave. When he and Dr. Maccabee were alone for a few seconds at the front door he said, "Don't bring up transhumanism, Bert. *Please*. And in this no-cloning, no-deleting thing, don't get into computer games again. Try and stick with how it could, or could not, possibly explain a soul on Myra's terms. In spite of all her frantic efforts to bring science into the picture, she was a nun for pushing twenty years. That has to run deep. If you really want to blend science with religion in any romantic sense, you're going to need a very light touch. Gently does it. In every way. Circumnavigate a bit. Know what I mean?"

Bert Maccabee nodded.

"And think of my problems," Charlie added, as he turned away. "I've got a dear, dead friend apparently come to life as a seven-year-old schoolboy. Plus, I could be falling in love with somebody who sees fairies in trees."

*****

The hail had stopped and the sky had cleared. He walked slowly back to the school, lost in thought. When knowledge runs out, we have only two choices: we either don't think about some things very much at all, or we live life according to a belief of choice. And, arguably, this belief of choice, this narrative that we create, becomes, in effect, a personalised metaphysics. Something, Charlie reasoned, that probably gets us through the pains of life - and of death - just as well as the truth itself would do, were we actually to be in possession of it.

Until recently, death was one of those things that Charlie had chosen not to think about. He wasn't, of course, alone in that. The entire western world was in a frenzy of activity - earning, spending, drinking, imbibing endless pharmaceuticals and generally adding as much and as varied sex and fun as it could to its bucket list. All to avoid any contemplation of the abyss.

After the accident, Charlie had built a wall of pain between him and this abyss. A wall whose shadow he'd lived in, but whose heights he'd never tried to scale in order to take a squint at the other side. His grandmother's death, a few years later, had merely added broken glass to the top of the wall. Unable to face more loss, he'd cheated on the hospital visiting. He'd chosen not to look death full in the face, or reflect in depth upon the nature of its evident finality. So, he had no real idea what Grandma Peterson had thought as she lay there at the end. Had any one ever asked her? he wondered, now. Did anyone ever ask these things of the dying? Was she afraid? Had she thought that there was the possibility of anything else? And if so, what?

She'd no longer been aware of much, his father had said. No point in going to the hospital to just to sit there. For what it was worth, he would sit there. He and Lottie would sit there. Charlie had been much in Grandma's life when she'd been able to enjoy him. That was what mattered. And it was true - nursemaid and babysitter, she'd been the one who'd always been there, open armed. The one who'd enabled his mother to go on working at the position she'd finally acquired in the posh art auction house when the unplanned baby arrived.

Three boys had been enough for the Petersons in terms of offspring, but his mother's long held desire for a girl child had, as she'd always claimed, apparently worked away in her unconscious to significant effect. Not quite significant enough to get the arrangement of the chromosomes right, but there he was with his penis and his testicles, and Grandma Peterson had stepped in, helping to rear him up on homily and home-made soup. And it had been like being reared up by a grandmother in a fairy story. Someone unaffianced to any religion, but with powerful convictions about how the universe worked. It existed, he'd gathered, in all its immensity, for the express purpose of keeping human beings in line. It was dedicated to comeuppance.

It visited misfortune upon children who did not eat up their greens. Their hair would not curl, nor their limbs grow straight. It cast shade upon the futures of liars and cheats, and took away toys from people who refused to live up to their responsibilities. Idiosyncracy it viewed with suspicion, and virtue had to be its own reward. Gold stars for spelling were the most that one could ever expect.

But to what ultimate end all of this toeing the line and getting the better of baser instincts, he wondered now. For thousands of years human beings had been telling themselves stories. Surprisingly similar stories. The hero goes out into the forest, overcomes his fears and his self-doubt, kills the monster, saves the world and comes home a better man, clutching the goose that lays the golden eggs. Or, if he's really lucky, a princess for the happily ever afters. But for the end of our personal stories, there is no happily ever after. That's what people like Freud and Richard Dawkins have taught us. Neither modern psychology nor biology as much as give a nod to the dying myth of eternal salvation. Nature simply dispenses with all the enormous effort of consciousness and spirit that a man has put into a lifetime, and flings his empty and exhausted carcass onto the carbon recycling heap. Ultimately, we labour for nothing but the transmission of the selfish gene, a pile of humus, and a hundred year legacy. For all our intellectual conceits we are, like ants, about nothing more than the survival and advancement of a species. That's the bet the smart money that doesn't live in Silicon Valley has placed. And there, Charlie reflected, was where he'd always placed his own.

But could Myra, in her dogged search for the eternal soul,

actually be right? Could our consciousness, our essence, be preserved? Was the 'conservation of information' law a postulate with a spiritual leg or two?

So what had Grandma Peterson accepted on her deathbed? Was it possible that her belief in comeuppance had been her version of karma or judgement day? Had she expected, after her death, some sort of synthesis to emerge from all her effort? He'd never asked, and Grandma Peterson had never told him. Be a good boy. For him, that was all her philosophy had ever seemed to boil down to. Only one thing was certain. Grandma Peterson had never thought she was a computer simulant.

But now there was Tempest min. And Dr. Deshpande. Offering what, exactly?

Still prey to such rambling, inconclusive thoughts, Charlie arrived at the school gates. The hail had stopped, the night had cleared, and the driveway looked like a ribbon of moonlight. Almost too soon, with the air so crisp and the sky a great unfathomable dome of beautiful stars, he found himself crunching across the gravel of the forecourt to get to the flat. And there he crossed paths with Mrs. Batt, stumping her way to somewhere in her headscarf, her old tweed coat and her support stockings. She was carrying a large shopping bag. She stopped in front of him. By way of greeting, he said that it had turned out a nice night.

Mrs. Batt put her shopping bag down. "Still wrestling with all that pain and unbelief?" she asked.

To his surprise, Charlie found himself replying, quite naturally as if the question had been merely another comment on the weather, "I'm afraid so."

Mrs. Batt nodded. "Don't turn it into a mountain …" She reached for one of his hands. "I'll give you sixpence for it." And with that she pressed something into his palm.

Before Charlie, closing his fingers automatically on the small, unfamiliar coin, had really grasped what she was doing, she was on her way. He looked quickly after her. The shopping bag suddenly appeared very heavy. He called out: "Can I give you a lift somewhere?" Something like a chuckle floated to him on the frosty air, but the receding figure of Mrs. Batt was now as far away and as insubstantial as a moonlight shadow.

Chapter Nineteen

"Ah, the man with the guitar. Your reputation for electrifying noise precedes you, Mr. Peterson."

This didn't sound to Charlie like an entirely auspicious start to things. He noted the distancing effect of being addressed as 'Mr. Peterson' but chose not to react to it. "I'm sorry if you feel I've trodden on your toes in any way," he said.

The head of music inclined his leonine head in acknowledgement. He had a shock of iron grey hair and slender, tapering fingers which could whirl and magick the air, drawing forth great sounds from his pupils. "No, Mr. Peterson, I do not feel that you have trodden on my toes in any way." He spoke in gracious, but rather regal tones. "I understand perfectly that you offered the lessons to Blake with the very best of motives. And I think a band would be an extremely good thing for him. He's not noted for playing well with others. I'm sure he could stand the practice." He paused, studying Charlie for a few moments. "But rock bands are not my area of expertise." (This last delivered with a pronounced lack of regret) "And though music is undoubtedly music there is, as always in teaching teenage boys, a credibility factor. In short, Mr. Peterson, though I fall asleep at night happily enmeshed in webs of music theory, and can play all of Beethoven's piano concertos and those of many composers besides, I lack the necessary wherewithal to keep Blake Vane Tempest interested. And that's because Blake needs more from me than music. I am not the sort of role model he can identify with."

Once again, Charlie declined the opportunity to feel ruffled by the ambiguity of tone, but that didn't mean he wasn't making a note of it.

"And neither is my colleague, Tony Ritson," the head of music went on. "Tony runs to jazz and brass, but Blake took care to point out to us when he came to broach the matter, that he wasn't interested in 'no trumpet playing bands' - it's not, apparently, what he calls rock 'n' roll. He assured me that that was some sort of famous quote, although I failed entirely to recognise it."

"Dire Straits," said Charlie. "The Sultans of Swing. Mark Knopfler had quite a distinctive guitar-picking sound, and the other Sunday we were listening to the various styles and levels of difficulty that have …"

The head of music held up a quelling hand. "And that's it," he said. "That is precisely why you are more qualified to help Blake in this matter than I am. Who, or what, are Dire Straits and the Sultans of Swing must forever remain one of life's great mysteries to me. But, nevertheless, do consider the music department as a collaborator - in terms of equipment, practice rooms, use of the stage perhaps and, of course, the ultimate vindication of your efforts - public performance. We have a little music festival here at the end of the summer term when the exams are all over. It's our winding down party for the leavers. But in spite of being what I believe is now, courtesy of the U.S. of A. called a prom, we have hybridised it with what used to be Speech Day and consequently it encompasses everybody. I like to think of it as our 'Proms'." He smiled thinly at his own joke. "So, we will look forward," he went on, "and with a pronounced tingly feeling, to hearing exactly what it is you have produced."

*****

"So now," said Charlie to the four expectant boys in front of him, "now we've all got a little problem, haven't we? It looks as if there has to be a lot more to this than whiling away a few happy hours pretending to be Deep Purple. Still ..." he glanced around the practice room, "we appear to be equipped to the eyeballs."

There was a formidable array of amps and pedals – the latest thing was for boosted vintage master volume Marshalls, he was informed. The on-trend experts had apparently decided that 'they don't make stuff like they used to'. Driven with a boost these Marshalls were going to give a better sound than the latest in high-gain amps ...

He nodded. Great. At least one of them was something of a techie. He looked at the set of Pearl drums before him – resplendent in red sparkle and glittering steel. Two thousand pounds worth, at least. He remembered, with a slight wince, Tom's first set of drums - an old set of Ludwigs bought for his eleventh birthday. They were hell to tune. It was the opinion of someone who sounded infinitely informed that that was because the drums were no longer perfectly round. It was Tom's father's opinion that the drums were quite round enough. This was before the family firm had suddenly flourished, and there had followed some bracing reminiscence about learning to drive in the seventies in an old Vauxhall Viva where the gear lever kept coming off in your hand. Challenges of this nature were, Tom's father had assured them, immensely character building.

The resplendent set of sparkly red Pearls was actually the property of the older brother of one Nate Greville, and Nate had been manoeuvred into the percussion seat by Paul Vane Tempest in an attempt to put an end to his own brother's increasingly moody search for a drummer. The set of Pearls had been duly retrieved from the attics of the Greville home - Nate's brother having gone off to university, lost his desire to be the drummer in Foo Fighters the sequel, and gone on to be something vague in the media. Nate, sitting behind them now, did not look too adrift. He'd picked up something from his sibling, polished it with a few lessons, and subsequently subjected it to a modicum of practice.

But that had been a while ago. The drums can be a lonely instrument. They do not lend themselves to convivial singsong. Nobody ever says: 'Oh, do get your drums and give us a tune'. So Nate, devoid of confederates and encouragement, had sort of given up. But he was smiling now. A bit nervously perhaps, but then he was a couple of years younger than the others and the testosterone wasn't flowing as freely. He was still in the more or less pretty phase, with floppy schoolboy hair and a becoming absence of spots. Overall, he was an amiable and obliging-looking youth – which somehow made Charlie think that, since he was apparently a friend of Paul Vane Tempest's, maybe Paul wasn't quite the worrisome dark horse that Myra O'Grady thought he was.

Booger, in spite of his unfortunate nickname, was another amiable-looking youth. Long and gangly, with patchy whiskers sprouting on his chin and a bouncy gait like a cartoon character, he peered myopically on the world through black-framed spectacles. Of an age with Blake, and unchallenging enough to get along with him, he had been billed as an adequate guitarist. Adequate but not scintillating.

The bassist had thick, slicked-back hair like a wet otter's pelt, and wore an earring when he wasn't in class. He wasn't very tall, and he was more unusual-looking than good-looking, but there was an air about him that hinted at competence. On the other hand, it could just have been bravado. He'd been rooted out from the deepest reaches of Gloucester House where he normally lurked in a lonesome murky way, playing cheesy slap bass to himself, and possibly working on some dream that involved computer hacking. One could imagine him as the one getting seized at his desk by the CIA. 'God,' people would say, 'I just knew Evelyn Hamilton was doing something he shouldn't.' But probably he was up to nothing more subversive than experimenting with sparklier earrings and alternative first names.

So, another Sunday afternoon and there was Charlie, presented not just with the challenge of Blake Vane Tempest, but looking at what could be callously described as the rag, tag and bobtail of the school's musical wannabes. Each one of them probably needing more from a Boulevard of Broken Dreams than the ability to deliver up a competent cover version of the song. Charlie taught none of these boys, and though he'd previously received some scattered details from Blake Vane Tempest, he had yet to form any opinions of them. And they had yet to form a real opinion of him. And, as his past was being thrust so thoroughly upon him through the medium of Tempest min, there no longer seemed any point in trying to avoid it. He looked at his boots for long moments while the drum stool went up and down some more, and the guitars got a further superfluous tuning, and Booger asked Nate why there was a pillow in the bass drum, and Nate said he wasn't sure there just always had been, and then finally Charlie looked up.

"Well, I've picked up a bit about you, so let me tell you a bit about me. I teach chemistry, as you no doubt know, but I'm not standing here because I teach chemistry. Or even because I can play the guitar. I'm standing here because I spent a large proportion of my life standing where you're standing now ..."

"We know, sir," interrupted Blake Vane Tempest. "As I said before, nobody gets that good at the guitar just to play it in his bedroom. We found out about you."

"My brother remembered you, right off," added Nate. "He said you were great. Endgame was great. You were great. He couldn't understand how come you'd ended up as a teacher, in spite of ..." He tailed off.

"But we can understand why you've never talked about it," said Blake quickly.

"Then we don't need to," said Charlie. "This is now about you, not me. Got it?" He paused for a moment. "Right then. So ... in preparation for this, I asked Blake to get the four of you to put together, as best you could, something that's a bit of a

364

rock classic. Just for assessment purposes. He's got the hardest part in this, which he assures me he's been practising, but it's nice and straightforward for our least experienced member ... Nate, isn't it? Right, let me hear it then, Nate. Just you on your own for a minute. Lay it down straight, AC/DC style, simple beat, no frills, no fills, snare on the two and the four."

But they weren't really concentrating. There were looks.

Charlie ignored them. "Nate," he said. "Are you listening to me? Nate! Don't make me have to keep repeating myself."

So Nate laid it down straight, AC/ DC style, and he was ... well, he could have been a lot worse.

Charlie nodded to him. "Not bad. Not bad at all. A bit tentative, but then we're really just beginning. However, you must keep in mind that this is not folk music, it's not country and western, it's not even pop. It's rock, if not metal. So there are going to be times when you're going to need to really hit those mothers. And equally, there are going to be times when you won't. There's a balance that is the difference between being a musician, and being a wanker with a set of drums. This is the kind of thing that all of you, in fact, will hopefully learn as we go along. Mr. Horton keeps telling you that there is no 'i' in team. Well there is no 'i' in band either."

"Couldn't you have gone on without your friends, sir?" asked Booger. It didn't seem quite the moment to ask, but presumably he couldn't help himself.

Charlie sighed. "I had the chance." He spoke dismissively. "But somehow, it didn't seem right. Okay? End of story." And without allowing for any more discussion he carried on. "Now Mr. Bassman, Evelyn, isn't it?"

"Unfortunately, sir."

"Any alternative?"

"Nothing that's an improvement," said Evelyn, amidst stifled sniggers from the others.

"Evie," said Blake.

"Or Lyn."

"Because he's such a girl."

Evelyn flushed and turned away, fingering his earring.

"Stop," said Charlie. "Let's not do this. We are trying to create something here, so let's do things a little differently. When we come into this room to practise, we don't have to be who we are out there. We can be a guy who is better."

A silence greeted this. If any of them knew a better guy they wanted to be they were being pretty cagey about it.

"For my last couple of terms at uni," said Charlie, "I was someone called Reuben Stuart. Because unlike Charlie Peterson, Reuben Stuart liked chemistry. He didn't play the guitar every hour God sent, and he got out of bed in the morning and got stuck into some books. He wasn't interested in women, or men, and he didn't drink or smoke weed. And when he was finally confronted with the exam papers, it turned out he'd learned some stuff. He passed those finals for me, which at least pleased my parents, even though Charlie Peterson wasn't fussy either way."

Another silence. Finally Nate Greville said, "Don't you think he must have been, sir? To go to the extent of thinking up Reuben Stuart?"

"There you go," said Charlie. "So, you see, we all have layers. Alter egos even. And we can find the one that will do the job we

366

need it to do, at the time we need it to do it. And we can give it a name, if we want, and that helps it to take on a life. And inside each of you, there is somebody who can get in tune with the music, hear it speak, and be creative with it. So, let's bring him to the party and leave the disgruntled, difficult guy back in the rooms. In doing my job at this school, I'm Mr. Peterson the chemistry master but, as you've no doubt worked out, the Charlie Peterson of Endgame was a rather different person. And now you've caused me to resurrect him, you might be in for a shock or two, because Charlie Peterson is a creature with a side that Mr. Peterson doesn't have. And to that end, in here, but only in here, you can call me Charlie. Because if you can each tune in to the part of you that really wants to be a decent musician, Charlie Peterson can turn you all into a fucking band."

There was silence then, in which the boys exchanged surreptitious half smiles with each other.

"And by the way," said Charlie Peterson, "there's a pillow in the bass drum because it muffles the overtones. Now, let's get back to where we were. Evelyn ..."

"BB," said Evelyn. "Short for bass boy."

"Well that was quick. Different name, different guy. You're sure you're going to be happy with this, BB?"

"Yes."

"Good," said Charlie. "Because I think he's got the air of someone who might be pretty decent. Is he ready to give this a go? Good. Booger, you ready? Okay. Now you get ready, Nate, you count us in, use the sticks - yes, that's the way ... one, two, three, four ..."

It wasn't the sharpest of intros but it could have been worse.

Then a minute or so in, Blake Vane Tempest suddenly stopped playing. "What's he doing in here?"

"Listening, stupid, and you're not tight. The beat is sticking, and him with the five string bass is not playing for the song. It doesn't need a fancy bass line. He's overplaying."

"What the fuck do you know about it?" asked Blake.

Charlie swung round in astonishment. Tempest min was standing right behind him. And he was absolutely correct. The song didn't need a fancy bass line, and it had never had one. A lot of the time, the bass in rock merely supported the lead. That was something Charlie knew he had to explain at some point. It was the wanking with drums story again but right now, with BB having already taken a hit or two over his name, this wasn't the moment to rerun it.

"Charlie and I were in a band together," Tempest min said to Blake in a shrill, offended voice. "In my past life. We were famous."

"Oh, for crying out loud," his brother snapped. "Have you been listening at the door, you little creep? You don't need an alter ego, you're a big enough pain when there's just the one of you."

For Blake, the fact that his little brother seemed surprisingly informed in the matter of bass lines had been consumed by the immediate flare of temper. And if it had struck the rest of the band at all, they were obviously too concerned with their own performance problems to register the fact in any significant way.

"It's a soundproof room, stupid," said Tempest min, flushing a tearful pink. "So I couldn't have been listening at the door. And I *was* in a band, and it was better than you lot will *ever* be!"

"Stop this now," said Charlie. He looked at Blake. "He's still half asleep from his afternoon rest, and you need to be a little more understanding when he's not well."

"He's never been any different," said Blake, under his breath. "Attention seeking little git. *I'm different. I don't really belong with you. I belong somewhere with special people.*' It started as soon as he could talk."

Charlie gave him a warning look and then took Tempest min by the hand and led him out into the corridor, where he squatted down beside him and looked into his face. "This past life thing of ours is going to be very hard for people to understand, you know," he said gently. "Think about it. They'd have to believe that not so many years ago, you and I were the same age, had been friends for virtually our whole lives, and were in a band together. Until you died. You can see how difficult this would be for them, can't you?"

Tempest min nodded.

"This is an incredible thing that has happened to us," Charlie went on. "But at the moment, it's a phenomenon that is not readily acceptable to most people. You know what a phenomenon is, don't you?"

"Is it something special?"

"Very special," said Charlie, "but it's something like, let's say ghosts or alien spaceships. Some people have seen them and believe in them, and others say that they don't exist. It's something that is still being investigated. Now, you have had this other life - just like somebody else has seen a ghost or a spaceship. And you and I are talking about it with Dr. Deshpande. We are investigating it. Trying to understand it. Do you see?"

"Yes."

"But it's not going to help us understand, or make us any happier, if we have to argue the point with the sort of people who'll never believe in ghosts or spaceships. Or other lives. We'll just get upset and angry, and make everything more difficult. I think we've been given a great gift, and we don't want it spoiled with arguments. So, maybe we ought to keep this a little more to ourselves. Let it be our secret for the moment, just like Dr. Deshpande suggested. Do you agree?"

"Yes."

"Then let's try to stick to that. But you're okay? You feel okay?"

"Yes."

"Good. Now, you go off and do whatever is you should be doing."

"Prep. I should be doing prep. I've got behind."

"You go and get on with that, then. You've got a whole new life to get through, and it'll work out a lot better if you can read and write and do the maths."

So, Mr. Peterson the chemistry master turned round and went back into the practice room and became the Charlie Peterson of Endgame again. And the little blonde boy, who'd built the bridge between the two, ran off down the corridor to catch up with his prep.

"Okay guys," said Charlie. "Highway to Hell. Let's try it again, one, two, three …"

*****

The daffodils were out in force along the driveway and round the edges of the sports fields, tossing their trumpets in breezy sunshine when Charlie finally found Ianthe in the walled garden again. She was sowing turnips into a drill made in some soil that had been pre-warmed under polythene - so she explained, as she straightened up and gave him a smile to rival the breezy gold of the daffodils. Sowing turnips doesn't sound like the sort of procedure that could be choreographed into a thing of grace and beauty, and yet that's just how it appeared to Charlie. "You're back," he exclaimed, unable to conceal his delight. He'd come, he'd found her, he was delighted. Full stop. To avoid the awkwardness of Rory's question about whether or not he was looking for something that could end in a trip to Holy Island, he simply hadn't thought about it. Didn't think about it. He'd just followed the dictates of his heart and come. What he'd probably told himself, but without actually forming the specific thought, was that the coming would be enough.

"I haven't really been away," said Ianthe. "Just a day or two here and there. Visiting relations and so on. I went across to the college at Pershore one day to hear about Pershore berries, otherwise known as June berries. They're the fruit of a type of Amelanchier and a sort of superfood. Somebody there imported plants from Canada. I was hoping she'd sell me a few of the young ones she's been propagating. For the garden here. Healthy food for the boys. "

"Well, your under gardener wasn't very forthcoming about where you'd gone," said Charlie, for whom, at this precise moment, the concept of a new development in British agriculture was falling somewhere short of riveting. "Nor was he particularly civil, for that matter. In fact he was extremely odd. The weirdest ears. And he certainly didn't encourage me to call again soon."

"I'm afraid that's Robin Goodfellow for you." Ianthe stepped carefully out of the vegetable bed. "But he's not the under-gardener. In fact, I'm surprised you caught him. He only puts in an appearance when he feels like it."

"Doesn't sound very cooperative." Charlie was still thinking he'd been actively discouraged.

"Well, cooperation is not a thing that Robin Goodfellow's ever been much noted for." Ianthe seemed amused at the very idea. "Would you like some coffee?"

"Will it be made from dandelions?"

"No. I bought some Nescafé, especially for you." She looked at him, laughing and delightful, the sun in her face, her hair lifting in the breeze. Irresistible. All earth and trees and flowers. The whole of spring in her eyes. And she'd bought him coffee. Was that significant? Or was he becoming a connoisseur of the nearly-nothing?

Lured out of his peeve about the lumpish Goodfellow, he followed her to the potting shed and watched as she rinsed out mugs and put on the kettle. He was so happy to see her again, it was as much as he could do to suppress the urge to reach out and touch her. Maybe just her hair … Just lift it up … Kiss the lovely curve of her neck. And then he'd certainly know her feelings, wouldn't he? No. There was the line. He had to keep one side of the line. To cross it with Ianthe involved answering the question about Holy Island first.

"Charlie?"

"Yes?"

"I asked if you wanted a biscuit."

"Please."

Ianthe handed him a tin. "I hear that you and Dr. Deshpande are rising to the reincarnation challenge."

Charlie didn't ask her how much she'd heard about what had eventually transpired. He just assumed that somehow she'd heard a lot. That's how it seemed to work at Puckrup. The people who needed to hear things, heard things. He wondered if the biscuits were bought for him. He'd never seen her eat one. Though that Robin Goodfellow creature probably ate more than he deserved.

"Dr. Deshpande is finding reincarnation a useful medium through which to pursue his therapeutic goals," he said. "I aid and abet him. It seems to be working. So far. For Tempest min, at any rate."

"But not for you?".

"I go along with it." But even as he spoke, he was inwardly acknowledging all the coincidences, all the inexplicable knowledge - of which the latest, the instant analysis of the new band's performance and the grasp of bass lines, was one of the least easy to shrug away.

"Just go along with it?"

"I keep thinking that there has to be some other explanation. Though I honestly don't know what. And, in spite of a pile of what you could call anecdotal evidence, and Myra O'Grady rummaging desperately through the book shelves of quantum physics with all the wild optimism of a true believer, it still feels like a giant leap of faith. And not an easy one. In fact, it's downright disturbing. Joe Beck and I were lifelong friends. We wrote together, celebrated together, cried together. As I told Dr. Deshpande, it was more than I ever shared with any of my own brothers. And then Joe was killed. While I stood in a passageway, waiting. It was never going to be easy to deal with, on any level."

"Of course not."

"But you believe, do you? In reincarnation?"

"Yes. But then, my opinion may not carry much weight. You think I'm a little peculiar."

"First of all," Charlie somehow found himself saying, (because he hadn't at all expected to say what followed, though it came out in spite of that). "I find you unbelievably beautiful. But that's not the only reason I come here. I like talking to you. To use Tempest min's words, you make my heart feel better. In fact, on occasion, you actually make it do somersaults." He paused, felt he was saying too much and decided to quickly cool it down. "Then way behind all of that I find you - yes, a little peculiar. But, as I seem to find myself saying ad nauseam these days, we all have layers."

"We certainly do," said Ianthe with a smile. "There's the chemistry you, and I'm always pleased to see him. He's polite and sweet and faintly uncomfortable with himself. And then there's the you who plays to me when I take the stamens - that's the male sexual parts by the way - out of Grandmama's hellebores to do the cross pollinations for her breeding experiments. And that's the you I've heard and felt, but never fully seen …" She paused for a second or two before going on. "But when I listen, I hear and feel someone much more at ease in his skin, maybe a little bit dark, possibly a touch difficult, but also," she paused again, "a bit hot. Would hot be a suitable word to use?"

"*Hot*?"

"Yes. But Grandmama and Mrs. Batt have always advised me to discourage any feeling like that. They say it's a hard feeling," she hesitated, "to get to go anywhere good."

Charlie swallowed. With some difficulty. Twice. "Depends on what you mean by good," he said finally. "The definition has changed over the years. Sometimes good can just be the same as fun. As long as everybody is careful and the situation is made clear ..." Jeez! What the hell was he saying? "I'm just generalising, of course," he rushed on. "About the way things are often done these days. And of course that was me then, but ..." Stop. For God's sake, Peterson, just shut up.

"Of course," said Ianthe. "These things don't have to mean anything, be anything. I understand."

"Please," protested Charlie. "Don't ... "

But at that moment the potting shed door was flung open and the shadow of Robin Goodfellow fell across them both. "I've come to do some jobs for you," he said, quickly turning unappreciative, aggressive eyes on Charlie and adding, "I don't mean you."

"Charlie was just leaving," said Ianthe.

Robin Goodfellow stood to one side, took a grubby, velvety green cap off his head and, with an ironic sweeping gesture, used it to motion Charlie outside into the garden. Then he slammed the door on him.

*****

By the time he got back to the flat, Charlie had worked himself into a mood bordering on sulphurous. He found Rory in the kitchen, emptying dead leaves and the odd bit of twig out of a green canvas sack into the pedal bin. "I've just done the stupidest thing," he said, flopping down on a stool.

"Oh aye?" Rory turned round and raised an eyebrow.

"I finally came across Ianthe again in the walled garden and, over coffee, during the course of conversation, you know, she said she found me a bit hot. Not me now, precisely, but, well that doesn't really matter. The disastrous point is that I picked her up on it as if I'd been talking to Blake Vane Tempest or somebody. I totally lost my wits."

"Blake Vane Tempest thinks you're hot? Get away …"

"Don't be ridiculous! Ianthe said that her grandmother and Mrs. Batt had positively discouraged her from viewing men as hot because it never went anywhere good. And I proceeded to qualify that with some reference to current sexual mores – how it wasn't necessarily good or bad, but could just be fun as long as both parties were careful and clear that that's all it was."

"Jeez," said Rory shaking his head in disbelief. "That's an invitation she's not gonna be able to resist."

"Exactly," said Charlie. "But before I could dig myself out of the hole, some filthy creature looking like Fungus the Bogeyman came into the shed and virtually forced me to leave."

"Fungus the Bogeyman?"

"Robin Goodfellow or some such name. Honestly, he looked like he could have been that boggart."

"What boggart?"

"The one that lives in the forest garden," said Charlie impatiently. "The one we were supposed to be hunting on Halloween. When you were having fisticuffs at Malvern School."

"He's usually just papier mâché," said Rory.

Charlie made a gesture of irritation. "It was some sort of gardening freak, anyway. Helping Ianthe out. And he turned up for work, so naturally she had to …" He gave up.

"Whereas you think she'd have much preferred to talk more to you about this casual bit of fun you could have together, if only she hadna' bin indoctrinated with outmoded ideas by two old ladies?"

"Stupid, wasn't I?"

"Very."

"I don't know what came over me. I was just realising that alongside Mr. Peterson the chemistry master, there was now the Charlie Peterson of Endgame - busy climbing back out of his grave like some sort of vampire, except without the bloodlust, but possibly with a few other lusts - well maybe not lusts exactly but, you know, a bit more life in him. But then there was the whole question of Holy Island, and whether I really wanted to go there. Whether it would be even possible to go there with a woman like Ianthe. And then suddenly, there was this remark about my being a bit hot, and it was so unexpected and potentially complicated that I just couldn't think. So I ended up resorting to … to … the sort of stuff the lady from LAFFAS might have said." Charlie gave a sigh and then, as the pedal bin lid crashed down yet again, snapped, "What in God's name are you doing with that bloody sack?"

"It's a bivvy bag. And does it make me a bad person that I find your new confused self and conversational cock-ups a wee bit pleasing?"

"No." Charlie looked at the kettle for an absent moment or two, then finally he reached across and felt it. It was still warm. Not yet entirely converted to Nespresso, he turned it back on and peered into a convenient mug to see if it was clean enough to use. "You're entitled after all the leg pulling I've inflicted on you. Plus, it's a well-recognised feeling. It's called schadenfreude. Horribly human."

"Good to know I'm human, then," said Rory. "I'll forget the word, but I'll remember it makes me human." He took another look in the sack.

"What are you doing, anyway?" Charlie finally asked. "Do I need a look in that sack? It seems to be pretty bloody fascinating in there."

"Christina and I might be having a weekend in London for the second exeat."

"Wow," Charlie was slightly taken aback. "The weekend away. It's that time, is it?"

Rory took another shake at the sack. It looked like an oversized duffel. Ex-military he explained, when further pressed as to the part it was intended to play in a romantic weekend. It was his luggage. He held it up with a degree of reverence. It had been to Iraq and Afghanistan and back with one of his cousins. Twice. It was extremely serviceable. It was just that bits of Kielder Forest had accumulated in the bottom.

"And you're actually going to stuff your glad-rags for the big romantic excursion in there?" Charlie studied it in disbelief.

Rory sat down on a neighbouring stool and laid the bivvy bag across his knees. For a man who had been aching from afar for at least two years, he looked surprisingly unenthused about this weekend away. And it was a lot more than the natural anxiety of anticipation. There may not be, he confessed between sighs, a lot of romance. Not quite what Charlie had been expecting him to say - at least not in tones that were so very far removed from his 'something embarrassing once happened in a hay barn' voice. "So what's going on?" he asked.

Rory explained that Christina had a small house in London - in some place called Parsons Nose.

"Parsons Green?" Charlie suggested.

"That's it."

"Expensive."

But maybe not back in the nineteen fifties when Christina's grandparents had bought it. Christina had inherited this house and lived in it during her tenure as a lecturer at the Slade. And then, and here Rory became conspicuously shy with the details, it seemed that Christina had been followed home one night by a random man who'd never been caught. What happened then had been horrific to endure and almost impossible to live with afterwards. At least in the same house. In the end, Christina had left London altogether, and the house in Parsons Green had been let. Now the tenancy had come to an end, and Christina felt that she ought to go and look at the place before re-letting. At least she felt, she'd said, that she ought to be *able* to go and look at the place. After the incident, as Rory called it, she'd gone from the police station and the hospital to her parents' home in Chiswick, and hadn't been back to Parsons Green since.

"God," Charlie felt more than shocked. Somehow, the fact of Christina's extreme fastidiousness made such an assault – even in his mind he avoided calling it rape – much more shocking. It felt like rank indecency to even talk about it without her permission. Which was, no doubt, why Rory was focusing on the house rather than on some intrusive mulling over of what, in detail, had happened.

"But do you think she really has to put herself through a visit?" Charlie asked. "Parsons Green is a nice enough area, but one could avoid it for a lifetime and never feel the miss. Couldn't the letting agent sort out the house for her? Or her parents?"

"It's a thing," said Rory. "She calls it her endeavour. She feels that it's something she has to do. Walk into that house, look around, and say: 'Fuck you, mister whatever-your-name-was. That was a different woman in a different life and I am no longer a victim.'"

"Closure," said Charlie.

"That's another word she used," said Rory with a sigh. "It's heartbreaking."

"But is it better for you both now it's out there, do you think?"

"I hope so. I find it difficult to know what to say. I'm not smart like that. Naturally she's talked, in the past, to people whose job it is to be smart like that. But things get triggered again, don't they? Years might go by, but things can always get triggered."

It seemed to Charlie that Rory, in spite of his touted lack of any ability to talk a smart line, was well equipped to deal with this. There'd been many noticeable omissions in his reminiscences. Omissions that Charlie had never commented upon. The pair of them were not naturally disposed to smearing their deepest emotional lives around like curry sauce on the kitchen surfaces. They drank beer, and aired certain frustrations, and told tales from which subtexts could be unconsciously absorbed. And it seemed to Charlie that Rory had stood a lot of pain and family trauma, and not let it ruin him. And, in consequence, he would be able to stand alongside Christina in her pain, and not let it ruin her. Or their relationship.

"You'd never really have guessed this," he said, finally. "To look at her. How she is, I mean. And to hear how she talks. She's always seemed so together. I just assumed that she was standoffish with us because she thought she was sophisticated, and we were from the less couth side of town. But I realise now, that maybe ..." He tailed off.

"She is sophisticated," said Rory. "She's just got a bit damaged as well." He laid the renewed pain of this damage at the door of the sexually incontinent university lecturer. A man, enabled by his position to have sex with a sequence of girls young enough to be his daughters was, in Rory's opinion, exerting a type of subtle coercion. This surely had to have set off an echo in Christina? Over and above the more obvious things she'd felt about her own experience at his hands, the undercurrent of exploiting impressionable young women could not have escaped her. Especially as he was the first man she'd had any dealings with since. "So I've no idea what this weekend is going to hold," he finished, after a long pause. "Assuming we end up going. There's certainly no likelihood of romance."

"No," agreed Charlie. "But you can get her through it. You're solid, and you're in love with her. And she'll feel it. Feel the empathy. I think you're perfect for this."

"Really? I mean, I feel so helpless ..."

"You're very far from helpless, Rory. Why do you think Christina finally took to you? Before she came up with the arte povera stuff?"

"I have no idea."

"Yes, you do. You hung back, spilling sugar everywhere, and looking as if you were just a bumbling bucolic which, to be fair, you probably were when it came to women. But then something dramatic and violent happened - at the dance, remember? And everyone else was floored, a couple of them literally, but you just stepped in and sorted it. The big bad world doesn't faze you, Rory. Not the badness of it. It's been trying for a significant part of your life, and it's failed. You might actively abhor certain things, but they won't ever cut the legs from under you. You'll stand at the door of that house in Parsons Green and, even though Christina may not frame the idea precisely, she'll feel that as a long as you're standing there, nothing else will be able to get in. And I mean that both figuratively and literally."

"Right." Rory passed a thoughtful hand over his chin. His concern for Christina had caused him to accumulate stubble. Maybe he was like Sampson. Hair gave him strength. He gave a great sigh. "You won't tell her I told you any of this, will you?"

"Of course not."

It was too personal a subject for them to feel easy discussing for long, so they had some coffee then, and afterwards Charlie suggested that if Rory wasn't too emotionally dependent on the bivvy bag, he give it a well-earned retirement in a drawer somewhere, and borrow his holdall.

Chapter Twenty

The ambitions of the school's new rock band, bearing in mind the youth and inexperience of its drummer, began to stream far ahead of its abilities. Led Zeppelin's Moby Dick moaned and hammered and stuttered its way to far distant and inconclusive endings that were followed by furious arguments. Drum solos didn't present themselves at every rock music turn, but Nate had stumbled across that one, and he thought he had as much right to indulge himself as anyone else. The alter egos (including his) came with temperament as well as musical commitment. Charlie didn't worry too much about this. Rock bands composed of teenage boys were volatile entities, and at least the arguments now concerned the music and not the personal. Over-heated enthusiasm was how young bands thrashed out their fantasies and their energies, and finally found their sound and honed their talent. But while the boys burned through calories and testosterone and guitar strings on their own time, they had to make some organised progress for the end of term performance on his.

He looked at them now, ready to call a halt so the Sunday

afternoon session with him could begin. Dr. Carlyle was standing beside him, rocking to and fro on his veldtschoens and covering his ears. "Energetic boys," he said finally. "Good to see such enthusiasm, but could we go out into the corridor for a moment or two?"

Outside of the practice room, he took in a lungful of blessed silence before proceeding. "Academies of contemporary music," he said. "The careers master has been getting to grips with them. Amidst a background level of consternation, I might add." He hesitated for a moment and then said, "Your friend Joe Beck actually went to one of these places, didn't he?"

"He did."

Dr. Carlyle nodded slowly. "There was always an innate musicality in Tempest min. We just never understood why he persisted in shying away from it."

He paused again, nodding to himself, evidently pleased to have tied up a loose end. Then he asked, "Did you suggest a contemporary music academy to Blake?"

"Not me." Charlie denied it fervently. "I'm very wary about what I suggest these days. Not least because my suggestions seem to come home to roost and bring their friends along."

"Well, the idea has got into him somehow," said Dr. Carlyle. "And David Borgsen. I suppose it's the age of the internet isn't it?",

"Is it bad that they've come up with this?"

"Not at all. It's just rather late in the day to be making such a decision. And late in the school year for applying. Initially, it threw the music department into a bit of a fluff. These boys aren't even doing A-level music, so there were some quite heated discussions concerning extra tuition and mysterious things, at least to me, called Sibelius and Cubase. But then on further investigation …"

Reading between Dr. Carlyle's diplomatic lines, Charlie came to the conclusion that the general opinion in the music department was that there had to be some serious abuse of the word 'academy' going on. The entry requirements seemed to amount to not very much, at least as far as examination results went. On the other hand, the colleges may have already made all the offers they intended to make. Nevertheless, Dr. Carlyle added, Mrs. Vane Tempest seemed disturbingly sanguine about her son's belated aspirations.

"What did she say?" Charlie asked.

"She said, 'If you press enough money into the hand of the maître d', you can get a table anywhere, at pretty well any time'."

"Oh."

"She's a very complicated woman," said Dr. Carlyle. "One never really knows quite what to make of her."

"I'm afraid I harbour a certain antipathy," said Charlie.

"Understandable," Dr. Carlyle nodded his head slowly, "but I try not do that. Though I worry that somewhere in London, there could be a college principal who's about to get very excited at the thought of some expensive new recording equipment."

"That would hardly be fair."

"Mrs. Vane Tempest tends to take viewpoints that are less fair than expedient," said Dr. Carlyle. "And I believe that in the current economic climate, most college principals could well be of a similar mind. But we must concentrate on getting bona fide places. It seems that Blake's technical ability on the instrument should be enough?"

"Hopefully," said Charlie. "And we must also hope that one of Mrs. Vane Tempest's 'expedients' is not listed as 'sex with college principals'. If Blake ever found himself in a position to even *imagine* that, it would result in nothing less than total bloody disaster."

"Dear, dear," Dr. Carlyle looked briefly alarmed. "What unsuspected problems we can find ourselves facing in this modern world. Quite soon I may no longer be up to outmanoeuvring them." He took one of his cogitative looks around the ceiling. "But, tell me - does Tempest min remember much about the course he did?"

"Not in great detail. There's a deal of emotional baggage that comes with Tempest min's memories, so Dr. Deshpande is very careful about how he resurrects them. We both are."

"Could he have given his brother the idea? Do you think they talk about the past life thing together?"

Charlie explained that because his past life memories were such a minefield, Tempest min had been actively discouraged from talking about them outside of the consulting room. Blake, in particular, had revealed himself as a highly unsympathetic audience, so it was unlikely that the idea of a popular music course had come to him from his little brother.

"Perhaps Dr. Deshpande could do something about their relationship," suggested Dr. Carlyle. "Pave the way for future harmony."

"Well, it's beyond me," said Charlie. "I have enough to hold together."

"So I hear," said Dr. Carlyle, flinching slightly as Moby Dick butted heads with the practice room door again. "Little Nathan

Greville is certainly giving it some stick, isn't he?" He put a finger in one ear and waggled it around with the presumed intention of bringing some sort of relief to his eardrum. "We do the earplug thing, don't we?"

Charlie nodded.

"Good. It's nice to hear youngsters expressing themselves, isn't it? More so when earplugs are involved. And I'm particularly pleased that David Borgsen is finally bringing himself to the surface. He's not academic, but it's never mattered because his father is a successful businessman, so there was always going to be a life for David in the family firm. But I think it's good for him to develop the self a little more before he gets totally absorbed into Borgsen and Sons. We must do all we can for his new aspirations. So many people end up going to their graves with the song still in them. Thoreau, I believe. Interesting chap." And he set off down the corridor.

But before he turned the corner at the end, he shouted, "Mothers and fathers and uncles and aunts and grandparents. Various siblings, some girlfriends, and a scattering of locals who will sneak in towards the end. That's our music festival. Our Prom, as it were. Do keep that in mind when you devise your performance."

"We call it a set," Charlie shouted back, as Moby Dick battered at the door again.

"Really?" Dr. Carlyle shook his head. "Like badgers, then. How very peculiar."

"I think you'll find it's spelt differently," Charlie called. But Dr. Carlyle had already disappeared.

After a moment or two's contemplation, Charlie took a deep

breath then flung open the practice room door and walked in to confront the four sweaty-faced boys. "Right," he said. "Time to stop dicking around."

*****

"Holdall?"

"So, you're going then?"

"We are."

Charlie went to get the holdall.

"You not going anywhere?" Rory examined it suspiciously.

Charlie watched him. "No need to worry. No dope. And I'm not going anywhere as it happens. For my sins, I get to spend the exeat here with the band."

Charlie wasn't quite sure how they'd got from the situation of 'rock band equals fun' to 'rock band equals half an hour on stage at the end of term where it will impress The Parents and a slack handful of all their friends and relations'. But it had happened. In fact he had allowed it to happen as a result of a verbal sleight of hand visited upon him in a disadvantaged moment and then somehow raised to the level of headmaster's decree. And without any further consultation as to whether he could actually turn it into an 'edge of your seat' reality. This is what happens, Charlie reflected, when you upstart into the egregious classical world of the music department. You get no marks for being helpful, but are expected to prove your worth by spinning straw into gold overnight like the miller's daughter. The head of music might not have been an expert on rock but he would certainly tell, and with mischievous glee to everyone within earshot, when a band was completely out of time. And, if half of this band was hoping to get into some sort of 'academy' in order to become further acquainted with the principle of playing out of time, then the pleasure would be untrammelled. And speaking of time, between preparations for GCSEs and A-levels there was a current shortage - which was why Dr. Carlyle had given special dispensation for the band to spend the exeat at school.

"Kit Kat wrappers," said Rory, ruffling in the side pockets of the holdall. "I was expecting condoms."

"You think you'll need them?"

"I don't know. Christina booked the hotel. I don't even know if it's one room or two. And it seems crass to ask."

"I suppose, whether or not you'll need the condoms depends on how the visit to Parsons Green goes," suggested Charlie. "And how closed she wants her closure to be. If I were you, I would play the boy scout and be prepared."

"You really think I'll need to be?"

"From driving primal need to source of comfort," said Charlie. "Sex is supposed to fill no end of emotional niches, isn't it? And create a few new ones while it's at it. No wonder it gets us into so much trouble ..."

"I'm confused," said Rory. "Are you saying she might want us to finally, well ...? It would seem a hell of a time to start."

"I don't know. I'm just telling you why I think it wouldn't be out of the question. Even though you might think it would be, given the circumstances. People supposedly have sex after funerals - some sort of subconscious need to confirm the fact they're still alive."

"You have to be kiddin'," said Rory. "Where d'ye get this

stuff? There's only ever fights after we bury a McEwan."

"I used to have goings-on with an anthropologist," said Charlie. "She was doing a bit in telephone sales to help pay for an M.Sc.. We kept in touch at odd times over the years. I called her after my grandmother's funeral and, as I happened to mention that I'd just been to it, she promptly explained to me why, exactly, I was calling. Then she said she was too busy to fulfil my life affirming primal needs, just at the moment." He glanced reflectively round the room. He'd felt unjustly spurned at the time. "But maybe Christina might at least want to go out for a nice meal. Somewhere uncrumpled. So don't stuff your good jacket and trousers into the holdall. Hang them up in the car, or lie them on the back seat."

Rory looked helplessly at him.

"Just be you," said Charlie quietly, relieving him of the Kit Kat wrappers. "And get the antennae up for God's sake. Try the best you can to pick up on the signals. She might not be in the mood to articulate them very clearly."

"Y'know," said Rory, "when Sandra Maguire jumped up from them hay bales that time in Thomsy Kerr's barn, she was of the opinion that, in terms of primal needs, warmth, physical comfort and a total absence of rats and Jack Russell terriers took precedence over sex. I know this because she explained it very thoroughly to me when I drove her home. Course, I might've heard her all wrong. As I said before, one of my ears was ringing something chronic." He paused. "The point I'm trying to make is this - am I that compelling? And I don't just mean for this weekend. I mean, at all. Am I enough to get Christina past what she needs to get past? The memories, y'know? All those rats and prickly hay bales she has piled up in her mind?"

Charlie studied him for a moment, and then he said, "Have you ever wondered why it is you ended up here?"

"I got offered a job," said Rory. "And it was very, very wet up in Kielder at the time. Is it relevant?"

"Just something Dr. Carlyle said to me the other day. About there being a synchronicity that seems to operate in this place. A synchronicity that borders on predestination."

"Some kind of destiny, you mean?"

"Perhaps," said Charlie. "You and Christina brought together ... Because you're what she needs. Do you think that's possible?"

"Seems incredible," said Rory. "Christina and a man like me. Seems an incredible thing for destiny to think up. I mean, it would be like I was actually chosen for this. Wouldn't it?"

"I'm pretty sure that Dr. Carlyle would think you were. What do you think?"

Rory shook his head. "I'd never been chosen for anything in this life, until Dr. Carlyle come along." He thought for a moment, before adding, "Sometimes though, when I'm holding her, y'know, when we're sitting quietly after she's been upset, she gives a little sigh and smiles up at me and then falls asleep. And I just stroke her hair a bit, and carry on holding her, and ..."

"And?"

"And then I feel all the love in the world. Welling up inside me, y'know. All the love in the world ... powerful ... and ... bottomless ... and ... and kind of invincible. But who would have credited it? Love like that in a bloke like me? Who would ever have credited it?"

*****

Mrs. Batt, apparently in charge of comestibles for the duration of the exeat, had brewed up a large vat of lumpy soup. Charlie watched with a degree of suspicion as she stirred it and then aimed a full and dripping ladleful in the direction of the bowl he was holding out. With only half a dozen people to occupy it, the dining hall felt an echoing and empty place. And the soup seemed to emphasise some undercurrent of sad unwanted children left in an institution for the holidays. But maybe that was just the soup. Something stirred into it by Mrs. Batt whose countenance was tending to the unsympathetic, if not frankly critical. The unwanted children however, wrestling over the remains of a French stick at a nearby table, seemed perfectly happy.

"The turnips haven't come through." Soup plopped accusingly into Charlie's bowl.

"Excuse me?"

"Ianthe's turnip seed. It hasn't germinated."

Recalcitrant turnip seed was well outside Charlie's sphere of expertise. "Is it the weather?" he asked politely.

"No."

"So?"

"So," said Mrs. Batt, dumping the ladle back in the vat and fixing him with a stern, interrogating eye. "Now what?"

Charlie had no idea but fortunately, at this point, one of the unwanted children called out in something that could have been pain, or at least was conveniently interpretable as pain, and so he had an excuse to turn away. He went to the table and sat down alongside the boys. "How are you getting on?" He nodded towards a sheet of paper.

"Sweet Home Alabama, for sure," said Blake. "Booger's mother requested it."

"Well, we spent this morning doing the equivalent of smoking weed and getting with the vibe," said Charlie. "So this afternoon we have to work on the set list. And then I'll have to do the unconscionable and teach to the test. Otherwise, we'll sound like crap. Or you will. I'll just feel like it. Any other requests? What else does Booger's mother like?"

"Robbie Williams."

"No."

"James Blunt."

"Absolutely not."

"My father likes the Eagles," said Nate. "He plays their 'best of' CD all the time in the car. He's old," he added, as if that explained something.

"We think maybe Hotel California," said BB.

"What's that about?" asked Nate. "He loves it, but I never get what it's about. Are they vampires at that hotel, or what?"

"It's a metaphor," explained Charlie. "For the state of California. It lures you there with its sybaritic lifestyle but then, when it doesn't live up to your hopes and expectations, you find that however hard you try you just can't leave. It's sucked you in."

"Tell me about it," said Blake Vane Tempest, with unconcealed rancour.

"What's sybaritic?" asked Booger.

Blake Vane Tempest snorted.

"You could even expand the idea," Charlie added, "and realise that the Hotel California could stand for anything that make us the false promise of happiness, but then won't release our psyches when it fails to ultimately deliver. Drugs and alcohol, for instance." He was learning. As a teacher you had to take the chance to plug things when the opportunity presented itself.

"Dad really likes another one of theirs as well," Nate offered, filling what could have been a sceptical silence. "Take It To The Limit." He looked diffidently around at the others. "But now I think about it, I never quite get that one either. 'You can spend all your time making money, or you can spend all your love making time.' How do you make time? That's impossible, isn't it?"

"Why don't you just shut up," Blake suggested. "And worry about the drum lines instead. Can you play them for instance? How about that for a problem?"

"I misremember the complete drift of that song," said Charlie, ignoring Blake. "But taking the second line in isolation, I could hazard a guess that making time was being used in the sense of making time with women. In other words chatting them up for one night stands. And the word spend was being used in the sense of 'to expend' or 'squander'. In other words, you are wasting your heart and soul, all your love, while you dally endlessly with things that lack any meaning and are therefore ultimately pointless."

"Now that I don't get," said Booger, whose chances of managing a string of one night stands were, at this period in his development at least, looking pretty slim. As a result, the concept naturally took on a high level of appeal. "Doesn't seem pointless to me."

"Maybe it'll come over you when you're older," said Charlie absently, not entirely comfortable with the fact that this second bit of teacherly opportunism was starting to niggle at him.

"Philosophy," interrupted Dr. Carlyle. "A contemporary philosopher then, this man, this singer."

"Just a competent lyricist," said Charlie, through the hasty scraping of chairs and attempts to stand up.

Dr. Carlyle motioned for them all to sit. "Don't undersell the modern troubadour," he said amiably. "The composer of songs has a worthy history, and the best of them often had a story to tell or a moral to impart. In this case, as Mr. Peterson was so adequately explaining," he paused to transfer his full attention to the boys, "our modern troubadour appears to be telling us that when all our aims are merely appetites, then all that we pursue is infinitely replaceable and therefore of no particular value. This is ultimately dehumanising, reducing personhood to a closed loop of stimulus and response. It is the nihilism of impulse satisfaction in the absence of context or meaning. I thought that a point worth emphasising." He beamed round at them. Dr. Carlyle didn't teach so his teacherly opportunism was mostly couched in terms that required more thought than the average teenager was prepared to give it. Charlie wondered whether it would be acceptable, at some point, to use popular music as a means of introducing him to the concept of a hook line.

"All having a nice weekend, then?" Dr. Carlyle added. "No unconquerable urges for computer games or searching for validation on Facebook?"

Apparently not.

"Excellent." More satisfied beams. "I'm not always in tune

with the existentialists but here I find myself suddenly thinking of Kierkegaard: 'The thing is to find the truth which is true for me; to find the idea for which I can live and die'. Noble work, Mr. Peterson, do carry on."

There was a polite silence as Dr. Carlyle took his leave then BB, obviously keen to hasten over the diversion into bits of moralising said, "Johnny B. Goode. My grandfather's coming and he really likes it. He says it was among the messages from Earth sent up on a Voyager interstellar mission in the seventies."

This assertion was met with some disbelief.

"No it's true," said Charlie, running his soup spoon idly round his bowl. "It was on the golden record with bits of Bach and various pieces of ethnic music."

"They'd never tell us if they ever got an answer," said BB. "I'm with the conspiracy theorists there. If there are aliens, the government would never tell us. If NASA got an answer, they would never let on."

"They did get an answer." Charlie looked up.

"What answer?"

"'Send more Chuck Berry'." Suddenly abandoning the soup spoon and pushing back his chair amidst the groans, he said, "There's a lot of boogie piano in the original. Kind of made it. But The Stones, The Beatles, AC/DC, George Thorogood and The Destroyers, covered it without. And Hendrix."

"How do you know all this?" asked Booger.

"Beats me," said Charlie. "I guess it's just who I was." He paused for a moment. "Anyway, listen to those while I'm gone. They could be on YouTube but, wherever they're lurking, I'm sure BB will be able to find them. Then decide if, between you,

you've got enough technical headroom to manage a version that won't ruin Grandpa Borgsen's day. And give some thought to the rest of the set. There's something I need to do for an hour or so."

*****

Charlie hadn't expected his sessions with the band to be overtaken by the existentialist urge to find the thing he wanted to live and die for. Once upon a time, a band had been a thing to live and die for. Quite literally, as it happened. But a man gets older and develops a broader spectrum of nagging needs. The great guitar solo is no longer a thing unto itself. And the feelings it precipitates, those soaring indefinable yearnings, are harder to satisfy. Yes, Charlie was a musician, yes he would always, at heart, be a musician - music was one of the greatest inventions of man. Or possibly a gift from the universe, depending upon whether or not you were with Pythagoras. But while there were times when it could be a source of great pleasure and solace, there were other times when its peculiar access to your deepest self could stir up a whole bunch of stuff that defied analysis. And you could put your boot through as many amplifiers as you wanted and you still wouldn't be able to define which demon it was that had been raised. And now, throwing guitars around and kicking amplifiers (and here we are speaking metaphorically because Charlie had always been fastidious with equipment) would be nowhere near as cathartic as it had been when you were twenty. Because the things that bother you when you are twenty are a lot easier to kick the hell out of, than the things that bother you when you won't see thirty again. Twenty has the gift of immortality and the problem of the now. Thirty starts looking at forks in the road and wondering how many options are left. And what, exactly, is there in this life that is really worth dying for?

So, one way and another, the discussion in the library had stirred things up for Charlie. The soil of confusion had been turned over again, and the Charlie Peterson of Endgame, half in and half out of his grave, was looking around and saying, *What the hell is going on here? Are we really abandoning a set list to investigate turnip seed?* … 'Looks like it, doesn't it?'

Crossing the football pitches, Charlie wondered briefly if there wouldn't, eventually, have come to be some weird kind of peace in the settled, if inhibited, heartbeat of a simple chemistry master. 'Show me a heart unfettered by foolish dreams …' Yes, he could maybe have been another teacher such as Dr. Boswell. *'And do you want to tell me more about this turnip seed ?'* … 'It's the precursor of turnips' … *'And we are concerned about this, why?'*

"Where are you going?"

He looked up. Tempest min and the trembly terrier had paused in their joint effort to dribble a football.

"I'm going to see about some turnip seed," Charlie said. "I thought you'd gone home with Crammond mi."

"I still have school work to catch up on. Also I've got a guitar to play now. A half-size one. Not a bass. I like tunes. And words. I'm sure I could always play the guitar, you know. Not like you, of course, but I think I could." He struck a pose and waggled his fingers.

"You could," said Charlie, unable to avoid marvelling yet again at the surreal nature of their exchanges. Exchanges that Tempest min now rarely failed to conduct with anything other than the untroubled credulity of childhood.

"I'm having a few lessons to remind me," he said. "There's a new guitar teacher. They had to get one. The guitar's a thing, now. He comes Wednesdays and Fridays."

"You didn't want *me* to help you?" Charlie felt a sudden pang.

"I wanted to surprise you. It was all supposed to be a surprise …" Tempest min tailed off, suddenly annoyed with himself.

"I look forward to it, then."

"Can I come with you to see about the turnip seed?"

"I think it's something I'll have to do myself. I may have upset Miss Keeble Parker and I need to find the right words to sort it out."

"My mother always says it's better when men are honest. Although she never really seems to like it when they are."

"I guess that about sums things up," said Charlie with a sigh.

"So can I come?"

"No. I need to think and you'll talk all the way."

"We used to talk a lot about women."

"Yes, but you were bigger then."

*****

Lady KP was in the walled garden remonstrating furiously with Schrödinger the cat, who was digging a hole for his toilet in a new seed bed. He looked unconcerned, scraping away with a paw while she waved her stick ineffectually at him from the path, and shouted in threatening but somewhat gnomic terms about more frequent and potent worm doses, and a new type of radioactive decay that would be less heavily weighted in his favour. "So you've come." She barely altered tone.

"Yes," said Charlie.

"A fact for which I must bear part of the original responsibility."

"Okay …" A little unclear as to her exact meaning here.

"I really like you," said Lady KP. "But you have dropped into my granddaughter's life like a meteor, and I'm not sure what size hole you're going to leave."

Charlie watched the cat for a thoughtful moment or two while he endeavoured to assemble a response. Immediately aware of fresh scrutiny, Schrödinger raised his head from his excavations and looked hard at him. His eyes glinted in the sun. *You come and shit in this garden at your peril, mate, so before you do it you'd better bear in mind that you are nowhere near as efficient a Houdini as I am.* And he turned his attention back to his hole.

"I'm not intending to shit on anybody," Charlie protested.

"Excuse me!" exclaimed Lady KP.

"I was talking to the cat."

"Well that's never very productive, as you must have already noticed." Lady KP considered things for a moment or two then proffered the information, in tones significantly lacking in encouragement, that Ianthe was in the orchard at the other end of the garden. "Don't disappoint me, young man," she called after him.

What would constitute disappointment for Lady KP? It might have been helpful for Charlie to know. Or not. Either way, he wasn't about to go back and ask.

He found Ianthe, as predicted, at the other end of the garden, walking slowly through a millefiori meadow under the fruit trees, picking spent heads off daffodils and examining, with obvious pleasure, the chequered petals of fritillaries that hung like magical fairy lanterns, drawing the light of the spring day into themselves. The blossom on the trees, the sunshine, and the jewel-like spangling of flowers invested her with a sort of poetic nimbus - something that could be, as Dr. Boswell had pointed out and Lady KP so clearly understood, very easily destroyed.

"Hello, Charlie," she said, without looking up. "I haven't seen you in a while."

"No," said Charlie, "and I suspect there may be a specific reason for that."

"Oh?"

"Last time I was here, I may have inadvertently offended you."

"Offended me how?"

No easy in there, for what he needed to say. "Well, let's just say that I was unhappy with the way things were left. The last thing I said was … open to interpretation, I think."

"In what way?"

No help for him there, either. No option but to press on. "When you vaguely - very vaguely, perhaps - implied that you might have found me attractive in some way, I was so surprised that I responded rather badly. And you might have thought, in turn, that I was suggesting something that I most certainly wasn't. Would never have even thought of suggesting to you. There are so many better things I could have said in the circumstances - and believe me I've probably covered all of them a hundred times a night, every night since - so I just want to apologise."

"Apology accepted." And she smiled. But it wasn't quite her

usual smile. "Though I wasn't offended, as it happened. I didn't over read what you said because I wasn't looking for anything in particular. I always understood that something in particular could never be."

"Oh?" Charlie's dismay was poorly hidden.

"You're just passing through, Charlie."

"I am?"

"Some of the staff are here because they are fundamental to the place's very existence. Some people come and then stay. They make it their home, their last resting place, even. Others ... well, others are simply passing through. And you, Charlie, are definitely one of the others."

Charlie tried to hide just how sickeningly his heart had lurched. "So," he said lightly. "This is not the Hotel California, then."

"Hotel California?"

"You can check out any time you like, but you can never leave."

"Right." She nodded. "I get it. It's a song. And yes, that's how it is for me. But not for you."

Charlie had had no real idea what could have come of this moment. No concrete expectations, just vague hopes and feelings conspicuously unexamined. And some persistent underlying longing for things that might ... develop. In that indefinable way he'd discussed with Rory. He'd decided, upon brief reflection, that the turnip seeds' failure to germinate was a metaphor - or even, in this strangest of strange worlds, a concrete expression of some disappointment that was nagging at Ianthe. And yet she didn't look disappointed. But he was now fully aware of how badly he'd wanted her to be.

After studying him for a moment or two, she said, "I've done enough here for now. Would you like some coffee?"

"I'd better not. I have to be getting back. There's a band waiting."

"There's always been a band waiting, Charlie," she said quietly, as he walked away.

*****

Back in the practice room, Charlie stared unseeingly at the latest set list. Johnny B. Goode had a question mark beside it.

"No good?" asked Blake Vane Tempest.

Charlie shook his head. "Why don't you all show me what sort of a shambles you can make of Hotel California before I say anything? I know you've at least had a go at it."

The boys looked at each other.

"Come on," said Charlie. "We haven't got all day."

Nate fiddled nervously with his drumsticks. "I can't do the fills, sir," he said.

"Then don't do the bloody fills." Charlie was looking at him, but he didn't really notice the sudden flush that came to Nate's face.

"Should we revise the list again, sir?" asked Booger, hesitantly.

Warily, they had stopped calling him Charlie. But in some ways, they were wrong. This was the Charlie Peterson they had summoned. The creative energies in this world are not exclusively dispensed by angels. Passion, passion for anything, so frequently comes at the price of peace. Even genius is rarely

403

without blemish - and never without pain. So what drove Charlie Peterson the rock musician was more Dionysian than Apollonian. He had his dark side. But he also had a job to do, and Grandma Peterson had made sure that he'd learned how to walk a line. And the pain? The turbulent, many-faceted pain that he was feeling as he looked at four anxious and dependent boys with guitars and drums? Well, as Dr. Carlyle had told him, he had to own it. Not it him.

He took a deep breath and shook his head. "No. Let's leave the set list as it is for now. And I didn't mean to pick on you, Nate. It's not your fault. I was asking the impossible. Just hoping for a nice surprise, maybe. But I should have known it's not that sort of day."

"Wait," said Blake Vane Tempest. "Listen. I can do the solo …"

So Charlie listened. "You have absolutely no idea," he said, when Blake had finished, "how much that has improved my afternoon. If Booger could manage the harmony part for the outro lead guitar lick we'd *really* be sounding like something. Who's got the iPod?" He looked around. "Let's listen to the track."

Five minutes later he turned to Nate. "Come on, you can do this. It's 4/4 time. Just play a simple backbeat, standard boom ka, same as Highway to Hell, snare on the two and the four. Keep it steady. Remember that steady is what your job is all about. You are the metronome. Forget the reggae fills for now, but try to pick up the accents in the solo. Blake will give you the nod. Let's give it a go from the beginning. Just the two of you, for the moment."

Rory came back from London smiling. He didn't yield up much detailed information but what he did say amounted to this: You can't dodge all the terrible things that come down the line in this world but, if you're loved, then they don't matter quite so much. And he met Charlie's eyes and nodded and smiled. And Charlie nodded and smiled in return. Happy for him. And just a little bit envious. It had been a long time since he'd smiled like that himself, and it had never been on account of a woman.

*****

"So why don't y'go and see her again?" Rory suggested few days later.

"What's the point? What could I say?"

"Y'could always try telling her the truth."

"That I find her more entrancing than any woman I've ever met? That I could actually be falling in love with her? That I want her to want me more than I can decently express? That making love to her would be like nothing I've ever known? That I'm terrified it would be like nothing *she's* ever known? That maybe she's just too different with her white witch potions and her defensive entourage of hobgoblins? That she really belongs to some weird yet innocent world that I can never touch? That I'm not sure I have what it takes to look deep into her eyes because I'm afraid I might be revealed to her as less than she'd hoped I would be? That we would, in essence, be the marriage of heaven and hell? That Dr. Boswell is probably right and she's best kept as an idea? A beautiful idea?"

"Jeez," said Rory, taken aback. "That's an awful lot. Maybe you just need to have patience and remember what you told me about destiny."

Chapter Twenty-one

"A sort of white witch," said Peter Peterson, in a voice that was just a note away from aghast. "Are you thinking seriously about what he's been saying, Lottie?"

They were conversing in rather strangled tones as they walked across their orchard towards Charlie, bearing breakfast bounty in the form of coffee and croissants.

"I am," replied Lottie firmly. "And mostly, I'm just relieved that he feels he can say it. And that he came home. He could have been brooding in isolation back at the school. Or sitting in a lonely corner in a pub. Look on the bright side. We must have done something right as parents. Not to mention your mother."

"My mother evidently told him too many fairy stories."

"She liked them," said Lottie. "Evil stepmothers and good princesses. Big bad wolves and innocent Red Riding Hoods. Nice clear messages. Not much of a one for the moral relativism, your mother."

"And she could be a real pain about it."

"It was the Lutheranism that lurked deep in her soul. She carried a powerful folk memory mix of one-eyed Odins and Norwegian Protestantism."

"She'd never even been to Norway," protested Peter Peterson. "Or had much of a regard for religion. Nor my father."

"Ancestral folk memory," said Lottie. "Unconscious affinity, not actual memory."

Peter Peterson snorted. "Look, he's sitting on those wild flower plugs you paid nearly a pound each for, and I spent an entire day planting into the grass on my hands and knees. Not to mention the subsequent watering it takes to keep them from shrivelling up. Why doesn't it rain, for heaven's sake? It rains all the time except when you want it to. I wonder if the white witch woman lays on rain-making ceremonies? For a suitable fee, of course."

"He's getting to be in love with her," said Lottie after a further moment of contemplating their son. "I can tell."

"How? How can you tell?"

"I gave birth to him. I can tell."

Peter Peterson sometimes felt that his wife had an altogether too fanciful take on life. He snorted again. Charlie looked in their direction. Peter lowered his voice. "You'd think, wouldn't you, that if, as a basically decent guy, you got a job at a private boarding school, you would fall naturally into conservative channels. Drift towards the solid and the unimaginative. Fall in love with the Latin mistress, or somebody else with an appreciation of dead languages. Or geology. Geology would be good. And if you had to take a walk on the wild side, you'd go and join the ramblers' association. But not Charlie. It has to be rock bands. *Again*. And now witches. He's ended up in the only school in the country with a sanctioned sideline in the occult. Somebody needs to explain to me why this feels inevitable."

"Well it's hardly Aleister Crowley stuff," said Lottie. "For goodness sake, Peter. It's just a bit spiritual. Marginally eccentric, if you prefer. And the music is just who he is. Whether you like it or not, it's part of him."

"But why does it have to be so loud? And … and …." He broke off for a second or two. "Why couldn't he have been the accountant? Craig was the only one of them with his feet on the ground, you know."

"But Craig is dead," said Lottie. "And we should just be extremely grateful that Charlie isn't." Drawing close, they were whispering now.

Charlie stood up. He'd been sitting with his back against an apple tree, staring unseeingly across the grass. He hadn't differentiated the wild flower plugs from the rest of the green sward, and was totally unaware that he could have been sitting on a couple of carefully nurtured rarities. All he'd registered was that he felt nearer to Ianthe when he was outside than when he was inside. There'd been solace in the rough rub of the bark against his back and the sweet, early morning smell of the earth.

The Easter recess was not proving a pleasurable respite. Mostly it felt like a sojourn in a world where certain things suddenly became much harder to understand or accept. He'd talked about Ianthe because his mother had asked and was sympathetic in her opinions. He had not talked about Tempest min because no one had asked. No one knew to ask, and he preferred it that way. A couple of his brothers, his sister-in-law and his little niece and nephew were still in bed. He did not want the subject of reincarnation dissected and ridiculed. No one, perhaps excepting his mother, acknowledged Easter much beyond chocolate eggs and the bank holiday. It was Easter Sunday but there would be no talk of resurrection, let alone reincarnation. So he kept to himself the strange circumstance of Tempest min and the way the pain that was still mixed up with it came and went in unfortunate complicity with the 'second time around' feeling of the school rock band. But it was harder to keep a steady perspective without the relentless daily timetable of lessons and the constant necessity to attend to things other than his own thoughts.

"Can we sit at the picnic table?" Lottie said to him. "The grass has to be damp and your father's getting rheumaticky."

"I am not," protested Peter Peterson. "I just can't see the point in sitting on the ground when there's an alternative."

"He hasn't quite got the point of nature, as yet," said Lottie, handing Charlie a mug of coffee. "Croissant?"

*****

Dr. Boswell was halfway down the drive at Puckrup. He and his country walking stick with the blackthorn knob on the end, and the trembly terrier nearby rooting determinedly in a molehill. Charlie stopped the car and lowered the window. "Good Easter?"

"Oh yes. Hot cross buns and simnel cake. And a trip to church to hear the vicar tell me that when I die this graceless earthly body could be replaced by one of glorious light."

"And do you believe him?"

"I continue to subscribe to the idea of a greater hope. In fact, now I'm nearer to seventy than sixty, I pay the subscription automatically by direct debit." He paused to scrutinise Charlie for a moment or two. "And you? Did you have a nice break away from here?"

"Yes, thank you."

Dr. Boswell shook his head. "I said to Heart: 'How goes it?' And Heart replied: 'Fit as a Ribstone Pippin'. But it lied'."

And with a wave of his stick he continued on his walk.

The flat was empty. Rory had gone to London. It was another big moment for him. Now that the memory of Parsons Green had lost much of its power to hold Christina fast in the countryside, London seemed to be calling to her again. She wanted Rory to meet her parents. They lived in Chiswick, where they had a fashionable antique shop which was stocked with French furniture and kitchenalia that they selected themselves during cross-channel expeditions. As trial by parents went, it had the potential to be a difficult one for Rory, but Charlie thought it was highly significant that Christina had wanted him to undergo it. And, as incongruous as the notion of Rory sipping tea from Sèvres porcelain amongst artefacts intended for the discerning metropolitan decorator had initially appeared, Charlie had come to think that he would manage perfectly well. Rory loved beautiful things, and he saw right to the heart of them. There would be practical talk of dovetail joints and inlays and marquetry, and silent moments of pure aesthetic emotion while he ran his big red fingers over delicate details as gently and smoothly as raindrops slide down glass. And maybe, he would find himself so much at home that he and Christina would gradually slip into the ranks of those who were not destined for a life at Puckrup, but merely passing through.

So Charlie sat for a while on one of the futons in the

411

uncommunicative flat, and contemplated the wistful light of the spring evening as it fell in golden shafts onto the coffee table. He felt achingly lonely. Then suddenly he got up and clattered downstairs, made his way through the stored games equipment and the stage props, past the papier mâché donkey's head worn by innumerable Bottoms to be wooed by the queen of the fairies, and let himself out of a rear access which cut a hundred yards off the walk to the walled garden. Just then, a hundred yards felt a lot. He was almost running when he bumped into Dr. Boswell, who was evidently on one of his cogitative circular walks. Dr. Boswell caught him by the arm. "I think you should let her come to you," he said.

Charlie came to a halt. "You think she will?"

"I very much doubt it."

Charlie looked at him. What did he know?

"A man can only live one dream at once, Charlie."

"One dream?"

"At once," said Dr. Boswell. "One big dream at once."

"So which is my other big dream?"

"The one that conflicts."

"And which is that, exactly?"

"The one you're living at the moment."

"And that is?"

But Dr. Boswell had already stepped off the path, and the primordial woodland had closed impenetrably around him.

Somehow, Charlie knew that he had to listen. With a heavy heart, he turned back the way he'd come.

*****

412

And so the busy summer term got underway. The boys with life-deciding examinations coming up ran through cycles of mild concern, exaggerated nonchalance and frank panic. The staff steered and soothed and counselled, and Julius Harvey took up deep-breathing exercises and meditation. Charlie found him, eyes closed and cross-legged, on the floor in a corner of the common room in Hereford House. At a distance he looked like some illustration from The Elves And The Shoemaker. "Julius?"

Julius leapt to his feet. Being a wiry little man, he did not find such manoeuvres difficult, and the meditation hadn't been of sufficient duration to slow him down. With all the boys out of the house for afternoon games, he'd sunk to the floor to make some brief capital out of the silence. Had he done this in his adjoining quarters his wife would have inevitably found him and said, "What on earth are you doing, Julius? You must get up earlier and practise this kind of thing before breakfast. This is no way."

"Blake Vane Tempest …" Charlie began.

"*Oh, God no …*"

"No. No cause for alarm. Everything is okay. It's just that Dr. Carlyle has given the band permission to skip games a couple of times a week and have a practice session instead. It's partly about the prom, but mostly about trying to get Blake and David Borgsen up to speed for getting them into a music academy. I need to get some music theory and some technology into them." He paused. "Though on the technology front they're probably ahead of me. Evelyn Hamilton is like a robot that you plug into a computer. Barely reads the manual. He and Sibelius became as one animal the moment they were introduced. Can't compose worth a damn, but he loves showing Blake Vane Tempest how to work the programme. Sorry, that's all irrelevant. Not intending to get between you and your efforts to contact infinite peace. Dr. Carlyle just wanted me to check that skipping games would have your consent."

"Anything," said Julius fervently. "*Anything* to keep Blake from doing something that will discommode the entire house before the exams."

"I can't guarantee it," said Charlie. "But I'll do my best."

*****

Tempest min had no examinations apart from a spelling test and some multiplication tables to learn. His sessions with Dr. Deshpande were now more widely spaced, and a preoccupation with his new guitar had entirely replaced his compulsion to produce agonised drawings of car crashes. Every so often, at moments appropriately devoid of other people, he would run up to Charlie and fling his arms round him. And sometimes Charlie had to stop himself from stooping to kiss the top of his head. Something was happening.

"These psychological shifts take place during therapy," Dr. Deshpande explained. "The unconscious mind starts knocking things into an acceptable form. It's distilling the feelings you had for Joe Beck and the feelings you have for Tempest min into a happy solution."

"What sort of happy solution?"

"I have an opinion, but it's not my opinion that counts. This flood of affection you feel towards the little boy. How would you define it?"

"I don't know."

"Yes, you do. Just think about it for a moment or two."

"Fatherly," said Charlie finally, and somewhat to his own surprise. "*Fatherly*. Which is ridiculous, isn't it? I'm not his father, which was definitively proven. And furthermore, I've never had the remotest urge to be anybody's father."

"And yet, when you look at your relationships with Joe Beck and Blake Vane Tempest and Christopher, isn't it remarkable how many times you've found yourself functioning like one?"

"I've functioned like a friend and a schoolmaster," said Charlie, slightly confused.

"These roles we play are never as distinct in life as they are on paper." Dr. Deshpande studied him for a moment or two. "And strangely enough, some of the more esoteric writings about reincarnation claim that groups of souls can progress through sequential lives together, their relationships changing from life to life. Sometimes you're somebody's father, next life you're their husband. Sometimes you're just a friend. Or even a wife. Interesting, isn't it?"

"No," said Charlie. "It sounds like you're getting creepy again."

"He's not having bad dreams anymore," said Dr. Deshpande.

Charlie shook his head and sighed. "That's probably because I'm having them instead."

"You were Joe Beck's anchor," said Dr. Deshpande. "Both his anchor and his safe space. Christopher talks about having tea at your house, with your family, as far back as when he was in primary school as Joe. Evidently, he felt very secure there. You are still his safe space. Wherever you are, that is where he wants to be."

*****

Meanwhile, the exams drew closer. Rory and Christina also drew closer. They spent the final exeat in France with Christina's parents going around antique markets. Rory took to reading Miller's Antiques Handbook & Price Guides which he professed to find fascinating. He stopped talking about carving pieces of oak and lime, or how he was never working with sequoia again because it made his hands all red when they were already red enough, and started using words like rococo and rocaille. Charlie worried about that when he had worry to spare because he'd always seen Rory as some creatively inspired wild woodsman, not an antique dealer. It was hard to imagine him tethered to the leg of a Louis Quinze chair. But it seemed that Rory was happy to be tethered anywhere alongside Christina. It was the first time in his life that anyone had given a damn where he was.

*****

The band worked up solid performances of Hotel California for Nate Greville's father and Sweet Home Alabama for Booger's mother and Johnny B. Goode for BB's grandfather, and Seven Nation Army for people more aware that they were in a new century, and Back in Black and Paranoid because Blake didn't want to look like too much of a pussy and Nate, who was not yet John Bonham or Taylor Hawkins, could manage the drum lines.

But Nate, who was taking ten GCSEs and had a lot to juggle, still kept sitting bolt upright during the night shouting, '… boom ka, boom ka, boom ka …' Charlie told him not to worry about

416

the drums, they weren't his future. He had to look on them as relaxation. And Nate said he didn't feel very relaxed when he was playing them because Blake Vane Tempest turned the evil eye on him whenever he made mistakes. So Charlie mentioned to Dr. Carlyle that he thought exams plus the prom performance was maybe too big an ask, and Dr. Carlyle said that Blake Vane Tempest appeared much more amenable to everyone else, and he and David Borgsen finally had something to work for. Something they actually *wanted* to work for. And Evelyn Hamilton had flourished like the rose helping them do it. Music technology today, the Pentagon tomorrow. If GCHQ didn't recruit that boy soon …

"We'll be careful to keep Nate Greville's head above water," he finished, "then all will be for the best, in the best of all possible worlds." And after these Panglossian reassurances he clapped Charlie on the back and went cheerfully on his way.

So Charlie concentrated on doing what he could do - including keeping his chemistry students calm as they fretted and studied and had last minute panics. But inevitably the day came when it wasn't up to him, it was up to them …

*****

Then suddenly the exams were over and, before any sense of anticlimax or result anxiety could set in, it was time to prepare for the great prom. It was always held out of doors, a compulsory prerequisite for generating proper festival feeling. So in annual defiance of the British weather, a stage was erected on the huge hairy lawn behind the house. The school's maintenance men huffed and puffed and the big metal trusses refused to come

417

together properly, and one of the men called to Charlie, "Where's that fucker McEwan hiding? He was a lot more use before he got hisself involved with that smart piece from the art and design block."

So Charlie, who had been thinking that this was a very professional-looking stage, went and winkled Rory out of his cubbyhole, and brought him to the scene to apply the natural affinity he had with things that needed constructing. Dr. Maccabee produced two or three rather geeky boys, who seemed to have a comparable affinity with the sort of electrical circuits that could power impressive lighting set-ups and sound systems, and Charlie had a chat with a specially anointed geek, coincidentally one of his chemistry pupils, who had lately revealed a flourishing alter ego as the school's named sound man.

A hire firm came and erected a marquee at the other end of the lawn, and teams of boys endeavoured to erect the school's own canvas gazebos down either side. People who couldn't even screw things together were sent to lug trestle tables out of the stores and carry hundreds of chairs across the grass, while the kitchen staff worked double time piling up cakes and scones, and a man in a pork pie hat came to talk about laying on a hog roast for the evening. The concept of veggie burgers confused him for a moment or two, but he was a geezer of the first water so he soon saw how, in spite of being primarily a man who cooked pigs, he could accommodate what he referred to for the remainder of the discussion as 'the queer people'.

The head of music, meanwhile, spent a lot of thoughtful moments on the sidelines, apparently envisioning the glory of the coming performances. Charlie found himself hoping to God that the band, especially Blake Vane Tempest who, as front man, was absolutely pivotal, had more of the big match temperament than he'd been expecting it to need.

"Hall of Fame," said Blake. "wouldn't that be good to finish off with? Maybe as a sort of encore."

"Good idea," said Charlie. "Highly appropriate and like a sweet course to help them digest AC/DC and Sabbath. Also, I'm very impressed that you think you're going to need an encore. And that you think you can learn it in time."

"It's basically a four chord song," said Blake. "How hard can it be? We'll just need to rejig the keyboard intro and some other bits, for the guitar. Won't you?"

"You'll do that yourself," said Charlie. "I'll help because of the time factor, but I'm not the one here trying to get into music college."

*****

So finally, at 4 p.m. on a glorious Saturday in mid-July, a brilliantly attired, bird of paradise crowd began to build up on the great, hairy lawn which had somehow, during its conversion into an arena of substance, developed the miraculous striping of a lovingly mown, virtuoso sward. And through some equally obscure transformation, Charlie found himself wearing a dinner jacket - the dress code for staff and senior boys.

"This is a do, isn't it?" remarked Rory, now a border chieftain, his muscular calves magnificently revealed by a kilt. So impressive was he, that he even managed to draw the eye away from Christina in her perfect summery dress.

"It certainly is." Charlie glanced around.

"Band going to be okay?"

"I hope so. They're on last. At nine."

"Best keep Blake away from the booze, then."

"The riot act has been read," said Charlie grimly. "Several times. Still, bright side, the sound man seems to be pretty good." He cocked an ear. Perfectly relayed fine music from a string quartet of bow-tied seniors was floating gently over the crowd.

People were emerging from the tea tent with loaded plates, and settling into congenial groupings at the trestle tables which were now dressed with white linen, flowers and candles. The head of music, standing attentively by the stage, was looking regal in tails. Charlie wondered if he'd put the band, billed as 'The Rock Juke Box', right at the end of the evening in the expectation that most people would have gone home. He glanced at the programme. Between various musical offerings there were assorted speeches and prize-givings. A small herd of junior boys in specially pressed trousers and sponged-clean barathea blazers suddenly galloped past. "Walk!" Rory growled at them. "*Walk*!"

"They'll knock somebody's grandmother over," he assured Charlie. "As sure as eggs is little chickens."

"Mr. Peterson!" A large lady in a blue silk suit was advancing upon them. "Could I just have a word?"

"Now it starts," said Christina. "Gird your loins. This might all look fabulously celebratory but it can be hell. And," she glanced at her watch, "an endlessly enduring hell. Long enough to expiate even your sins, Charlie."

Charlie conjured his most charming smile. "Mrs. Leadbetter," he said, "how nice to see you."

By six o'clock Charlie had parried numberless parents, half of whom were under the impression that he was somebody else, and carried on a nonsensical, intermittent conversation with a peripatetic three-year-old who, presumably impressed with the new dinner jacket, repeatedly waylaid him. In amongst it all, he had some quiet moments during which he caught Für Elise, Moonlight Sonata and Clair de Lune being performed on the piano. Now the prizes for music and art were being handed out and fervently clapped. Strawberries, he thought suddenly. Maybe there were some left. There weren't. The marquee looked as if a few plagues of Egypt had passed through it.

"Were they from the walled garden?" he asked, wistfully. "The strawberries?"

Freshly picked at the crack of dawn and delivered by Miss Keeble Parker herself. They worked miracles, they did, in that garden.

"Is she here, anywhere?"

Could be. Most likely not. But the hog roast was starting at seven.

Charlie ate a forlorn, damaged sandwich left on a platter and looked listlessly at the programme again. God! Tempest min! He hadn't noticed that before! Jeez! *Tempest min?* Playing the guitar? On his own? No back up? And in five minutes time? He almost ran out of the tent, manoeuvring his way, as politely as he could, towards the stage.

Somebody had just finished a rather stuttering but rapturously received performance of The Flight of The Bumble Bee on a flute. Charlie negotiated himself into a more advantageous position.

"And now we have Christopher Vane Tempest," announced the head of music, "giving us a song on his guitar. Christopher is a beginner, and he says he wrote this song himself, and is playing it especially for a friend. So let's give him a big round of applause!"

Everyone clapped furiously.

Tempest min, fair hair brushed neatly back, face a little pink, tie a little askew, looked tiny on the big stage. He gave his Fender Mini a tentative strum. The microphone was barely low enough. Charlie's heart began to thump.

"This song," said Tempest min in a high clear voice, "is called 'Slow Learners'." Looking up from a sudden quick twiddle with a guitar peg, he added, "It's not about school."

A few people laughed. But Charlie's heart almost stopped. Then Tempest min began to sing. And his voice carried the magic of angels. Evoking beauty amidst incurable sadness, it wafted over the audience like a spell. Tea cups were put down. Glasses stopped clinking. Jaws stopped working. Even the breeze held its breath. Dr. Carlyle's eyes misted over. He seemed to know exactly what he was hearing, even though he could have neither recognised the tune, nor been privy to the ultimate significance of the lyrics.

But Charlie both recognised and understood. The tune was exquisite, with an arrangement so spare that there was room to engage deeply with the words. And they were words that Tempest min could never have known, never have stumbled upon by accident. Words that were scribbled on a piece of paper amongst a pile of dusty mini discs in an old box somewhere. Words to the last song that Joe Beck had ever written. Words that said things, as they so often do in this kind of song, about love. About heartache and pain, about slow learning boys and slow learning girls, and the weight of the chains that they inevitably managed to forge from the golden threads of what could have been, had they only had the wisdom to do things differently. Had they only been able to bring into reality the eternal dream that, in some magical somewhere, there is for each of us a perfect soulmate whom we will love forever and desire infinitely.

Everyone on the lawn was caught in the moment. And each held breath, each misting eye, each bitten lip, spoke of the endless, universal search for something, someone, to fill the hole that lies in every human heart.

But over and above their poignant poetry, what the words of the song said to Charlie Peterson was this: 'I am Joe Beck. Hear me and believe'.

Finally, there was a moment of profound silence before tumultuous applause. When Tempest min descended the stage he ran unerringly to Charlie who picked him up and swung him round with tears in his eyes. No more words were necessary. Everything that needed to be understood was understood.

"Hello, Mama," said Tempest min over Charlie's shoulder, as he was set down. "I'm pleased you came. Did you like my song?"

"I thought it was genius," said Mrs. Vane Tempest.

"Thank you, Mama," said Tempest min, without any great feeling. "I think I'll go and play with my friends now." And he disappeared into the crowd without a backward glance.

"Sometimes," said Mrs. Vane Tempest, "I wish my children liked me more."

"I dare say you're not alone in that," said Charlie. And having got hold of himself and blinked away the tears, he turned round.

"I'm Alicia Vane Tempest." She held out a hand.

"I'm Charlie Peterson." He shook it.

Alicia Vane Tempest was stunningly beautiful, the daughter of Zeus and Leda, 'the face that launched a thousand ships and burnt the topless towers of Ilium'. Charlie knew little about Helen of Troy beyond her name, but he could recognise her when he saw her. Yet her beauty made no impact on him over and above the automatic act of observation. Nor did it serve to reduce in any way his accumulated animosity. If she sensed that at all and, supreme female that she was, it's unlikely that she didn't, Alicia Vane Tempest kept it well hidden. Instead she glanced in the direction of her youngest son's departure and said, "Henry Ford - he of 'any colour as long as it's black' fame - didn't believe that genius was a gift. He believed that it was the accruement of learning across lifetimes."

"Really?" It was casually delivered and carefully disinterested. Charlie did not want to volunteer Joe Beck and Tempest min for discussion.

"Could we talk, do you think?" she asked. "Could you spare me fifteen minutes? I think Tony has found us a quiet table."

Crowds did not pile up alongside red carpets expressly for Alicia Vane Tempest. She was not that well known. But once she was glimpsed, her beauty meant that they parted like the Red Sea to accommodate her. She led the way to a small empty table at the edge of the lawn. Charlie recognised Tony as the handsome, unpopular man who ferried the Vane Tempest boys and their luggage to and from the school, but his status was not further elaborated and, after delivering a couple of glasses of locally produced prosecco, he quickly excused himself.

"So," Alicia Vane Tempest wrinkled her nose slightly at the prosecco. "Do you think Christopher will want to take up music like Blake?"

"I hope not," said Charlie. "He's nowhere near physically robust enough, or dark enough, to be a rock musician."

"Which brings us nicely to the point," said Mrs. Vane Tempest. "And do call me Alicia, by the way, I'm hoping we can be friends."

Charlie said nothing. He took a diversionary sip of the prosecco. Didn't seem too bad to him. A barbecue smell suddenly floated past. There was a gap between performances. People were moving around a bit. Getting refreshments.

"I can see that you don't particularly want to talk to me about the reincarnation issue," said Alicia. "Fine, that's your prerogative. It doesn't really have a lot to do with the main matter in hand, and I believe it's been essentially resolved for all practical purposes. What I really want to know, Charlie Peterson, is what you intend to do with the life *you're* living at the moment."

Charlie didn't immediately answer.

"Teaching chemistry is very worthy, of course," she paused, watching him. "But for the next thirty years, Charlie? *Thirty years?* Have you no more fires to burn? Life should be in some measure intoxicating, otherwise it's just time passing. It's burn or rot, I believe. Burn or rot."

Charlie couldn't actually imagine Alicia Vane Tempest burning. He had the distinct impression that her pleasure would come from wielding power - sexual or otherwise - with a compelling, cool detachment. "I like this school," he said.

"Of course." Alicia was in complete agreement. It was a remarkable school. Quite astonishing, in fact. But was it everything?

Nothing was everything, Charlie said.

"When we're young," said Alicia, "there are things that seem to be everything, aren't there? But it doesn't last, of course. One becomes," she paused for a moment, "somewhat harder to set on fire."

Charlie declined to comment.

"I dare say a man could leave this school and come back later, if he wanted to."

"Oh?" It was a very bland 'oh'. Little more than polite punctuation.

"There are a lot of people who can teach chemistry, Charlie."

He noticed the repeated use of his name. It was a technique. He'd learnt it in telephone sales. Somebody had started playing Smoke Gets In your Eyes on a jazz saxophone.

"However," Alicia Vane Tempest went on, "there are very few people, and by very few I mean virtually nobody, who can get through to Blake. But *you* can." At this point, she obviously decided to stop looking for responses that weren't forthcoming and just lay the matter out. "Blake wants to go into the music business. As a performer. You've been there. You must know how easily he could end up in rehab, or dead at the bottom of a swimming pool. It can be a ruthless world. That's why it's called a business. So, I'm asking something really big of you. Something that I have no right to ask, over and above the fact that I can pay you handsomely to do it. Plus, it may chime somewhat with your own inclinations."

426

Charlie said, "Oh," again.

Smoke Gets in Your Eyes segued into Stranger on the Shore.

"Come back to London," she said. "Put yourself between my son and his worst instincts and his penchant for disaster." She paused for a moment or two before going on, but still Charlie said nothing. "Pragmatically speaking, of course, I'm not oblivious to the fact that you're a hell of a guitarist and a good song writer but, that said, I could probably find another. What I would be hard pushed to find, though I assume one could be manufactured, is a guitarist and songwriter who has such a poignant back story. You know the one - band killed when poised for glory … lifelong friends, etc., etc.. I understand publicity machines, Charlie. I know a good headline when I see one. And when it's a true headline, well, so much the better. And a fresh incarnation of the band, Endgame? It could be a story with legs." She paused again, but still Charlie didn't respond. "However, that being said and acknowledged with all due cynicism, what I cannot get elsewhere, at any price, is *you*. Get Blake through the music academy. Keep him focused. Help him put together a band. Manage it. Get it there …"

"Get it there?" Charlie suddenly baulked. "I can't guarantee that. Nobody could … What can be got there, as you so pragmatically put it, varies with the zeitgeist. And it's a fast moving zeitgeist these days. Endgame could now be viewed as rock dinosaurs. Special dinosaurs, possibly, but dinosaurs nevertheless."

"Notes are notes, Charlie," said Alicia Vane Tempest. "And I'm told that you consider yourself a musician. Put the notes together in a different way. Catch the zeitgeist."

"I never wrote, Joe and I never wrote, specifically to catch anything other than ourselves. We wrote what we felt."

"That was then," said Alicia Vane Tempest. "This is now. Feel something different."

Charlie just looked at her.

"Put together whatever you have to put together. Help Blake create what music proves necessary for him to create. The rest - the managing and the getting there - you won't be alone in that. Obviously, Blake sees himself as the front man in all of this, but whether you choose to hold things together from the wings or from somewhere else on the stage, would be your choice."

Truthfully, Charlie didn't know what to say. He didn't even know how to view the principle. Put together what was necessary for Blake because it was popular? Or put together what was necessary for Blake, because it welled up inside Blake? He suspected the former. As Dr. Carlyle had said, Mrs. Vane Tempest was a dedicated proponent of expedience. Did he want to connive at one of her expediences?

The saxophonist finished. There was applause.

"Blake was never prepared to accept anyone as a substitute father," said Alicia. "There's a lot more of the Hamlet in him than is easy to deal with. You're in receipt of the most acceptance he's ever given another man. Truthfully, you're probably the only person who stands a chance of preventing him from taking the highway to hell. I doubt his peculiar friend Booger, though he may well be alongside him, will have much of an influence."

Charlie acknowledged her use of the song title with a flicker. "Did he have something special with his biological father?"

"His father died when he was a baby."

"I'm sorry."

"No need. He was an old man. He was due to die. One could almost say he lasted longer than he deserved, considering the way he lived. He was, however, extremely rich. That's why I married him. I was very young. What can I say? Except that the baby was an accident. I didn't think the old boy had it left in him - a case of ignorance rather than innocence on my part, I have to confess. I felt no particular guilt in marrying him for money. Still don't. I entertained him for a year or two and he made me rich. Blake's father owned the biggest porn empire on the west coast. He was English, by the way, a rather dissolute and disowned blue blood. But he had very clever financial advisors. We met during one of his trips back to London. And, at barely twenty years of age, I became an extremely rich widow with very clever financial advisors. What's to regret?"

"Blake?" suggested Charlie.

"Maybe I could have done better with him. But then, look at the genes."

"And Paul's genes?"

"Paul's father turned out to be rather boring. Something he may well have passed on, but he never had another son, or indeed, another child so his prepotence in the matter of being boring never really got tested. Testicular cancer, I think. Anyway, a few years ago, he felt the need come back into Paul's life. I suppose the threat of death can do that to a man. But he's still alive, and still in business somewhere in New York. It seems to be working out for Paul."

"That's good," said Charlie.

"It is."

There was a silence. A few more sips of prosecco went down,

then Alicia Vane Tempest said, "After some of Blake's stories, I expected you to be chattier."

"Tell me about Christopher's father."

"That's rather more difficult. He was one of those 'long ago, in another country and besides the wench is dead', situations."

"Dead?"

"Unmemorable."

"Right." Charlie was carefully confining himself to neutral comments. Alicia Vane Tempest was a difficult woman to get in focus. She spoke incredibly well, she was clearly a long way from poorly educated and, if she'd been driven to attach herself to someone like Blake's father by any demons other than those of avarice, it was by no means obvious what they were. Amongst other imponderables were her pregnancies. She seemed to have had children, as Myra O'Grady had asserted, by this one and that one without any very clear motivation - offering them little or nothing of herself, or her time. On the other hand, having honed motherhood down to a mere walk-on part, she appeared industrious enough in the getting and paying of an extensive and varied supporting cast.

"Do you think boys need fathers?" she asked, suddenly.

Charlie shrugged. "I've never had a particular opinion on the matter."

"Christopher seems to think that he does."

"So are you going to get him one?" He thought fleetingly of Tony the chauffeur.

"A father figure, maybe." She sought his eye over the rim of her glass. "Someone Christopher can have meaningful contact with. And he's very attached to you. And you to him, apparently. That means you qualify."

Charlie said nothing.

Alicia Vane Tempest stood up then. "You've arrived in our lives," she said, "courtesy of some peculiar agency that I wouldn't even *try* to understand, and I just want to organise an outcome that could suit all of us." She laid a card on the table. "Call me. Blake starts at the Rock Academy in September. We need to have sorted out accommodation and money by then. And Dr. Carlyle needs a new chemistry master."

"So you're fairly sure I'm going to do this?"

Alicia Vane Tempest studied him for a moment or two. "My faults may be legion, but I rarely fail in reading people," she said, finally. "Especially men. When I look at you, I don't see a chemistry teacher. I believe it's burn or rot for Charlie Peterson now. Your choice, of course."

It wasn't really the kind of remark designed to sway Charlie in her favour but then it wasn't her he would be doing this for. "You're staying to see Blake play?" he asked.

"I fly back tonight," she glanced at her watch. "No doubt Paul will make a video. He seems to like doing that kind of thing." And she walked away.

Charlie stared after her with dislike.

At this point the herd of junior boys, evidently refuelled by fumes from the hog roast, came galloping past again. As Charlie automatically shouted, "Walk!" Tempest min detached himself from the stampede and came across to hear more about what Charlie had thought of his song.

"Has Mama gone?" he asked, though it was far from the first thing he said.

Charlie explained that she'd had to rush off to catch a flight.

431

That had obviously been accepted before it had even been raised, so it cast no pall over Tempest min's happy chatter about the impact of his performance and the compliments he'd been receiving. At no point in this chatter did he appear aware of any dissonance between his age and the nature of the song's contents, or of any other implication that the song could have had. And Charlie could clearly see what previously he'd only felt - that through the alchemy of that one last performance, Joe Beck had pretty much gone. Dr. Deshpande's work was complete, and now only the grown-ups would remember.

"I was good, wasn't I?" said Tempest min. "Because I'm over being poorly now, you know. I wasn't myself for a while, was I?"

"No," said Charlie. "You certainly weren't."

"Did you like Mama?"

"She was ... em ..." Charlie paused uncertainly.

"Men always follow her around," said Tempest min. "But they're never around for long. Nobody ever stays to be my father."

Charlie reached out and ruffled his hair without saying anything.

Tempest min smoothed it down again. "And Mama can never make me feel better about things. I don't really think she knows how."

"That's because you're an annoying little creep," said Blake Vane Tempest, dropping into the seat his mother had vacated. "Nobody could ever work out how to make you feel better. Now push off and join your horrid, noisy pals."

"Don't listen to him," said Charlie. "He's just starting to worry about his own performance because yours was so good."

Tempest min took on his brother's dismissive remarks with his legs defiantly braced. "When I get a father, you won't be allowed to speak to me like that."

"People don't get fathers," said Blake. "Mothers bring home men they want to fuck, not fathers."

After the word 'mothers', Charlie's powers of prediction had enabled him to have a sudden coughing fit. Then he took hold of Tempest min's shoulders and turned him round. "Look, here come your friends on another of their mysterious circuits, so you go along with them and let me deal with Blake's performance anxiety."

The galloping herd swept past, beckoning excitedly, and Tempest min flung himself into its midst.

Charlie turned to Blake. "Don't say things like that to him," he said. "It's really unpleasant and not what you should be saying to a child. You know this, for heaven's sake, so just stop it."

Blake turned angry eyes on him. "If you ever have sex with my mother, I will fucking kill you."

"You won't get the chance," said Charlie. "Because I'll have killed myself first."

"She'll pull you in," Blake warned him. "She spins mens' heads. They can't help themselves."

"Believe me," said Charlie fervently, "your mother is pretty well bottom of the list of things that could spin my head. Compared to some stuff that's turned up lately, she classes as unremarkable. So forget your mother, I'll probably never see her again, in any case. But do you need a final run through of any sort before you play?"

"No. We're cool."

"Are we indeed," said Charlie. "That sounds disturbingly complacent. A touch of adrenalin never comes amiss, you know."

Blake sat silent for a few moments then he said, "You will see her again. What about the coming to London thing? Don't you want to?"

"I don't know," said Charlie, slowly. "What do you want?"

"Well, in terms of the music, you'd obviously be a great help. Critical even. One day I'll be better than you, of course, but in the meantime …"

"In the meantime," said Charlie, "I gather that my job would be mostly to stop you from dying of a heroin overdose."

"Hell," said Blake, "nobody's going to be able to do that, but if somebody has to try, I would really, *really*, like it to be you."

And he got up and walked away.

Chapter Twenty-two

Finally alone, Charlie stayed at the table staring into space. Music washed over him. And laughter. And applause. And his own thoughts. The music industry, the Vane Tempests, Ianthe, chemistry, his parents, the school, Ianthe again, Tempest min again, Joe Beck, a three minute guitar solo … disjointed pieces of his life floating through in no particular order. Some talented senior was playing Liszt's Liebestraum - Love Dream - on the piano. It was agonisingly beautiful. Presently Tempest min came and stood beside him again, leaning slightly against his shoulder. Charlie went to put his arm round him and then stopped. He wanted to pull the little boy onto his knee and hold him while they listened together. But he couldn't do that. He was a teacher. Guidelines had to be observed. And yet, in all of that great gathering of staff and mothers and fathers and sisters and brothers and grandparents and friends, Tempest min turned only to him for emotional respite and reassurance. Charlie was still, apparently, both the anchor and the safe space.

"You okay?" he asked. "You need me to find Matron or anything?"

"No. I just came to see you." And then, like a puppy or a kitten, Tempest min had had his few minutes of rest and comfort, and was ready to play again. Charlie stared unseeingly after him.

"He's more than just attached to you, you realise." It was Dr. Carlyle. Charlie made to stand up, but the headmaster pressed him back down with a hand on his shoulder.

"Won't that fade?" Charlie asked. "Now he's not Joe anymore?"

"I've learned," Dr. Carlyle replied, "that people will forget what you said, people will forget what you did, but people will never, *ever* forget how you made them feel. Maya Angelou, I believe, but I couldn't put it any better. The real question is, Charlie, what do you do about it?"

*****

"What's wrong?" Rory was bending over the table peering into his face. "Why are you sitting over here all on your own? Why aren't you fussing over the band like an old hen?"

"I'm thinking."

"What about?"

Charlie didn't immediately answer.

"Has something happened?" Christina asked.

Charlie told them about Alicia Vane Tempest.

"Wow," said Rory. "That's a hell of a decision to have to make. And I doubt anyone will get Blake to straighten up and fly right. Not without some savage talk, the odd busted lip, and nervous breakdowns all round."

"You need some coffee, Charlie," said Christina. "You look dazed."

436

Charlie felt dazed. Over and above the decision he had to make, he was still dealing with the psychological impact of having Joe Beck virtually speak to him from the stage. It was a lot to process and he hadn't, under the immediate circumstances, got either the clarity or the space to do it. Rory offered to get the coffee but Christina said she would go because she wanted to assess the palatability of the pork buns. She was hungry, and Rory would be nothing of a judge. When it came to food, he had the discernment of a hound and the immune system of an alligator.

"She's amazed by my ability to eat out-of-date food and not get sick," said Rory, when Christina was out of earshot. "She picks the oddest things about me to be amazed by. Bothers me sometimes. I'd like to be amazing like she thinks Jude Law is amazing."

Charlie nodded absently. This inconsequential and mundane talk about Rory's appetites and digestive system, coupled with the solidity of his pork bun presence was slowly bringing him back to earth, but he wasn't yet fully focused.

"We're thinking of having a threesome," said Rory. "Jude Law turned us down but you were our second choice. Will you do it?"

"*What?*" Charlie jumped into life. "What the hell are you talking about?"

"Aha! I thought that might bring you round." Rory burst into guffaws. "So now I've penetrated the daze," he went on, still laughing. "I'll tell you something in confidence. Something real, this time." He laid a suddenly solemn finger alongside his nose. "Christina wants me to move to London with her - if she can get

437

back into the Slade. Or somewhere like Saint Martin's or Goldsmiths. So we, you and me, could both end up in London."

Charlie looked at him. "What would you do up there?"

"Antiques. Help the parents."

Charlie didn't react.

"It's good. It's all good." Rory leaned encouragingly across the table. "And does it help your decision at all?"

"I don't know," said Charlie. "I just can't seem to think straight."

Christina set a tray of coffee and buns on the table. "Perhaps this will help," she said. "But it better work quickly because the band is getting ready to play."

Charlie gulped down the coffee and took a bun with him. The band, as it happened, seemed gratifyingly organised. Everything was set up, guitars were being given a last quick adjustment - probably more to ease the nerves of the performers than to correct any aberration the instruments might have developed in their two minute trip the stage. Signals were flying back and forth to the soundman. Bow ties had been ditched, shirts were open at the neck. Blake was wearing a black T- shirt. Nate Greville was looking a bit tense. Booger and BB seemed to have worked up an effective line in overt nonchalance. Blake was actually grinning. If it was a nervous grin, it wasn't possible to tell.

Charlie jumped down from the stage. He didn't feel too worried. The set was supposed to begin with The Stones' Satisfaction - recognisable to a high proportion of the demographic, catchy, and straightforward enough to settle the band. An unchallenging introduction to a change of mood. But as he walked across to take up a position beside the sound man, the opening chords of Johnny B. Goode blasted through the two thousand watt PA system and hit the audience like a wave of electronic cocaine. A great roar went up. BB's grandfather, waving his stick, knocked somebody's hat off as he lurched to his feet. A group of teenage girls started to scream. Everybody was suddenly grinning or tapping or jumping up to dance on the central strip of clear grass.

"Turn the bass up," Charlie said to the sound man. "It's getting a bit lost and Grandpa Hamilton needs to hear his grandson." He shook his head. Blake Vane Tempest certainly had balls. But it had it worked. And didn't he look good. No wonder the girls were screaming. As long as Grandpa Hamilton didn't give himself a heart attack reliving his youth, everything was going to be alright.

Sweet Home Alabama and Hotel California followed - soothing the startled head of music back into some sense of security. Parents and grandparents nodded and smiled and applauded enthusiastically. The head of music nodded and smiled and applauded with them. He even joined in the war chant that echoed the riff of Seven Nation Army, beating it out with one foot. Then Back in Black and Paranoid hit him where it really hurt. Wincing, he covered his ears, grinning apologetically round at everyone while the youngsters stomped, played air guitar in the solos, and did brain scrambling things with their heads.

All too soon for everyone, it seemed, it was time to round off the performance with something that reflected the nature of the occasion. The Script's Hall of Fame floated tunefully and peacefully from the stage:

'You can be the greatest,
You can be the best …'

The head of music took his hands tentatively from his ears …

'You can go the distance,
You can do the mile,
You can walk straight through hell with a smile …'

The head of music smiled too. He could recognise a finale. The end was in sight.

'Do it for your people,
Do it for your pride,
Never gonna know, if you never even try …'

*****

"Well done, Charlie." Dr. Carlyle put an arm around his shoulders. "I think we had a real touch of group transcendence there. Pity poor old sick Nietzsche couldn't have been here to feel it. All his years of searching …" He gave Charlie's shoulders a squeeze and nodded towards Blake Vane Tempest. "El duende, eh? Almost the perfect vessel, isn't he?"

"It could be kill or cure," said Charlie.

"You must endeavour to make it the latter," said Dr. Carlyle.

"Redemption through heavy rock? It's a hard one. They once played music to a bunch of white mice as part of an investigation into its effect on the brain. The ones that got Mozart became very smart at finding their way through mazes. The ones that got stuff like Paranoid finally ate each other."

Dr. Carlyle burst out laughing. "Oh, Charlie, we're really going to miss you, you know."

*****

Nobody rushed to leave. Slowly, people started gathering up their belongings, folding travelling rugs, dropping empty champagne bottles into bins, shaking hands, thanking the staff, indulging in prolonged goodbyes with people they wouldn't see until the following year, and others they would probably never see again. A crowd of teenagers gathered round the stage, one or two aspiring performers trying out the instruments, but eventually pupils were herded back into the school and the rest drifted away with friends and relations in the direction of the cars.

When he had done all he had to do, Charlie sat down in a deckchair and stared up at the sky. The pink wash of sunset had long since faded from the west and there was a luminescence to the night just where a silver moon was hanging above the tree line. Bats, fragments of blackness, flitted through the shifting halos of light cast by guttering candles. A member of the kitchen staff, towing a last bag of rubbish, headed back to the school.

Finally he was alone. Or so he thought.

"You have to go," she said, just a shadow in his peripheral vision.

He stood up.

"You know that." She looked up at him. "For Blake, of course, but also for yourself. Otherwise all those unwritten songs, all that unplayed music … You can try and push it away, but it will eventually break your heart. And you realise, surely, that you've been given licence to go back to it all without guilt?"

"I know." He sighed. "And I will go."

And as he said it, he suddenly felt the situation quite clearly.

441

He'd go for Blake, and he'd go for himself. But what he'd come to realise, without really understanding all that had happened, or why it had happened, and certainly not *how* it had happened ... what he'd finally come to understand, he explained, was that he had to go, above all, for Tempest min. For Joe. He needed better parental care than he had, and he needed love. And last time around, he'd never had much of either in a worthwhile form.

"I can't let that happen again," he said. "I have to be in a position to do more – more than I would be able to do as a teacher at this school. I can't immediately see how to make it work, but I have to try."

"I'm pleased you've come to see it like that," she said.

There was a long pause. "Not that I want to leave here," he said, finally. "And I have one especially enormous regret." He thought about reaching for her hand but he didn't. "Tell me," he went on. "Tell me there was something real, something special, between us ..."

"There was ... but ..." She stopped.

"I know. There never seemed to be just the right moment." He shook his head. "We are so different. There always seemed to be something getting in the way."

"The doctrine of unripe time," she said. "Other things were meant to be done first, and who are we to refuse the universe? We were not the journey."

"Could there be a time for us? Ever?"

"If it's meant," she touched his cheek, just for a second, "and you were truly ready, then there's nothing in this world that would be able to stop it. But for now ..." She nodded towards the school.

"Charlie, *Charlieeee*!!!" Tempest min, in red striped pyjamas,

442

was running towards them, barefoot through the grass. As he flung himself forward, Charlie turned to catch him up. And in those couple of seconds, Ianthe slipped away. He said a quiet goodbye into the shadows. A woman he would willingly walk the earth to find again, and he'd never even kissed her. For just one painful stabbing moment, he felt he'd paid a steep price for what he needed to do. Later, before he finally left the school, he would go to the walled garden to conduct the sort of goodbyes that courtesy demanded. But he knew she wouldn't be there. So that one goodbye, whispered into the dark, had to carry everything he felt, everything he might ever get to say.

He looked at Tempest min. "I thought you'd stopped this." He set the little boy down and ruffled his hair again. "These bedtime escapades. You're past this now."

"I wanted to see you," Tempest min sounded breathless and excited. "Paul told me you were coming to London. To look after Blake and his music. Does that mean you're going to be our father? Blake's and mine?"

"Not in any literal sense," said Charlie. "But I certainly intend to be around."

"Then I want to go to school in London," said Tempest min.

"We'll need to consult your mother."

"It must be near you. A school near you. And full of music. Big music."

"*Big* music?"

"Yes. I'd like to write *big* music. Big as the sky." Tempest min waved an arm in the air, carving out the universe, conducting the planets. "With cellos and violins and trumpets for the angels. Do you think I could do that?"

Charlie took his hand and squeezed it. "I'm absolutely certain you could."

"And you'll come and listen to it, won't you?"

"I'll be there," Charlie promised. "I'll always be there."

And so they stood together on the dew soaked grass, heads tilted to the heavens, contemplating the vastness of the cosmos, seeing eternity in the stars, and hearing really big music.

Acknowledgements

The inspiration for this book came from reading Return to Life by Jim B. Tucker M.D., Associate Professor of Psychiatry and Neurobehavioral Sciences at the University of Virginia. Return to Life is, of course, a work of scientific investigation and The Music of the Cosmos is entirely fictional. So whilst there was inspiration there is no correlation, except in the preoccupation of one character - Dr. Deshpande's 'friend' from academia who investigated the phenomenon of reincarnation as it presented in the Western world. His findings, however, I mixed freely with myth and esotericism. For real case histories and scientifically presented facts, you must read Return to Life. I need, however, to acknowledge a couple of sentences which Jim Tucker attributed to Charles Richet, a Nobel Prize winning physiologist who, in dealing with the details of various phenomena, once responded to a sceptic with this: "I never said it was possible. I only said it was true."

Now I must extend particular thanks and gratitude to another American - artist Todd Young of Fort Wayne, Indiana, who so generously and freely gave me permission to use his magically appropriate 'MAESTRO' for the cover. To see more of his delightful pictures go to www.toddyoungart.com.

For musical corrections (and snorts) including aspects of the popular music industry, I must thank my sons Max and Todd - only one of whom communicates with fairies.

And finally, as always, and perhaps even eternally, I owe an enormous debt to my husband Andrew.

Lightning Source UK Ltd.
Milton Keynes UK
UKHW040819260419
341658UK00001B/9/P